Books by Deborah Crombie

DEBORAH
CROMBIE

IN A DARK HOUSE

AVON BOOKS
An Imprint of HarperCollinsPublishers

This is a work of fiction. Names, characters, places, and incidents are products of the author's imagination or are used fictitiously and are not to be construed as real. Any resemblance to actual events, locales, organizations, or persons, living or dead, is entirely coincidental.

AVON BOOKS
An Imprint of HarperCollins*Publishers*
10 East 53rd Street
New York, New York 10022-5299

First Avon Books paperback printing: January 2006
First William Morrow hardcover printing: October 2004

Avon Trademark Reg. U.S. Pat. Off. and in Other Countries, Marca Registrada, Hecho en U.S.A.
HarperCollins ® is a registered trademark of HarperCollins Publishers Inc.

Printed in the U.S.A.

10 9 8 7 6 5 4 3 2

To the memory of Fleur Lombard
Who died in the line of duty
February 4, 1996
Avon Fire Brigade, England, U.K.

Why have you suffer'd me to be imprison'd,
Kept in a dark house . . .

—William Shakespeare,
  Twelfth Night

Acknowledgments

Thanks are due to all the good people at William Morrow for their support and enthusiasm, especially to Selina McLemore and my brilliant editor, Carrie Feron.

Thanks as well to Nancy Yost, best of agents and friend, for her good advice and infinite patience; to Laura Hartman Maestro for bringing the book and its setting to life with her map; and to Canon Bill Ritson for his hospitality and knowledge of Southwark.

To those who have read the manuscript—Steve Copling, Dale Denton, Jim Evans, Diane Sullivan Hale, Gigi Sherrell Norwood, and Viqui Litman—thanks for your dedication, suggestions (and our many dinners at La Madeleine), and to Kate Charles, Marcia Talley, and particularly Diane Hale for your creative input.

Jan Hull provided moral support, as always. My husband, Rick, kept all my IT systems up and running, and my daughter, Kayti, kept my *life* running smoothly while I wrote. I'm sure I couldn't have done it without you all.

The Globe Theatre

Thames St.

Southwark Cathedral

Paul's Walk

City of London Sch.

The Millennium Bridge

The Queen's Walk

Bankside Pier

Southwark Bridge

Cannon St. Railway Bridge

Shakespeare's Globe Theatre

and Exhibition

Tate Modern

BANKSIDE Street

The Rose Exhibition

Park

Vinopolis Street

The Clink Prison Museum

Winchester Palace

St. Mary Overie's Dry Dock

The Golden Hinde

London Bridge

Southwark Cathedral

London Bridge

Summit

Southwark St.

Southwark Bridge Road

Southwark Street

Borough

London Bridge Sta.

Old Operating Theatre Museum

London Bridge Duke St. Hill

London Bridge Station

London Dungeon (under railway)

Little Dorrit Window at St. George the Martyr

SOUTHWARK

Union Street

Ironwood Space

Copperfield

Loman Street

Crown Court

Pocock Street

Hallows Street

Southwark Fire Brigade Station

Little Dorrit Court

Marshalsea Road

Crossbones Graveyard

Union Street

Borough High St.

The George Inn

Guy's Hospital

Greenwood Mkt.

Snowfields

Library

Suffolk Street

Southwark Bridge Road

Great Suffolk St.

Webber Street

Pickwick Street

Charles Dickens Prim. Sch.

Borough Sta.

St. George The Martyr Church

Dorrit St.

Marshalsea Prison

Long Lane

Guy Street

St. Hugh's

Kipling St. Estate

Leather Market

Pickwick Street

Gravel Lane

Suffolk Road

Borough High

Chaplin Close

Great Dover St.

Sterry St.

Quilp St.

Marshalsea

Dover St.

Borough Road

Police Station

Harper Road

Holy Trinity Church

Trinity Street

Inner London Crown Court

Nebraska

Newington Gardens

Bath Terrace

Dickens Square

Rockingham St.

Elephant & Castle

Kennington

Ontario Rd.

Gaunt St.

Southwark Bridge Road

Illustrated map by Laura Hartman Maestro 2004 ©

Scully & Martinelli

IN A DARK HOUSE

1

London . . . Smoke lowering down from chimney-pots, making a soft black drizzle, with flakes of soot in it as big as full-grown snowflakes—gone into mourning, one might imagine, for the death of the sun.

CHARLES DICKENS
Bleak House

It took no more than a match, nestled beneath the crumpled paper and foil crisp packets. The flame smoldered, then flared and crackled, and within seconds tongues reached out for the bottom layer of furniture stacked so conveniently on the ground floor of the old warehouse. Nothing burned like polyurethane foam, and the cheap chairs, sofas, and mattresses removed from the flats on the upper floors of the building were old enough not to have been treated with fire retardants.

A gift. It was a gift. He could hardly have asked for more if he had assembled the ingredients for a perfect fire himself. The furniture would generate enough heat for flashover, then the old wooden floorboards and ceiling joists would blaze with a beautiful fury. The fire would take on a life of its own, separate from its creator.

And the fire had power, that he had learned early on, power to exhilarate, power to transform, power to induce wonder and terror. He had first read about the great Tooley Street fire of 1861 in school, which seemed to him now an odd place to have discovered a life's calling.

The conflagration had burned for two days and consumed over three hundred yards of wharf and warehouse, damage unequaled since the Great Fire of 1666, damage not to be seen again until the Blitz.

There had been other fires, of course: the Mustard Mills in 1814, Topping's Wharf in 1843, Bankside in 1855; it seemed to him that fire was as necessary to Southwark as birth and death, that it provided an essential means of growth and regeneration.

Heat began to sear his face; the skin across his cheekbones and forehead felt stretched, his nostrils began to sting from the smoke and escaping gas. The blaze was well under way now, burrowing deep into the pile of furniture, then licking out in unexpected places. It was time for him to go, but still he lingered, unable to tear himself from the energy that gave him more than a sexual charge—it was a glimpse into the heart of life itself. If he gave himself up to it, let it consume him, would he at last know the truth?

But still, he resisted complete surrender. Shaking himself, he blinked against the stinging in his eyes and took a last look round, making sure he had left no trace. Satisfied, he slipped out the way he had come. He would watch from a distance as the fire mounted to its inevitable climax and then . . . then there would be other fires. There were always other fires.

Rose Kearny liked night duty best, when the station was quiet except for the muted murmur of voices in the staff room as everyone went about their assigned tasks. There was something comforting about the camaraderie inside held against the dark outside, and in the easing of the adrenaline rush after a call-out. And she considered herself lucky to have ended up at Southwark, the station where she had trained, and the most historic in the London Fire Brigade.

She and her partner, Bryan Simms, were checking their breathing apparatus after the first bell of the night—a little old lady in a council flat, having decided to make herself a bedtime snack, had dozed off with the chip pan on the burner. Fortunately, a neighbor had seen the first sign of smoke, the blaze had been easily contained, and the woman had escaped serious injury.

But every fire call, no matter how minor, required a careful examination of any equipment they had used. Tonight she and Bryan had been assigned BA crew and their lives depended on the efficiency of their breathing apparatus—and on each other. Simms, at twenty-three a year older than Rose, was as steady and reliable as his square, blunt face implied, and not inclined to panic.

He looked up at her, as if sensing her regard, and frowned in concentration. " 'What's in a name?' " he asked, as if continuing a conversation. " 'That which we call a rose by any other name would smell as sweet.' "

For a moment, Rose was too startled to respond. Not that she wasn't used to being teased about her name, or her fair looks, but this was the first time one of her fellow firefighters had resorted to Shakespeare.

Taking her silence as encouragement, Bryan went on, grinning, " 'But earthlier happy is the rose distilled, than that which withering on the virgin thorn grows, lives, and dies in single blessedness—' "

"Piss off, Simms," Rose interrupted, smothering a laugh. She had to admit she was impressed he'd gone to the trouble of memorizing the line. "I'd never have taken you for a Shakespeare buff."

"I like the second one. It's from *A Midsummer Night's Dream*," said Simms, and she wondered if she had imagined a blush in his dark skin as he bent again over his task.

"You don't say," Rose retorted with a smile. "And *Romeo and Juliet* as well. Aren't you the clever one." Her father, a high school English teacher, had begun quoting Shakespeare to her before she could talk. "Look sharp there," she added, glancing at his neglected equipment. "You don't want to miss a crack in that hose."

She'd started with the Southwark Fire Brigade six months before Bryan, and she never missed an opportunity to remind him of her seniority. It was hard enough, being female in what was still basically a man's profession, and she certainly couldn't afford a partner with some half-baked romantic idea about their relationship.

Rose meant to go far, perhaps even divisional officer one day, and she wasn't about to let an entanglement stand in her way. Not that she was averse to a night out and a bit of a recreational cuddle, but not with someone on her own ground. And the job left no time for a real relationship. If you wanted to be good, you had to eat it, sleep it, breathe it. She wanted more than the ability to put a fire out; she wanted to understand the why and how, and fire investigation was a way to move up in the ranks.

It was now after midnight, and she intended to use her downtime to study if things remained quiet. She'd just stowed the BA set and pulled out her books when the bells went for the second time that night.

Rose felt the familiar jolt of adrenaline, and then she and Bryan and the rest of the watch were running for the pole-house. Descending to the appliance bay, they began rigging in fire gear as the duty officer called out "Pair" over the tannoy, meaning that both the pump and the pump ladder were needed. As if of their own volition, Rose's hands performed the familiar rituals: fastening her tunic, tightening the throat buckle, pushing back her hair before slipping on her helmet and adjusting the chin strap, clasping her belt so that the weight of the small axe rested against her hip.

The station officer, Charlie Wilcox, ripped the call slip off the teleprinter. "It's just round the corner—warehouse in Southwark Street," he told them. "Sounds like it's well away—we'll need sets on this one."

Within seconds they were aboard the appliance and rolling into Southwark Bridge Road, sirens wailing and blue lights flashing. A fine drizzle blurred the September night, slicking the tarmac and haloing the street lamps. As they swung round into Southwark Street, Wilcox called out from the front, "It's showing."

As the pump came to a stop, Rose saw a bank of smoke hanging heavily over the street, and in the lower windows of a brick Victorian warehouse, the telltale red-orange flicker of light. Acrid smoke stung her nostrils as she leapt from the appliance and pulled on her mask. She caught a glimpse of huddled bystanders as Wilcox said, "Rose, Bryan. It looks as though the worst of it is still confined to the ground floor. Take in a guideline and check for occupants." He turned to his sub officer, Seamus MacCauley. "Check round the back, will you, Seamus? See what we've got."

The other BA team from the pump ladder was already laying hose line as Rose and Bryan tallied in their breathing apparatus, checked their radios. "Door's open," she heard Wilcox shout as she pulled her visor down, and she registered a faint surprise before focusing again on her task.

They went in low, Rose leading, peering through the smoke, feeling their way into the dense blackness. The heat seared, even through their coats, and she could hear the groaning and cracking of a well-established fire. She fell against something soft and bulky, went down on her knees. Through a momentary thinning of the smoke she saw shapes piled above her like a giant child's tower of blocks. The disjointed images suddenly coalesced.

"It's furniture," she said. "Someone's piled up bloody furniture." The polyurethane foam used in furniture cushions and mattresses was highly flammable—the thought of the devastating fire that had started in the furniture department of the Manchester Woolworth's crossed her mind, but she banished it, concentrating on the job at hand.

Still on her knees, she moved forward, feeling her way round the obstacles, trying to find a suitable place to tie off the line. Suddenly, there was a loud crack, then a series of pops, and the heat bloomed as debris rained down on them.

"Flashover," shouted Bryan. She felt him grab her waist belt. "We've got to get out of here. Forget the line, Rose."

Even with Bryan's weight dragging at her, her momentum carried her another foot, her hand still outstretched with the line.

"I said forget the fucking line, Rose. Evacuate! Evacuate!"

Even though her stubbornness, her refusal to let the fire get the better of her, was one of the things that made her good at her job, she knew he was right. Going on would be suicidal, and nothing could have survived this blaze without protection.

Hemmed in on one side by a sofa, on the other by what seemed to be stacks of lumber, Rose tried to turn back the other way. As she maneuvered her body round, her gloved hand came down on something that yielded beneath her fingers. It felt malleable, like flesh, with the brittleness of bone beneath.

Rose looked down, blinking eyes burning and swollen from the heat, and felt the bile rise in her throat. "Jesus Christ," she said. "We've got a body."

On this morning there had been no drifting slowly into consciousness, no lingering in imagined wholeness, no savoring the memory of life as it used to be.

Fanny Liu opened her eyes and took stock, reluctantly. It was later than usual, that she could tell by the angle of light in the sitting room window, but still overcast, as it had been the previous day. She slept, as she had since she'd become unable to manage the stairs, on an old velvet-covered chaise longue that had belonged to her mother. For once in her life her small stature was a blessing—a few inches taller and her feet would have hung over the end of her makeshift bed. At night the arms of the chaise cradled her, offering a solid comfort; in the daytime her bedding could be tucked away, allowing her to maintain an illusion of normalcy.

Elaine had argued with her, of course, wanting to put a bed in the sitting room, but for once Fanny's soft refusal had held sway over her roommate's brisk efficiency. The wheelchair was bad enough. For Fanny, a bed in the sitting room would have meant admitting the possibility that she might not improve.

Her cat, Quinn, still lay curled on her feet. The only sound in the flat was his faint purring. It was the silence that had awakened her, Fanny suddenly realized. There were no footsteps upstairs, no sound of movement in the kitchen. Elaine was always up first, making coffee and puttering around the flat. Before leaving for her job as an administrative assistant at Guy's Hospital, she allowed time to make Fanny tea and toast and helped her with her morning routine.

Perhaps Elaine had overslept, thought Fanny—but no, Elaine was as punctual as Big Ben. Could she be ill? "Elaine?" Fanny called out tentatively, pulling herself up by using the arms of the chaise. Her voice seemed to echo emptily, and a spark of fear shot through her. "Elaine?"

There was no answer.

Suddenly, Fanny remembered her dream, a jumbled nightmare of doors closing softly, and felt again the dream's inexplicable sense of loss. It made her think of the deathbed watches she'd kept as a private nurse before her illness, of the way she'd felt when she'd awakened from an inadvertent doze and known instantly that her patient had died while she slept.

Just as she knew, now, as the silence closed around her, that the house was empty. The sound of the door closing in the night had been no dream.

Elaine was gone.

There was nothing Harriet Novak hated more than having to tell strangers that she attended Little Dorrit School. Grown-ups would smile and coo as if it were disgustingly sweet—which made Harriet wonder how many of them had ever actually read *Little Dorrit*—and kids looked at her as if she'd just teleported from another planet.

Not that the school itself was all that bad, she allowed, digging the toe of her trainer in the play yard dirt as she waited for the first bell. It was just that it sounded so God-awfully sickening—like telling people you were called Tiny Tim.

It helped to be prepared, Harriet had learned, knowledge a necessary defense against living in a Dickens-infested neighborhood. She'd read the biography in the school library and could tell people more about Dickens than most wanted to know. Charles Dickens's father had been briefly imprisoned in Marshalsea Prison, just up the road, and twelve-year-old Charles had lived in lodgings nearby. This experience had stayed with him all his life, working its way into many of his books, and then his creations had come back to haunt the Borough. Not only did the area boast a Little Dorrit Court and a Little Dorrit Street, there was a Marshalsea Road, a Pickwick Street, and a Copperfield Street.

At least there was nothing named after Oliver Twist. Harriet thought Oliver a right little tosser, too sweet to be borne. Davey Copperfield she liked better. He was a bit soft on his dead mum, but at least he *had* bitten his horrid stepfather. Davey knew how to stand up for himself.

Harriet scowled, only half aware of the smoky tang in the air and the students straggling in the school gate. Her thoughts settled into a well-worn groove. Would it be better to have a wicked stepfather, like Davey, rather than a father who had walked out? He said he loved her, her dad, but if that was true, how could he have left them?

He told her lots of parents got divorced, that it was just something they would all have to learn to live with, but that didn't stop her missing him. Nor had his moving out stopped her parents' rows. She heard them when he came to pick her up, and other times she heard her mum on the phone with him.

The last argument had been the worst, when her dad had taken her home hours late after her last weekend at his flat. Her mum had been sitting on the doorstep of their house, watching for them, and she'd run to the car as Harriet was getting out.

"You bastard, Tony, you selfish little shit," her mother had shouted—her mother the surgeon, who was always in control, who had never raised her voice before this began. Her curly dark hair bloomed round her head as if energized by her anger; her jeans and jumper hung loosely on her too-thin frame, making her bones look as sharp as her voice. "You're late, you don't answer your bloody phone—does it ever occur to you that I might worry? Anything could have happened."

Harriet stood frozen on the pavement. She'd glimpsed a movement in the open window of the flat next door and knew their neighbor was listening. In the street, a couple walking by with their dog pointedly looked away and increased their pace. She felt her face flush scarlet with embarrassment. "Mum, we only—"

"For God's sake, Laura," her father broke in. "We went to the bloody zoo. It was a nice day, and we stayed longer than we meant. Is that a crime?" His voice was level, tight, his face pinched.

"You were supposed to have Harriet back hours ago. You know the rules—"

"Mum, please," said Harriet, hearing the mortifying quaver in her voice. Her throat ached, and a sharp pain seared her chest. "I'm fine, really. Can we please go in?"

Her father shot her an anguished glance. "Laura, let it go, okay? You're upsetting Harriet—"

"*I'm* upsetting Harriet?" Her mother stepped back from the car, looking suddenly, dangerously, calm.

"Listen, it won't happen again," Tony said quickly, as if realizing his mistake. "Next time I'll—"

"There's not going to be a next time," her mum had said quietly, taking Harriet's arm in a viselike grip and turning them both towards the door. As they reached the building, Harriet looked round and saw her dad pulling away, and if he had tried to ring her since, her mum hadn't told her.

Harriet hadn't dared ask her mother what she'd meant, but the words had stayed with her over the past few days, disturbing her sleep and haunting her waking hours.

She shifted her backpack and frowned again, aware of a headache coming on. She hadn't eaten her breakfast and her empty stomach was starting to cramp.

That was one of the worst things about her parents' separation—now, with her dad gone, when her mother had to work night duty at the hospital, she left Harriet with old Mrs. Bletchley, who lived in one of the cottages across from the school. Mum said Mrs. B. was lonely and enjoyed having children stay with her, but the woman reminded Harriet of the witch in *Hansel and Gretel,* and her house smelled of cats. That morning she had given Harriet some sort of unspeakable hot cereal for breakfast, which Harriet had mushed around in the bowl and tipped in the bin when Mrs. B. wasn't looking.

A shiny black Range Rover pulled up to the school gate and a boy climbed from the back, shrugging into his backpack with impossible-to-imitate eleven-year-old cool. Shawn Culver was a year ahead of Harriet, and the most popular boy in school.

"Hey, Harry," he called out, seeing her watching. She nodded without smiling, determined not to appear impressed, but she didn't protest his use of the hated nickname. She tugged her hair more tightly into its bunch, suddenly aware that she looked as if she hadn't bothered to wash that morning—which she hadn't. And if her hair weren't bad enough at home, when she could smooth it down with some of her mum's gel, on a Bletchley morning it was impossible.

The bell rang. She'd turned to follow Shawn with a studied nonchalance when the sound of a car braking fast made her look back. It was a dark green Volvo, like her dad's—no, it was her dad's. As she made out his face through the tinted glass, she saw that he was motioning to her. What was he doing here, before school?

She started towards the car slowly, aware of the second ring of the bell, of the play yard emptying behind her. As she neared the car she realized there was a second person in the passenger seat, a woman, and for a moment her heart flared in wild hope.

Then her dad reached back and swung open the rear door, and she saw that the woman was not her mother, but someone she had never seen before.

"Want some coffee, guv?" asked Doug Cullen, popping his head into Detective Superintendent Duncan Kincaid's office. "I mean real coffee, not that slop," Cullen added, nodding at the mug on Kincaid's desk.

Kincaid grimaced at his sergeant and laid down his pen, stretching the stiffness out of his shoulders. "You just want an excuse to get out, and we've not been here an hour." They'd come in early the past few days, catching up on accumulated paperwork, and the warren of cubicles that made up Scotland Yard's CID had begun to seem more like a prison than an office.

"Guilty." With his thatch of straight blond hair and wire-framed spectacles, Cullen looked more like a schoolboy than a detective sergeant. But in the year since Kincaid's former partner, Gemma James, had been promoted to detective inspector and posted to the Metropolitan Police, he had learned to work well with Cullen, respecting the younger officer's intelligence and dogged persistence when faced with a problem.

Not that Cullen or anyone else could truly replace Gemma as a partner. Although he and Gemma had been living together since the previous Christmas, he found he still missed working with her.

Glancing out his window, he was tempted to play truant along with Cullen, but the pile of paper on his desk argued against it. Besides, the day had gone perceptibly grayer since he'd come in, and he wasn't in the mood to get drenched. "Okay," he said, stifling a sigh. "A coffee. But just coffee, mind you, no poncey lattes."

Cullen grinned and gave him a mock salute. "Right, boss. Back in a tick."

It was a bad sign, Kincaid thought, when going out on such a dreary morning seemed preferable to work, but administrative reports had never been his strong suit. Not that he didn't have the aptitude for it; he just lacked the patience. He hadn't joined the force to become a bloody bureaucrat, yet that seemed more and more the case. And he had reached the point in his career where he felt increasingly pressured to seek promotion, but such a move would mean still less work in the field.

Could he stay where he was, watching the university fast-trackers like Cullen pass him by, without becoming bitter? It was not a prospect he wanted to consider, so with a scowl he turned his attention back to the performance survey on his desk. But when his phone rang a moment later, he leapt on it like a drowning man.

It was his guv'nor's secretary, summoning him to a meeting with the chief superintendent. Kincaid straightened his tie, grabbed his jacket from the coatrack, and was out the door with only a twinge of regret for his missed coffee.

Chief Superintendent Denis Childs had moved office recently, now commanding a view of the parks and the river, but in spite of his elevated status the man remained as Buddha-like as ever. His round, heavy face betrayed little emotion, but Kincaid had learned to read the slightest flicker in the deep brown eyes half hidden by folds of skin. Today he detected apology, annoyance, and what might have been a trace of worry.

"I'm sorry to put this on you, Duncan," said Childs, his voice surprisingly soft for a man his size.

Not a promising start, Kincaid thought, settling himself in a chair. Perhaps he should have stayed with the paperwork, after all. "But?"

"But as you have nothing pressing on at the moment, and as you have a knack for soothing ruffled feelings . . ."— Childs's lips turned up in the smallest of smiles—"you seemed the best man for the job."

"I'm not going to like this, am I?"

"You can look on it as a diplomatic challenge. It will mean liaising with the Fire Investigation Team and Southwark CID. A fire broke out in the early hours of this morning, in a warehouse on Southwark Street. Do you know it?"

"Southwark Street? That's near London Bridge Station, isn't it? But why send me?"

"Patience, boyo, patience. I'm getting there." Childs leaned back in his chair and steepled his fingers together, a familiar gesture. "This particular building is Victorian, and was in the process of being made over into luxury flats. The fire apparently started on the ground floor, but by the time the brigade got there it had done considerable damage to the upper floors and had begun to threaten the building next door."

"The warehouse was empty, then, if it was undergoing renovation?"

"Not quite. When the brigade got inside, they found a body among the debris. Quite badly burned, I'm afraid. And no identification."

"A tramp, smoking—"

"Possibly, although tramps aren't usually found naked with no effects. And it gets a bit more complicated. This particular building happens to be owned by one of our more illustrious MPs, Michael Yarwood."

"Yarwood?" Kincaid sat up a bit straighter in surprise. "I didn't know Yarwood was developing property." The vocal and abrasive Yarwood leaned far to the left of the government's moderate Labour party and was often heard publicly castigating anyone capitalist enough to make a profit. "This could be awkward for him, I take it? And the press will be on it like flies."

"An understatement. A public relations nightmare in the making, to be more accurate, especially with an important by-election coming up. Not to mention that the loss adjusters are already sniffing round and muttering about possible insurance fraud. And I've heard rumors from other quarters—one of my golfing mates who's in the property market—that Yarwood hasn't had the early interest in his leases that he expected."

"Ouch." Kincaid winced. "So he might have a very costly boat anchor on his hands—or he did until last night."

"Not that he'd admit it. But the powers-that-be are worried enough that someone from Number Ten rang the assistant commissioner and called in a favor."

"And that's where I come into it?" Kincaid said, enlightenment dawning.

"The word is, they only want to be sure the investigation is given high priority—"

"Meaning they want to be sure Yarwood's interests are well represented." Kincaid weighed the prospect of taking on such a politically sensitive case against going back to his performance reviews. It could prove messy, both literally and figuratively. He hated self-important politicians, and fire scenes had always given him a bit of the creeps.

"You can refuse, of course," said Childs, with a deceptive gentleness Kincaid recognized. Not only did Childs want him on the investigation, he knew that Kincaid could use the good mark in the AC's book.

"Is the body still in situ?" Kincaid asked.

Childs permitted himself another small smile. "I told them to wait for you."

2

"But let him look at me, in prison, and in bonds here. I endure without murmuring, because it is appointed that I shall so make reparation for my sins."

CHARLES DICKENS
Little Dorrit

THE REVEREND WINIFRED CATESBY MONTFORT was finding it more difficult than she'd expected to adjust to life in London. After the past few years at her country church outside Glastonbury, the concrete and grime of urban South London seemed a barren landscape to a soul parched for the gentle spread of green across the Somerset Levels.

But her exile was only temporary, she told herself for the hundredth time as she searched the unfamiliar cupboards of St. Peter's Rectory, hoping that something would materialize for her lunch. She also reminded herself that her exile was of her own making, and that she had no real cause for complaint. When her old friend and theological college mentor, Roberta Smith, had developed asthma so severe that her doctor ordered her to leave the city for a few months, Winnie had suggested that they swap parishes.

At the time it had seemed the right thing to do, as if God had offered her an opportunity to serve too obvious to refuse, but now she wondered if it had been merely her ego jumping at a chance to be seen as a rescuer—*St. Winnie saves the day.* And so she had abandoned her husband of less than a year, as well as others at home and in her parish who depended on her, to minister to what she had imagined as the poor and huddled masses.

Instead, she found a fairly comfortable and disinterested parish, the same round of bureaucratic meetings she'd left behind, and an ache of homesickness and longing for Jack that plagued her like a missing organ.

Well, there was nothing for it now but to get on with things, she chided herself as she rooted out a tin of tuna from the cupboard shelf and checked its use-by date. Too much self-examination smacked of self-absorption and was unproductive to boot—and her situation did have its compensations.

The rectory, a flat in Mitre Road across from St. Peter's Church, was cozy, filled with the bright wall hangings and artifacts Roberta had collected on her trips to Africa and Asia. Southwark Cathedral was only a few streets away, and Winnie found the frequent exposure to cathedral life both fascinating and moving.

Then there was Borough Market, nestled up against the side of the cathedral, its bustle and color an unending source of culinary and sensual delight. When Jack could get up to London for the weekend, they began it with a trip to the market.

She now had a family connection in London as well, Jack's cousin, Duncan, and Duncan's partner, Gemma, and their two boys. With the zeal of the newly wed, Winnie hoped that she might encourage the couple to take the same step. She knew the dangers of meddling, of course, but she also knew that sometimes a sympathetic ear and a bit of a gentle nudge were all it took to set things in motion.

And then there were her parishioners, some of whom she was beginning to know and like. One in particular was her neighbor, Frances Liu, a woman near her own age who had been stricken a few years ago by the mysterious and debilitating Guillain-Barré syndrome. As Fanny remained partially paralyzed and housebound, Winnie had quickly got into the habit of stopping in after work as often as she could, and she took the sacraments to her on Sundays.

On the latter occasions, Winnie felt the disapproval of Fanny's flatmate, Elaine, but she hadn't discovered whether the woman's hostility was personal or ideological. Nor had she quite worked out the exact nature of the relationship between the two women, but she sensed that Elaine perceived her as a threat and knew she must tread carefully. Winnie had no wish to make Fanny's life any more difficult. Perhaps if she could learn more about Elaine, she could draw her out—and then there was the fact that Elaine was a striking woman, and Winnie's curiosity was naturally piqued.

Resolving to make more of an effort next time she saw the two flatmates, Winnie finished her sandwich and began tidying up. She'd just dried her plate and cup when the rectory phone rang.

"I was just thinking of you," she said when she heard Fanny Liu's voice. "I thought I'd pop by after work—"

"Winnie, can you come now?" Fanny's words were hurried, breathy.

Winnie frowned in concern. "Are you all right?"

"I—it's Elaine. She wasn't here this morning, and when I called the hospital, they said she hadn't shown up for work."

"You mean she wasn't in the flat at all?" Winnie asked, puzzled. "Perhaps she went for a walk—"

"At daybreak, in this foul weather, when she never goes

walking? Why would she do that?" Fanny's voice rose. "And even if she had, why not come home or go to work?"

She could have felt ill, Winnie thought, but doubted the suggestion would dampen her friend's growing panic. "Did she leave a note?" she asked instead.

"Not that I can find," Fanny said tightly, and Winnie imagined her frustration, her search limited by the range of her wheelchair. Nor would Fanny have been able to check upstairs, she realized, thinking of a young woman in her home parish who had died suddenly of an aneurysm. What if Elaine, upstairs, alone, had fallen ill and been unable to call for help?

"Look, I'll be right over." She gathered up her bag and jacket, forcing a lightness she didn't feel into her tone. "But I imagine she's just decided to play truant for a day. Everyone deserves to play truant once in a while, even Elaine."

"No," said Fanny, refusing to be placated, her voice level now. "Something dreadful's happened to her. I know it."

The rain began as they crossed Waterloo Bridge. Kincaid had been glad to let Cullen drive, and now could look out at the Thames with the pleasure he always felt when crossing the river. He glanced upstream, at gray water melding into gray sky, then downstream, towards Blackfriars Bridge obscured by the curtain of rain. Beyond the bridge lay the Tate Modern, the Millennium Bridge, the Globe, all part of trendy new Bankside, which so recently had only been crumbling dockside. The transformation had been due, in part, to the vision of men like Michael Yarwood.

Cullen, who had been quickly briefed, seemed to pick up Kincaid's thoughts. "Have you ever met Yarwood?"

"No, just seen him on the telly." Yarwood was not easily forgotten—stocky and balding, with a face mashed flat like a bulldog's, his speech and manner as blunt as his looks. In spite of his ingrained skepticism towards all politicians,

Kincaid had found himself both impressed and intrigued by the man.

"Why all the fuss about him making a bob or two on a real estate venture?" asked Cullen, deftly negotiating the turn from Waterloo Road into Stamford Street.

Kincaid thought about it for a moment. "It's not that he's ever taken an antidevelopment position, but he's supported projects that benefit the community as a whole—"

"And bringing in yuppie flat owners with money to spend doesn't?" Cullen asked with evident sarcasm.

"Yes, the new tenants patronize restaurants and shops," Kincaid said, finding himself in the role of advocate. "But what happens to the lower-income residents displaced by the renovation? They can't afford alternative housing in the area, and it's these people who are the backbone of Yarwood's constituency." Yarwood had come from just such a working-class Southwark family, with roots in the neighborhood that went back generations.

"Well, I'd be happy enough to contribute to the economy by leasing one of his flats, if I could afford it." There was an edge of bitterness in Cullen's voice. Kincaid knew how much his sergeant disliked his dreary Euston flat, and he suspected that Cullen's girlfriend, the well-off and well-connected Stella Fairchild-Priestly, had friends with flats in the Borough or Bankside.

"How *is* Stella, by the way?" Kincaid asked.

Cullen glanced at him as if surprised by his apparent non sequitur, but answered readily enough. "Bloody insufferable. She's been promoted."

Kincaid knew that Stella, a buyer for an upscale home-furnishings shop, would only be content with Cullen's choice of job if he were suddenly and miraculously promoted to chief constable, and he suspected that her impatience would only increase as her career advanced. "Bully for her," he told Cullen, keeping his reservations to himself.

"We'll have to have you over sometime soon, to celebrate," he added cheerfully, knowing Gemma would view the prospect with as much enthusiasm as for a root canal. Although Gemma got on well with Cullen, her few encounters with Stella had not been successful.

The traffic began to back up as they reached Blackfriars Road, slowing to a crawl as they eased into Southwark Street. "Looks like they've still got things partially blocked off," said Cullen.

Ahead, Kincaid could just make out the red bulk of the brigade appliances and the blue flash of lights on the Met patrol cars. A brigade utility lorry was pulled up behind the fire engine. "There's no bloody place to put the car," Cullen grumbled.

"Then you'll have to make one, won't you, Dougie?"

Cullen flashed Kincaid a grin and pulled the Astra up, half on the double-yellows and half on the pavement. As a uniformed constable trotted over to wave them away, Cullen held his ID up to the window.

Kincaid saw with relief that the rain had eased to a drizzle and he abandoned his umbrella, merely turning up the collar of his mac as he climbed from the car.

With his first breath, the smell hit him in a tangible wave, the bitterness of charred wood mingling with the darkness of wet ash in the back of his mouth. Looking up to the right, he saw what remained of Michael Yarwood's Victorian warehouse. He recognized the building immediately, having noticed it when passing by because of its particularly attractive architecture.

Its four stories were a solid gray-brown brick belied by the graceful arches of large windows. The square edges of its corners were softened by gentle curves, its dark facade lightened by touches of cream brick round windows and roof.

Now the roof sagged and the front door hung crookedly

from its hinges. The shattered windows glared like blind eyes, those on the front of the building ringed by the black stain of smoke. A firefighter in helmet and tunic raked through the broken glass and smoldering debris littering the pavement. Hoses still snaked inside from the brigade engine, along with cables from the utility lorry.

The building and the surrounding area had been cordoned off with crime scene tape. Pedestrians milled outside the barrier, a few sporting the telltale notebooks and cameras of the press. A sole television van remained, waiting, Kincaid assumed, for the removal of the body and a statement from the police.

Well, they could wait a bit longer, but he'd have to deal with them eventually. Speaking to the media was a necessary part of a senior police officer's job, but he didn't particularly enjoy it. Giving a brief thought to the tie he'd put on that morning, a loud Liberty print Gemma's mum had given him the previous Christmas, he shrugged and smiled to himself. Maybe he'd set a police fashion trend.

As they neared the warehouse entrance, Kincaid saw a uniformed firefighter with an Alsatian dog. Beside him stood a tall man wearing a firefighter's tunic over civilian clothes and a woman in a suit and tan wool coat. The tall man Kincaid pegged as a member of the Fire Investigation Team, and there was something in the woman's bearing that marked her unmistakably as CID. There was a tension in their postures, as if they'd been arguing.

"You'll be Scotland Yard, I expect," said the tall man, turning towards Kincaid and Cullen with an air of relief.

Kincaid introduced himself. "And you're—"

"Fire Investigation Officer Farrell, Southeast FIT," the man acknowledged. He was balding and bearded, with a lined, intelligent face and eyes that seemed narrowed in a permanent squint, as if he'd spent too many hours poring over minute fragments of evidence. "I was just telling Inspector Bell here that we'd wait until you arrived to view the scene—the less disturbance inside, the better. My team and the Home Office pathologist should be here any moment."

The woman nodded at them but kept her hands firmly in her coat pockets. "Maura Bell, Southwark CID." Her voice held a trace of Glasgow Scots. She was dark-haired, thirty-ish, with a thin, sharp-boned face and a less than welcoming expression. "I've been asked to help you coordinate the local area investigation. We'll set up an incident base for you at Southwark headquarters."

Bell might have been asked to assist, Kincaid thought, but that didn't necessarily make her happy about having Scotland Yard on her patch. He'd have to tread carefully if he wanted more than minimal cooperation from her. She must have guessed why they'd been called in, even if she hadn't been told outright—Southwark CID would have been responsible for informing Yarwood of the damage to his building.

Farrell turned to the uniformed firefighter. "This is Sub Officer Jake Martinelli, and Scully."

"That's a name to live up to," Kincaid acknowledged, admiring the dog. She was black and tan, with dark comma-shaped patches above her eyes that gave her a quizzical expression. "Search and rescue, or explosives?" The Alsatian sniffed his proffered fingers, then went back to gazing expectantly at her handler.

Martinelli gave Kincaid a friendly grin. Olive-skinned and dark-eyed, he had broad cheekbones, which hinted at a dash of the exotic mixed with his Italian heritage. "Neither. Scully's an accelerant detection dog. Her nose is a hundred times more sensitive than the mechanized hydrocarbon sniffers—"

"Don't let him start," broke in Farrell. "He'll bend your ear till it's blue. Not that Scully isn't a good advertisement, but as I was just saying to Inspector Bell, we can't take her in until the scene has cooled down sufficiently." The dog whined and moved restively, as if aware her name had been mentioned, and Martinelli stroked her head.

"Easy, girl," he said to her, then added, "she knows what she's here to do, and she's eager to get started."

"Do you have reason to suspect arson at this point?" Kincaid asked.

"There's always a possibility of arson with a fire, but no one's reported a man running from the scene with a can of petrol." Farrell grinned. "We should be so lucky."

In Kincaid's experience, fire investigation officers tended to be a cautious species, refusing to commit themselves to anything less obvious than whether or not the sun was shining until they had irrefutable evidence, and sometimes not even then. At least this one appeared to have a sense of humor. "What *do* you have so far?" Kincaid asked without great expectations.

"The alarm came in at twelve thirty-six," Farrell began deliberately, ignoring the impatience radiating from the angular Inspector Bell, as well as the drizzle, which was steadily growing heavier again. It occurred to Kincaid that perhaps Inspector Bell's temper was not improved by being wet.

Nor was his, and he was beginning to sympathize with Cullen's craving for hot coffee.

"Called in by someone next door, a resident in one of the flats who looked out the window and saw flames," Farrell went on, nodding towards the adjacent building, of similar but less elaborate architecture. Together, the two structures had formed a bastion of grace among an array of concrete shop fronts.

"Could it have been the torch?" Kincaid asked, knowing that sometimes arsonists called in their own fires.

"Not likely. According to Control, it was a woman, and there were small children audible in the background."

"No sign of anyone hanging about when the brigade arrived?"

"No, and the response time was under three minutes. The appliances came from Southwark Fire Station, just up the road. The station officer believed the fire had been in progress ten to fifteen minutes when they arrived. It was well established on the ground floor and beginning to take hold on the upper floors."

"The door wasn't locked." The soft voice came from behind Kincaid and he turned, startled. A young woman stood there, dressed in jeans and anorak. Her corn-fair hair was tied back in a ponytail and she looked tired, her eyes red-rimmed. "I'm Leading Firefighter Kearny, Southwark station," she explained, seeing their expressions. "My partner and I were first on the scene, BA crew."

Farrell seemed to assess her disheveled appearance. "You're just off your watch, then?"

"Yes, sir. Thought I'd make sure the relief had it all under control." Kearny smiled but shifted on her feet, as if she felt a bit awkward under their scrutiny. "And I thought, if you had any questions, I'd save you waiting until the watch came back on duty tonight."

"You're interested in fire investigation?" Farrell asked with a trace of amusement.

"Yes, sir." The girl met his gaze squarely, her chin up. Although her face was scrubbed pink, her bare neck still bore traces of soot, and the contrast struck Kincaid as rather endearing. Both Cullen and Martinelli were eyeing her with obvious interest, but she didn't seem to notice.

"Were there persons reported when you went in?" Farrell asked.

"No, sir. We were just doing a routine search, trying to lay a guideline for the hose. But it got really hot, and when Simms and I started to evacuate, I crawled into . . . it." She made a faint grimace. "We could see there was no point in rescue."

"Any smell of petrol before you went in?" Martinelli asked.

Kearny frowned, then shook her head. "Not that I remember. And then afterwards I had my mask on . . ."

"You said you found the front door open," Kincaid said. "Is there more than one entrance?"

"There's a side door," Farrell told him, gesturing towards the narrow street on their right. "It was open when we got here, as well. There's no sign of damage to it, and none of the crew reported forcing entry."

"So someone with legitimate access opened the doors?"

"Too soon to say," Farrell cautioned.

"The builders' crew might have left them open accidentally," offered Cullen.

"One, maybe, but both?" Farrell shook his head. "I suppose it's possible, but not all that likely, in my opinion. Which takes us back to an illegitimate entry, but if that's the case, we've not turned up anything noteworthy on the preliminary outside search."

The station officer came up and spoke to Farrell. "The SOCOs have finished their preliminary examination, guv, and the structure seems stable. I think it's cool enough for the dog, if she wears her booties." He gave the dog a friendly pat, but she ignored him, all her attention focused on the building. When Martinelli pulled a set of paw protectors from his tunic pocket, she began to dance and strain at her lead.

"All right, girl, all right," he soothed, kneeling to slip the rubber boots over her paws.

"Let me get my kit from the van, will you?" Farrell said, adding, "It's Rose, is it? Since you're here, Rose, you can go through the scene with us, tell us if anything strikes you."

Farrell strode to the brigade van, returning with a bulky evidence collection bag and a notebook. "Right, then, let's have a look."

They queued up behind Farrell single file—Indian file,

Kincaid would have said as a child, and he felt a flicker of regret for a politically correct age in which his children would never be encouraged to play cowboys and Indians, or army. He had done both, and had still grown up relatively civilized.

But any pleasant thoughts of childhood were quickly banished as he stepped through the warehouse doorway behind Farrell and Rose Kearny. If the smell had been bad outside, in here it was choking, a physical substance that permeated skin, hair, clothing, sinuses. As he blinked his watering eyes, he detected another odor beneath the pervasive char, the faint, oily sweetness of roasted flesh.

Water from the firefighters' attack had pooled on the warehouse floor, standing several inches deep in places, and Kincaid made a mental note to be careful where he placed his feet. Swallowing hard against the burning in his throat, he focused his attention on Farrell, who had stopped a few feet into the interior.

"Stay behind me if you can," Farrell said. "We don't want to muck things up more than necessary."

"I'm not sure *muck* is the appropriate word," Cullen muttered, and Kincaid heard what might have been a snort of agreement from Inspector Bell.

They stood in a large, open area, lit by arc lights powered from generators on the brigade lorry and by what weak daylight filtered in through the intact windows, but the illumination made only a feeble sally against the encroaching blackness. Walls, ceilings, floors, the unidentifiable objects that filled the room—all might have been black holes, absorbing light into a dense and solid darkness.

As his eyes adjusted, Kincaid began to differentiate shapes. To his left, near the windows, a long object resolved itself into a stack of lumber, but Kincaid couldn't tell if it had been new or salvage from the renovation. Four posts, equidistant from the room's center, rose floor to ceiling, and he assumed they were the structural supports left behind when interior walls had been removed. The charring on the posts seemed fairly shallow, but he still gave an anxious glance at the ceiling.

Then, to the left of the posts, he saw a large, lumpy pile of objects, an obscene parody of furniture. Blackened coils and springs protruded from the mass at odd angles, like a bizarre modernist sculpture.

Martinelli moved away from the group, murmuring words of encouragement to the dog as he began a careful circuit of the area's perimeter.

"Tell us what you saw," Farrell said to Rose Kearny.

"We *couldn't* see. Not more than a foot or two. The smoke was low, and black." She turned slowly in a circle, examining the space. "We must have come straight in, but after a few yards, there was nothing but the line to anchor us. We didn't know there weren't any walls, so when I bumped into that"—she gestured towards the furniture—"I thought I'd hit a wall or some sort of room divider. Then I realized it felt soft, but it still didn't make sense for a few seconds—you don't expect furniture to tower over your head."

At the invitation of a mate in the fire service, Kincaid had once suited up and gone into a burn house on a training exercise. The memory of the searing heat and complete disorientation still made him shudder, but the experience had given him tremendous respect for anyone who could face such a situation on a daily basis.

"Where was it burning hottest?" Farrell asked. "Could you tell?"

"The fire was everywhere—it must have been close to flashover. But"—Kearny frowned, nodding towards the furniture—"I'd say it was most intense there."

Turning to his little group of followers, Farrell said, "The first thing we do in a fire investigation is identify the point of origin. Look." He pointed at the floor surrounding the furniture. "See, the char is deepest here, as if it burned the longest. And there"—he nodded at the rear wall, a few feet behind the piled furniture—"see the V pattern?"

Kincaid found that he could make it out, now that his attention had been directed to it, a faint lightening of the soot in a pattern wider at the top than at the bottom.

"Fire tends to travel upward and outward, and to burn longer and more intensely near the point of origin. The expanding gases typically leave such a pattern, but there are other indicators, of course."

"You're telling us that the fire started in the furniture?" said Inspector Bell, sounding interested in spite of herself. She edged forward so that she stood in front of Kincaid.

"That would be my guess, but that doesn't tell us whether the cause of ignition was deliberate or accidental."

"But surely if it started in the furniture, it must have been arson," Bell insisted.

"Not necessarily. First off, until we interview the job foreman, we don't know whether the furniture was stacked up by the builders or by an unknown party." Farrell ticked one forefinger against the other, striking off an imaginary list. "Then, even if the work crew left the furniture this way, that still doesn't tell us if the fire was started by accident or design. The foam in these cushions and mattresses is highly flammable. One of the workmen could have dropped a cigarette, left it to smolder. Or there might have been a spark from the wiring they've torn loose." He pointed to a flex hanging from the ceiling, shrugged, then called out to Martinelli, "Any hits yet?"

"No. She's not picking up anything definite," Martinelli answered. "She's feeling a bit frustrated," he added as the dog whined and nosed at his tunic pocket.

"If the dog doesn't find an accelerant, can you rule out arson?" asked Cullen.

"Oh, no." Farrell sounded almost gleeful. "The accelerant

could have burned off completely, or the fire could have been started without an accelerant. Amateur torches love to splash the petrol around, but often more practiced arsonists prefer to start a fire using only what's available at a scene. More of a challenge that way, I should think."

Kincaid was beginning to sympathize with the dog's frustration and Inspector Bell's impatience. "Well, we do have one without-a-doubt fact here. Someone died, whether it was before, during, or after the fire. What do you say we have a look at the body?"

"There." Rose Kearny stepped forward gingerly. "We must have gone past the furniture, then turned slightly to the right."

Kincaid followed her, and as they edged into the gap between the furniture and the rear wall, he saw it.

The remains were identifiably human, at least. The body lay on its back, arms and legs drawn up in the pugilistic pose caused by muscular contraction, the skin blackened, the teeth showing in a grotesque parody of a smile. The few remaining tufts of hair were charred, and there were no traces of clothing. Although the tissue damage was extensive, the breasts were still recognizable, and that somehow made it worse. Kincaid swallowed against the sudden rise of bile in his throat.

Rose Kearny's hand had flown to her mouth, but as Kincaid glanced at her she forced it back to her side.

"Bloody hell," Cullen mumbled, looking a bit green, and even Inspector Bell seemed momentarily to have lost her composure.

When a light female voice spoke from the warehouse doorway, they all spun round as if they'd been caught at something unspeakable.

"I take it I've the right address?" said the white-suited figure, and with a flash of pleasure Kincaid recognized Kate

Ling, his favorite Home Office pathologist. Now they might get some answers.

Tony Novak pulled things from the bureau drawers and threw them into the open suitcase on his bed, the largest he'd been able to find. Laura would have criticized his untidiness, but then Laura would not only have packed neatly, she would have made a list of essentials for the journey and checked it off as she stowed each item.

And, of course, Laura would have criticized his impulsiveness, but there were times when impulsiveness could be a virtue. And, he reminded himself, it no longer mattered what Laura thought.

They had been polar opposites from the beginning of their relationship, first attracted by their differences, then, as time went on, just as fiercely repelled. If she'd teased him at first, saying he'd bluffed his way through medical school, he'd thought there was some part of her that had admired his recklessness. Later, she had seen that quality only as a character defect to be mended.

What she had never understood was that his failings were also his strengths, interwoven with an intuitive understanding and an ability to make quick decisions, and it was these qualities that had made him a success at emergency medicine.

When they'd closed down the Accident and Emergency at Guy's, his loyalty to the hospital had kept him on in Minor Trauma, but days spent dealing with flu and broken fingers, with objects inappropriately placed in body orifices, had quickly soured. He missed the adrenaline rush, the sense of flow that came only in a crisis, when time seemed to telescope in on itself. Glancing up, he caught a glimpse of himself in the bureau mirror, his face lean and tired, with new lines about the mouth.

Work was only a small part of the discontent he'd felt lately—it was nothing compared with the gaping hole left in his life by the absence of his daughter since he and Laura had separated. He looked down at the suitcase, at the few things Harriet had accumulated on her weekends in his dreary rented flat on Borough High Street, and felt the familiar despair.

For a moment, his courage failed him. But no, he had gone too far, and he knew Laura too well. He knew about her increasing involvement with the women's shelter, and he knew that the agency made it possible for women to disappear with their children. And he'd known, when she'd threatened him on Sunday, what it was she meant to do.

Well, she'd lost her chance, he thought, his resolve returning. Hadn't it occurred to her that two could play at that game, and that he had the advantage? There was no place easier to vanish into with a child than Eastern Europe, and he had family in Czechoslovakia who would help him. A change of name, a new set of papers, a job in a backwater town where doctors were desperately needed, all easily accomplished. He and Harriet would start a new life together, and nothing would separate them again.

The hospital would be in a crunch for a bit, no doubt, losing him without notice, but there were other doctors who could bandage cuts and prescribe antibiotics.

It was Harriet that mattered, and he had Harriet safely tucked away—he hadn't dared wait until later in the day to pick her up. Once he'd set things in motion, he'd been driven by a mounting sense of urgency. Now, all that remained was a trip to the bank, and Harriet's passport. The passport meant he had to get into Laura's flat, and he had to do it when he could guarantee no one would be home.

Nor could he take Harriet with him, as he hadn't yet told her what he meant to do, so he'd been forced to call on the one person he felt he could trust to take Harriet for a few hours. He'd arranged to meet them at London Bridge Station at noon, and then he'd tell Harriet he had a surprise planned for her, an adventure. The truth could wait until they were across the Channel, away from England and all the misery of the past months. He would tell her when he felt the time was right, and he smiled at the thought that from now on, as far as his daughter was concerned, only his decisions mattered.

3

... trifles make the sum of life.

CHARLES DICKENS
David Copperfield

WELL, WE'RE NOT likely to get an accurate temperature on
this one, are we?" Kate Ling said dryly. She squatted beside
the body, balancing on the balls of her feet with an ease that
made Kincaid envy her thigh muscles. On anyone else the
position would have looked awkward, but the Home Office
pathologist even managed to carry off her white crime-scene
boiler suit with grace.

Kincaid had worked with Kate Ling on a number of cases,
and found her not only good at her job but genuinely interested
in helping the police with their investigation, a trait not every
pathologist exhibited. Some of them seemed to become almost
territorial about the bodies in their possession, behaving as if it
were a point of pride to reveal as little information as possible.

Kate pulled on her thin latex gloves. "Anything to go on
here? Witnesses? Missing person connected with the
scene?" She probed the corpse gently with a gloved finger.

"Nothing so far," Kincaid told her, with a glance at Farrell for confirmation.

"And no identifiers?"

"Nothing obvious." Farrell squatted beside her, his notebook open. "Unless there's something under the body. We'll do a grid sift, of course, once you're finished here."

"Odd." A tiny crease puckered Kate's forehead. "I've seen clothing literally fused to the skin, but the condition of the body doesn't indicate that sort of heat. Nor is there any jewelry that I can see." She lifted what remained of the victim's left hand, and Kincaid heard a stifled protest from someone in the group. "Some trace of a wedding ring usually survives a fire, even if the digits are completely destroyed."

"Any guess as to the victim's age?" Kincaid asked.

"Hard to say without X-rays and measurements. She seems on the slight side, but the heat can cause shrinkage as well."

"Race?"

"The lab analysis will tell us, and I'd rather not speculate in the meantime."

"A homeless person would explain the lack of jewelry," Cullen suggested. "Someone sheltering from the rain, maybe starting a little fire to keep warm, not realizing the furniture was highly flammable."

"When have you seen a rough sleeper without a bin liner or a shopping trolley full of possessions?" Inspector Bell said dismissively. "And surely someone would have noticed a naked person wandering the streets?"

"You've a better suggestion?" retorted Cullen.

"Any lividity visible?" Kincaid asked, heading off an altercation. He wondered if she was as sharp with her own officers—it was not the best technique for fostering confidence in the ranks.

Kate lifted one side of the torso gently. There was a distinct lack of charring on the floorboards beneath the body, but the underside of the corpse still looked dark to Kincaid. "There might be some bruising, yes, but I'll have to get into the tissue to be sure. And there is something else," Kate added, lowering the torso and edging her fingertips beneath the head. "It feels like there may be quite a severe fracture to the back of the skull, but there's no way to tell whether it's postmortem or antemortem until I can have a look in the lab. The heat alone can cause shattering of the skull."

Kincaid knew that even if the pathologist could verify that the trauma had occurred prior to death, that wouldn't rule out an accidental injury. His gut instinct, however, told him that this death had not occurred by chance.

With that knowledge came the realization that his likelihood of spending the weekend with Gemma and the boys was rapidly evaporating. They had planned a Saturday morning excursion to Portobello Market, weather permitting, with a particular mission in mind.

After having shared a bedroom with five-year-old Toby since they'd moved to the Notting Hill house, Kit had asked if he could move into the third bedroom, the room they had meant for the nursery. When Kincaid had started to object, Gemma had stopped him, saying, "That's fine, Kit. We'll do it up for you."

"Gemma, are you sure—" Kincaid had begun, but Gemma had stopped him with a shake of her head. "No, it's all right. Kit needs his own space."

That was true, Kincaid had to admit. Since Kit had turned thirteen at the end of June, he'd been finding it increasingly difficult to share with Toby, and now, with the beginning of the new school term, it was becoming clear that he would need a more private space for his schoolwork.

Gemma had gone on brightly, throwing herself into planning and decorating the room, but to Kincaid her enthusiasm seemed brittle. It had been almost a year since her miscarriage, and on the one occasion he'd gingerly brought up the idea of trying again, she'd looked away and changed the subject. It was still too soon, he'd told himself, but now he wondered if her willingness to give up the nursery to Kit meant she'd rejected the idea altogether. The thought struck him with a fierce and unexpected sense of loss.

"I think that's all I can do here," said Kate Ling, drawing him back to his surroundings. "Let's bag and tag, and I'll get to the postmortem as soon as I can."

Kincaid chided himself for letting his attention wander, and as he gazed at the charred remains of the body, he felt a twinge of guilt for his aggravation over the change in his plans, surely a trivial thing when a human life had been so brutally snuffed out.

"Can you rule out self-immolation?" Doug Cullen asked as Ling stood and stripped off her gloves.

Farrell answered, "Again, it seems unlikely unless we turn up some trace of clothing or a positive on accelerant. Let's give the electronic sniffer a try," he added, removing the bulky hydrocarbon detector from his evidence collection bag and taking Ling's place beside the body. After running the collection nozzle over the remains and the surrounding charred area, he shook his head. "I'm not getting a reading."

He motioned to Martinelli, who had almost completed the outer circuit of the room. "Jake, try over here, will you?"

The others edged out of the way as Martinelli brought the dog over, giving the team room to work.

Kincaid found himself standing beside Rose Kearny. The young woman stood with her hands shoved firmly in the pockets of her anorak, her shoulders hunched. "Is this your first body?" he asked quietly.

When she glanced at him in surprise, he saw that her eyes were a clear cornflower blue. "How did you know?"

He shrugged. "I'm not sure. I've seen a lot of coppers at their first crime scene."

She seemed to consider this for a moment, then she

looked back at the group surrounding the victim and said thoughtfully, "I've pulled people from buildings who I knew weren't going to make it, tried to revive them. And I've worked my share of fatality road traffic accidents. But this is different, somehow. Maybe it's not having a job to do. In a fire or a rescue, you only have time to think about what you're going to do next."

"It must have been bad in here." As Kincaid looked round the ruined space, he realized that water was seeping into his shoes.

"The worst I've seen," Rose agreed. "I didn't realize how fast you could lose it, you know? One minute you're on top of it, you're in charge, then the next it all goes to hell."

"Do you want to go back?" he asked, studying her, his curiosity roused by her candor.

An unexpected smile lit her face. "Oh, yeah. Absolutely. There's nothing like it."

"No joy," Martinelli called out, patting the dog, who looked as if she took her failure personally. "If anything was used here, it's burned up. We'll keep looking, but if there's nothing at the seat of the fire, I'm not hopeful."

The station officer appeared in the doorway and signaled to Farrell. "The mortuary van's here, Chief."

"About time." Farrell turned to the others. "Let's move out, let them get on with it. Try to keep to the same track you used coming in."

Kincaid felt an unanticipated shudder of relief as they stepped out onto the pavement again. He realized he'd been tensing his shoulders as if personally preventing the ceiling from collapsing.

As the mortuary attendants and the white-suited crime scene specialists conferred with Farrell, he decided he'd grab the opportunity to ring Gemma. It was still raining, a steady and relentless drizzle. Ducking across the street, he sheltered in the doorway of an office building and dialed Gemma's mobile number.

He'd been half expecting her voice mail, but she answered herself, a lift of pleasure in her voice. "I wasn't expecting to hear from you until later today. Don't tell me, you're off early." Her tone was half teasing, half hopeful, and he hated having to puncture her mood.

"No, sorry, love. Something's come up. A special request from the guv'nor. It's a fire in Southwark, with a possible homicide. I'll fill you in on the details later."

There was a moment's hesitation before she said, "You'll be tied up for the weekend, at least. Kit will be disappointed about tomorrow."

"Go to the market without me. It's better than postponing."

"And tonight?"

It was only then that he remembered they'd had plans to take Gemma's friend Erika out for a meal. "Oh, bugger. You'd better cancel, at least on my part." Erika Rosenthal was an older woman of whom Gemma had become quite fond, and Kincaid had been promising to meet her for months. "Maybe we can reschedule for next weekend."

"Right. Look, I've got to dash," Gemma said a bit abruptly. "Ring me when you can."

Winnie pushed the bell at the Ufford Street house, then let herself in when she heard Fanny's voice, knowing it was hard for her to negotiate the front door from the confines of her wheelchair.

She stepped directly into the sitting room, marveling, as she always did when she came here, that a woman of Chinese descent would choose to create a room that was more English than the English. Shelves on the pale green walls held pottery jugs filled with dried flowers, 1930s green glassware, clocks, and hand-painted china; the open spaces between shelves were filled with cottage watercolors, crewelwork still lifes, and, in the place of honor above the mantel, a large print of a contemplative black-and-white cat among pots of flowers.

The furniture was pine, the squashy settee chintz, and in the back of the room, strategically placed for the view into the tiny garden, was a green velvet chaise longue.

Beside the chaise, Fanny sat in her wheelchair, and if her cotton print dress and beaded cardigan seemed accessories to the room, the metal frame of the chair provided a harsh contrast. Her delicate hands were twisted in the cashmere shawl on her lap, the smooth oval of her face etched with worry.

"Thanks for coming," Fanny said, her voice quavering as Winnie came across and clasped her cold hands. "I didn't know who else to call."

"Let's start with some tea, shall we?" said Winnie. "You can tell me everything, then we'll see what's to be done." She went into the kitchen at the rear of the house. Toaster and kettle, along with the necessities for both, were arranged on a low table in front of the window. Although Fanny had had a small bathroom with roll-in shower built off the scullery, she'd told Winnie she refused to have the cabinets and worktops refitted to wheelchair height. Nor had she put in a wheelchair lift for the stairs. To her, both those things had seemed like admissions of defeat.

Fanny was determined to walk again, and while Winnie had learned that people often did make at least a partial recovery from Guillain-Barré syndrome, she knew it could be a slow and laborious process.

"Is there anything you need doing?" she called out as she put the kettle on to boil.

"No. I can manage the basics pretty well on my own," Fanny answered from the sitting room, her voice steadier. "It's just the getting out that's difficult."

As she gathered the tea things, Winnie looked round for anything odd or out of place in the small kitchen, but everything seemed the same as on her previous visits. Carrying the steaming mugs back into the sitting room, she pulled a worn wooden chair up to Fanny's and sat down.

"Let's go back a bit," she said. "Was Elaine at home last night?"

"Yes. Although she was a bit late getting in from work, but she's been late several times a week the past few months, and I didn't think anything of it."

"Was there anything else unusual? Did she seem upset or worried?"

Fanny wrapped her hands round the mug and frowned into its depths. "No, no, not really. She made us scrambled eggs on toast for supper, then we watched a bit of telly. She didn't stay down to watch the ten o'clock news with me, but she made my milky drink before she went up."

"Could she have been feeling unwell?" Winnie asked, remembering her earlier fears.

"Not that she said." Fanny looked up, fear in her dark eyes. "You don't think . . . Surely I'd know . . ."

"Why don't I start by having a look upstairs." Forcing a reassuring smile, Winnie found a spot on the mantel for her mug and crossed the room to the stairs, which rose from near the front door. She climbed quickly, trying to ignore the dread tingling at the base of her neck.

There were three doors in the upstairs corridor. She opened the first door on the right with trepidation, then gave a small sigh of relief. The room, obviously Fanny's, with its inlaid mahogany bed covered by a lilac quilt, was tidy and had the slightly musty odor of disuse.

Winnie closed the door softly and tried the next. It was the bathroom, tidy as well. Both the towels on the rack and the soap in the dish on the sink were dry, and cold air poured in through the partially opened window. An escape route? Winnie wondered, but as she pulled the window closed she saw that it was a straight drop down to the small paved patio outside the scullery. Not unless Elaine had grown wings.

That left the third door, the room that faced the front of the house. Winnie knocked softly, then, realizing she was holding her breath, exhaled deliberately and pulled open the door.

The room might have been a monk's cell. The starkness came as an almost physical shock after the cocooning clutter of Fanny's house. A single bed stood against the wall, its worn white matelasse bedcover reminding Winnie of the one on her parents' bed when she was a child. An unfinished pine nightstand held a clock and a small lamp—nothing else. The surface of a matching chest of drawers held nothing other than a faint layer of dust. Beside the chest, a straight-backed chair stood awkwardly, like an uninvited guest. No prints or pictures graced the magnolia walls, and there was no mirror.

The bed looked as if it had been made hastily, a lack of care that seemed oddly in contrast to the rest of the room. Winnie opened the wardrobe doors. A few hangers hung empty among the neat ranks of skirts, coats, and dresses, but she had no way of knowing whether the bare spaces indicated clothing removed for flight or the ordinary breeding of hangers in cupboards. There were no other signs of packing or of hasty departure.

Winnie left the room and descended the stairs more slowly than she'd gone up, wondering what could possibly have happened to Elaine.

"She's not here," she said when she reached the sitting room and saw Fanny's anxious face. "And I can't tell whether or not she's taken anything away. Are you sure you didn't hear anything in the night?"

"No." Frowning, Fanny picked at the fringe of the shawl in her lap. "I only remembered sensing something wrong as soon as I woke this morning. It's odd—I don't usually sleep quite so soundly. Oh." She looked up, her eyes widening. "I dreamed I heard a door close."

"It must have been Elaine, as it doesn't look as though she went out a window, and she can't have vanished into thin air. Have you any idea what time this was?"

"No. I'm sorry. I'm not usually so groggy."

"And you said you rang Elaine's work and she hadn't come in? Did they tell you if she'd called?"

"No. Only that she wasn't there. They're not allowed to give out more information than that over the phone."

"Well, that's the first thing, then," Winnie said with relief, glad to have a goal. "I'll go have a word with them. She works at Guy's?"

"Yes, in medical records."

"What about family? Does Elaine have anyone you could ring?"

Fanny shook her head and a strand of her fine dark hair came loose from its clip. "No. There's no one. Her parents are dead and she hasn't any siblings. That was one of the things that—" She stopped, her eyes filling with tears. "We were both alone."

Winnie knelt by Fanny's chair and gave her hand a squeeze. "You're not alone. I'll help any way I can."

Returning the pressure, Fanny forced a smile. "Thanks. Sorry for being so wet."

"You're just fine," Winnie reassured her, then added hesitantly. "Fanny, if we find that Elaine hasn't been in touch with the hospital, I think we should call the police."

"No!" Fanny jerked her hand free.

"Why ever not?" Winnie asked, startled.

"But . . . surely that's not necessary. If she's just out for a lark or something, she'd be furious."

"You're afraid that if she's all right, she'll be angry with you? Wouldn't she understand that you were concerned?" Winnie was beginning to feel there was something very odd here.

"Yes, but . . . you have to understand. Elaine's a very private person. She doesn't like . . . I don't think . . . I think we should wait. After all, she did leave of her own accord," Fanny added, but she looked even more worried.

"It does seem that way, but—" Winnie stopped, deciding this was not the time to express her own uneasiness. And hadn't she heard that the police wouldn't allow a person to be reported missing until twenty-four hours had passed? She needed advice, and suddenly she knew exactly whom to call.

"Look," she said to Fanny. "Don't worry. I've a much better idea."

There was no point taking her disappointment out on Duncan, Gemma told herself, regretting her hastiness as soon as she'd hung up the phone. She'd sounded a right cow, and it wasn't as if she hadn't had to cancel out of family plans herself, especially in the past few months, but somehow that didn't make being on the receiving end any easier.

She knew the investigation that had lately consumed so much of her time and energy had disturbed her balance, but that was no excuse for acting the harpy.

A child had gone missing on her patch, a six-year-old girl, and the current slacking of her workload was due not to a resolution, but to the fact that the case had gone cold. Not only was it the first time Gemma had dealt personally with such a case, but as SIO, she felt responsible for her team's failure.

The parents' grief and anger had been particularly hard to bear, and she'd not been able to shake off the case outside working hours, something she knew to be essential if one were to survive the job. Her fears for the missing child seemed to have transferred themselves to Toby and Kit, and she found herself worrying whenever they were out of her sight.

Which was all the more reason she should take the boys

to Portobello on her own, where she'd have both of them under her nose for the day. She'd promised Kit they'd look for an antique specimen cabinet for his room, and having begun the redecorating project, she didn't dare falter. They'd already framed sets of nineteenth-century botanical and zoological drawings they'd unearthed at one of the market's print stalls; she'd painted the walls a strong aqua, and set up bookcases and a desk complete with microscope and dissecting instruments.

Although Kit had seemed thrilled with the idea of focusing his new room around his scientific interests, Gemma hadn't neglected a concession to adolescent fashion—she'd covered a portion of one wall with cork squares, ready for his growing collection of music posters.

But in spite of Kit's enthusiastic response to her efforts, she knew that nothing she did could compensate for Duncan's lack of participation. It shouldn't matter, she told herself, slamming her desk drawer and pinching her finger in the process. She swore loudly and shook her injured hand, realizing she'd failed to find the pen she'd been rooting for in the drawer when her phone had rung.

There was a knock on her office door and Melody Talbot, the PC who often assisted her, looked in. "You all right, boss?"

"Just a little accident with the drawer," Gemma said, embarrassed by her outburst. "What's up?" she added, as Melody seemed inclined to linger.

"It's the sergeant's birthday. Some of us were planning to go along to the pub after work, buy him a round or two. Want to come?"

Gemma had worked hard to improve her relationship with Sergeant Talley, who had initially resented her posting. It would certainly be politic to join in the festivities, even if only for a few minutes. Could she juggle things with the children, now that she knew Duncan would be late—if he got home at all? "I'll try—" she began, when her mobile phone rang again.

Melody gave her a little wave of acknowledgment and slipped out the door.

Assuming it was Duncan ringing her back, Gemma flipped open the phone without checking the ID. "Look, I'm sorry. I was—"

"Gemma?" The voice was female and puzzled. "It's Winnie. I've a favor to ask."

He mingled with the crowd, moving around the fringes, careful to keep his expression neutral, careful not to watch too greedily. He'd left the scene last night before the brigade arrived—staying to watch a burn was a luxury he'd long since learned to deny himself—and had only come back after full daylight, when they'd begun to clear up.

A purposeful air was an essential part of his camouflage. A morning coffee, a bit of shopping, a paper from the newsagents—he'd even brushed deliberately against one of the detectives as the man sheltered in the doorway of an office building, making a phone call.

He'd seen the CID arrive, of course, and smiled to himself as they poked through the debris, looking for clues he hadn't left.

He'd seen the pathologist, too, and had watched the removal of the body bag with a mild surprise. The body was a first, a bonus, like the prize in a Christmas cracker after the pop. He felt no remorse, only curiosity, and an unexpected spike of excitement. The future might prove more interesting than even he had thought.

4

The Borough of Southwark . . . consisteth of divers
streets, ways, and winding lanes, all full of buildings.
As a subsidy to the king, this borough yieldeth
about . . . eight hundred pounds, which is more than
any one city in England payeth, except London.

JOHN STOW, 1598

AS SHE HUNCHED her shoulders against the persistent drizzle, Maura Bell grimaced at the stench coming from the
damp wool of her coat. Even in the relatively fresh air outside the building, the cloth held the rankness of smoke and
a faint scent of corruption. The coat was new, as well, carefully budgeted for, and put on for the first time early that
morning. To think she'd been pleased at the drop in temperature, unusual for September, that had allowed her to wear
her purchase early. Now, she'd have to send the coat to the
dry cleaners as soon as she could change, and God knew if
even that would salvage it.

It amazed her to think that there were those, like Farrell
and Jake Martinelli, who chose to work fire scenes on a

daily basis—but then there were plenty who'd say the same about her choice of profession. Not that there weren't days when she'd agree with them, and this was certainly looking like one of them.

She'd organized the uniformed constables into search teams for the house-to-house—or rather building-to-building—and was now awaiting the arrival of the warehouse's construction foreman, one Joe Spender. In a futile effort to keep out the damp, she hitched her collar up, and wished it were possible to organize a crime scene while holding a brolly. That was all she needed, to prance about like Mary bloody Poppins when she had Scotland Yard on her patch.

In retrospect, the day had begun well enough. She'd got into the station early, beating the traffic from her flat on the Isle of Dogs. She liked to drive rather than take the train and the tube; the time cocooned in her car allowed her to sort her thoughts, gear up or unwind, and having the car in the Borough gave her the freedom to follow up case leads without depending on the station motor pool.

First on the rota, she'd been pleased to draw a major case, a suspicious fire with a possible homicide, and when a trace of the building's ownership had returned a holding company linked with Michael Yarwood, she'd felt a shiver of excitement. Sensitive, yes—Yarwood was an important presence in the Borough—but this was the sort of case that could add rocket fuel to a career.

Then her chief superintendent had called her into his office and told her Michael Yarwood had requested that the Yard be brought in, and she'd been fuming with resentment ever since. Power and influence, that was what it was all about, and if she'd thought the job was proof against it, she'd been a fool.

And what had high-and-mighty Scotland Yard accomplished so far? They'd slouched through the crime scene, the superintendent had nipped off to make a phone call, and the sergeant was chatting up one of the female SOCOs. Even had she been disposed to feel charitable towards the Scotland Yard superintendent sent to pour oil on the waters, his casual demeanor would have raised her hackles. You'd have thought he was out for a walk in the park, for all the urgency in his manner, and he was too good-looking by half. Maura distrusted handsome men in general, and found the combination of looks and rank particularly threatening.

The sergeant, now, he wasn't so bad, although a bit rabbity with his fair English coloring and his Harry Potter glasses. Not her type, of course; she liked her men big and brawny; but he seemed friendly enough and not too full of himself.

She fished in the pockets of her coat for the cigarettes she'd been trying to give up. Might as well be hung for a sheep as a lamb, she thought with a grimace. Surely no one could complain that her hair and clothes smelled of cigarette smoke, not after her exposure to the fire reek. Not, she reminded herself, that there was anyone likely to complain . . .

"Inspector Bell." It was the sergeant, Cullen, followed by an enormous man in a flat cap and yellow safety jacket. "This is Joe Spender, the job foreman."

"Mr. Spender." Maura hastily stuffed the unlit cigarette back in her pocket and forced herself not to step back as Spender loomed over her. He must have been all of six foot five, with a belly that hung over his belt, and the florid complexion indicative of high blood pressure. "What can you tell us?"

He was shaking his head even as she spoke, his eyes flicking towards the ruin of the warehouse. "I can't believe it. Couldn't believe it when Mr. Yarwood rang me this morning." His accent was East End, comfortable. "Yesterday, when we finished up, everything was shipshape."

Kincaid, the Scotland Yard man, had finished his phone

call and come across to the group, but he stood a few feet back, listening.

"You didn't leave anyone behind in the building?" asked Maura.

"No. But that's the first thing I thought when I heard. What if one of my blokes forgot his lunch pail or something and went back, but I checked right off, and all my crew are accounted for. Crazy idea, anyway, as I'm the only one with a key."

"And you locked the premises before you left?"

"'Course I did," Spender said vehemently, but Maura thought she saw a bit of the color leach from his flushed face. "I always lock up, side door and then the front. Yesterday was no different."

"Anyone else have access to your key?" asked the superintendent. When Spender gave him a startled glance, he introduced himself. "Scotland Yard. I'm Superintendent Kincaid."

Spender glanced at his warrant card, shaking Kincaid's hand a little more enthusiastically than he had Maura's. "Not unless you count my wife and my two girls at home in Poplar. They're eight and six, by the way, my girls."

"What about the furniture?" Maura put in quickly, determined not to lose control of the interview. The man would be pulling out wallet photos of his kiddies if she wasn't careful. "Where did it come from?"

Spender turned back to the building. "Cheap furnished flats, that's how the place was being used when Mr. Yarwood bought it. Not much better than squats. He had a time getting the last of the tenants out, had to cut the power and water, but then we were able to get in.

"We started on the ground floor, pulling out walls to make the restaurant space. Then we moved all the furniture from the flats downstairs, ready for the rubbish skips. Should have come yesterday, the skips, but there was a delay with the delivery."

"Restaurant space?" Kincaid asked, frowning.

"Luxury flats upstairs, restaurant downstairs. A celebrity chef, you know, like what's his name, the cheeky chappy. But now . . ." Spender sighed, shrugged. "Who knows how long it will take to get this sorted, if at all."

"Problem with the insurance?" Kincaid commented easily, as if it was to be expected, but Spender's reply was wary.

"Not that I know of. It's just these things take time. You know how it is."

Kincaid gazed at the building, hands in the pockets of his Burberry. "Word has it the leases haven't sold as fast as Mr. Yarwood had hoped."

"It's too soon to say that." Spender's voice held the first trace of irritation. "There's no doubt they'd have sold, a place this close to the South Bank and London Bridge Station."

"Let's get back to the furniture, shall we?" said Maura, grinding her teeth. "How did you leave it yesterday?"

"Piled in the middle of the bloody room, wasn't it? To give us as much working space as possible."

"It didn't occur to you it was a fire danger?"

"What else were we going to do with the stuff? Put it out in the street for a traffic hazard?"

"What about your crew? Any of them smoke?"

"Look, Inspector." Spender took a breath and seemed to gain another inch or two in height. The friendly aura had vanished. "None of my lads left a fag end to smolder and set that furniture alight, if that's what you're thinking. They've more sense than that, and I've told you I checked the building over before I locked up. We left nothing out of place."

"And you're absolutely positive you locked both doors?" she asked.

"Of course I'm bloody sure. Do you take me for an idiot?"

Maura saw Sergeant Cullen glance at her and thought she

read a trace of amusement. "Mr. Spender," she began tightly, "we do need your cooperation here—"

"Mr. Spender, excuse me," Kincaid broke in with his easy smile. "You may be able to account for your key, but surely there's more than one?"

Following Winnie's instructions, Gemma took the tube to Waterloo and walked south along Waterloo Road, passing the hulk of the railway terminal and the grimy brickwork of the lockups that abutted it. The rain had let up, but puddles stood on the pavement and the sky was still as solidly gray as gunmetal.

How odd, she mused as she picked up her stride, that she should find herself on the edge of Southwark, when Duncan had only that morning been summoned out to a case in the same borough. And odder still, the call from Winnie Montfort, who was not one to make spur-of-the-moment demands.

Fortunately, Gemma hadn't anything too pressing for a Friday afternoon, and as her lunch usually consisted of a sandwich brought up from the canteen, she didn't feel terribly guilty about taking a longer than usual lunch break. She had, in fact, been feeling rather restless and unsettled, and was glad for an excuse to stretch her legs and breathe in the cool, damp air flowing from the river.

She and Duncan had managed to see Winnie only once since Winnie had come up to London from her Somerset parish, and that had been on one of the weekends when Jack had joined her. Winnie and Jack had come to Notting Hill, duly admiring the house, and giving Gemma the opportunity to try out her very unpolished cooking and entertaining skills. Gemma had never had much time to cook and, until now, had certainly never lived anywhere with the space or the atmosphere conducive to giving dinner parties.

There had been times that evening, watching the group

around her candlelit dining room table, when she'd felt like a child playing dress-up. But if she'd felt like an impostor in her own home, she had also, rather to her surprise, enjoyed herself. Not that she was in any danger of turning into Stella Fairchild-Priestly, the queen of hostesses, but perhaps her social life had begun to evolve past spag bol and a bottle of plonk.

Of course, she and Winnie had ended the evening with promises to get together soon, but then work had intervened on her part and she supposed the same had been true for Winnie. It was a shame, she thought now, as she was beginning to realize how desperately she missed having a close female friend now that Hazel Cavendish had gone.

Reaching The Cut, she turned left, passing the Old Vic Theatre on one side and a council estate on the other. Winnie had suggested they meet for a quick lunch at a pub called the Hope and Anchor, near her church and her temporary accommodation. Then, Winnie had promised, she'd explain why she'd rung.

The Cut, for all its unusual name, was an unremarkable street, lined with small grocer's shops, cafés, dry cleaners, newsagents. Damp squares of betting slips littered the pavement outside a bookie's premises, like giant confetti, and Gemma thought she smelled a faint tang of smoke beneath the traffic fumes.

Just as she spotted the pub's name above an unassuming shop front, she saw Winnie standing outside, watching for her. If Winnie Montfort was not strictly beautiful, most people forgot it as soon as she smiled. Her pleasant face radiated honesty and humor, and she had the knack of making those she spoke to feel they had her undivided attention. Today, her soft brown hair curled about her face in the damp, and her clerical collar provided a slash of contrast beneath her cherry-colored raincoat.

Her face lit with pleasure at Gemma's approach, and she

gave her a quick hug. "Gemma, thanks for coming. They're holding a table for us—I've just checked."

"Busy place?" Gemma asked as she followed her inside.

"It's gaining quite a reputation as a gastro pub," Winnie told her, grinning. "Awful term, isn't it? Always makes me think of some unmentionable complaint. But the food *is* good, and it's more or less my local."

The bar, with simple wooden tables and an upright piano in the corner, took up the right-hand side of the space, while partially drawn velvet drapes marked off the restaurant area to the left. A waiter seated them at a small table near the back of the restaurant and handed them laminated menu cards.

When they'd ordered—pollock and greens for Gemma, a chicken and mushroom pie for Winnie—they settled back with their drinks. "All right, first things first," said Gemma, spreading a piece of brown, crusty bread with pale fresh butter. "How's Jack? Is he coming up to town this weekend?"

"'Fraid not. The commission in Bristol is keeping him busy. He may not get away again until the job's complete."

"Can you not go to him?"

"I only have one day off a week—not long enough to go to Glastonbury and back. And even that day is subject to emergencies."

"Sounds a bit like the police," Gemma said ruefully. "Good thing you picked an understanding bloke."

"It is, isn't it?" agreed Winnie, sipping at the small glass of Pinot Grigio she'd ordered with her meal. "Although sometimes I wonder if I'd feel less guilty about juggling the job and the relationship if he *weren't* so understanding. What about Duncan and the boys? Any news on the Eugenia front?"

"We've a preliminary hearing scheduled next week." As if their family situation weren't already complicated enough, Kit's maternal grandmother, Eugenia Potts, had filed for custody of thirteen-year-old Kit. Since Kit's legal guardian, Ian McClellan, had moved to Canada, he had allowed Kit to live with Duncan, his natural father, and Gemma.

Eugenia, however, appeared to blame Duncan for her daughter's death, and could not bear the idea of her grandson living happily with his father. And although Kit despised his grandmother, he'd not been willing to take the DNA test that would prove Duncan's paternity without a doubt, thus giving Duncan clear legal rights.

Kit's stubbornness over the testing meant that Duncan and Gemma would be forced to rely on the understanding of the family court judge, and on the hope that the judge would see Kit as old enough to decide where, and with whom, he wanted to live. It was all very worrying, and since Eugenia had filed her petition the previous May, tensions had been running high in their household.

"We had an outing planned to Portobello Market tomorrow to look for some things for Kit," Gemma told Winnie, and found herself expressing feelings she hadn't been able to articulate to herself. "I really thought we should all be together, as a family, to reassure Kit that we'll continue to be a family . . . But Duncan can't make it . . ."

"Work?"

Gemma nodded. "A case came up. Here in Southwark, as a matter of fact."

"I wouldn't worry about your outing," said Winnie. "Kit knows how committed you are, and the last thing he needs now is to feel any sort of divisiveness between you and Duncan."

"I'm sure you're right," Gemma admitted. "It's just nerves. I suppose I hate the idea of being put on show as a model family. What if we don't measure up?"

"You measure up as far as Kit's concerned, and I'm sure that's what counts." Winnie buttered a slice of bread for herself. "What about your friend Hazel? I'm sure she'd testify on your behalf."

"She would, but she's in Scotland."

"Trying to make a go of her distillery?"

Gemma nodded, fighting back the sudden, mortifying prickle of tears. After the tragic events of the previous spring, she'd encouraged Hazel to do what she thought right, even if it meant staying in Scotland, but she hadn't realized what it would mean to lose the supportive presence of her closest friend.

She took a sip from her half pint of cider, concentrating on the feel of the bubbles against her tongue, hoping that her voice wouldn't betray her. "She and Tim are talking, at least, and they've agreed for the time being not to sell the Islington house."

"Any hope of a reconciliation?"

Gemma sighed. "I don't know. It would be hard, after what's happened, for either of them." Their food arrived, and Gemma was glad of an excuse to change the subject.

"Now, why don't you tell me why you rang?" she said, picking up her cutlery, but a cloud of steam rose from the perfectly arranged food on her plate. "I'm dying of curiosity."

"Well, I hope I haven't been hasty," confessed Winnie. "But this is outside my experience, and I wasn't sure if it was a matter for the police, so you seemed the obvious person to consult. And my parishioner wasn't too keen on the idea of going to the police . . ."

"I was the unofficial solution?" Gemma asked, a little amused, imagining a teenager caught stealing, or an accumulation of traffic citations. She hoped she hadn't been called out for a kitten stranded on a fire escape, but in any case it looked as if she was going to get a good lunch for her time.

As Winnie began to tell her about Frances Liu's missing roommate, her amusement quickly faded.

"I've been round to Guy's Hospital, where Elaine works,"

Winnie continued, "and got them to tell me that not only did she not show up for work this morning, she didn't call in. Her coworkers say she's very punctual and dependable; she's seldom missed work at all, and never without notice."

"Does she have family you could ring? Boyfriend? Ex-husband?"

"Not that Fanny knows of, and that strikes me as a bit funny as well. I mean, how many people do you know without connections of some sort?"

"Had she been behaving oddly?"

"Not that Fanny noticed . . . or not that Fanny admits noticing, anyway."

Deciding her food had cooled enough to taste, Gemma took a bite of meltingly tender white fish and sautéed greens. "Blimey," she said, closing her eyes in bliss. "This is wonderful." Swallowing, she forced her attention back to the matter at hand. "What about the local hospitals? Did you check to see if she'd been admitted?"

"I checked Guy's and St. Thomas's," answered Winnie. "No one by that name, nor any Jane Does. And that left me at a dead end. I thought that perhaps if you were to talk to Fanny, you could convince her to file a missing-persons report."

"Do you know why she's so reluctant?"

The pub had filled to capacity since they'd come in, and Winnie leaned a little closer in order to be heard above the rising babble of voices. "She said Elaine's very protective of her privacy, and would be angry if Fanny had called attention to her unnecessarily." Winnie frowned and toyed with a forkful of her chicken pie. "But I also think that Fanny has a horror of making a fuss, of being seen as the hysterical invalid."

"That's understandable, I suppose," Gemma said thoughtfully. "But although the most likely explanation is that her friend has done a runner, the situation is odd enough that I think she's justified in sounding an alarm. Does she live nearby, then?" she added, thinking reluctantly of the work that would be piling up on her desk at Notting Hill. She wouldn't be getting away early enough that evening to toast Sergeant Talley's birthday.

"Not five minutes from here, just across from my church." Winnie smiled. "It'll give you a chance to show you where I slave away my days."

Kath Warren shut herself in the toilet adjoining her office and leaned against the basin, holding on to the cold porcelain edge as if it were the only anchor in an unstable universe. She took deep breaths, counting in, counting out, and after a moment she turned on the cold tap and held her wrists beneath the stream. When the faintness began to pass, she shut the water off and reached for the towel, only to find it had disappeared from the hook—nicked by one of the shelter residents, she supposed, as per bloody usual. Tearing off a bit of toilet tissue from the roll, she dried her hands and gazed at herself in the fly-specked mirror over the basin.

She saw carefully streaked hair, expensively feathered over her ears and at the nape of her neck. Regular features, nose a bit turned up, skin taut and evenly tanned from weekly sessions in the tanning salon. A good face, she told herself, an attractive face, but in the cold light filtering through the toilet window, there was no denying it was the face of a forty-five-year-old woman.

How could she possibly have convinced herself it didn't matter? She'd risked her job, her marriage, her children, her comfortable semidetached house in Peckham, all for a few quick encounters on the stained and threadbare sofa in her office.

Encounters. That was a euphemism even shabbier than *passed on* or *developmentally challenged.* She could at least be honest with herself. It had been *sex*—sweaty, pulseracing, heart-pounding, skin-tingling sex—and she had wanted it with a ferocity she hadn't known she possessed.

And she had believed that it mattered as much to him as it did to her. She had been an utter fool, a stupid, pathetically middle-aged fool, and now she would have to deal with the consequences.

The phone call had come that morning as Michael Yarwood was downing a last cup of coffee in his Birmingham hotel room before beginning the first day of a three-day Labour conference. While the official agenda held topics such as "Communicating with Your Constituents" and "The Question of Tax," the real purpose of the meeting was to meet and greet, to make or cement alliances that would further one's political ambitions. If he had been naive enough in his early days as an MP to think that his own convictions mattered, he had long since learned the error of his ways. But if he'd learned to play the game, he'd also learned to enjoy it for its own sake, and he'd been looking forward to the weekend as a way to take his mind off more personal troubles.

Then the police had rung his London office, and the dominoes had begun to topple. His secretary had rung him, her voice squeaky with distress; he had taken the first available train, then a taxi from the station, stopping only to drop off his overnight bag at his flat. Now, he stood staring in disbelief at the remains of his building, struggling for breath as if he'd just been kicked in the chest by a draft horse. He hadn't imagined it would be so bad, hadn't really visualized the gaping windows, the piles of rubble on the pavement.

Reduced to rubble. Maybe it was fitting for a bricklayer's son with aspirations above his station. He'd been eighteen when he'd bought his first small delivery van with the earnings from his second job; twenty-five when he'd stood for his first council seat. He'd balanced his anomalous roles as

small-business owner and Labour activist by his personal re-
jection of the greed-driven principles of big business and his
unswerving dedication to improving his borough. Until,
driven by his worries over Chloe, he'd given in to the temp-
tations of the property market, and now he was facing financial disaster.

Or worse. His secretary had informed him that the prime
minister's office had unofficially requested that Scotland
Yard oversee the case, and that was the last thing he needed.

A movement caught his eye. Turning, he saw a reporter
coming towards him, accompanied by an assistant wielding
a handheld video cam like an unnatural appendage. For a
moment he wondered wildly if he had conjured them up
from the depths of his imagination. But no, they were real
enough. The red eye of the camera held him mercilessly, and
he struggled to resurrect his public face as the reporter held
out a mike.

But before the reporter could speak, there was a touch on
his shoulder and a quiet voice said, "Mr. Yarwood? I'm with
the police. If we could have a word."

Kincaid had recognized Yarwood immediately, but had been
content to observe him for a few moments. The man was
smaller in stature than he appeared on television, nor did he
seem to have the assurance that had always leapt from the
screen. Was it shock, Kincaid wondered, or did the camera
amplify certain character traits?

Yarwood wore no overcoat—he had not, perhaps, planned
to spend his day standing in the rain—and the fit of his dark
suit suggested Savile Row. No amount of tailoring, however,
could really make the man look as though he belonged in a
suit. He was too burly, too barrel-chested, his arms and
shoulders out of proportion to the rest of his body, his legs
short as a wrestler's.

It had seemed strange to see Yarwood's bulldog face

wiped clean of its usual cheerful belligerence; stranger still to see his expression of dismay at the journalists' approach.

Seeing no advantage to letting the press have their way with Yarwood just yet, Kincaid hurried to the rescue. When he'd introduced himself, deftly turning Yarwood away from the camera, he looked round for a place where they could talk.

The rain seemed to have stopped for the moment, at least, making shelter less of a necessity, but it was still difficult to find somewhere that afforded privacy and the least likelihood of being trampled by firefighters with rakes and axes. The side street between Yarwood's warehouse and the similar building next door had been blocked off completely with crime scene tape. Making a quick decision, Kincaid ducked under the tape and led Yarwood towards a spot by the facing building's side door.

Cullen was busy taking details from Spender, the job foreman, but DI Bell caught his eye and came to join them. Kincaid introduced them, but Yarwood seemed not to take it in. He stared at the burned building as if mesmerized.

"The body—they say you found a body—is it still . . ." His eyes shifted towards the building, like an involuntary tic.

"No," Kincaid told him. "It's been taken to the morgue, for examination. Have you any idea how a woman ended up dead in your building, Mr. Yarwood?"

"A woman?" Was it Kincaid's imagination, or had he seen a jolt of panic in the man's eyes? If so, Yarwood managed to disguise it, shoving his hands in his pockets and rocking on the balls of his feet. "My guess would be that the construction crew left the building open and some poor soul wandered in off the street."

"That occurred to us as well," Kincaid said agreeably. "But Mr. Spender, your job foreman, says he checked the locks himself when they finished up for the day, and both doors were well fastened."

"Well, perhaps he's mistaken," Yarwood ventured after a moment's pause. It was obvious he didn't want to call his foreman a liar.

"Or maybe someone came along later and unlocked it again," suggested Bell, her Scots accent sounding clearly. "Where were you last night, Mr. Yarwood?"

Yarwood stared at her in surprise. "You're not suggesting—"

If Kincaid had needed a partner in good cop/bad cop, he had certainly got it. "It's routine, you understand, Mr. Yarwood. We have to ask these things, and it's to your benefit to get things clear from the beginning."

"My benefit?" Yarwood sounded puzzled.

"We have a possible homicide and a possible arson here. As you are the owner of the property, the Fire Investigation Team will naturally need to rule you out—as will your insurance company. Insurance fraud is more common than you'd think."

Yarwood ran a hand through his short, thinning hair, and seemed to gather himself. "Of course. I understand that. I was in Birmingham, at a party conference. I had dinner in the hotel restaurant with some other attendees, then went to bed."

"Mr. Spender says you have the only other set of keys to the warehouse. Did you have them with you?" asked Bell.

"No, they're at home in my flat. Why would I carry them with me?"

"Why indeed?" agreed Bell lightly, but there was no humor in her voice. "We'll need the details, of course, Mr. Yarwood, but even if you were safely put up in the Midlands last night, that doesn't rule out a bit of professional help."

"Now look, Inspector, you can't accuse me of setting my own warehouse alight." Yarwood glared at her with a return of his characteristic attitude, as if he were suddenly on firmer ground.

"No, not at this stage, anyway." Bell allowed herself a small smile. "But there are rumors going round that you were in financial trouble, that your leases weren't selling fast enough to cover your construction costs."

"That's simply not true," Yarwood said with assurance. "The project's barely off the ground, and we'd never expected to sell off all the leases until the flats were finished." He frowned at Bell, his heavy forehead creasing. "You said *possible arson.* That means you've no proof that the fire wasn't an accident."

"Not yet." Bell's tone implied that it was only a matter of time, and she gave him a challenging stare.

Kincaid thought he should intervene before they resorted to head-banging. "Mr. Yarwood, let's just say that we find that the fire was started deliberately. Have you any idea why someone would want to burn your warehouse?"

"*No.* Absolutely none." Yarwood's denial was firm, accompanied by a sharp shake of his head, but this time Kincaid had no doubt. He'd seen the flash of fear in the man's eyes.

5

The chief features in the still life of the street are green
shutters, lodging-bills, brass door-plates, and bell-
handles; the principal specimens of animated nature, the
pot-boy, the muffin youth, and the baked-potato man.

CHARLES DICKENS
The Pickwick Papers

GEMMA AND WINNIE left the pub, crossing the busy road,
then soon made a jog into the aptly named Short Street.
Winnie pointed out her church, a nondescript brown brick
structure that paralleled the street on their left.

"And that's Mitre Road." Winnie gestured to the street of
neat Victorian terraces that ran off to the right. "My flat's
about halfway along, first floor. It's quite nice—cozy compared to my drafty vicarage at home. I promise I'll have you
both over for a meal.

"And Fanny's house is just there," she added as Short
Street came to an abrupt end at Ufford Street. "Practically
on my doorstep."

They were neat as dolls' houses, thought Gemma as she

studied the two-storied terraces lining Ufford Street. The houses looked cheerful even on such a gray day, the red tile roofs steeply peaked, the gables white, the narrow front doors a glossy black. Most of the houses, she noticed, sported flowered number plaques and hanging baskets. A black iron fence ran the length of the terrace, separating tiny front gardens from the street. A glance towards the end of the street revealed a massive gray brick warehouse and, looming above it, the unexpected silhouette of the Millennium Wheel.

"It's easy to forget how close we are to the Thames," said Winnie, following Gemma's gaze as they crossed the road. "And that everything here in Southwark used to revolve around the river. The churches still hold remembrance masses for those lost at sea." She opened one of the iron gates and led Gemma up to a covered porch. A wheelchair ramp bridged a slight incline to the front door. She rang the bell, then opened the door and called out, "Fanny? It's Winnie. I've brought a friend."

"Oh, what a lovely smell," exclaimed Gemma as she followed Winnie into a sitting room as green and flowery as a cottage garden brought indoors.

"Do you like it?" The woman in the wheelchair rolled towards them, her small oval face lit with pleasure. "It's one of my candles. I make them, from soy wax and essential oils. This one's a blend of bergamot, lavender, and ylang-ylang—it's meant to be calming." On a small table near her chair, a candle burned in a green glass jar. Beside it lay a walk-about phone.

"Fanny single-handedly supports the church bazaar," added Winnie, when she'd introduced Gemma. "Her candles are the biggest seller. It's not only the scents that are wonderful—she uses all sorts of things for containers. Teacups, antique glass jars, flowerpots—"

"Basically, anything I can get my hands on," Fanny explained. "I used to haunt car boot sales; now I have to make do with what friends bring me. Elaine—" She stopped, her voice suddenly unsteady.

Winnie pulled up a chair for Gemma before sitting on the end of the chaise longue. "Have you heard from her?" she asked Fanny.

On closer inspection, Gemma saw that Fanny Liu looked tired, and that her dark eyes were red-rimmed as if she'd been weeping.

"No." Fanny shook her head. "Nothing. I tried her office again, just in case."

"And you've rung her mobile phone?" Gemma asked.

"She doesn't have one. An unnecessary expense, she said. Elaine likes to mind her pennies." Fanny studied Gemma for a moment, her head tilted to one side. "Winnie said you had something to do with the police, that you could advise us. But you're not quite what I expected."

"No uniform?" Gemma smiled. "I'm in CID. We wear plain clothes. Why don't you tell me about your friend?" she added, leaning forward in her chair, her hands clasped on her knee. "Start from the beginning."

"Her name is Elaine Holland. She—" Fanny's voice wavered and cracked. "She—she works in the medical records department at Guy's Hospital. She's an administrative assistant."

"Winnie said she rents a room from you," prompted Gemma, when Fanny paused. "How did the two of you get together?"

"I posted a notice on the hospital board. I was a nurse before my illness, so I knew it was a good way to find someone compatible. I offered a reduced rent, in return for help with chores around the house and shopping. Elaine was the first applicant I had and we made a deal on the spot."

"How long ago was that?"

"Almost two years."

Gemma smiled. "So you must have got on quite well."

"I—yes, we did. We do."

"You said this morning that her parents were dead, and she hadn't any siblings," put in Winnie. "But what about a boyfriend or an ex-husband? Or a school friend? Is there anyone else she might have gone to?"

"Elaine didn't—Elaine doesn't like to talk about personal things," Fanny said quietly, not meeting their eyes, and Gemma thought that Elaine's reticence must have hurt her. "But I don't think she's ever been married. Somehow I can't imagine her married," she added, trying for a smile.

"And she never brought anyone here, to the flat?"

Fanny shook her head. "Never. I told her she was welcome to have her friends in, when she first arrived, but then after a while the subject just never came up. I suppose we got into a routine."

A slight thump came from the kitchen, and a black-and-white cat appeared in the sitting room doorway. It regarded them seriously for a moment, as if assessing their suitability as guests, before jumping into its mistress's lap and curling into a ball. "This is Quinn," Fanny explained to Gemma, stroking the cat. "He has his own cat flap so that I don't have to let him in and out of the garden. Elaine's allergic to cats, so it's better if he doesn't spend all day in the house. Then she's all right as long as he stays out of her bedroom, but you know how cats are—it's a battle of wits between them. If she leaves her door open for a minute he's in like a shot."

Gemma smiled, thinking of their cat, Sid, and his unerring talent for picking out those with feline phobia. "Did Elaine have any other health problems that you know of?" she asked. "Seizures? A bad heart?"

"No, not that she ever mentioned. But she was good at looking after others—I mean, she knew how to do . . . things." A flush of embarrassment rose in Fanny's cheeks. "I asked her once, in the beginning, if she'd done any nursing,

but she said no. She was a bit sharp about it, to be honest."
She looked up, meeting Gemma's gaze. "You think she's
fallen ill somewhere. But Winnie's already rung the hospitals . . ."

"I think it's a possibility we have to consider." Gemma
looked round the room, suddenly aware of the one thing
missing in the clutter. "Fanny, do you have a photo of
Elaine?"

"No." She frowned, as if the realization surprised her. "I
can't remember there ever being an occasion to take one."

"She didn't bring any photos of her own?"

"Not unless they're upstairs in her room."

Winnie gave Gemma a quick negative shake of her head.

Glancing at her friend, Gemma thought it was no wonder
Winnie had rung her. All her instincts told her there was
something not quite right here. "Why don't you give me a
description, then?" she suggested to Fanny.

"Well, she's about my age, midthirties, I'd say." Fanny
looked at Winnie as if for verification and Winnie nodded.

"You don't know exactly?" Gemma asked, curious.

"Elaine didn't hold with birthdays," Fanny murmured, her
hands twisting in the cat's fur, but he only stirred a little and
narrowed his eyes.

"Okay." Gemma smiled, trying to put her at ease. "What
else?"

"Um, she's tallish. Fair-complexioned. Brown hair, about
like this"—Fanny held a hand level with her chin—"with a
bit of wave to it. Light brown eyes."

"I think that's good enough for a report. We can just ring—"

Fanny was shaking her head, her eyes wide with distress.
"I told Winnie I didn't want anything official. I don't
want—"

"Look, I understand you don't want to upset your friend."
Gemma tried to soothe the woman's agitation. "But I think
you have a serious welfare concern here, and for Elaine's

sake, you must report her disappearance to the police. What if she's lying ill somewhere and needs help? We'll ring the local station, then Winnie and I can wait with you until they send someone round."

"You'd do that?" Fanny sounded surprised, and Gemma wondered how much support Elaine had actually provided.

"Of course we would," Winnie assured her.

Fanny closed her eyes for a moment, her hands still on the cat's back. Then she sighed, as if coming to a decision, and looked up at Gemma. "Okay. But will *you* call?" She nodded towards the phone. "I—I don't want to have to explain why I can't come in to the station."

"It's all right. They won't expect it," Gemma told her, but she was happy enough to comply. She rang the local station directly, as she hated to tie up a 999 line with a nonemergency call, and identified herself. The duty officer said he'd send someone round as soon as he could, but they were a bit shorthanded because they'd had a fire.

"Yeah, got half my constables tied up with house-to-house and perimeter control," the officer responded. "Southwark Street, not far from your address."

It was close, Gemma thought as she hung up, visualizing the page of the *A to Z* she'd glanced at before meeting Winnie. Why not take the tube from London Bridge Station, rather than Waterloo, when she returned to the office? Her route would take her right past Southwark Street—she could see what was going on, have a word with Duncan.

In the meantime, however, she had another idea. As Winnie volunteered to make them all a cup of coffee, Gemma said, "Fanny, do you mind if I have a look at Elaine's things? I might see something that Winnie missed this morning."

Fanny gave her a bleak smile. "If something's happened to her, it won't matter that she wouldn't like it. And if she's okay, she'll be so furious with me for making a fuss that I might as well be hung for a sheep as a lamb. Go ahead."

Gemma climbed the narrow stairs and looked in the first room at the top. The flowers and antiques identified it as Fanny's, but it had the desolate feel acquired by rooms whose inhabitants had died. An ornate mahogany dressing table held the personal photos she had expected to see downstairs—Fanny as a girl, posed between a well-dressed Asian couple who looked both proud and rather stiffly formal, as if the portrait had been an occasion. Fanny playing in a garden with a Border collie, laughing into the camera. Fanny alone, in a nursing sister's uniform, her expression grave. Gemma touched the photo with a fingertip, then went out, closing the door firmly behind her.

She examined the bathroom more closely, this time looking for traces of Elaine Holland. The medicine cabinet held paracetemol, plasters, cotton swabs, a bottle of over-the-counter cough remedy. There were no prescription medications, no hairbrush, no toothbrush. Frowning, Gemma tried the cupboard above the toilet. It held only toilet tissue, tampons, a few bars of inexpensive soap, and a bottle of Boots brand bubble bath.

Perhaps Elaine kept her personal things in her bedroom, Gemma thought, moving on to the third room in the corridor and opening the door. Winnie had told her over lunch that the room was bare, but the description hadn't prepared Gemma for the bleakness that met her eyes as she stood on the threshold.

In Gemma's experience, the need to stamp one's personality on one's living space seemed a basic human need, one that surfaced as soon as the essentials of food and shelter were provided. She'd seen prostitutes' rooms decorated with ribbons, pictures—only bits of tat from the street markets, but much loved tat nonetheless. She'd seen nursing-home quarters filled with personal mementos. She'd even known rough sleepers on the streets to guard their few possessions as fiercely as they did their blankets, as if those possessions allowed them to keep a remnant of the identity life had stripped away.

But this room bore no more imprint than a cheap hotel room slept in for a night—it was as if Elaine Holland had vigilantly erased herself every day of the two years she had lived in this house. There were no photos, no books, no magazines or CDs, no clothes left haphazardly strewn across the bed or the chair. Gemma crossed to the bureau and ran a finger across its surface—there was only a light coating of dust.

Methodically, she opened the drawers. At least the woman wore underwear, she thought with a grin, although they were nondescript Marks and Spencer's cotton knickers and bras. One drawer held a pad of cheap writing paper with matching envelopes, a few stamps, elastic bands, and pens marked with the hospital logo, but there were no bills or personal documents.

She went on to the wardrobe with as little success. A few pairs of sensible shoes, trousers and jackets in neutral colors suitable for work and, Gemma noted, in the same size she wore. A shelf held neatly folded blankets and bed linens. The wardrobe was quite deep, and on an impulse, Gemma lifted down the linens, then pulled over the bureau chair and climbed up on it so that she could reach all the way to the back of the shelf.

Her fingers closed on a small cardboard box and she drew it into the light, exclaiming as she saw the bright colors. It was the manufacturer's container for an Orange phone, and it was empty.

So, in spite of her protestations to Fanny, Elaine owned a mobile phone. But why had she lied?

Flushed by her success, Gemma climbed down from the chair and stood back, surveying the storage space. There had to be more—she was sure of it. Pushing all the hanging clothes aside, she was rewarded for her diligence. A low

door was set into the back wall of the cupboard, a not unusual feature in many old houses. The extra storage space
was remarkably easy to access, once you knew of its existence, and the latch was a simple hook and eye.

Kneeling, Gemma swung open the door. A faint odor of
old mothballs wafted out, and she saw immediately that she
had hit a treasure trove. Some of the open shoe boxes on the
floor held strappy, high-heeled sandals, others an assortment
of lacy lingerie. Folded over hangers on a low bar were se-
quined tops and sleek skirts, a few low-cut cocktail dresses,
a beaded vintage cardigan.

Gemma sat back, wondering what to make of her find.
One thing was certain—there was more to Elaine Holland
than her housemate had dreamed.

When asked by her fellow firefighters why she still lived at
home, Rose would say the decision was purely practical—
there was room in her parents' house, after all, and why
should she waste money paying rent when she could be sav-
ing towards a deposit on a place of her own? Living in London was prohibitively expensive, and firefighters' earnings
ranked on the low end of the scale.

She didn't talk about her father's unexpected death from
heart failure the previous year, nor about her reluctance to
leave her mother alone in the house her parents had shared
for the thirty years of their marriage. She was even less
likely to admit that she couldn't yet bear the thought of leaving the house that still bore such tangible reminders of the
father she'd adored.

The drive from Southwark southeast to suburban Forest
Hills usually came as a relief at the end of her watch. With
some of the money she saved on rent she'd splashed out on
her car, a fire-engine-red Mini with a Union Jack painted on
the top. She loved the way the little car handled, and the
sense of physical engagement she felt as she drove helped

her shed the stresses of her shift. The blokes teased her about the car, of course, but it was the good-natured ribbing of approval. They could understand her attachment to a collection of nuts and bolts.

But today not even the drive had helped her unwind, and as she pulled up in front of the semidetached house not far from the main parade in Forest Hills, she realized she had the steering wheel clenched in a white-knuckled grip. She flexed her fingers and stretched the kinks from her neck, making a conscious effort to ease the tension from her body. It was a ritual with her, trying not to take the job inside, even though she knew her mum would be at work. The house was sanctuary, the one place she could be entirely herself.

She gazed at the familiar curve of the bay window, the gingerbread of the porch gable with the distinctive crosses at the bottom ends, the stained glass of the front door. At work, only Bryan Simms knew she lived in a "Christmas" house, as no explanation would allay the teasing if the rest of the watch were privy to that little tidbit. It wasn't that she was usually thin-skinned—in most cases she actually welcomed the firehouse banter and the practical jokes because they were a sign of acceptance—but the passion for the house had been shared with her dad, and it was an area still too tender for public exposure.

Edward Christmas's company thrived between 1888 and 1930, and while his houses weren't as well known as those by Arts and Crafts architects such as Voysey and Lutyens, they had a wealth of detail and a unique charm. Her parents had bought the place cheaply in the late seventies, before the resurgence of interest in the builder's work, and throughout her childhood her father had spent his spare time lovingly restoring each distinctive feature. And she'd helped him, becoming comfortable early on with woodworking and power tools, brick pointing and glass repair—all things that had stood her in good stead in the male culture of the firehouse.

Hey, will ya look at that? The flower can use a chain saw!
The memory of her sub officer's surprise still made her
smile.

A magpie lit on the gate a few feet from her car and examined her, its bright, beady eye mocking, as if it knew the
truth about her. She'd worked so hard at showing she could
do the job, at fitting in—had she blown it all that morning?
What would her station officer say when he heard she'd
gone back to the scene, off duty, without clearing it with him
first? Charlie Wilcox was a good boss, a fair man who preferred encouragement to criticism, but she had a sinking
feeling that she'd violated some unwritten protocol, made a
fool of herself, and by association, of her watch. There was
nothing worse than that. The magpie took off with a sharp
clap of wings, and her shoulders jerked involuntarily.

What had possessed her? Had she been afraid she'd
missed something, made some mistake that would come to
light? In the three years she'd been in the fire service, she'd
only worked half a dozen large structure fires, and last night
was one of the few times she'd had the nozzle. To have the
nozzle, be first on the hose, that was what every firefighter
lived for—it was the ultimate experience, it was what made
you real. She could still feel the exhilaration in her veins,
and in an instant of clarity she knew she hadn't done anything wrong, she'd simply done what she'd been trained to
do, and she'd never felt more whole in her life.

Then why did her brain keep replaying the spongy feel of
flesh beneath her gloved hand, the glimpse of the contorted
face with the bared and blackened teeth? She'd seen worse,
for God's sake—why did *this* one somehow seem to be her
responsibility?

She had to let it go. She had to sleep or she'd be useless
on her watch tonight. That she couldn't afford, especially
with the FIT coming in to question the rest of the watch. Her
visit to the fire scene was bound to come out; there was no

avoiding it. She'd just have to take her lumps from Wilcox and the others, if necessary, and put the whole episode behind her.

With that resolution, she blew a few stray hairs from her face and got out of the car. But as she let herself into the quiet house, she found herself thinking about the coming evening, wondering if the FIT officers would have any new information, and if the superintendent from Scotland Yard would be there as well.

Not wanting to say anything about her discoveries in front of Fanny, Gemma waited until the constable had come and gone, then spoke briefly to Winnie as they stood outside the church office.

Winnie shook her head in bewilderment. "Why go to so much trouble to secrete things away, when she knew Fanny couldn't climb the stairs? And why hide the things at all? Don't most single women have a few pairs of sexy knickers?"

"If they don't, they should," Gemma replied, grinning. In spite of her newly married status, Winnie could still display an endearingly innocent honesty. "What about the phone?" she asked. "Do you suppose Elaine thought Fanny would be a nuisance if she knew she could reach her on a mobile?"

"It's always seemed to me that Fanny goes out of her way not to make demands on Elaine." She shrugged. "But maybe Elaine perceived it differently. I can't guess at this point. Should we have told the constable about these things?"

"I don't think having a stash of slightly tarty clothes and a mobile phone constitutes significant detail. But it has made me curious," she added. "Will you let me know if she turns up? Do you think Fanny will be all right?"

"I'll look in on her this evening," Winnie told her. "Thanks for all your help."

After a quick hug, Gemma went on her way, cutting up

Blackfriars Road into Union Street. The rain had begun again, a drizzle too light for umbrellas but heavy enough to be annoying. She turned up the collar of her coat and clutched it closed at her throat, trying to keep the occasional drops from slipping down the back of her neck.

There was one thing she'd noticed that she hadn't felt comfortable sharing with Winnie. Fanny had frequently used the past tense when talking about her friend, although she'd corrected herself a few times. Did she know more about Elaine's disappearance than she'd let on?

"That's a nasty suspicious mind you've got," Gemma chastised herself aloud, earning a surprised glance from a passing man in a pin-striped suit. The woman was confined to a wheelchair, for heaven's sake, she went on to herself— she couldn't possibly have had anything to do with her friend's mysterious disappearance.

And Gemma certainly had enough on her plate, with her own caseload and Kit's hearing coming up on Monday, without taking on another problem. She'd lost half her afternoon as it was, and she imagined Melody Talbot beleaguered, ready to send out a search party for her. Fishing her phone from her bag, she gave Melody a quick call, explaining that something had come up but that she was now on her way back to the station.

Her ruminations and her phone call having taken her as far as Southwark Bridge Road, she took a moment to orient herself before turning north, towards the river, then right into Southwark Street. She caught sight of the distant cluster of emergency vehicles almost immediately, but it wasn't until she was almost upon them that she was able to see the scene of the fire itself.

Her first thought was one of regret, for the building had been beautiful, its form and symmetry a striking example of the best of Victorian architecture. How could someone willfully damage something so lovely? she wondered, then remembered that Kincaid had called it a *suspicious* fire. It might not have been arson.

The appliances had gone, but the generator lorry remained, and against the gray sky the lower windows of the warehouse glowed with the eerily bright light of the arc lamps. Piles of blackened rubble had been raked out onto the pavement, and even from a distance the stench made her throat constrict.

There were several marked police cars and a couple of unmarked but vaguely official-looking vans. She recognized Doug Cullen's slightly battered Vauxhall Astra pulled up over the curb. She was about to ask one of the constables guarding the perimeter where she might find Kincaid when she saw him, standing a few yards down the side street with Cullen and a dark-haired woman in a tan coat.

Gemma's lips curved in an involuntary smile; familiarity hadn't dulled the jolt of pleasure she felt on seeing him after a few hours' separation. Then he looked up and saw her, his eyes widening in surprise.

"Gemma!" he said, hurrying towards her. "What are you doing here? Is everything all right? The boys—"

"No, no, they're fine," she hastened to reassure him. "It's just that I was in the area—Winnie rang and asked me to lunch—and I thought I'd stop by and see how you were getting on."

"Very slowly," he said, slipping an arm round her shoulders for a quick hug and giving her a grin that told her he was glad to see her as well.

Gemma realized that the dark-haired woman was watching her with a less than welcoming regard. "I don't want to trespass on your patch. If it's inconvenient—"

"You're fine. Don't worry about the grim-visaged Inspector Bell," he added in her ear. "She improves as she thaws. We're just about to have a word with the woman who reported the fire. Come along with us—I'll be glad to have your take on this. Then you can tell me about Winnie."

They'd reached the others. Doug Cullen took her hand warmly, then introduced her to DI Maura Bell. Bell put out her hand in response to Gemma's, but jerked it free after the slightest press of fingers. *Slam-bam-thank-you-ma'am*, Gemma thought, amused. This was a woman who obviously did not relish physical contact or having an uninvited investigator on her case.

"While we're waiting for the fire investigation officer, Bill Farrell, I can give you a quick rundown of what we have so far," Kincaid said, ignoring Bell's scowl. "The building belongs to Michael Yarwood, the MP, who was in the process of turning it into luxury flats with a restaurant on the ground floor. The emergency call came in just after half past twelve last night, and the fire was well involved by the time the brigade arrived. They entered through the front door, which they found unlocked, and they later discovered the side door unlocked as well." He gestured towards the door facing them across the narrow side street. The rear of the building jutted out in a sort of attached tower with a window at each level, leading Gemma to assume that the door opened into a rear staircase.

"The firefighters found their progress into the ground-floor space impeded by a pile of soft furniture gathered in the center of the room," Kincaid continued. "Behind the furniture they discovered the charred body of the victim. Bill Farrell, the FIO, thinks it likely that the fire started in the furniture, but they've found no obvious signs of arson."

"Does that mean the death may have been accidental?" asked Gemma.

"Possible, but I'd say not likely, as Kate Ling found a massive fracture to the back of the skull."

"Kate was here?" Gemma felt a twinge of jealousy. She knew that Kate fancied him, but how he felt about Kate she'd never quite been able to work out. Obviously, he respected the doctor professionally, and just as obviously he found her attractive, but it never seemed to occur to him that the feeling might be reciprocated. Men could be so clueless, thought Gemma, but in this case Kincaid's blind spot was a blessing. She just hoped he never saw the light where Kate Ling was concerned.

"Been and gone. She'll get to the postmortem as soon as she can." He turned to greet a tall, balding man. "Here's Farrell now."

"Are these flats, then?" asked Gemma when she'd been introduced, looking up at the building they were about to enter. It was larger than its burned neighbor, and a bit more ornate, but it showed obvious signs of decay and neglect. "You said someone called from here after midnight."

"Not flats," Farrell told her. "It's a family violence shelter." He pointed out a small plaque near the door, which bore the legend HELPING HANDS. "It was one of the residents who called in the fire. We're going to have a word with the director before we interview the young woman. I've got the entry code from the constable who took the original statement."

The street door stood open, showing a small entry hall fitted with stained coco matting, but as Gemma tailed after the others, she saw that an interior door had been fitted with an expensive new security keypad. Farrell entered a code and, when the door swung open, led them into a dingy stairwell. Looking back over his shoulder, he said, "First off, we need to make sure they haven't misplaced a resident who fits our victim's description."

"I doubt they were expecting a delegation," Maura Bell muttered as they climbed.

"A delegation of detectives?" Kincaid quipped. "Or would a murder of detectives be more appropriate? I rather like that."

Gemma touched Kincaid's arm. "Wait. Are you saying your victim was female? I just assumed, when you said you had a possible homicide, that the victim was male, someone to do with the site."

"No. We've got a Jane Doe. Female, no ID, and burned beyond recognition. Why?"

Gemma's mind raced. Surely it was too much of a coincidence—but was it? The fire scene was only a few streets from Fanny Liu's house . . . but what would Elaine Holland have been doing in an empty warehouse at night?

Unless she'd been moonlighting as a prostitute, and that might explain the hidden clothes and shoes, the secret mobile phone. Gemma remembered hearing that call girls worked Union Street at night—a doorway in nearby Southwark Street might have provided a quieter rendezvous, a bit more privacy. But then—

"Gemma?" Kincaid's voice snapped her out of her speculations. They had reached the top of the stairs.

She shook her head. "Nothing. Just a wild idea. I'll tell you later."

A woman awaited them in the first-floor corridor. "Hi, I'm Kath Warren, Helping Hands' director. You're the police?" She'd started to offer her hand but let it fall to her side, seemingly daunted by their number. Gemma guessed the woman to be in her well-preserved forties, with an air of no-nonsense competence softened by an attractive face with a slightly upturned nose. She wore a honey-colored trouser suit that complemented her streaked blond hair, and her green eyes held a hint of wariness.

Farrell stepped easily into the breach. "I'm Bill Farrell, from the fire brigade." He nodded at the others, clustered behind him like ducklings, as he made the introductions. "Superintendent Kincaid, Scotland Yard. Sergeant Cullen. Inspector Bell. Inspector James," he added last, with a questioning glance in her direction to assure he'd got it right.

Kath Warren looked round the corridor, as if realizing its unsuitability for conversation. "Um, perhaps we'd better go

into my office. It's not much larger, but at least there's somewhere to sit."

"I should say *our* office," she added as they followed her
into the first room off the corridor. "This is Jason Nesbitt,
the agency's assistant director."

The room held two utilitarian desks, a sagging sofa, several mismatched straight-backed chairs, and ranks of metal
filing cabinets. A young man sat at the second desk, one
hand on the telephone, the other balancing a manila file
folder. At their entrance he returned the handset to its cradle
and stood up.

"It's the police, Jason," said Kath, motioning them to the
assorted furniture as she slipped behind the other desk.

"So I gathered. We must really rate." His grin was sar-
donic but engaging. He was tall, rail thin, with blond-tipped
hair and a wide, expressive mouth. His dark shirt and tie
hinted at a certain vanity, and a closer look made Gemma re-
vise her estimate of his age to nearer thirty than twenty.

"Please sit down. You'll have to excuse our lack of ele-
gance," said Kath, with a shrug that indicated the office.
"The place is a bit of a tip, but we're funded primarily by the
council, and that leaves no room for frills."

Cullen and Bell sat rather awkwardly together on the sofa,
while Farrell and Gemma perched on two of the hard-
backed chairs. Kincaid remained standing, resting his hip
against a filing cabinet.

"You take in women who've been abused by their husbands?" said Gemma, forgetting for a moment that it wasn't
her place to ask. Bell gave her a dark look.

"Women and their children, more often than not." Kath
Warren seemed more comfortable behind her desk. "Not
that men aren't sometimes victims of spousal abuse, but the
council makes other arrangements in that case. We give
women a safe haven, a chance to sort things out, and if that's
not possible, we help them move on to new lives."

"How many rooms do you have?" Kincaid asked.

"Ten, all full at the moment. Not the most salubrious of accommodations, but that may not matter for much longer. It looks as if our time here is limited. This building, like the one next door, is ripe for redevelopment. The front half is already vacant, and the asking price for the property will be much more than the local council can afford."

It seemed to Gemma that what had begun as a practiced spiel had become personal, that the impending loss of the agency's premises affected Kath Warren in some intimate way. "What will happen then?" she asked.

"Oh, they'll find a new spot for us eventually, but it may mean our shutting down for some time. The council will do their best to find places for our residents with other agencies, of course." She forced a smile. "But I'm waffling on about things that don't concern you, when I'm sure you have questions."

Jason Nesbitt had been listening, his eyes darting occasionally from Kath to the others, but his mobile face was unreadable. It occurred to Gemma that the impending closure of the facility might mean that both Nesbitt and Kath Warren would be out of a job.

"Your residents, Miss Warren," interjected DI Bell, almost springing from her seat in her impatience, "are they all accounted for?"

"Yes, of course. The residents must sign a log when they exit or enter the building, and we do have a ten P.M. curfew. Sometimes at night the women start to miss their husbands and the curfew helps prevent lapses. And it's Mrs. Warren, by the way," she added, but she looked down at her hands as she spoke, twisting her wedding ring, rather than at DI Bell. "We saw the mortuary van, you know, and the attendants loading the . . . body . . . into it. Does this mean you don't know who it was?"

"An unidentified female, ma'am," said Bill Farrell. "That's been released to the media and is really all we can say at the moment. Now, we understand that one of your residents notified the fire brigade of the fire?"

"Yes, Beverly Brown-Mouse, we call her. Both her kids have got bad colds at the moment, and she was up with one of them when she looked out the window and saw the flames. She had to use the phone in the hallway—we can't allow residents to have mobile phones. Again, it makes access too easy for both parties."

Nesbitt stood up. "I'll just go get Mouse, shall I?" Without waiting for an answer, he eased his way round his desk, and as he passed her, Gemma caught the musky scent of expensive cologne.

"That seems rather an infringement of their rights," ventured Cullen, speaking for the first time.

"They come here voluntarily, but to enter the program they must agree to the rules. It's a waste of our time and theirs if they're not willing to make changes—that's the only way to break the patterns of habitual abuse." Kath Warren stood, as if the waiting made her nervous. "Can I get you all some coffee? We keep a pot going in the scullery."

By the time they had all refused, Jason Nesbitt had come back with his charges. He ushered the woman and the two children into the room, then stood behind them protectively.

If ever someone looked in need of protection, it was this woman, thought Gemma. She was small and slight, appearing hardly more than a child herself, playing dress-up in her T-shirt and combat trousers. Her skin had a junkie's pallor, and a streak of pure white hair sprang from her widow's peak, making her look more like a little badger than a mouse. Her face was pinched with fright, and Gemma guessed that talking to a roomful of coppers was not her idea of a good time.

The children were girls, perhaps two and five, pale as their mother and snotty nosed. They clung to their mother's legs, ducking their faces behind the meager barricade she provided. A good thing, too, thought Gemma, as she had to fight the temptation to pull tissues from her bag and give their faces a good scrubbing.

"Do you want to sit down, Beverly?" asked Kath Warren, but the woman shook her head. "These people are trying to find out what caused the fire last night, and they need to ask you a few questions. I'm sure it won't take long."

"It's all right, Mouse," said Jason Nesbitt. "They won't bite you."

Beverly nodded, eyes wide, but didn't speak.

Bill Farrell shifted his chair to face her. "Beverly, can you tell me exactly what you saw last night? You can start by describing what you were doing beforehand."

"It was Brittany," she said in a soft, high voice that made the reason for her nickname evident, pulling the older child out from behind her leg as if wanting to prove her existence. "Her cough was that bad, she couldn't sleep." The child coughed on cue, a racking sound that made Gemma cringe. "I went down to the kitchen to steam a pan of water for her to breathe. When I came back to the room I made her sit over it, you know, with a towel to keep the steam in. Ten minutes, I told her, and I promised to watch the clock. That's when I looked out the window." Her voice had grown stronger, as if she was encouraged by their interest. "At first I thought it was weird, you know, there was a red light in the building across the street. I thought, why would someone have a red light, must be a wild party. And then I saw it flicker, and suddenly I go, wow, it's not a light, it's a fire."

"And that's when you called 999?"

"Yeah. They were fast, you know. Couldn't have been much more than a minute before we heard the sirens."

"And you kept watching?"

"Well, yeah, it was exciting, you know?" She ducked her head, as if not sure that was an acceptable response. "Brandy woke up, too, so we all watched."

Farrell smiled at her. "There's nothing like a good fire. I'd be the first to agree with you on that. Now, did you see any-thing else before the brigade arrived? Anyone on the street or coming out the side door?"

"No. There wasn't nobody."

"The building would have burned down if it hadn't been for Mummy," piped up Brittany. She wiped a fist across her nose and glared at Farrell, as if daring him to contradict her.

"That's right, sweetheart," Farrell said kindly. "Your mummy saved the day. Now, you know what to do if you see a fire, don't you?"

"Call 999," Brittany informed him, puffing out her little chest in its stained Scooby-Doo T-shirt. "I know where nine is on the phone. Three nines. I can count them."

"That's great, sweetheart." Farrell turned back to her mother. "Beverly, did you see anything before you noticed the fire? Or hear anything unusual?"

Beverly shook her head, perhaps a bit too quickly, Gemma thought. "No. I was asleep. It was only Brittany's coughing that woke me up."

"What about earlier in the evening, before you went to bed?" Kincaid asked. "Did you see anything then?"

"No. I didn't look, did I? I was putting the girls to bed." She turned to Kath Warren. "Can I go now, Kath? I have to take Brittany to the clinic."

Kath glanced at Bill Farrell, who nodded.

Farrell handed Beverly a card. "There's my number, if you think of anything else," he told her.

"Yeah, okay," she said, with an obvious lack of enthusi-asm. She slipped out the door, her children still clinging like limpets, and Gemma noticed that she adroitly managed to avoid touching Jason Nesbitt.

"Is there somewhere we can talk?" Gemma shielded her eyes against the rain, which was coming down harder now, the drops stinging her skin like biting midges.

Kincaid looked round at the warehouse frontages and at the office buildings across Southwark Street, none of which offered any protection from the downpour; then he shouted at Doug Cullen, who was conferring with Farrell and a fire-fighter with an Alsatian. "Hey, Dougie! Lend us your keys for a minute, will you?"

Cullen tossed them over with a grin. "Careful you don't fog up my windows."

They sprinted for the car, and when Kincaid had managed to get the doors unlocked, fell inside, laughing.

"I left my brolly at the office," he admitted, wiping his face.

"Me, too," said Gemma. "I thought it had stopped." She could almost feel her hair curling from the moisture, springing free from its clip.

"Here." Kincaid retrieved a box of tissues from among the gum wrappers and crisp packets littering the car floor. "Will these help?"

Gemma tried not to touch the box as she pulled out a few tissues and dried her face. Then, looking round for some-place to put the soggy remains, she grimaced at the mess. "This car's a tip. I wouldn't have thought it of Doug."

"I think he's rebelling against having to keep his flat spot-less for Stella. Now." He turned towards her. "Tell me what's up with Winnie? Are she and Jack all right?"

"Of course." Touching his cheek, she remembered his re-action when he'd seen her. She was so close she could see the tiny patch of stubble he'd missed when he'd shaved that morning and smell the damp warmth of his skin. "You're a bit mother-henish today."

"Maybe I don't like fires," he confessed with a shrug. "There's something about a burned body, as illogical as it is."

Gemma felt the lump of Fanny Liu's candle inside the bag on her lap, a sudden burden, weighted by possibility. "Okay.

I know this is going to sound far-fetched." She took a breath and proceeded to tell him about Winnie's phone call, about Fanny Liu and her missing roommate, Elaine Holland, and about her theory that Elaine might have been moonlighting on the street and somehow ended up in Yarwood's warehouse.

Kincaid tapped his fingers on the steering wheel for a moment when she'd finished, gazing out at the warehouse through the slanting curtain of rain. "It is far-fetched, I'll give you that," he said slowly. "But it's the first report of a missing woman we've had that fits the time frame. I think that alone makes it worth consideration. But say, just for the moment, that you're right and she was with a john, sheltering in the doorway. How did she end up inside the building?"

"Maybe the client had a key?"

His eyes widened. "Right now, that would narrow it down to Michael Yarwood and his foreman, Spender. We're already checking their alibis for last night. But there are other possibilities. Estate agents, former owners, janitorial services . . ."

"I don't envy you that," Gemma said, thinking of the massive paperwork involved in following up these leads. "What about Elaine Holland? Will you want to speak to Fanny again today? What about a proper search of the house?"

He thought for a moment, then shook his head. "No, let's wait until we get the results of the postmortem. There's no point in jumping the gun here. For all we know, at this point the PM may tell us something that would rule her out entirely—say, the victim was a teenager or nonwhite. Kate said she'd try to schedule the PM tonight or first thing tomorrow, and she'll keep me informed. We'll go from there. But in the meantime, I'd better fill in the others." He turned back to her and reached out to cup her cheek in his hand. "I don't know when I'll get home."

"I know."

"Then we'd better make the most of the moment," he said, sliding his fingers down to her chin and turning her face so that he could brush his lips against hers.

He tasted very slightly of coffee. Gemma struggled, laughing, as he nuzzled her neck. "Don't do that. Someone will see us."

"That's the idea. You wouldn't want to disappoint Doug, would you?"

Why the hell didn't the woman answer her bloody phone?

Tony Novak stood in London Bridge Railway Station, mobile phone in hand, panic rising in his throat. He'd told Beth to bring Harriet to meet him at the flower stall at twelve o'clock, and there he'd been standing for the last hour.

After half an hour had passed, he'd started ringing Beth's mobile, but the stupid fucking thing went directly to voice mail. It was only then that the truth began to dawn—he had a name and a mobile number, nothing else, and he'd left his daughter with her.

Dear God, what had he been thinking? Sweat stung his armpits, stuck his shirt damply to his back, and his knees felt suddenly as if they might give way. He sank down onto the large suitcase, rubbing his face with his free hand. People milled past him, wheeling luggage, shouldering briefcases, as if the world hadn't come to a dead stop. A pretty girl slowed, gave him a tentative smile, then looked away and hurried on as if something she'd seen in his face had frightened her. Good bloody riddance.

They had always been his downfall—girls, women. He attracted them like flies to honey, and in spite of the best of intentions, he had never learned to say no. This little weakness had ruined his marriage to Laura, as well as every other relationship he'd had since adolescence.

And that was how he'd met Beth, in the bar at the George Inn in Borough High Street, near his flat. An attractive woman, obviously looking for company; he in the throes of postseparation shock, an easy mark. When she'd chatted him up, he'd seen no reason to refuse. He'd taken her back to his flat that night, surprised but intrigued by her ferocity.

Afterwards, lying naked in his bed, she'd told him she was married, her husband a commercial traveler, a jealous man. She said she would come to him again if he wanted, and he *had* wanted it. It helped fill the hours, numbed his mind, and he had liked the fact that she was married, unavailable for more than their regular trysts.

Lately, though, things had begun to change. He should have seen it coming—he'd never known a woman to remain satisfied with simple sex. He recognized the signs easily enough—hints of dissatisfaction with her marriage, hints that things might be different between them—and he'd begun to think of finding a way to terminate the relationship.

Then things had blown up with Laura and his life had spun out of control. His plans hastily conceived, he'd realized he needed someone to watch Harriet while he retrieved her documents from Laura's flat and withdrew his funds from the bank, and Beth had seemed the logical choice.

It was only now that he remembered the odd look on her face last night when he'd told her what he meant to do, but then she'd smiled and said yes, of course she'd help him, and in his hurry and his relief he'd quickly buried any uneasiness.

A garbled announcement came over the tannoy, a train departing for some unidentifiable location. The sound made his head hurt. He rubbed at his face again, trying to clear his mind, trying to bring back any little tidbits of information that Beth had revealed in postcoital conversations.

She worked in an estate agent's in the Borough, she had told him that much. She'd grown up in South Africa, a daughter of missionaries, and had only come to London in her late teens. She'd been married once before, but it hadn't worked out.

Fat lot of good any of that did him. What was he going to do, go round to every estate agent's in the Borough, hoping to find her? He might as well ring directory inquiries and ask for a listing for *Beth*. It was madness.

Mary, mother of Jesus, how could he have been so stupid? He stood again, looking round wildly, as if his daughter's face might suddenly appear in the crowd.

Had Beth taken Harriet to the authorities? But in that case, wouldn't she have also told them where he was? He'd been waiting in the same spot for close on an hour and a half now, and no one had approached him.

But the alternative was more terrifying still. If she had not reported him, what in hell had she done with his child?

6

Five jails, or prisons, are in Southwark placed,
The Counter once St. Margaret's Church defaced,
The Marshalsea, the King's Bench, and White Lyon,
Then there's the Clink where handsome lodgings be.

JOHN TAYLOR, 1630

ROSE HAD DRAWN kitchen duty for that night's watch, her
least favorite chore. Growing up, she'd not had any interest
in cooking, while her mother had enjoyed it and had been
content to let her help her dad with his projects rather than
insisting she do her share in the kitchen.

But cooking, she quickly discovered, was an essential
skill in the fire service, and she'd set out with her usual diligence to become competent. Now, at least the other members of the watch didn't roll their eyes and suggest Chinese
takeaway when it was her turn to prepare meals.

She'd come in a half hour early, hoping to have a word
with Station Officer Wilcox before the tour of duty began. It
would be better if he heard about her visit to the fire scene
from her rather than the FIT.

But Wilcox hadn't yet come in, so she decided to get the dinner ready to go in the oven before roll call. That way she had more chance of getting the meal finished if they had a busy night, and it would give her something to do while she kept an eye out for Wilcox. Using a mallet, she pounded chicken breast halves into an even thickness before coating them in seasoned bread crumbs and drizzling them with olive oil. Then she scrubbed and quartered potatoes for roasted potato wedges; both dishes could be popped in the oven later. She could throw a salad together at the last minute, and there was ice cream in the freezer for a sweet.

Yawning as she finished her tasks, she rubbed at eyes burning from lack of sleep. Although a nap and a shower had helped, she still felt frayed round the edges. It would be a long night, but she knew better than to wish for a quiet one—that only seemed to guarantee that the bells would go nonstop.

Bryan Simms wandered into the kitchen as she was finishing up, carrying a takeaway coffee. "You look knackered," he offered after examining her critically.

"Thanks." She shot him a sour glance. "You really know how to boost a girl's confidence."

"Anytime." He grinned at her. "Dinner looks good, though." He reached for a slice of raw potato, but she snatched it back.

"Don't eat raw potato, it's disgusting. You'll get a disease or something."

"Hasn't hurt me yet." Lounging against the oven, he sipped his coffee and watched her wipe the worktops. "Besides, I need something to keep my strength up. I've got phone duty, and I hear the press calls about last night's fire have been coming in nonstop." He'd have checked with the previous watch's duty officer for any ongoing problems. "I'm to refer all queries to Lambeth PR."

Rose dried her hands on a tea towel, debating whether to tell him about her visit to the scene that morning. "Bryan—"

The blare of the tannoy drowned out her words as Seamus MacCauley, the sub officer, announced roll call. "Never mind," she said, patting her hair to make sure it was tucked up in regulation fashion. "Tell you later."

But later never seemed to materialize. During roll call, MacCauley informed them that the FIT was expected at seven o'clock and would be debriefing the entire watch in the lecture room, so from roll call they scattered to complete their routine maintenance of the equipment and appliances.

Wilcox was closeted in his office with MacCauley, and as she'd caught up on her kitchen chores, Rose offered to fill in for one of the pump ladder's crew on a call to a nearby office building, a person stuck in a lift. By the time they returned and she'd dashed into the kitchen to put the food in the oven, the rest of the watch had gathered in the lecture room. Having missed her chance to talk to Wilcox, Rose slid into a chair in the back. The tension that had been temporarily dissipated by the call returned with a vengeance.

As she looked round the room, she thought how seldom she saw them all gathered together, except on the rare occasions when both crews managed to sit down to a meal at the same time. It was a good watch, the best she'd ever had, due in part to the personalities of the men themselves and in part to Charlie Wilcox's scrupulous refusal to tolerate any sort of hazing or bullying on his team. Rumors of Wilcox's potential promotion to divisional officer circulated with distressing regularity. What might be a gain for the fire service administration would be a loss for Southwark Station.

Their sub officer, Seamus MacCauley, at fifty-four the oldest member of the watch, was nearing retirement, and Rose suspected he had never actively sought promotion. A whipcord-thin Geordie with an unlikely Scots-Irish name, he was a good and patient teacher, a mediator whose easygoing manner helped keep conflict to a minimum.

As if aware of her regard, he looked over at her from his

position by the door and smiled. "You ready for the inquisition, flower? Mean bastards, this lot," he added, and winked.

"Just as long as they don't keep me from my dinner," said Simon Forney from the row in front of her. Simon and the man beside him, Steven Winston, although not in fact brothers, were usually referred to as Castor and Pollux because of their uncanny resemblance to each other. Round-headed, barrel-chested, and proud of their strength, they'd only begun to accept her when she'd proved she could swing an axe and haul hose as well as any bloke.

The buzz of conversation in the room died away as Wilcox came in with the investigators. He introduced Station Officer Farrell and Sub Officer Martinelli, then the three detectives Rose had met that morning. Kincaid, the superintendent, caught Rose's eye and nodded in recognition.

Rose hadn't really noticed Martinelli earlier that day—any attention she'd turned in that direction had been focused on his dog—but now she realized he was younger than she'd thought, perhaps only in his early thirties. His Italian heritage was evident in his dark coloring, but the slant of his cheekbones and the shape of his eyes hinted at another racial component, Asian or maybe Polynesian. He gave her a friendly grin and she looked away, embarrassed that she'd been caught staring.

"We'll keep this informal," Farrell told them as he hitched himself up on the table at the front of the room. The others stood about a bit awkwardly until Kincaid took charge, pulling chairs from the empty front row and flipping them round so that they could sit facing the group. "You'll need to make individual statements for the coroner's report," Farrell continued, "as is always the case with a fatality fire, but first I'd like to hear if anyone noted anything unusual at the scene last night. We've already heard from Firefighter Kearny earlier today about her discovery of the victim."

Rose felt a sudden intensifying of attention in the room.

Simms gave her a surprised glance, frowning as he turned back to Farrell.

"No one saw anyone loitering near the scene?" Farrell prompted. "Or smelled anything unusual?"

After a few silent minutes, Simms spoke up. "Sir. You think it was arson, then?"

"We haven't found any obvious use of accelerants, but of course that's not conclusive," replied Farrell evasively.

"What about the videos from the appliances?" Simms continued, undiscouraged. The pump and pump ladder carried cameras mounted in their cabs that provided investigators with a view of any suspicious activity en route to a scene.

"No joy there, I'm afraid."

"What about CCTV, sir?" put in MacCauley.

"Those tapes are still being collected," answered Superintendent Kincaid. "We'll be having a look at them in the morning, but our findings shouldn't prejudice your observations. We would appreciate your cooperation on this," he added.

A ripple of bodies shifting in chairs and a few mutters signaled the watch's interest.

From the doorway, MacCauley directed a comment to Farrell. "It seems we've had an unusual number of structure fires in the Borough the last few months, guv. Might be worth checking to see if there's some sort of pattern."

"We'll keep that in mind." Farrell stood. "Okay, if there's nothing else, we'll get your statements. It shouldn't take long."

Superintendent Kincaid and the other detectives stood as well. Kincaid murmured something in Farrell's ear, then flashed a smile at Rose as the three detectives left the room. The FIT officers moved round to the far side of the table to take statements. As she slipped into the rough queue formed by the firefighters, Rose wondered at the generous police presence. She'd been too frazzled that morning to pay much attention to the rumors flying round the scene that the building belonged to Michael Yarwood, the Labour MP, but she supposed that would account for the amount of attention being given the case.

Beside her, Steven Winston said quietly, "You oughta remember to wipe your nose, Kearny."

She reached up instinctively, then flushed and dropped her hand as she realized what he meant. Although his tone had been teasing, his eyes were cold. Before she could respond, he nudged her and added, "Boss wants you."

Turning, she saw Wilcox watching her from the door. When he had her attention, he jerked his head in the direction of his office. "Rose. A word."

She followed him, her throat tight, very much aware of the stares directed at her retreating back. Expecting the worst, she stepped into the room and, at Wilcox's nod, closed the door behind her.

He stood behind his desk, studying her for a moment, then said quietly, "Initiative is a good thing, Rose, up to a point. But we don't need freelancers on the watch. No loose cannons, on the fire ground or off. If you know, or remember, anything that might be relevant to last night's fire, you talk to me first and from there we'll take it through the proper channels. Understood?"

Rose swallowed and resisted the urge to explain herself. "Yes, sir."

The days when aggression in a firefighter was prized above all else were gone. Freelancing—charging into a fire, or any situation, without thought for partner or team—was as frowned upon now as going into a fire without a mask.

"I don't want any unnecessary entanglements with the FIT on my watch. It complicates things. And you don't want the rest of the team feeling you've gone behind their backs. You're a good firefighter, and you handled yourself well last night. Don't do anything to screw up your record." Wilcox sat down at his desk and picked up a stack of reports, effectively dismissing her.

"Sir." Knowing she'd got off lightly, Rose breathed a sigh of relief and headed for the door. Then, her hand on the knob, she turned back, her curiosity overcoming her better judgment. "Guv, about those other warehouse fires. Wouldn't the brigade database—"

"Let the FIT do their job, Rose," growled Wilcox, looking up at her with irritation. "You've done yours. Leave it alone."

The phone rang twice before the voice mail clicked in, just as it had the last dozen times Yarwood had called. "You've reached Tia and Chloe," the soft, drawling voice informed him. "We're busy at the moment, but leave a message and we'll get back to you."

It was not Chloe's voice, but Tia's. The girl's Sloane Ranger upbringing was apparent in her stretched vowels, and Yarwood had recently noticed that Chloe had begun to imitate her flatmate, a fact that made him furious. He slammed down the phone in frustration.

He'd been trying to reach his daughter, either at her flat or on her mobile, since he'd left the fire scene that morning, with no success. The only possibility he hadn't tried was Chloe's mother, Shirley. He might be worried, but he wasn't yet desperate enough to call his ex-wife.

Yarwood went back to pacing the sitting room of his flat, stopping to stare out the window at the fading light in Hopton Street. He felt edgy and confined. It was ironic, really, as until Shirley's last decorating binge had swathed the room in pale blue and green fabrics and filled it with ornate gilded furniture, he'd always found the small space comforting.

That was just before she'd run off with the interior designer, damn the bitch. The pair was now living in happily wedded bliss, according to Chloe, catering to the tastes of the blue-rinse set in Brighton. Good riddance to them both as far as he was concerned.

It was a shame about the flat, though. The building was one of the oldest in Southwark, and deserved something more in keeping with its character. He'd bought the flat years ago, when the Globe Theatre had been merely Sam Wanamaker's dream, and living in the hulking shadow of Bankside Power Station had not been seen as an advantage. Now the Globe had become a reality, the power station had metamorphosed into the Tate Modern, and Bankside had become a major destination for the tourists and the trendy.

Of course, the value of the flat had increased exponentially, and Shirley had nagged him incessantly to sell it. They could buy a place in the country, she'd said, or one of those new flats on the river.

But he hadn't wanted to let the old place go. It was part of Bankside, part of who he was, part of what he believed in. And trying to make him into a country gentleman was about as ridiculous as putting a pig in a tutu.

After what had happened last night, however, selling up might be his only option. How else could he get his hands on the cash he needed, and get it quickly enough?

A current of fear snaked between his shoulder blades and he clenched his fists, as if he could physically subdue it. He'd always considered himself tough, a self-made man who could tackle anything that came his way, but the thought of the charred remains of his warehouse, and of the body he'd seen loaded into the mortuary van, made him feel sick.

Had the fire been a warning, the body a reminder of what could happen to his daughter if he didn't ante up?

He strode to the sideboard and poured himself a tumbler of whisky from the bottle he kept mostly for guests. He'd never been much of a drinker, on the theory that it took a clear head to get on in the world, but tonight he needed something to numb the worry clutching at his gut like a claw.

Did Chloe have any idea what she'd got herself into? Or did she think she could wheedle her way out of this, as she had everything else in her life?

The girl had always preferred her mother's company—not that he'd given her much choice, with his schedule—but when her mother had taken off with that ponce of a designer, Chloe had chosen to stay in London with him. She'd been eighteen then, and she'd thought exile to a seaside town like Brighton a fate worse than death.

But nothing Yarwood had done in his life had prepared him for dealing single-handedly with a spoiled and angry teenager, and he'd failed miserably. He'd insisted she get a job or stay enrolled in some sort of college or university course, but she didn't seem able to stay with anything long enough to make a success of it. After two years of her failures, his patience at an end, he'd told Chloe he'd no intention of continuing to support a layabout, and he'd kicked her out.

He hadn't counted on Tia Foster taking her in as a charity case. Tia, whose wealthy parents had endowed her with more money than sense, had moved Chloe into the spare bedroom in her flat, and Chloe managed to survive by scrounging off Tia and begging the occasional handout from her mother.

Christ, how could he not have seen how vulnerable his daughter was? Or how vulnerable she had made him?

Now he could do nothing but pay for the consequences of his own stupidity, and try to keep Chloe safe. He picked up the phone and jabbed a blunt finger at the keypad once more.

He knew the value of a uniform. Clothes made the man. Or so his mum had always told him—the old cow—and then she'd reinforced the maxim with a few well-placed smacks. It had been years since he'd had to put up with that, but he still ironed his shirts as if his mother were watching over his shoulder.

Collar first, then shoulder, then sleeves. He slipped a fresh section of pale blue cloth over the end of the board and shot it with spray starch. His routine never varied. Every evening before reporting for work, he unfolded the old ironing board in the middle of his sitting room and labored over his uniform shirt until it could stand on its own; then he touched up his navy-blue trousers and jacket.

Radio Two droned in the background, not quite loudly enough to cover the murmur of traffic that drifted up from Blackfriars Road through his partially open window. His mum had been big on fresh air in all weather, convinced that sealing up a dwelling would result in a buildup of deadly gases. Bollocks, of course, he knew that, but still the habit stayed with him, and he liked the way the smell of curry from the takeaway beneath his flat mingled with the exhaust fumes and the clean soapiness of the starch.

It was odd the way the mind could divide itself, one part occupied with the identifying of familiar scents, the motion of his arm holding the iron, the babble of sound from the radio—while the other part seethed and bubbled with excitement from last night's burn.

It had been—what was the word he'd read somewhere?—serendipitous, that was it. The walk home after his half shift, the sliver of darkness beckoning him from the open door, the interior prepared for him as if by some grand design.

Could it be that his own carefully prepared plan fit into something larger, dovetailed within it like a nut inside its shell? The thought was so heady it made him shiver. "Careful, careful," he whispered, his voice a thread of sound in the empty room.

The possibilities were laid out in his mind like a series of *jewels on a map of the Borough, all carefully researched and explored, waiting to be plucked when the time seemed right. Did last night's gift mean he should act sooner than he'd planned?*

Anticipation pumped his heart, made the breath puff from his nostrils. He whipped his shirt from the board and switched off the iron—no one knew better than he the dangers of fire—his mind alight with the thrill of choice.

"That was a frigging waste of time," Maura Bell muttered as she walked out of the fire station into Sawyer Street, Kincaid and Cullen on either side of her. The rain had stopped at last, and above them a few patches of dusky purple sky showed against the banks of pewter cloud. The temperature had dropped with the sunset. Glancing back, she saw warm light spilling from the windows in the fire station's red bay doors, a glimpse of a closed and comforting world.

She shrugged the collar of her coat closer around her throat.

Kincaid glanced at her, raising an eyebrow, as Cullen said easily, "Maybe, maybe not," as if he'd nothing better to do than sit around watching a bunch of surly firefighters shuffle their feet and look clueless. "Somebody may remember something. Never hurts to plant a seed. Listen," Cullen added as they reached his car, left in the fire station car park, "we'll give you a lift back to the nick. There's not much more we can do tonight."

"I've a better idea," Kincaid said. "Why don't we all have a drink. My treat. We can map out our agenda for tomorrow."

Her response was automatic, instinctive. The last thing she wanted to do was have a chummy pint with Scotland Yard. "I've things to do at the station."

"Surely they can wait a bit," Kincaid said lightly. "Call it conference time, if it will ease your guilty conscience, but I think we could all use a break."

"The CCTV films—"

"That's what constables are for," chimed in Cullen, opening the car's back door for her. "You have to learn to delegate."

Maura shifted some of the papers that had slid back into the space she'd cleared in Cullen's backseat on the short ride from Southwark Street to the fire station. The task gave her a moment to think.

She'd checked in with the incident room staff just before their meeting at the fire station, so she knew there were no breaking developments that urgently needed her attention.

She was also aware that her refusal to socialize with the other detectives could mark her as a bad sport, and possibly a prig—not the reputation she wanted to establish on her first outing with Scotland Yard. "Okay, just a quick one, then," she said, trying to give in gracefully. "I know a good pub in Borough High Street. Or there's this one." She pointed at the pub that occupied the bottom corner of the fire station premises. "The Goldsmith—"

"If I'm buying, I get to choose," interrupted Kincaid, sounding amused. He glanced at Cullen. "The society?"

Cullen nodded. "Right."

"But—"

"Don't worry," Kincaid assured her. "We'll have you back before you turn into a pumpkin."

With this, Maura had to be content. She sank back into her seat, curiosity beginning to override her indignation.

In moments they were crossing Blackfriars Bridge. The river caught the remnants of the sunset in a gleaming swath of gold, and beyond it the floodlit dome of St. Paul's was haloed by the fading pink sky. Cullen drove with an assurance she had somehow not expected, and Kincaid sat beside him without criticizing, unlike some of her superior officers.

Once in the City, Cullen sped up New Bridge Street and around Holborn Circle, into Hatton Garden, the heart of the diamond district. Maura knew this part of town only by reputation. "Doing a little after-hours shopping, are we?" she asked as Cullen slipped the car into a vacant parking space on the street.

"We should be so lucky," said Cullen, his fingers barely brushing her elbow as they followed Kincaid across the street. "But this is almost as good. You'll see."

Maura relaxed a bit as they came to a cheerful-looking pub, but Kincaid passed it by, ducking into the narrow alleyway that ran alongside it. He stopped at a sleek door made of pale wood and keyed an entry pad.

Maura hung back. "What—"

"Never fear, it's not a brothel." Grinning, Cullen guided her inside. The pair reminded her of her older brothers playing a prank—not an auspicious omen.

The foyer opened directly onto a staircase made of more blond wood and brushed steel. "Private club," Kincaid tossed over his shoulder as he started to climb. "The Scotch Malt Whisky Society. Good whisky's the best antidote to the taste of a fire scene."

She knew what he meant. The acrid smoke seemed to have settled permanently in her sinus cavities and the back of her throat, and the sandwich she'd managed to snatch for lunch had tasted of ashes.

They had reached the first floor. Maura followed the men through a cloak area and into a large room that contradicted all her preconceived notions of a private club. There was a handsome bar down one side, but the furniture was contemporary, more Habitat than gentleman's club, and the white walls were splashed with bright, abstract paintings. The room was quite full, but Kincaid spied an empty table in the far corner and led them to it. "Shall I choose?" he asked as they settled into their chairs.

Picking up a booklet from the low table, Maura found it filled with pages of whiskies identified only by numbers and rather fulsome descriptions.

"The society does its own bottling, straight from casks it buys directly from the distilleries," Kincaid explained. "It assigns a number to each bottling, but there is a key that links the numbers with the names of the distilleries, if you're interested."

She shook her head and closed the booklet. "I'll trust you on this. So, are you some sort of whisky connoisseur?"

"Not really. It's just that we've a friend who's trying to get a small Highland distillery back on its feet, so I'm doing my bit to support the industry."

"Very noble of you, I'm sure."

"Yeah." He grinned at her, and for the first time she was aware of the power of his smile. She suspected he used it like a weapon and dislike surged through her. "Why don't I see what they have on special tonight?" Kincaid added, then stood and threaded his way to the bar.

"Your superintendent's quite the charmer," she said to Cullen.

"He has his moments," Cullen agreed, as if unaware of her sarcasm. "He's a good guv'nor, the best I've had."

How like a man, she thought furiously, to defend another male no matter how inexcusable his behavior. "And does he snog all his female officers when he gets them in a car?" she blurted.

"Snog?" Cullen looked at her as if she'd lost her mind. "In a car—oh, you mean Gemma?" Enlightenment dawned in his face. "In my car. Did he really? Good for him." He gave a whoop of laughter.

"How can you—"

"Look, Inspector—Maura—I'm afraid you've got the wrong end of the stick. Duncan's not Gemma's boss. She works out of Notting Hill Division, not the Yard. They live together. She was in Southwark today for personal reasons. And I've never seen Duncan behave inappropriately with any female officer under his command, if that's what you're thinking."

Maura felt the blood rising in her face. "But—I thought—"

Kincaid returned at that moment, balancing three tumblers. She gave Cullen a pleading glance, hoping he wouldn't mortify her further by repeating her comment.

"This is a lighter Speyside," Kincaid said as he handed round glasses filled with pale gold liquid. "I thought it might be more to your taste than some of the heavily sherried or peated whiskies." She had no idea what he was talking about but forced a smile. She opened her bag to reach for a cigarette, then, realizing that neither of them smoked, thought better of it and closed the bag.

Kincaid took a small pitcher of water from the table and added a splash of water to his glass and Cullen's, but Maura shook her head when he offered it to her. She was a Scot, in case he hadn't noticed, and the one thing she did know was that Scots drank their whisky neat. "Cheers," she said, and tipped back her glass for a hearty swallow.

Fire ripped at her throat and knifed down into her chest. A spasm of coughing racked her, and by the time she caught her breath, her eyes were streaming. "For Christ's sake," she gasped. "What is this stuff, turps?"

Both Cullen and Kincaid were barely containing their smirks. "It's cask strength," Kincaid told her. "I should have explained. The alcohol by volume is well over fifty percent on most of these. Here, have some water."

This time she accepted the pitcher and added a good dollop before attempting another very small sip. "Have I passed some sort of initiation, then?" she asked, scowling at them.

"With flying colors," said Cullen. "At least it's not the Hellfire Club."

She wasn't sure whether it was the effects of the whisky or the fact that she didn't see how she could possibly make a bigger fool of herself than she already had, but Maura felt a pleasant sense of ease spread through her muscles.

"Now." Kincaid set down his glass and leaned forward. "I had a call from Kate Ling while I was at the bar. She's scheduled the PM for nine in the morning, at St. Thomas's. We're to meet her at the morgue. After that, we'll at least have something to go on. Maura, you've not heard anything new from missing persons?"

"Not as of an hour ago."

He frowned. "Gemma's report must not have been processed yet—either that or it didn't get flagged."

Cullen looked surprised. "Gemma's report?"

"I haven't had a chance to tell you," Kincaid explained, including Maura with a glance. "And I'm not at all sure it's relevant. My cousin's wife is an Anglican priest on a temporary assignment here in Southwark. She rang Gemma today, wanting some advice because one of her parishioners said her flatmate had disappeared overnight. That's why Gemma was in Southwark. She talked to the woman, convinced her to file a report."

Cullen gestured excitedly, sloshing a little whisky over the edge of his glass. "But that's—"

"Gemma also said it looked as if the woman might have decamped voluntarily. It sounds as if she stole out of the house sometime in the night—by which time our victim may already have been dead—and that she might have taken personal items with her, perhaps an overnight bag. Nothing like that has turned up at the scene." He paused, sipping his drink. "I thought we should wait until we knew a little more about the victim before we pursued it further."

"What's the woman's name?" Maura pulled a notebook from her bag and was surprised to find it took a bit more effort than usual to grip the pen.

"Elaine Holland. Midthirties. White. Lives in Ufford Street and works at Guy's Hospital.

"Right now, however, I'm more concerned about Michael Yarwood and his foreman. I want to make sure their alibis are solid."

"I've asked Birmingham to send someone to make inquiries at Yarwood's hotel," said Maura, glad to have her notes handy. "And I've got a DC from our station checking on Spender."

"What do you know about Yarwood?" Kincaid asked.

She shrugged. "Just what you read in the papers or see on the telly. I'd never met him before today, but I've never heard anything dodgy about him, either. Seems to be a pretty straight guy. I think he's divorced, with a twenty-something daughter. He started up his own fleet of delivery vans when he was just a kid, before he went into politics. I think this warehouse is his first venture into real estate."

"He didn't strike me as the sort to go in for insurance fraud," Kincaid mused, swirling the dregs in his glass. "And I think he was genuinely distressed over the loss of the building, but he was also nervous. I want to know why."

"You think it was more than knowing the press would be on him like sharks?" asked Cullen.

"Yarwood's spent his whole career dealing with sharks. That's what politicians do. My guv'nor—that's Chief Superintendent Childs," he explained to Maura, "mentioned rumors that Yarwood's leases weren't selling as fast as expected, but both Yarwood and Spender denied it. We need to find out where that's coming from and whether or not it's true."

Cullen looked pleased. "That's right up my alley. I'll see what I can dig up on the Internet tonight. Then I can follow up leads tomorrow."

"And I'll have a word with Childs. We also need to talk to Yarwood's insurance agent, if we can track him down on a Saturday." Turning to Maura, Kincaid added, "And you've got the CCTV in hand?"

As was her habit when collecting her thoughts, she started to reach again for a cigarette, then checked herself and sipped at her drink instead. "We should have the tapes collected and scanned by morning. There's only a view of the front door, though, and even that was a lucky break. The office building across the street recently put in a camera, as they've been having some security problems. We've also collected tapes from the other cameras in the area, just in case they've picked up something suspicious."

"What about the fires the sub officer mentioned tonight?" Kincaid asked. "Do you know anything about that?"

She frowned, trying to recall snippets of talk she hadn't given much attention. "I do remember hearing about a couple of fires in the past few months, but I don't think they were tagged as arson."

"Nor is this one yet. But my gut tells me that Farrell is certain of it; he's just not willing to commit himself without evidence. Farrell's sharp, and if there's anything to this, I think he'll ferret it out." Kincaid glanced at his watch. "Blast. I'd better dash. Toby'll be in bed, but I'd like to at least say good night to Kit, since our plans for tomorrow are shot to hell."

"I can run you back to the Yard, guv." Cullen started to rise, but Kincaid waved him back.

"I'll get the tube from Chancery Lane; worry about the car in the morning. Can I get you two another round before I go?"

Maura shook her head. She'd be legless if she had another.

"I'd better not," said Cullen, and she noticed his whisky was barely touched. He seemed to hesitate before adding, "How *is* Kit, guv?"

"As well as can be expected, I suppose, under the circumstances." Kincaid stood, and although his response had been polite, Maura sensed it was a subject he didn't want to pursue. "I'll leave things in your capable hands, then." He nodded at them both. "See you in the morning."

Maura watched him walk away, her curiosity aroused. "Who's Kit?"

"His son," Cullen said, his expression guarded, as if he regretted bringing it up, and he quickly changed the subject. "Are you sure I can't get you another drink? I can have them put it against Duncan's membership."

"No, thanks. I'd better get the tube as well. I left my car at the station, and I've things to check on before I go home."

"Then let me run you back to Borough High Street. It's right on my way."

She gave him a quizzical glance. "Where do you live?"

"Um . . ." He grinned. "Euston."

"You've an odd way of getting there. Over the river and back again."

"I find driving relaxing," he told her, poker-faced. "What do you say we get a bite to eat first? I'm starved, and the pub downstairs is brilliant."

"No little missus waiting dinner for you at home, Sergeant?"

"That'd be a fine thing." He grimaced. "My flat runs to a bit of moldy cheese in the fridge, along with a beer or two if I'm lucky. What about you?"

She took a mental inventory. "Olives, shriveled. Some *good* cheese from Borough Market. A half bottle of wine going bad."

"Does that make us even? I think the least we could do for the sad state of our affairs is to join forces for a decent meal."

Maura thought about the dark flat awaiting her, considered the prospect of cheese and biscuits eaten in front of the flickering light of the telly, and suddenly rushing home didn't seem all that appealing.

She knocked back the last of her Scotch, her eyes watering, and set her glass down on the table with a thump. Some small part of her mind wondered if it was only the whisky talking, but she found she didn't really care.

"Okay," she said. "Why not?"

Winnie stirred a heaping spoonful of Horlicks into the mug of milk she'd heated for Fanny in the microwave, then popped the drink back in for a few more seconds while she rooted in the cabinets for a packet of biscuits. She'd made them both omelets for dinner, then helped Fanny get ready for bed and settled her on the chaise longue.

She'd been surprised to learn that Fanny could stand on her own, if only briefly. "It's not like a spinal cord injury," Fanny had explained as Winnie helped her into her night-dress. "Although I was completely paralyzed the first few months. I even had to have help breathing the first weeks in intensive care."

"How long were you in hospital?" Winnie asked.

"Six months, although I don't remember much of the first part. GBS comes on very suddenly, and they still don't know the cause. I am getting better, though," she'd added brightly. "It's just that . . . sometimes it's hard to be patient."

Winnie had been about to say, "I can imagine," when she realized she couldn't, and that there was no aphorism adequate for Fanny's everyday struggles.

Silently, she'd tucked Fanny up under her faded quilt. Then she'd come into the kitchen and rattled things in an effort to vent the anger she was feeling towards Elaine Holland. If Elaine had been dishonest with Fanny about a small thing like the mobile phone, what else had she lied about? Although Winnie cautioned herself against jumping to conclusions, she couldn't shake the feeling that Elaine had been using Fanny in some way.

She'd located the biscuits, on the low table that held a toaster, an electric kettle, bread, tea, and most of the other necessities that allowed Fanny to function fairly independently during the day. When the microwave dinged, she carried the mug and biscuits into the sitting room, breathing in the malty aroma of the Horlicks with a smile. "Isn't it odd how smells seem to connect with our memories so directly?" she asked as she positioned the things on Fanny's table. "One sniff of Horlicks and I'm five years old, staying the night with my gran, just as if it were yesterday."

"We drank cocoa when I was a child, but after I got sick I couldn't tolerate the caffeine," Fanny said, pushing herself up on the chaise so that she could reach the cup. "The Horlicks was Elaine's idea. She made it for me every night, even when she was late getting in."

Winnie tried to reconcile this small nurturing act with what she'd seen of Elaine, without much success. "Fanny," she asked slowly, pulling up a chair, "what do you and Elaine find to talk about? It doesn't seem as if you have much in common."

"Oh, well . . . we talk about her work, and the hospital—it makes me feel I'm still a bit involved—and about the daily household things, you know, what we need from the shops, what to have for supper. Sometimes we watch telly together." Fanny's face took on a faraway look. "Sometimes we'd plan holidays we were going to take when I was well enough, somewhere in the sun. Italy, or Majorca. I always liked to imagine Elaine on the beach, going brown as a nut, and I thought that if she could get away for a bit, she wouldn't *mind* things so much."

"Mind things?"

"Oh, you know. She'd get her feelings hurt easily . . . if someone said something at work or if she felt she'd been passed over. And sometimes she'd take against people for no real reason, like—" Fanny stopped, a little color rising in her pale cheeks.

"Like me, you mean?" asked Winnie gently. "It's all right, I don't mind."

"I don't think it was you personally. More the church in general."

Winnie had suspected Elaine of being jealous of her. Now she wondered if Elaine had been afraid of having her own relationship with Fanny too closely inspected.

"I thought she was beginning to soften up a bit recently, though," Fanny went on. "At least she stayed when you brought the Eucharist on Sundays. She'd always made a point to be out of the house when Roberta came."

"I'm flattered," Winnie said with a smile. "Although I can't imagine anyone not liking Roberta." She took Fanny's empty cup. "Will you be all right on your own tonight? I can stay if you like."

"You've done too much as it is." Fanny reached out and gave Winnie's hand a squeeze. "I do have some tablets, though, that I take sometimes when I have a bad night. Maybe I should take one of those."

"Good idea. I'll fetch it for you."

Having been directed to the drawer in the kitchen, Winnie found the bottle and shook a small oval white tablet into her hand. She recognized the name of a mild sedative hypnotic, but frowned as she glanced at the prescription date. The prescription was only a week old, but the bottle seemed at least half empty. She poured the remaining tablets out in her palm and counted them—there were ten left out of thirty.

She suspected this type of medication was addictive. Was Fanny taking more than the prescribed dose? And how could she go about asking her?

The room had grown dark. Harriet lay on a narrow bed, still half dreaming, disjointed images flitting through her mind.

Beneath her, a musty, sour smell rose from the mattress when she moved. It made her think of the time her friend Samantha had come for a sleepover and had wet the bed, and of old Mrs. Bletchley.

A spark flared in her mind. Mrs. Bletchley's, that's where she was. She'd overslept for school. But no—the images came crowding back, fuzzy and jittering like an old newsreel she'd seen in history class.

Her dad—she remembered seeing her dad, and ducking down to slide into the backseat of his car. Her backpack had caught on the door frame, and the lady in the front seat had looked back at her and smiled.

She drifted again, riding a current of flickering movement—her dad saying something—she could see his lips moving, but she couldn't hear the words.

More darkness. A lamp globe made of swirly orange glass swam into view. Coffee, she'd smelled coffee. It made her think of their flat in the morning, of her mother getting ready for work . . . but no, that wasn't right . . .

She struggled to pull herself out of the dream. Not home. Starbucks. The lady had taken her to Starbucks. But where was her dad?

Movement again, the world tilting. Another car ride—no, a taxi. She remembered the shiny black door. A man's face asking a question, his blue eyes kind. She felt the warmth of a body against hers, heard a woman's voice saying, "She's not feeling well . . . bit of a bug . . ."

Walls rose, taller than she could see, blocking out the light. Gray brick, topped with broken glass and strands of wire that curled.

Then a gate—or had it been before? Her mind fixed on it, trying to hold the image. A silvery arch, like a keyhole, filled with black flowers. And through the keyhole, a flash of green.

The bright color receded and winked out, as if a door had closed at the end of a tunnel, and the darkness descended like a weight.

7

> "Now, what I want is, Facts . . .
> Facts alone are wanted in life."

CHARLES DICKENS
Hard Times

ARE YOU SURE you don't want me to run you to the tube station?" Gemma asked as Kincaid gulped at a cup of scalding tea, and folded toast and bacon into a makeshift sandwich. "Then you'd have time to eat your breakfast sitting down."

"Thanks, love, but I think I'd rather walk. Make hay while the sun shines—isn't that what they say?" The morning had dawned bright and windy, but with a promise of more rain later in the day.

"Have you been listening to *The Archers* again?" she teased, turning from the fridge with a carton of juice in one hand.

"I confess. It's my secret vice." He set down his mug and gave her a one-armed hug. "No, seriously, I don't mind the walk, and you've got to get the boys up if you're going to make it to Portobello before the market's jammed." What he didn't say was that he needed that brief time on his own to fold away the morning's images, the bright kitchen filled with comforting smells, Gemma disheveled before the warmth of the Aga, the boys still safe in their beds upstairs. These were not things he wanted to carry too close to the surface when he walked into the morgue at St. Thomas's.

"I'm sorry about this morning, about not going with you," he added as she disengaged herself to turn a second batch of bacon cooking in the frying pan.

"You know it can't be helped," she answered, not glancing up from her task.

He hesitated, knowing this was not the time to discuss it, but he couldn't be sure when he'd have another chance. Tess and Geordie were underfoot, tails wagging as they watched him expectantly, so he divided the last bite of his sandwich between them. "It worries me that Kit won't talk about Monday."

This time she did look at him. "He'll be fine." She gave him a reassuring smile. "We'll be fine. We'll have our treasure hunt at the market, maybe lunch at Otto's, then after my piano lesson I'm taking them to tea at Erika's." Putting down her tongs, she came to him and grasped the lapels of his jacket. "Ring me when you know something. I'll keep my phone with me."

Her hair was sleep-tousled, her skin still free of the light makeup she wore during the day. With his thumb, he traced the faint pattern of freckles on her cheekbone. She turned her face into his hand. The tenderness of the gesture moved him to say what he'd been keeping back for weeks. "Gemma, are you sure about giving up the nursery? I think we should talk—"

"We can't disappoint Kit now. You know that." She stepped back, the momentary softness of her expression replaced by a bright smile. He had ventured onto forbidden ground and she'd withdrawn again. "Now go," she added briskly, "or you'll be late."

She was right, of course, he admitted to himself a few minutes later as he walked up Lansdowne Road, towards Holland Park tube station. Kit had to come first just now, but acknowledging that didn't make it any easier to deal with Gemma shutting him out—or the realization that she was, whether consciously or not, using the situation with Kit as an excuse to avoid talking about her miscarriage and the possibility of having another child.

And to add insult to injury, he'd had no luck trying to get Kit to discuss his feelings about Monday's impending hearing. Arriving home a bit before ten the previous evening, he'd found Gemma at the piano in the dining room, practicing for her Saturday afternoon lesson. She'd been working on a simple Bach piece, and although she didn't have much time to play, he could tell she was improving. Her tempo was still a little slow, but her fingertips moved lightly and surely over the keys.

Pausing, she'd looked up and smiled, but he'd waved her on. "Don't stop. I'm going to check on the boys."

He'd started up the stairs, and the dogs, having dutifully met him at the front door, settled back into position on the first landing. This had become their usual strategy for dealing with divided loyalties when the family was split between up- and downstairs. Their cat, Sid, on the other hand, operating on the principle of *all things come to those who wait,* would be curled on the foot of their bed.

First, he looked in on Toby, now sleeping alone in the room he'd shared with Kit until a few weeks ago. The five-year-old lay sprawled on his stomach, covers thrown back to reveal his train-printed pajamas, his stuffed bear tossed to the floor. Kincaid carefully tucked in the bear and pulled up the duvet, but there was no change in the rhythm of Toby's slightly whuffly breathing.

Kincaid moved on to the room down the hall, once intended as the nursery. When his light knock brought no answer, he opened the door. Kit sat at his desk, hunched over a sheet of paper, drawing. A set of headphones explained his lack of response, and Kincaid could hear the tinny, muted sound of the personal CD player from across the room.

Rapping more loudly on the open door, Kincaid called out, "Hey, sport."

Kit turned, startled, and yanked off the headphones. "Sorry. Didn't hear you."

"I'm not surprised." Kincaid thought of all the times his mother had told him he was going to ruin his hearing, and refrained from further comment on the volume. "What are you listening to?" he asked instead, sitting down on the bed. Tess, Kit's terrier, had followed him upstairs and now jumped up beside him.

"The Mighty Diamonds." Kincaid must have looked blank, because Kit added, in the *don't you know anything?* tone that had been creeping into his voice more frequently of late, "It's reggae. Classic eighties."

"Oh, right. I must have been listening to the Police in the eighties, myself."

"But the Police were influenced by reggae, and by Bob Marley," Kit told him with great seriousness, and Kincaid congratulated himself on inadvertently getting something right. He suspected that would become more and more difficult, but he meant to keep trying.

"Did you borrow the CD from Wesley?"

"He said I could." Kit's reply was unexpectedly defensive. "I haven't scratched it or anything."

"No. I'm sure you haven't. You're very good at looking after things," Kincaid assured him, thinking he'd have to ask Wes for a crash course on reggae on the sly. In the meantime, he'd try an easier topic. He glanced at the paper on Kit's desk. "Are you sketching?"

Kit held up a drawing of a tortoise, copied from the open zoology book beside it. "Galápagos tortoise." The boy's latest hero was Dr. Stephen Maturin, the surgeon/naturalist from Patrick O'Brian's *Master and Commander* novels, and he'd become determined to learn to draw.

"Wow, that's terrific," Kincaid said, and the sincere admiration in his voice elicited a smile from Kit.

"I could use some better watercolor pencils. There's an art supply shop off Portobello, near Otto's. I thought maybe I could get them tomorrow."

"Listen, sport. About tomorrow. I'm going to have to miss out on our shopping expedition. Something's come up—"

"I know. Gemma told me." Kit's expression was neutral, reserved.

"I'm sorry. I wanted—"

"Don't worry about it." Kit shrugged and turned back to his desk. "It doesn't matter."

The absolution cut Kincaid to the quick.

When Kincaid arrived at the morgue, Farrell, Cullen, and Bell were there before him, and Kincaid suspected that Cullen, at least, derived some satisfaction from getting one up on his boss.

He joined them in the postmortem theatre gallery, where they looked down on Kate Ling and her assistant, and on the grotesque and blackened form on the steel dissection table. The smell made Kincaid wish he'd forgone even his light toast and bacon breakfast.

Dr. Ling and the assistant pathologist wore long green plastic aprons tied over their scrubs and, viewed from the back, made him think of gunslingers in chaps. Perhaps it was something in the assurance of their stance, feet apart, ready to take on the grim reaper himself.

Ling turned and saw him, her eyes crinkling in a smile above her mask. She switched off her mike. "Duncan, I was just saying to your colleagues that we've finished the preliminary exam. As I'm sure you all know, we can learn a good bit simply from measurements and radiology, even when the corpse is quite severely damaged." She gestured towards the far wall, where a series of X-rays were mounted on light boards. "These things tell us that our victim was an adult female, of medium height—probably five-five or -six. Although fire can cause some shrinkage of bone, in this case I don't believe the heat was that severe."

"Could you narrow 'adult' down a bit, Doc?" Kincaid asked.

"Postadolescent, definitely. In females, by the age of twenty, the lower epiphysis—that's one of the bony plates at either end of the forearm—and radius have fused. Shortly thereafter the upper epiphysis and radius fuse as well, as is the case here.

"The collarbone gives us our next marker—it has usually finished growing by the age of twenty-eight or so—but as the victim's upper torso has suffered the most severe fire damage, I can't give a definitive opinion on that.

"As to the upper end of the spectrum, older subjects show signs of degeneration around the edges of the vertebrae, and joints may show signs of arthritis. Neither of those are evident here, but we may want to have a forensic anthropologist take another look."

"So you're saying twenty to—"

"Midthirties, possibly forty."

Kincaid winced at the idea that, according to a pathologist's estimate, he was already going downhill. He caught a glimpse of the pained expression on Bill Farrell's face and guessed the thought had occurred to him as well.

"Twenty to forty. That's a big bloody help," Cullen muttered in Kincaid's ear. While his sergeant might approach the most tedious and time-consuming data search with equanimity, postmortems made him cranky.

"Any chance the victim could be older than forty, Doc?" Kincaid asked.

"With good genes, maybe. As I said, I'm no expert. Let's move on to the exterior physical examination. Although it's not unusual to find a burn victim's clothing fused to the skin, we were unable to discover any fabric traces. Officer Farrell, has your team turned up any evidence of clothing at the scene?"

"Not so far. Even if the fire destroyed all fabric, we'd expect to turn up a bit of button or zipper, or a fragment of shoe leather. I'd say this woman was stripped and her clothing taken away from the scene, or she arrived there starkers."

Ling nodded, as if he were a promising pupil. "That leads us to another interesting point. The stripping of a female victim usually implies some sort of sexual assault, but this woman shows no obvious signs of sexual trauma. Of course, that doesn't completely rule out a sexual motive, but it does narrow things down a bit. We'll know more when we get the results of the swabs."

"What about race, Doctor?" asked Maura Bell. "The skin looks black, but the hair that's left seems reddish."

"Neither skin nor hair are good indicators here. The dark color of the skin is due to charring, but the hair color is also misleading. Dark hair can often lighten due to oxidation. My guess is that this woman was a Caucasian brunette."

Bell looked puzzled. "Caucasian? But you've just said you couldn't tell the color of the skin."

"We can't." Ling smiled. "But we can tell the shape of the skull, both from visual assessment and from X-rays." She touched a gloved finger to the head of the corpse. "This skull is high and wide. The nasal opening is narrow. The cheekbones do not project, nor does the jaw. These are all defining Caucasian characteristics."

"Okay, Doc," said Kincaid. "We've got white, female, brunette, medium height, between twenty and forty. But did she die in the fire?"

"Patience, Duncan, patience. I'm just getting to the interesting bit. Let's take a closer look at the skull. We noted at the scene that there was fracturing, but we also know that intense heat can cause fracturing. In that case, however, the plates of the skull tend to separate at the sutures. What we can see here, on closer examination, is more consistent with a depressed fracture due to blunt force trauma."

"Clear as mud," Cullen said, and Kincaid gave him a silencing frown.

"Microscopic examination of the edges of the fractured bone will tell us more," Ling went on. "But there's also evidence of frontal trauma, moderate Le Fort fractures. The nose has been broken"—she traced the bridge of the nose with her finger—"as has one cheekbone."

"Excuse me, Doctor." Bell stepped forward, resting her hands on the gallery railing. "Are you telling us this woman was killed by a blow—or blows—to the head, rather than by the fire?"

"No, I'm merely saying that it's more than likely the skull fractures were not *caused* by the heat from the fire. That doesn't rule out the possibility that the victim was alive at the time of the fire, or that these injuries were sustained *during* the fire. Although the last scenario is unlikely, I'll admit, as there was no evidence of structural collapse at the scene, and it's not very plausible that the victim could have fallen and injured both the front and back of her head at the same time.

"There is some soot visible in the nose and mouth, which could indicate that she was still breathing, but it might also be a result of settling, as she was lying faceup. We won't know for sure until we've examined the airway and lungs. So let's have a look." Switching her mike back on, Ling turned to her assistant, who had been patiently standing by, and accepted a scalpel. "Thanks, Sandy. Let's begin with the larynx and trachea."

Kincaid had never quite got over the instinctive flinch brought on by the pathologist's first incision, but he forced himself to watch as Ling made a precise cut, murmuring a detailed description into the microphone. The mortuary cold had begun to make his bones ache, but at least, he realized, his nose had gone numb, acclimatized to the smell. Stealing a glance at his companions, he saw that Cullen looked increasingly cross, Farrell impassive, and Bell wore a glazed expression that made him think of a deer caught in the headlamps of a car.

"Ah, now this is interesting," said Kate Ling, glancing up at them. "There's no sign of soot in the windpipe, but there is something else—bruising of the underlying tissues of the throat that was not visible on the skin."

"She was choked?" Kincaid asked, surprised.

"The hyoid bone is intact, but yes, I'd say so. She could have lost consciousness long enough to have been bashed in the head and face."

"And the absence of soot means she was dead when the fire started?"

"Well, there is always the possibility of vagal inhibition—that's a reflexive constriction of the pharynx—from inhaling hot gases, but considering her other injuries, I'd say yes, it's likely she was dead when the fire started."

"Hallelujah!" breathed Cullen, and a smile flickered across Bell's face.

"Can you tell us what was used to inflict the blunt trauma injuries?" asked Farrell.

"We'll know more when we get into the skull, of course, but I'd say something with a fairly large surface area."

While Kate Ling continued with her examination, Kincaid let his mind wander over the implications of what she'd told them. Although Farrell still hadn't found any definitive evidence of arson, this made it look as if they were dealing with a fire started to cover up a homicide—which in turn made it less likely that insurance fraud was the motive. But did that mean Michael Yarwood was out of the frame?

It didn't explain how the murderer had gained access to the building, and Kincaid still harbored a strong feeling that Yarwood was somehow involved.

It hadn't escaped him that he'd been asked to look after Yarwood's interests, but if Yarwood's bosses had thought that appealing to their connections at Scotland Yard would guarantee favoritism, they'd been much mistaken. As far as Kincaid was concerned, his brief was simply to make sure Michael Yarwood was not accused without grounds.

Kincaid also realized that Ling's description of the victim could fit the profile of Winnie's friend's missing flatmate. He'd have to ring Gemma as soon as they were finished at the hospital and arrange to get a sample of the woman's DNA for the lab. He could put in a sample request through official channels, of course, as a report had been filed, but out of consideration for Winnie he preferred to take care of it in person.

And he had to admit his curiosity had been aroused by Gemma's description of the house and the missing woman's odd lifestyle. If there was any chance the woman in the warehouse might turn out to be Elaine Holland, he wanted to see both house and flatmate for himself.

As Dr. Ling began the Y-incision that would allow her to remove and examine the victim's internal organs, Maura Bell's phone rang. She stepped back, shielding the phone and speaking quietly so as not to disturb the procedure, but when she rang off her face shone with barely suppressed excitement.

"That was Borough station," she said. "About the CCTV footage. They've found something."

Congratulating herself on her luck, Gemma slipped the car into a parking space in Pembridge Gardens, just off the top of Portobello Road. A spot so near Portobello Market on a Saturday morning was not to be passed up, although the location meant she'd have a struggle with Toby when they walked past the library. He'd begun to read simple books on his own, and their usual Saturday visits to the library were the highlight of his week, but today they had another agenda.

Having let the boys skip breakfast at home in the interests of speed, she distracted Toby with a reminder of her promise to buy them hot cocoa and croissants from the street stall at Mr. Christian's Deli. That way they could eat and shop at the same time.

Soon they joined the lemminglike flood of pedestrians pouring into the top of Portobello Road. With one hand firmly gripping Toby and the other her handbag, Gemma relaxed into the flow, letting herself enjoy the color and bustle of the crowd. Beside her, Kit looked happier than she'd seen him in weeks.

She loved the view from the top end of Portobello Road, and it was never more beautiful than on a sunny autumn morning. Below them the street curved gently, lined on both sides with houses and shop fronts painted every color of the rainbow.

It made her feel she'd been picked up out of ordinary London and plunked down in the middle of somewhere more exotic—a village in Italy, or maybe the south of France— except that this, too, was typical of London, where it was not unusual for colorful and eccentric pockets to butt up against sedate Victorian villas. Snatches of music came from the buskers farther down the road, fading in and out, as if someone were twirling the dial on a cosmic radio, and the odor of garlic cooking wafted up from a basement kitchen as they passed.

It took Gemma a moment to put a name to the feeling that welled up inside her. With a start of surprise she realized it was contentment. It wasn't only the view she loved, but all of Portobello, and Notting Hill, and the house she shared with Duncan and the boys. She loved the connections they had made—friends, neighbors, shopkeepers—and it came to her that she had never before felt so at home. Not in Islington, not even in Leyton where she had grown up.

Her parents had known that sense of community, of belonging, she was sure, but she'd always been focused on moving on, getting out, making her own life. Then, during her marriage to Rob, her pregnancy, Toby's babyhood, she'd always been looking round the corner, anticipating what came next. Her life had been a litany of afters—*after the wedding, after the baby, after she returned to work, after the divorce, after the promotion.* Even living in Hazel's garage flat, her perceptions had been colored by the knowledge that it could only be a stopgap, a temporary measure.

But now . . . now she didn't want to move on. Perhaps it was partly her worry over Kit; perhaps it was the sense of life's fragility that still lingered from her miscarriage; or perhaps it was watching the collapse of her friend Hazel's seemingly perfect marriage.

Whatever the reason, she knew only that she wanted fiercely to hold on to things just the way they were and not take any risks that might bring about change.

The crowd thickened as Gemma and the boys crossed Chepstow Villas and entered the heart of Portobello's antiques market, and she gripped Toby's hand a little tighter. When Kit veered off to the right, towards the antique sporting goods shop that was one of his favorites, she pulled him back firmly. "Food first. Then we shop."

A few minutes later, armed with hot drinks in paper cups and flaky chocolate croissants, they started a thorough perusal of the street stalls and arcades.

Gemma hadn't expected finding an antique specimen cabinet would be easy, but three hours and four arcades later, she was beginning to despair. As the clock crept towards noon, the heat in the arcades had become suffocating, the crowds aggravating rather than exhilarating. Kit's face had grown longer and longer, and Toby was whining because he was hungry and because she'd refused to buy him an outrageously expensive Matchbox car. If she hadn't been so hot and tired, she'd have laughed at the look on his face when she'd tried to explain that the toys were not meant to be played with, only looked at. The concept of collecting made no sense to a five-year-old.

"What do you say we take a break for lunch?" she said, sighing with relief as they emerged once more onto the pavement. "We could go to Otto's. Is Wes working today?"

"Yeah, I think so," answered Kit, displaying none of his usual enthusiasm for food or for a visit to their friend Otto's café. "Couldn't we look just a bit longer?"

"Maybe after lunch—" Gemma broke off, realizing that the tinny sound she'd been hearing above the noise of the mob was her mobile phone. It was Duncan, she saw as she fished it from her bag, and she had a sudden sinking feeling that it was not good news.

She answered, and when she'd heard him out, said, "I'll have to get in touch with Winnie. I'll ring you when I've connected with her, and you can meet us there."

"Gemma, you don't have to come," Kincaid protested. "You said the house is right across the street from Winnie's church. Why don't I just ask her to pop over and meet me?"

She thought of the boys, and of another missed piano lesson, and for a moment she was tempted to agree. But then she recalled Fanny Liu's frightened face and the comfort Fanny had seemed to derive from her presence, and she felt ashamed of her selfishness. "Yes," she said reluctantly. "I think I do."

When she rang off, both boys were watching her.

"You have to go, right?" Kit said flatly.

"Yes," she admitted ruefully. "But maybe we can grab a bite of lunch first."

"And the cabinet?"

"What about next Saturday?"

"Next Saturday? But—" Kit shrugged and turned away, studying the display of antique jewelry on a street stall table with great concentration, but she'd seen the flash of panic in his eyes. Was he so worried about Monday's hearing at the family court that he feared there wouldn't be another Saturday?

Gently she said, "Kit, there's no reason we can't do this next Saturday. Maybe Duncan can—"

"Gemma—" Kit was pointing at the jewelry display.

"—come with us. You know he wanted—"

"Gemma, look."

"At the jewelry? Whatever for?" But frowning, she followed his gaze, and then she saw what he had seen.

The glass-fronted display case lay on its back, covering most of the table's surface. But the cabinet, although large, was shallow, and its interior was divided into dozens of small, square compartments. In the case's current position, the compartments formed pockets, each of which held a small display of jewelry, but if it were stood upright, it would make a perfect specimen cabinet.

Their exchange had drawn the dealer's attention. Gemma gave Kit's shoulder a warning squeeze and said as casually as she could manage, "This for sale?"

The man lit a cigarette and squinted at her through narrowed eyes. "Well, now, that depends, luv. I'd have to find something else to put my stock in. Just how much are you willing to offer?"

The three detectives and Bill Farrell sat huddled round the video monitor in the room they'd been temporarily assigned at Borough High Street Station. After Bell's phone call, they'd left Kate Ling to finish the postmortem. Ling had promised to let them know immediately if she found anything else significant; otherwise, she'd get the report to them as soon as the lab results came back. Kincaid, for his part, had been just as glad for an excuse to miss out on the sawing and slicing.

The CCTV tape had been loaded into the VCR, and even with the videotape in pause mode, the black-and-white image on the television screen looked blotchy and faded. Kincaid silently cursed the cheap security measures that encouraged reusing videotapes until they were bloody well useless.

"This is from the building across the street and a few yards to the east of the warehouse's front entrance," said the DS in charge of running the tape. "We were lucky to find a private camera scanning more than the building's foyer, but as this is a credit reporting business, they tend to be a bit paranoid about external security. Unfortunately, the view isn't great, as you can see."

It took Kincaid a moment to match what he was seeing on the screen with his memory of the warehouse entrance. Then he realized that the camera's field of vision ended at the western edge of the warehouse door. This meant that not only could they not see the side door, but they had no view of the street on which it faced.

"Any luck finding a view of the side door?" he asked.

"No, sorry." The sergeant, a young Asian woman, sounded as if she took the failure personally. "There's nothing there except the shelter, and they said that although they'd considered a security camera, they hadn't managed to work it into their budget." She picked up the remote control and continued more briskly, "Now, we're just coming up to the critical time, if you'll bear with me." The time stamp in the screen's bottom corner read 9:55. As she rolled the tape, a figure popped into view on the left-hand side of the screen and moved quickly across—a man, head down, coat collar pulled up high—then vanished on the right. "A harmless pedestrian," said the sergeant, "but then things get more interesting." She fast-forwarded the tape until 10:00 showed on the screen, then slowed to normal speed.

This time the figures came from the right, walking more slowly, and stopped before the warehouse door. Although their backs were to the camera, they were recognizable as male and female. The woman wore a short skirt with some sort of blousy jacket; the man was several inches taller and wore what looked like a set of motorcycle leathers. There was something oddly lumpy about the back of the man's head, but Kincaid couldn't quite make out what it was.

The couple shuffled and bumped against each other, as if they were a bit tipsy, while the woman dug in her handbag, and the man threw an arm briefly across the woman's shoulders. Something glinted in her hand as she let the bag drop to her side, and then, for just an instant, she turned round and surveyed the street.

The sergeant froze the frame and they all gazed at the face looking eerily back at them, as if the woman were aware of their regard. The image was blurred and grainy, but still an identifiable likeness.

At first, Kincaid thought that she was too young to fit their profile, but as he studied her face more closely, he decided she could be in her early twenties, maybe even older. Although it was hard to be certain because of the poor quality of the image, she appeared to be white, and brunette. Her lips were pursed in a pout of concentration.

"Anyone recognize her?" the sergeant asked. When no one responded, she said, "We've printed photos from this frame—it's the best shot—and so far none of our regular beat officers have recognized her, either. That makes it less likely she's a hooker, but doesn't rule it out altogether. I had my doubts about the skirt anyway—doesn't look short enough for a girl on the game."

"Were those keys in her hand?" Kincaid asked.

"She did pull something from her handbag. It might have been keys or lock picks, but it could just as well have been a small torch or even a light saber."

"A warrior princess." Kincaid grinned, then just as quickly sobered as he thought of what might have happened to this woman. "Okay, what next?" he asked.

"Go forward again, slowly, Sarah," instructed Maura Bell.

As the tape jerked into motion, the woman turned back to her companion. Having evidently decided the coast was clear, they both stepped forward into the doorway. After a moment, the shadows round them seemed to darken. Then the couple disappeared.

The man's face had never been visible to the camera.

"We've got two more hours of tape before the fire," explained Sarah, "and neither of them comes out again—at least not by this door." She pointed the remote at the screen. "I'm going to fast-forward again. You'll see a few pedestrians, then, at a few minutes past ten, this man." A few jerky figures crossed the screen without giving the doorway so much as a glance; then, as the tape slowed, a man in a dark coat came into view, again from the right. His head swiveled towards the doorway as he passed. He seemed to hesitate for an instant, then went on. "And that's it," said Sarah, "until the fire brigade arrives two hours later." The camera had never caught the man's face, and nothing else distinguished him.

"Did he see the open door and disregard it?" Cullen mused aloud. "Or hear someone moving about?"

"We can't very well ask him, can we?" Kincaid said, venting his frustration in sarcasm. "And troops could have been moving in and out on the side street, for all we know, with a marching band and Hannibal's elephants."

"We've a photo of the girl that's good enough for an ID," Maura Bell said sharply, as if wanting to make sure her team got the credit they deserved. "I say we start by showing it to Michael Yarwood and his foreman."

"I can take a batch and canvas the street," offered the DS, showing commendable initiative.

Kincaid thought of the arrangements he'd made to meet Gemma. Could this woman possibly be old enough to fit the description of Elaine Holland? The camera could be deceiving, and it was dangerous to make assumptions at this stage of an investigation. And even if Winnie's friend did not identify the woman in the photo as her missing roommate, they had no proof that the woman was in fact the victim found in the fire more than two hours later.

As much as he wanted to question Yarwood and the job foreman about the photo himself, it made more sense to delegate. "Doug, why don't you and DI Bell try to track down Yarwood and Joe Spender? I'm going to follow through on the missing roommate, and I'll need an evidence collection kit."

Kincaid was tempted to regret his decision a few minutes later when Gemma rang to say she'd been delayed.

"Something came up," she said enigmatically. "And I had to get the boys some lunch. Besides, Winnie's tied up on a pastoral visit and won't be free for another hour."

"We could go without her," suggested Kincaid, chafing at the delay.

"I'd rather not," Gemma told him. "Fanny Liu is going to need all the support she can get. Besides, by the time I get the boys situated and get there myself, it wouldn't save us that much time. I'll ring you back when I've hooked up with Winnie."

With that he had to be content, and a moment's thought reconciled him to the setback. As efficient as Bell's young DS seemed to be, he wanted to show the photo to the shelter's staff himself, and the delay would give him time.

Although Kath Warren had assured him that all the current residents were accounted for, the woman could be a former resident, or have some connection with one of the current residents.

Bill Farrell was also heading back to the fire scene to supervise the ongoing collection of evidence. "I've got a murder weapon to find," he told Kincaid, "and at least now I have some idea what to look for."

Kincaid found a parking space near Farrell's van and walked down the side street to the shelter's entrance. The front door stood open, as it had the previous day, but the inner door was closed, and there was no answer when he rang the bell. There was no sound or sign of activity, and he doubted the residents answered the bell when the staff was out.

Glancing at his watch, he decided to grab a sandwich, then give it another go. He walked back to Southwark Street and stood for a moment, trying to decide which direction offered the best prospect of food. As he scanned the street, he noticed a girl standing in the shadow of an office doorway. Something furtive in her posture drew his attention; then he realized her face was familiar. Her straight blond hair was loose today, half hiding the curve of her cheek, but he'd no doubt it was the young firefighter he'd met yesterday.

"Rose?" he said, going up to her. "It is Rose, isn't it? What are you doing here?"

8

They mounted up and up, through the musty smell of
an old close house, little used, to a large garret bedroom.

CHARLES DICKENS
Little Dorrit

THE PATCH OF light moved across the wall above Harriet's
bed. She watched its slow progress for a long time, thinking
about the roses on the wallpaper. They were old roses, faded
roses, on a background the color of tea stains. Sleepily, she
wondered how her mum could have forgotten that she hated
flowery, girly things, but the thought drifted lightly away.

She felt very odd, as if she were hovering outside her own
body, watching herself, but when she gave her toe an exper-
imental wiggle, it moved reassuringly. It was only then that
Harriet realized she was still wearing her shoes. Why had
she gone to bed in her shoes?

Frowning, she pushed aside the rough blanket covering
her chest. Where was her duvet? And why was she still
wearing her sweatshirt, the same one she'd put on for school

that morning at Mrs. Bletchley's? Wait . . . was that this morning? Or had that been yesterday morning? It had been dark, and she knew, somehow, that she had slept for a long time.

She felt a sickening lurch of panic as fragments of memory coalesced. Her dad . . . the lady in the front seat of the car . . . the gray walls . . . being half carried, half dragged, up narrow and twisting stairs . . . the darkness closing in . . .

Harriet sat up, her heart pounding. Her eyes focused on the light pouring in from the rectangle of window on the far wall, but her relief was short-lived. There was daylight pouring in through the window, but it wasn't her window. Her mind finally wrapped itself around the truth it had been refusing to accept. It wasn't her room.

She forced herself to look around. Assess things, her mother was always telling her—have all the facts before you act. The room was larger than her bedroom at home. There was the window on the wall opposite the bed, and on the right-hand wall, a door. The left-hand wall sloped down, as if it was set into the eave of the house. The walls were lined with odds and ends of old discarded furniture, and a bookcase under the eave held a few tattered clothbound volumes. There were a stool and a tin pail in one corner, and beside the window, a chest of drawers. On the chest stood a china basin and ewer, patterned in faded pink roses, like the wallpaper.

Carefully, Harriet slid from the bed, and as she moved, the sour, musty smell rose again from the mattress. The odor brought back the memory of the darkness, but she pushed it away.

The bare floorboards had once been painted gray, but the color had aged to the color of dust, and the surface was marred with scuff and drag marks. She placed her feet carefully, afraid to make a noise. Making her way to the window, she looked out of the grimy, spider-snared panes.

A grim prospect greeted her. Below, she saw a dirt yard

infested with weeds and rubbish. Across the yard, another wall of gray brick, featureless. Beyond the wall, she could make out the peaks of higher roofs, but nothing looked familiar. She tried the window, but it had been nailed or painted shut. Not that she'd have been able to get out that way, anyway—she could see that it was too high, and a straight drop of several floors. Nor did it look as if anyone would hear her if she called for help.

The choking panic rose in her throat again.

Where was she? What was this place? Why was she here?

Harriet gripped the windowsill as dizziness swept over her. She realized suddenly that she was starving. How long had it been since she'd had anything to eat? A day, two days? The fact that she wasn't certain frightened her even more.

And she had to pee. The thought made her screw up her courage to try the door. The unpainted wood looked ancient and scarred, and there was a web of scratches around the old-fashioned keyhole. The knob turned in her fingers, but the door didn't budge.

Gripping the knob more tightly, she turned it hard to the right and leaned back with all her weight, but the door didn't even quiver. She let go and rubbed her smarting palms against her jeans, then crouched down to peer through the keyhole. There was nothing to see but darkness.

For a moment, the urge to call out was almost overpowering, but she pressed her hand hard to her mouth. A shout might bring worse than being alone and hungry.

Then she heard a noise. A creak, and then another, the soft footfalls of someone climbing the stairs. Harriet's first instinct was to hide. She looked round wildly, but there was no cover, even beneath the frame of the old iron bed.

Her logical mind told her it wouldn't matter, that whoever was coming knew she was there, but her body obeyed a different instruction. She ran to the bed and wrapped the blanket around herself, as if the tattered fabric could give her a layer of protection, and huddled back against the wall. Then came the sound of bolts being thrown back, and the clicking of the tumblers as the key turned in the lock. The door swung open.

"Superintendent." Rose Kearny looked as though he were the last person she wanted to see. Kincaid might have been tempted to take it personally, except that she'd been friendly enough yesterday, and her behavior seemed decidedly odd. She didn't strike him as the type to be skulking in doorways.

"Are you all right?" he asked, when she didn't step forward. She was dressed much as she had been at the fire scene yesterday, but with her hair loose rather than pulled back in a ponytail she looked younger, less professional.

"I—" She glanced past him, as if seeking a means of escape, then appeared to resign herself to the conversation. "I was hoping to have a word with Station Officer Farrell."

Kincaid nodded towards the warehouse. "He's there now, working on the crime scene."

Rose looked more uncomfortable still. "I—it's just that— if my guv'nor finds out I've been here without clearing it with him, he'll be livid. But our next duty's not until tomorrow morning, and there's something I thought Officer Farrell should know."

"Something you've remembered?" Kincaid asked, his interest quickening.

She shook her head. "No. But I've been looking into some things . . ." She drew farther into the doorway. "It's nothing, really. Probably a stupid idea. And if any of the lads from my watch see me here—"

"Look." He recalled now that there was a tea shop a short way up the road. If he was lucky, the place might have sandwiches, too. "Let me buy you a cup of tea, and you can tell me about it. Then I can pass your idea along to Farrell if you don't want to speak to him yourself."

After considering for a moment, she said, "Okay. I don't suppose it's likely I'll run into anyone I know in a tea shop." She smiled for the first time.

"Any rule against you being seen with a detective?" he asked as they headed east on Southwark Street.

"Not as long as it was you wanting to talk to me, but I'd rather not have to explain."

They reached the place Kincaid remembered. He saw that it was a museum as well as a tea shop, housing displays on the history of tea and collections of teapots, but they could use the restaurant without buying a ticket for the tour. Rose ducked inside with obvious relief.

When they'd found a table near the back and placed their orders—tea and sandwiches for him, tea and a scone for her—he said, "Anyone would think you were hiding from a jealous boyfriend."

"Rather that than get on the wrong side of my guv'nor. Or the lads—that's even worse. But no. No boyfriend, jealous or otherwise."

He wondered what had motivated her to risk discipline, or being ostracized, but thought it better not to push until she'd relaxed a little. "Are you the only woman on your watch?" he asked.

"Yeah, at the moment. We had another, a probationer, when I first transferred in, but she got posted to another station."

"It must be hard."

Rose shrugged as the waitress brought their tea. "Sometimes, but not like it used to be. The fire service is changing. Some of the old-timers may not like women coming in, but they know there's nothing they can do about it. And the good officers, like my guv'nor, realize that women have things to offer that are as important as brute strength. Not that I'm not strong, mind you," she added, with another small smile. "But I think the strength thing is overrated. I can haul hose and lift ladders with the best of them, but there are techniques that women, or smaller men, can use to make things easier. It seems to me that should be the point—getting the job done as efficiently as possible. Safer for personnel, safer for victims, safer for property." Her face was alight with enthusiasm, and Kincaid found himself hoping that the wear and tear of the job wouldn't erode too much of her crusading spirit.

"What about hazing? Is that still a problem?" Kincaid asked as their food arrived.

Rose considered for a moment. "There's teasing, of course. It's part of the culture, and I think that if you're going to make it as a woman in the fire service, you have to let a certain amount roll off your back." She frowned and added slowly, "The tough part is knowing when you have to draw the line, because eventually you will, with someone. I'm sure it must be the same for women in the police."

Kincaid thought of the difficulties Gemma had had with one of the sergeants under her command at Notting Hill. It had taken a delicate combination of tact and authority for her to establish a good working relationship with the man, but then she'd had the advantage of rank.

He was watching Rose slather butter on her scone, and congratulating himself a bit because he'd never felt particularly threatened by female police officers, when it occurred to him that he'd never worked with a woman who outranked him. If he did, would he find he was a hypocrite, and a self-righteous one at that? It was an uncomfortable thought. He made an effort to concentrate on his sandwiches, but he couldn't help wondering if he'd condescended to Maura Bell in a way he wouldn't have if she'd been male.

"What about you?" asked Rose. "We've established that I don't have a jealous boyfriend. Are you married?"

Kincaid looked up, startled, and tried not to choke on his tuna sandwich. "Um, no. But I live with my partner and our two sons."

"That sounds very progressive of you." Her smile was a little too quick, and he saw a telltale flush of color stain her cheeks, as if she'd embarrassed herself by asking. "Bohemian."

"It's not, really." He hesitated, imagining himself trying to explain their family situation, or telling her how hard it had been just to persuade Gemma to live with him. God forbid he should mention marriage. That was a can of worms he didn't want to contemplate himself, much less reveal to a stranger. "Long story," he said at last, then, not wanting to seem abrupt, added, "we're both in the job, so it complicates things. We used to work together."

"Really?" Rose sounded interested. "What happened?"

"She put in for promotion and a transfer." More than ready to change the subject, he said quickly, "Why don't you tell me what it was you wanted with Bill Farrell?"

Now, Rose seemed to feel awkward. With her fingertip, she pushed scone crumbs into a pile on her plate. "I don't want to sound like I'm trying to tell Station Officer Farrell how to do his job. But after the meeting last night I was curious, so I started looking back through the fire reports for the Borough in the last year." She pulled some folded papers from her jacket pocket and spread them out on the table. "I found five structure fires in the past seven months that seem to fit a pattern."

He could see that the top pages were fire brigade incident reports. "I'm sure Farrell will have checked for arson reports as a matter of routine—"

"But that's just the thing," interrupted Rose. "None of these fires were ever definitely flagged as arsons. They were all listed as undetermined cause. Here, I've marked them on a map." She pushed the bottom sheet across the table to him. It was a photocopy of an area map, showing six scattered red rings. He recognized one location, the Southwark Street warehouse.

"They started small," Rose said, tapping the ring on the map's western boundary. He noticed that her nails were short and unpolished, her hands slender. "The first one was in a lockup behind Waterloo Station. Accumulated rubbish, no sign of accelerants, no more than one point of origin. Multiple points of origin are usually a dead giveaway for arson."

He frowned. "So you're saying it *did*n't look like arson?"

"No, wait, hear me out." She tapped another circle, this one to the east, near the top of Borough High Street. "Number two was a vacant basement flat in a council estate. Same scenario, more bang. Keep in mind that basements are ideal for starting a good fire, because fire spreads upwards.

"Then a small grocer off the Borough Road. The fire started in accumulated polystyrene meat-packing trays, a great accelerant. That's how the fire was started in Leo's Grocery in Bristol. Anyone with an interest in fires would know that."

"Number four, a paint store." She touched a spot near Blackfriars Road. "That burned for two days, and took two adjoining buildings with it."

"And the fifth?"

"A warehouse near the Hay's Galleria. Stored fabric for a clothing manufacturer. Went up a treat."

"And you think last night's fire was the sixth," Kincaid said, intrigued now. "What about access in the first five?"

"No sign of forced entry in any instance. The only place with an alarm was the warehouse, but it was an old building and the system wasn't sophisticated."

"So what makes you think there's any connection? Why not a series of accidents? Or if they were arson, unrelated attempts at insurance fraud?"

"You can rule out insurance fraud on the first two. The lockup was abandoned, the flat vacant. It's a possibility with the others, but the investigators would have looked for financial problems or insurance irregularities. As for connections . . ." Rose ate the last bite of her scone and leaned towards him. "What do all these fires have in common?"

Kincaid felt like a slow pupil. "Besides the fact that they weren't proved arson? I don't know. But I think you're dying to tell me."

"Okay." She gave him a cheeky grin. "Most people think that arsonists go about splashing petrol all over the place and setting off timing devices, but that's not always true. A pro will use fuels available at the scene, and the simpler the ignition, the better. If you have a good fuel load, you can use a very small amount of accelerant to get things going and there won't be a trace left after the burn. You put a bit of petrol or paraffin on a pile of loose paper or some plastic cartons, light it with a cigarette lighter, and presto!" She sat back, looking pleased with herself.

Kincaid popped his last bite of sandwich into his mouth while he thought it over. "And all these places had the right sort of material for fuel, and were pretty well guaranteed to burn on their own from a small ignition?" She nodded. "Say you're right," he continued. "What makes you think last night's fire fits the pattern?"

"It would be hard to find a better fuel load than a pile of old furniture filled with polyurethane foam. The stuff was highly flammable, and arranged for maximum burn. It was a perfect set. And the time between fires has been getting progressively shorter. There were only two weeks between the last warehouse fire and this one."

He didn't like where this was leading at all. "So what you're telling me is that you think we have a pro, and that he's escalating? A serial arsonist?"

The satisfaction faded from Rose's face. "I could be wrong. But . . ."

"But if, by some chance, you were right, it would be impossible to prove."

"Well, yeah. Unless there were witnesses that haven't come forward. Or some forensic evidence left at the scenes that no one knew to look for." Looking less happy by the minute, Rose traced a pattern on the tablecloth with her tea-spoon, then set the spoon down and began gathering up her papers. "I'm sorry. This isn't much use to you, is it?"

There were arguments against her theory, but he certainly didn't think they could afford to dismiss it. "Maybe not," he said, "but that doesn't mean you shouldn't discuss this with Bill Farrell. He's been concentrating on the crime scene, so he may not have had a chance to research these fires as thoroughly as you have."

She stopped, papers halfway folded, and looked up at him.

"If I give him your number and he rings you, then you won't be in trouble with your boss, right?" Kincaid continued. "After all, you can't refuse to talk to the FIT." Farrell, he thought, might want to encourage her, regardless of whether her theory was pertinent to last night's fire. Rose Kearny had the makings of an investigator. Although her station officer might consider her insubordinate, Kincaid had found a streak of independence essential in a good detective.

"No, I suppose not." The corners of her mouth curved up, and he found he liked making her smile.

"Are those photocopies?" He gestured towards the papers, and when she nodded, said, "Why don't you give them to me, and I'll pass them along to Farrell along with your number. But, Rose . . ." He debated how much he could tell her. "There are reasons why this fire may not fit your pattern. I can't give you any details from the postmortem, but it looks as though this fire may have been set to cover up a homicide."

Her face tightened. "I hadn't forgotten the body. But it's not unheard of for serial arsonists to escalate to murder."

"No, but think about it. You saw the victim. She'd been stripped. The most logical explanation is that the killer wanted to conceal her identity. Why would a serial arsonist care to hide his victim's identity?"

"For the same reason anyone would. To prevent a connection being made between killer and victim. Do you have any idea who she was?"

Kincaid pulled the CCTV photo from the folder he'd carried with him and handed it across the table. "This woman entered the building a couple of hours before the fire. We've no way of knowing when—or if—she left. Do you recognize her, by any chance?"

Rose studied the photo for a long moment before reluctantly shaking her head. "No. She looks young, doesn't she? I hate to think . . ." She started to hand the photo back, then stopped and looked at it again. "There is something about her, though, that looks familiar. I just can't quite put my finger on it. Maybe she looks like someone on the telly?"

As the waitress came with their check, Rose gave an apologetic shrug and let him slip the photo back into his folder. Glancing at his watch, Kincaid realized he was running short of time if he meant to go back to the shelter before meeting Gemma.

Rose scribbled a number on the photocopied sheets, then stood and handed him the papers. "I won't take up any more of your time. I've put down my mobile number if Station Officer Farrell wants to talk to me. Thanks for the tea." She met his eyes. "And thanks for not telling me I'm crazy."

"I don't think you're crazy. But I hope you're wrong."

"Yeah. Me, too," Rose said slowly. "Because the thing is . . . if I'm right . . . there are going to be more fires."

This time, when Kincaid buzzed at the shelter's entrance, Kath Warren answered immediately. When he identified himself and asked if he could come up, however, she hesitated, then said she'd come down. A moment later the door clicked open and she slipped into the vestibule.

"I'm sorry," she said a bit breathlessly. "It's just that having the police in yesterday upset a number of the residents. You have to understand that these women live on the edge of paranoia at the best of times, and anyone coming into their space is perceived as a threat. It's my fault—I should have realized."

The crisp efficiency she'd displayed the previous day seemed a little frayed round the edges, and her careful makeup didn't quite conceal the shadows beneath her eyes.

"I'm the one that should apologize," he told her. "We shouldn't have tramped in like an invading army."

Kath smiled and seemed to thaw a bit. "We've conspiracy theories going round like a virus, I can tell you. First, it was that someone's husband had set the fire so that the women would have to evacuate the building. Now, it's some sort of police infiltration plot, but I haven't quite figured that one out."

"Do the women's husbands know where they are?" Kincaid asked, curious.

"No—at least we hope not. We don't advertise what we do here, but the women do go out during the day; they're not prisoners. There's always the chance of a slipup, either from someone being seen and followed, or—and I'm sorry to say it's more likely—from one of the residents giving out the location in a weak moment. It's not a perfect system, but we do the best we can."

"You don't place any credence in the evacuation idea?"

Kath shrugged. "I suppose it's possible. But in that case, why not start the fire in this building? The front half is vacant, and I imagine it would be easy enough for someone to break in."

"Would one of these men be desperate enough to endanger his own children?"

Kincaid's skepticism must have shown in his voice, because Kath said sharply, "These men are abusers. Many of them beat their children as well as their wives or partners. And they're very good at justifying what they do, both to themselves and to other people."

She was right, Kincaid knew, and right about the security risk from the derelict front half of the building. Uneasily, he thought of Rose Kearny's hypothetical arsonist. This building would make a perfect target, and he wondered how easily the shelter's families could be evacuated in case of a fire. He'd have a word with Bill Farrell about it when he passed along Rose's papers.

"It's not just the fire, of course," continued Kath, "but the woman's death. It's upset everyone. I don't suppose you've any idea yet who she was?"

"Nothing definite, as yet." Kincaid pulled out a copy of the photo. "But a CCTV camera caught this woman entering the building a couple of hours before the fire. That's why I came by. Do you recognize her?"

Kath took the paper from him and studied it carefully before shaking her head. "No. No, sorry. I don't think I've ever seen her."

"Not one of your former residents?"

"No. Not since I've been here, and that's been five years."

"Would you mind showing the photo to the residents, and to your assistant? Maybe it will ring a bell with someone."

"Jason's out today, but I'll be glad to hand it round the wom—"

Kath was facing the outside door. Kincaid saw her eyes widen in surprise. He spun round just as a tall man pushed roughly past him and grabbed Kath by the shoulders.

"Hey!" Kincaid called out. "What do you think you're doing? Let her—" He fell silent as Kath held up a cautionary hand.

"Where's my wife?" the man shouted at Kath, giving her a shake.

Before Kincaid could intervene, Kath said, "Tony?

What's wrong? What's happened?" She looked concerned, but not frightened, and Kincaid checked himself, waiting to see what this was about.

"You know bloody well what's happened," said the man she'd called Tony, his voice rising to a sob. "She's gone, and so is Harriet. I want to know what you've done with them."

"Laura's gone?" Kath gave Kincaid a startled glance. "Tony, I haven't seen her. I don't know anything about it."

Stepping forward, Kincaid said quietly, "Hey, mate. Why don't you let Kath go. Then we can talk about this."

"I don't want to talk about it. I want to find my daughter," Tony snapped back, but he seemed to take in Kincaid's presence for the first time. After a moment, he dropped his hands and stepped back a pace.

Kincaid got his first good look at the man. He was tall and thin, with a long face and the sort of dark, brooding looks Kincaid suspected women would find appealing under better circumstances. Now, however, he looked exhausted, and his well-shaped mouth was twisted in an effort to hold back tears.

"This is Tony Novak," explained Kath, making a game attempt at normality. "His wife is on our board of directors. Harriet's his daughter. Tony's a doctor at Guy's. He's helped us with some of our residents—"

"I'd never have lifted a finger if I'd known what I know now. Laura told me, you know. And she threatened me. She knew you'd help her."

"Help her do what, Tony?" Kincaid asked, forestalling Kath.

"Disappear. Disappear with my daughter. That's what they do here. They help women disappear. But I'm not standing for it." He turned back to Kath Warren, menace visible now beneath the hysteria. "You're going to get me my daughter back."

"Tony, I've told you. I haven't seen her. I haven't seen either of them. This is Superintendent Kincaid from Scotland Yard. You should tell him—"

Kincaid's phone rang, startling them all. Pulling it from his belt, he glanced at the name on the caller ID and jabbed the Send key. "Gemma," he said quickly, "I'll ring you right back— Hey!"

In the instant Kincaid had been distracted, Tony Novak had turned and vanished into the street.

9

*. . . a smattering of everything,
and a knowledge of nothing . . .*

CHARLES DICKENS
Sketches by Boz

KINCAID SPRINTED TO one end of the short street, then to the other, but there was no sign of Tony Novak in either direction. When he returned to the shelter, he found Kath Warren standing on the pavement, looking out for him anxiously. "Did you see him?" she asked.

Shaking his head while he caught his breath, he resolved to take up jogging. His weekly games of football with the boys were obviously not keeping him in as good a shape as he'd thought. Nor did the climate help—a dark bank of cloud was building to the west, and the char-tinged air felt heavy as treacle in his lungs. "No, not a sign," he told her when he could speak. "Who the hell is this guy, anyway? Is he completely barking mad?"

"No. At least I don't think so," Kath qualified, frowning. "I've certainly never seen him act like that. He really does work in Trauma at Guy's, and his wife—his ex-wife—is one of our board members. Laura helps out in our office when she can, but I haven't seen her in several days."

"Do you think there's any truth to his abduction story?"

"I can't imagine Laura would do something like that. But then . . ." Kath hesitated. "You never really know about people, do you? I got the impression it was a bitter divorce, but I believe they had a shared custody arrangement that worked well enough. Laura's not the type to air her dirty laundry in public, though."

"She wouldn't have confided in you?"

"We're not close friends. I'm not sure Laura *has* any close friends, to tell the truth. She's very focused on her job, her child, and her volunteer work. She's a doctor, too, a surgeon at Guy's."

Kincaid studied Kath. Her words were polite enough, but her body language said she didn't much care for Laura Novak. "What did Novak mean when he said you helped women disappear?" he asked.

Her throaty laugh sounded forced. "We don't bury bodies in the cornfields, Superintendent, in spite of how Tony made it sound. It's all perfectly legitimate. Sometimes it becomes obvious that counseling and trial separation are not going to do the trick. At that point, if it seems that a resident, or a resident and her family, are in serious physical danger, we make arrangements for them to start over someplace safe. In these cases it's essential that the husband or partner not be told their whereabouts. Unfortunately," Kath added with a sigh, "as I said earlier about the shelter, the system's not foolproof. We've had several cases recently where the man has discovered the family's new location. In one instance a woman was killed.

"Even if the woman is convinced she mustn't contact her abusive partner, there's a chance she won't be able to resist staying in touch with someone else, say, a mother or sister, and"—she shrugged—"the information invariably leaks out."

"Okay. I understand that. But that still doesn't explain where Tony Novak would get the idea you were going to help his wife 'disappear.' "

"I don't know." Kath looked genuinely puzzled. "I can't believe Laura would tell him something like that."

"Did she ever give you reason to think he was abusive?"

"No. But as I said, she keeps herself to herself, and I've enough experience with these things to know that abuse can happen where you'd least expect it. Look." Kath touched Kincaid's arm. "Shouldn't we make sure she's all right? If she and Tony had a fight that got out of hand, maybe she's hiding from him. She could be hurt."

"I'll need an address," Kincaid told her with an inward sigh. This was just what he didn't need—a domestic, on top of an unidentified homicide victim, a possible arsonist, and a disabled woman's missing roommate. But he couldn't ignore it, especially if Laura Novak really did turn out to be missing. "And a description," he added, fishing his notebook from his jacket pocket.

"I can give you her address without looking it up," said Kath. "She lives in Park Street. We talked about it often enough, because Laura's always involved in all the neighborhood issues. Her latest project was Crossbones Graveyard— you know, the old cemetery just a street over." She nodded in the direction of London Bridge Station.

"I'll need a specific address," Kincaid said, trying to steer her back to the subject. Time was passing, and Gemma and Winnie would be waiting for him.

Kath gave him a house number, adding, "The house is unmistakable. It's early nineteenth century. She's very proud of it."

"Can you describe Laura for me?"

"Um, I'd say midthirties . . . I know her daughter is ten,

and I think Laura had finished med school when Harriet was born."

"Looks?" prompted Kincaid.

"Medium height. Thin and wiry. Dark curly hair. Naturally curly, not permed."

"But light-skinned?"

"Oh, yes. Freckles. Brown eyes, I think—I never paid that much attention."

Kincaid realized with an unwelcome chill that Laura Novak matched the pathologist's description of their homicide victim. He'd have to move this up on his priority list. But the woman in the warehouse had been alone, which didn't account for a missing child. "And the daughter?" he asked. "You said her name is Harriet? Can you describe her, too?"

"Not really. I've never met her. But from what Laura says, she sounds a precocious kid. I think she goes to Little Dorrit School, though, over on Redcross Way. That's one reason Laura was up in arms about the graveyard. Harriet had to walk right by it going to and from school, and it's just the sort of place where perverts or drug dealers might hang out."

"And what about Tony? Do you have an address for him?"

"I remember Laura saying he'd taken a flat in Borough High Street, near the George Inn, but I'm afraid that's all I know," Kath offered apologetically.

"Don't worry. I'm sure we can find him," Kincaid assured her. "What concerns me more at the moment is *you*. This guy is obviously volatile, and he's targeting you as having something to do with his wife's disappearance—or supposed disappearance. He knows how to find you. What if you walk out of this building by yourself and he's waiting for you? Next time he might do more than give you a shake."

Kath paled. "I hadn't thought of that. He was a little scary. If you hadn't been here . . ."

"Is there anyone who can escort you in and out of the

building for the time being, make sure you get home safely? What about your colleague—Jason, isn't it?"

"Jason's gone to Kent for the day, to his aunt's. A family emergency." Her lips tightened, as if she weren't happy about Jason's absence, excuse or not.

"Is there anyone else?"

Kath brightened. "I could get my son to come in on the train and drive back with me. He's sixteen—"

"I'm not sure a sixteen-year-old—"

"And he has a black belt in kickboxing," Kath finished with a grin. "I'll be fine."

Kincaid's phone rang again. When he looked at the caller ID, he said, "Maybe I should keep your son with me. I could use a little protection from my partner about now."

When he reached Gemma on the phone, she and Winnie were waiting for him at Fanny Liu's house. Her voice sounded strained, and he guessed the visit was proving awkward.

"Something came up," he explained, "but I'm on my way now." He'd not taken time to speak to Bill Farrell about Rose, so he would have to track him down later.

"Are you all right?" Gemma asked. "I was worried about you."

"Yeah, I'm fine, but we may have another candidate for our mystery woman. I'll tell you about it after we've seen your friend."

The drive to Ufford Street was short, but he took time to check in with Doug Cullen. His sergeant informed him that he and Bell had seen Michael Yarwood's insurance agent, but had had no luck finding either Yarwood or his foreman, Joe Spender. "We've left messages," Cullen told him, "asking them to call back as soon as possible." Kincaid promised to meet Cullen and Bell at Borough High Street as soon as he'd finished at Fanny Liu's.

He found the house in Ufford Street easily, parking his ancient MG behind Gemma's orchid-colored Ford. As he removed his small evidence collection kit, he gave the car an affectionate pat. One day soon he was going to have to part with the old thing. It was a testament to the Midget's condition that Cullen preferred driving them about in his battered Astra to riding in it. The car was completely unsuitable for family life, as well, and needed more work than Kincaid was willing to invest in it, but he hadn't quite brought himself to contemplate joining the SUV-wielding hordes.

Gemma had apparently been watching for him, as she answered the door before he could push the bell. "We haven't told her yet—about the fire," she whispered as she led him inside. "We've just arrived, and besides, we thought it would be better coming from you."

"Thanks," he muttered, taking stock of his surroundings as she led him into a cluttered, flowery sitting room. The room's fussiness brought on an instant claustrophobia, made worse by the sweet smell pervading the air. Near the back of the room, Winnie sat beside a tiny Asian woman in a wheelchair.

"Winnie," Kincaid said as she stood to greet him. He gave her a peck on the cheek, thinking how trim and tidy she looked in her clericals.

"Fanny," Gemma was saying as he turned back to her, "this is Duncan Kincaid. He's a superintendent with Scotland Yard."

Kincaid found himself towering awkwardly over Fanny Liu, who looked up at him with frightened eyes. "Do you mind if I sit down?" he asked.

"Oh, I'm sorry. Excuse my lack of manners." Her voice was soft, her words carefully enunciated. As Kincaid pulled up a chair and sank down to her level, she went on. "It's just that I can't imagine Gemma and Winnie would have asked you here to give me good news."

"We've nothing definite to tell you about your friend," he

said quickly. "But there is a possibility we think needs looking into." There was no gentle way to present the situation, and he knew from long experience that it was best to get the shock over as quickly as possible. "Night before last, there was a fire in a warehouse in Southwark Street, not far from here. A woman's body was found. I'm afraid she was badly burned, and she had no identification."

"Oh, no." Fanny shook her head in denial. "You can't possibly think it's Elaine." Her words held an anguished appeal.

"It's an option we need to rule out, at least. The victim fits your flatmate's general description, but there are several other possibilities we're exploring as well." Seeing Gemma's quick glance, he realized he'd had no time to tell her about the woman captured by the CCTV.

Fanny's skin, pale when he had come in, had blanched to the color of parchment, but she asked steadily, "What do you need to do?"

"First, I need to show you a photo, an image captured by the closed-circuit security camera in the building across the street from the warehouse." Gemma came to stand behind his chair as he opened his folder and took out a photocopy.

Fanny took it with a trembling hand, a pulse beating visibly in her slender throat. She stared at the photo for a long moment, then leaned back in her chair and closed her eyes. "It's not her," she whispered. "That's not Elaine. This woman's much too young."

"We had to be sure. But even if the woman in the photo isn't Elaine, it doesn't necessarily rule out Elaine as the victim. This woman entered the warehouse at least two hours before the fire. She may have left again by the door not covered by the security camera, and by the same logic, someone else may have entered."

"But why would Elaine have been in this warehouse?"

"Do you have any idea if Elaine knew Michael Yarwood?" he countered.

"The MP?" Fanny looked startled. "No. Why would you think she did?"

"The warehouse where the body was found belongs to Yarwood. It was under renovation as luxury flats. If Elaine knew Yarwood, it's possible she might have met him there."

Fanny looked from Kincaid to Gemma. "I don't understand."

"We don't either," Gemma said gently, and from her tone Kincaid suspected she thought he was handling Fanny a little roughly. "Listen, Fanny," Gemma went on. "The only way we can positively eliminate Elaine is to compare a sample of her DNA against the victim's."

"How can you get Elaine's DNA?" Fanny asked. "I thought that was only from blood, or you know, from rape cases."

"People leave traces of themselves behind all the time—in the bathroom, in the bedroom. If you'll let me have a look, I'll see what I can find," Kincaid said.

"It can't be Elaine," Fanny protested. "That's just not possible." They all waited silently, giving her time to come to terms with the idea. After a few moments, she glanced at Winnie, as if for confirmation, before letting her breath out in a sigh. "Okay. Do whatever it is you have to do."

"Good." Kincaid gave her a reassuring smile. "Believe me, the sooner we get this done, the better for everyone. Now, I understand you don't use the upstairs bathroom. Is that right?" When Fanny nodded assent, he turned to Gemma and Winnie. "Did either of you use the basin or throw anything away in the bathroom?"

Winnie shook her head as Gemma said, "I didn't. But I think we both looked in the medicine cabinet, and I looked in the cupboard over the toilet."

"Your hair should be fairly easy to rule out if you shed one or two in the basin." He shot her an affectionate glance. "But I'll try the tub first, as that way we can eliminate Winnie more easily. What about the bed? Did either of you turn back the sheets?"

Gemma gave Winnie a questioning look before answering for them both. "No."

Kincaid turned back to Fanny. "Anyone else have access to the upstairs?"

"No. I can't remember when anyone else has been up there, until Winnie and Gemma came yesterday. Elaine did the cleaning herself. I told her I'd pay someone to come in, but she always wanted to save me money."

"Right, then. I'll get started."

As Kincaid climbed the stairs, he felt a profound sense of relief. It wasn't just the suffocating atmosphere in the room, he realized—Fanny Liu herself had made him uncomfortable. He was accustomed to dealing with people suffering from the grief and shock that accompanied a tragedy. Was it her illness that put him off? Of course he felt sorry for her. But if forced, he'd have to admit his pity was tinged with revulsion.

Feeling a flush of shame at his reaction to someone handicapped, he stopped at the head of the stairs. For a moment, he imagined Gemma struck down with some unexpected and devastating disease, confined to a wheelchair. Would he respond the same way? The thought horrified him.

But Gemma would rail against fate—she would be cranky and cross and difficult, and she would find a way to get on with her life. It was not Fanny's physical condition that bothered him, he realized, but the fact that she radiated neediness. The woman wore her vulnerability like a flag. If Elaine Holland had taken advantage of her, it would come as no surprise. But if Fanny Liu was the victim in that relationship, what had happened to Elaine Holland?

Gemma had to force herself not to follow Kincaid as he left the room. Her natural instinct was always for action. She wanted to be doing something, not sitting in the too-quiet room, watching as Fanny seemed to shrink before her eyes. It seemed to her that the woman's flesh had melted away from her bones just since yesterday, and with Kincaid's departure Fanny had sunk even further into herself, as if she'd used up all her energy reserves.

The creaking of Kincaid's footsteps as he moved about above them was clearly audible. Gemma found herself straining for the next sound, willing him to hurry. Beside her, Winnie sat quietly, and Gemma envied her supportive patience. But then she'd never been much good at hand-holding, even as a constable—and fortunately, these days her job allowed her to delegate such things to those more suited for it.

Then Winnie's phone rang, breaking the silence. After a murmured conversation, Winnie rang off and stood. "I'm sorry. I've got to run over to the church office for a bit. Fanny, I'll be back as soon as I can." She leaned down to give Fanny a brief hug, then said quietly to Gemma as she went out, "Stop in at the office before you go?"

Winnie's departure seemed to have roused Fanny. She sat a little straighter in her chair and focused her dark gaze on Gemma. "I still don't understand why Elaine would have been in a warehouse. It doesn't make any sense."

"Maybe she didn't know Michael Yarwood, but could she have been meeting someone else?" suggested Gemma, quick to take advantage of the opening.

"Who? Elaine went to work and came home. She didn't socialize."

"Someone from work, then?"

"She didn't really like anyone in her department. She never went along when the other women met at the pub, or got together for birthday lunches. They invited her, but she said they were cats, all of them, and she'd rather spend her time with . . ." Fanny faltered for the first time. "With me.

And even if she had met someone, what happened to the other person? Why weren't they burned in the fire?"

Gemma wasn't about to tell her that, according to the pathologist, the woman in the warehouse had been brutally murdered and left to burn by her companion. Maybe by the time that information was made public and Fanny's knowledge of it unavoidable, they'd have a positive ID on both murderer and victim. "We don't know," she said simply. She did, however, think it was time Fanny knew a little more about her flatmate. "Fanny, you said Elaine never went out. But when I was checking her room yesterday, I found a number of evening things." When Fanny looked at her blankly, she elaborated. "You know, dressy outfits, high-heeled shoes . . . Did you ever see her wearing them?"

"Elaine?" Fanny smiled. "No. I can't imagine. Maybe she used to go out more, before we . . . before she moved in with me."

Gemma was unconvinced. She could have sworn that some of the things she'd seen were a good deal less than two years old. "The really odd thing," she continued, "was that these clothes were hidden away. Did you know there was a storage cupboard in the back of the wardrobe in that room?"

Fanny shook her head. "No. I only bought this house after my parents died, and I got sick not long after. I never really used that room for anything. But why would Elaine want to *hide* her things?"

"Why would Elaine tell you she didn't have a mobile phone?" countered Gemma. "I found the box on the shelf in her wardrobe."

"Elaine has a phone?" Fanny whispered.

"It certainly looks that way." Gemma thought for a moment. "Fanny, didn't you say that the evening before Elaine disappeared, she was late home from work?"

"Yes. But that wasn't unusual. Elaine often worked late.

She said she could get more done when everyone else had gone home."

It was the classic excuse, thought Gemma, used by many an errant husband or wife, but it had obviously never occurred to Elaine's housemate to doubt her. "Did you never ring her at work after hours?" she asked, wondering how Fanny could have been so gullible.

"No. I wouldn't have wanted to interrupt her. She—" Fanny stopped as they heard Kincaid's tread on the stairs.

"I'll be off, then," he said from the doorway. "The sooner I get these samples off to the lab, the better. Miss Liu— Fanny—we'll let you know as soon as we have a result. Gemma, a word?" He jerked his head towards the door.

Gemma said a quick good-bye to Fanny and followed him out into the street, fuming at being summoned like a lackey. "Did I fail to notice the house was on fire?"

"What? Oh, sorry," he said distractedly as he unlocked his car and set the collection kit in the passenger seat. "I just got a call from Cullen. Michael Yarwood's coming into the station to look at the CCTV tape. They're waiting for me."

"Did you get anything?" She gestured at the kit.

"Yeah. Quite a bit of hair from the bathtub drain and a few from the bed. And I found some tissues in the bathroom waste bin. Looks like someone had a good cry, and if it wasn't you or Winnie, we'll have to assume it was Elaine Holland." He shoved a hand through his hair impatiently. "Listen, I've got to—"

"I'm going to stop by Guy's Hospital," said Gemma, making the decision even as she spoke. "I want to see if I can talk to someone in Elaine's department."

Kincaid stared at her, his momentum temporarily halted. "Gemma, it's not your case."

"Someone needs to do it. Someone should already have done it."

He frowned at the implied criticism. "We've had other

priorities. You know this is a long shot. If you were working the case you'd have a bit more perspective."

Gemma knew he was probably right, but she didn't like being dismissed. And besides, she was too curious now to let it go. "Maybe you need someone without perspective, then. And what harm can it do? It'll save your team a job."

"All right, go," he said after a moment's hesitation. "We'll talk about it when I get home. Then you can tell me how I'm going to clear this with DI Bell."

"Anyone would think the woman was going to bite your head off," Gemma retorted.

"Oh, I think she might do much worse than that." He flashed his familiar grin at her as he folded himself into the little car. "You'd better hope I'm still intact by the time this case is over."

It was only as he drove away that Gemma realized she was going to miss yet another piano lesson. "Bloody hell," she swore as she glanced at her watch, wondering if she could go by the hospital and still get back in time to take the boys to Erika's for tea. She could, she decided, if she didn't dally.

She rang Wendy, her piano teacher, and made her excuses, then went in search of Winnie.

Gemma found her in the tiny church office, staring in dismay at the stacks of leaflets covering her desk. "The printer's made a mistake on the Order of Service," she explained. "Again. Oh, well, perhaps no one will notice we're singing a hymn about crossing the barren *dessert*."

Gemma laughed. "Maybe they'll think you've run out of buns to serve at coffee hour." She went on to update Winnie on her plans, then added, "I feel guilty, leaving Fanny like that. If this were an ordinary case—if we had a definite identification of a victim, or even some evidence of foul play—I'd have a constable or a family liaison officer stay with her until we could get a friend or family member in."

With a sigh, Winnie said, "Except in this case, there doesn't seem to be anyone. It's usually only the elderly who are so isolated. I've offered to have volunteers from the congregation take it in turn to stay with her, but she won't have it. I'm learning that Fanny can be unexpectedly stubborn when she has a mind to it."

Gemma perched on the edge of Winnie's visitor's chair. "I know she lost her parents, but do you suppose she had any friends before her illness?"

"She lost touch with her coworkers, obviously. She was hospitalized for months. And I suppose other friends may have drifted away because they didn't know what to say or do—I suspect that happens more often than we care to think. But I've never heard her mention anyone other than Elaine. It's as if Fanny's life started when Elaine Holland moved into her house."

"Winnie, doesn't the relationship between these two women strike you as odd?"

"If you're implying that two single women living together must be lesbians," Winnie said a little tartly, "I thought that sort of sentiment went out with our parents' generation."

"And our parents may have been right more often than we credit," Gemma replied with a quick smile, "because it was socially unacceptable to tell the truth. But that's less true now, especially as neither Elaine nor Fanny has family to disapprove. And anyway, it's not their sexual orientation that worries me, it's the whole emotional setup. It just feels wrong. There's Elaine's secretiveness, and Fanny's dependence . . . At first, it seemed that Elaine was taking advantage of Fanny, but now I'm not so sure. I'm beginning to wonder who really pulled the strings in the relationship."

Winnie fingered the small silver cross she wore over her clerical collar, a habit Gemma had observed when she was thinking. After a moment, she said, "Fanny had no trouble going against Elaine when it was something that mattered to her, like having me bring in Communion on Sundays. Elaine didn't care for that at all."

"I think there was more going on here than Fanny's told either of us. The question is, does it have anything to do with Elaine's disappearance? Maybe if you could talk to Fanny—"

"Gemma, you know I couldn't pass on anything Fanny told me in confidence."

"No," Gemma agreed ruefully, "I suppose not. But you could encourage her to talk to *me*. That wouldn't be against regulations."

Winnie smothered a laugh. "It's not the God police, you know. It's my conscience that's the issue. But I promise I'll try." Then, sobering, she gazed at Gemma for a moment before she said, "Gemma, about this body in the warehouse. I know you said it was only a possibility . . . but do you really think Elaine Holland is dead?"

As he drove to Borough station, Kincaid rang his longtime contact in the Home Office lab, Konrad Mueller. Mueller, in spite of his Germanic name, was half Egyptian and, although in his late thirties, still lived the life of a lad in a flat overlooking the Grand Union Canal.

Kincaid had met him in his early days at Scotland Yard, when Mueller had been working as a crime scene tech, and had watched his rise through the forensic science service with interest. He'd kept up the connection, although he tried not to ask favors too often.

He'd made a point, however, of getting Mueller's home phone number when he discovered they were nearly neighbors, thinking he'd invite him round for drinks some weekend, and now his forethought came in handy.

Rather to his surprise, Mueller picked up right away. When Kincaid explained what he wanted, Mueller gave a gusty sigh audible over the phone.

"You do realize there's a football match tomorrow, mate?" he asked, sounding aggrieved. "Not to mention the fact that I just met this really hot chick at the supermarket and made a date for tonight."

The odd contrast between Mueller's olive skin and the gelled spikes of his bleached-blond hair didn't seem to deter women. Kincaid had never known him not to have at least two on the string.

"I wouldn't ask, Konnie," he said, "but I've got the AC's office breathing down my neck on this one, and I can't get anywhere with it until I have a positive ID on the victim. You won't have to run the sample against the database," he added, knowing that was the most time-consuming factor in the DNA testing process. "I just need a simple match."

After a pause in which Kincaid could hear the insistent thump of techno music in the background, Mueller gave in with another resigned sigh. "All right, mate. I'll see if I can get to the lab sometime tomorrow. But you owe me big-time for this one."

"Anything short of providing you with your own personal harem," Kincaid agreed, ringing off with a grin.

When he reached Borough station, he turned his samples over to Bell's sergeant, Sarah, with a request to send them directly to Mueller at the lab.

After taking down his instructions, she directed him to an interview room that had been set up with a television and a VCR in readiness for Yarwood's visit. As Kincaid opened the door, Cullen was saying something in Bell's ear and she was laughing in response. It was the first time Kincaid had seen her face lit by a genuine smile, and he realized she was actually quite pretty when she wasn't brooding like a disgruntled hawk.

Then the pair registered his presence. Both their faces froze into the instant solemnity of guilty children.

"Spoiled the party, have I?" Kincaid asked. Seeing their

blank expressions, he couldn't resist taking the piss a bit more. "Are you two going to let me in on the secret?"

Bell glowered at him and Cullen blushed an unbecoming blotchy red. "It's nothing, guv, just a joke," Cullen told him.

"I like jokes," Kincaid said, at his most innocent. "Do tell me."

"It wasn't that sort of a joke, sir." Cullen's face was now puce, and Kincaid thought he might explode at any moment.

Knitting his brows, Kincaid said sternly, "You're not telling rude jokes to the female officers again, Dougie? We've had words about this before—"

"I'll just let you two get on with it while I check on Yarwood," broke in Bell, giving them both a scathing glance as she marched from the room.

"What in hell are you on about?" Cullen hissed furiously as soon as the door shut behind her.

Kincaid had braced himself against the conference table and was laughing so hard he had to wipe his eyes. "Sorry," he managed to gasp. "It was just your faces. You looked like you'd been caught with your knickers down in the school-yard, and then you blushed—"

"You made me feel a complete idiot."

"I am sorry, Doug, really." Kincaid made a valiant effort to control his mirth, but the corner of his mouth twitched involuntarily. "You must like her. I didn't realize." He had wondered, when he'd left them at the club last night, if they might find more in common on their own, but they seemed to have exceeded expectations. If Cullen had actually managed to slip Stella's lead long enough to enjoy himself, he didn't deserve Kincaid giving him a hard time.

"I don't mind so much being made a fool," Cullen said with a return of his usual good humor, "but I don't think Maura takes well to being teased."

"Good God, Doug, how's she going to survive in the job

if she can't deal with a little friendly ragging? How's she stuck it out this long, for that matter?"

Bell came back in before Cullen could reply. "Got it all out of your systems, now, have you?" she asked. In spite of her poker face, Kincaid thought he saw a gleam in her eye, and he wondered if Cullen was underestimating her. "Yarwood's PA says he's on his way," she added. "He's coming from his office, apparently. Station Officer Farrell should be here soon, as well."

"Why did Yarwood offer to come in, rather than have us bring a photo round?" Kincaid asked.

"He didn't say, and ours is not to question why," Bell replied. "We're just the police flunkies."

"What did you find out from his insurance agent?"

Cullen took a chair at the table and rocked it back, in what Kincaid recognized as his "preparing to lecture" position. "He's not overinsured, according to Mr. Cohen. He hasn't changed the policy, and as far as Cohen knows, he's not having financial difficulties with the project. He suggested those rumors might have come from a competitor. Of course, their loss adjuster will be working with Bill Farrell, but at least for now they don't consider Yarwood a likely candidate for arson. But"—Cullen paused long enough to make sure he had their attention—"I did some phoning round this morning. I have a contact at one of the tabloids, who told me that *her* contact in Vice said there are rumors lately of Yarwood dealing with some pretty heavy hitters."

"What sort of heavy hitters?" Kincaid asked, trying to imagine the Michael Yarwood of reputation involved with drugs or prostitution. That would be a scandal worth murdering to cover up.

"West End gambling. Just because these posh club owners wear bespoke suits doesn't mean they don't collect their debts."

"Yarwood, gambling?" Kincaid supposed it was not unlikely that Yarwood's political connections frequented West End clubs, but it still seemed out of character for Yarwood himself. He turned to Bell. "Any luck verifying his alibi for the Thursday night?"

"I had a message from Birmingham CID. Yarwood was seen at dinner at his hotel, then in the bar until at least ten o'clock. There's no way he could have got back to London to start a fire a little after midnight."

"He could have hired someone," Kincaid mused. "But that wouldn't explain the body. Why would a paid arsonist have killed a woman before starting the fire?"

"If it was the couple in the video, maybe she protested when she realized what he meant to do," suggested Bell. "They struggle, he kills her, then strips her so she can't be identified."

"I've another possibility for our victim." Kincaid told them about his encounter with Tony Novak at the shelter and Novak's claim that his wife and daughter had gone missing. "We'll have to follow up. I've got an address for the wife, and we should be able to find the husband easily enough."

"You going to charge him with assault, guv?" asked Cullen with a grin.

"No. But I think he might be dangerous. I've told Kath Warren to watch herself until we can talk to the man again."

Before they could speculate further, the sergeant popped her head in the room. "Excuse me, ma'am. Mr. Yarwood's here."

"Bring him in, will you, Sarah?" said Bell. "I don't think we'll wait on Farrell," she told Kincaid and Cullen. "We can fill him in afterwards."

A moment later, the sergeant ushered in Michael Yarwood. If Yarwood had come straight from his parliamentary office, he had dressed casually for a Saturday's work. His polo shirt emphasized his massive shoulders and chest, and his heavy features seemed more prominent without the distraction of a tie. His eyes, however, still seemed as penetrating as they did on the telly, as he raked an impatient glance round the three of them.

"Your message said you found something on CCTV," he said abruptly, clearly in no mood for pleasantries.

Kincaid saw Bell bristle and guessed she wasn't about to relinquish control of the interview without a fight. The woman would give herself a heart attack if she didn't learn to ease up a bit. Before she could butt heads with Yarwood again, he said, "Why don't you have a seat, Mr. Yarwood, and we'll cue it up for you."

"I'll stand, thanks. Let's just get on with this, can we?" Yarwood was the picture of the busy politician, not bothering to expend charm on those who didn't matter, but there was a tension in his posture that made Kincaid wonder if his rudeness was due to worry rather than irritation.

Kincaid nodded at Cullen. "Let's have a look, then, Doug. As you'll see," he continued to Yarwood, "it's just coming up to ten o'clock on the night of the fire. Let us know if you want to freeze the image."

Yarwood stood with his hands plunged in his pockets as the screen came to life, his head lowered in the familiar bulldog pose. After a moment, the two figures moved into view, then stopped before the warehouse door. Yarwood suddenly reached out, his finger pointed as if he might touch the screen. Then, as the woman turned towards the camera, the color drained from his face. He reached blindly for the back of the nearest chair, grasping it for support.

"Are you all right, Mr. Yarwood?" Kincaid hovered with a hand near Yarwood's elbow, in case the man went all the way down, while motioning to Cullen to stop the tape.

Yarwood looked at him, as if trying to recall who he was. "Dear God," he whispered. "That's my daughter."

10

"I only ask for information."

CHARLES DICKENS
David Copperfield

HAVING NEITHER LIVED nor worked south of the river, Gemma had never before had occasion to visit Guy's Hospital. She knew that the two great hospitals, St. Thomas's and Guy's, had once faced each other across St. Thomas Street, until St. Thomas's had been moved to its present location in Lambeth to make room for an extension to London Bridge Station.

Winnie had told her to be sure to have a look at the chapel, so when she'd parked the car on St. Thomas Street, she entered the hospital's main quadrangle. It was an imposing vista, although the symmetry of the eighteenth-century buildings was marred, in her opinion, by the addition of a sixties tower block. After taking a moment to examine the statue of Sir Thomas Guy in the quadrangle's center, she saw a small sign designating the chapel on the right-hand side of the quad.

Gemma passed through the chapel's unassuming entrance with little expectation, then caught her breath in delight. She felt she might have stepped inside a Fabergé Easter egg. The cream walls were touched with gilt and aqua, the arched stained-glass windows glowed like living gems, the rich wood of the simple pews shone with years of polish. The air smelled faintly of lilies.

The chapel was empty, the quiet so intense it felt like a physical force. Gemma stood, letting the silence seep into her. How many had come to this place over the years, seeking solace from their worry or grief? Had they found comfort here . . . or did the air hold a weight of accumulated sorrow?

Her thoughts strayed to the parents of the child she'd failed to find. There would be no consolation for their loss, here or anywhere else. Gemma turned and went out into the gray austerity of the quadrangle.

"Mr. Yarwood, did you have some reason to think your daughter might have been in the building?" Kincaid asked, remembering the tension he'd seen in Yarwood's body before the tape began.

They had encouraged Yarwood to sit, and Cullen had fetched him a cup of water. Now, while Cullen and Bell stood back, Kincaid took the chair across the table from him. He could see Yarwood beginning to pull himself together, and he wanted answers while the man was still vulnerable from shock.

"No, no, of course not." Yarwood set down the plastic cup and scrubbed a hand across his face. "It's just that I hadn't spoken to her for a few days, and I was a bit worried."

The room, small and poorly ventilated, had become stuffier as the afternoon warmed. Kincaid thought he detected, beneath the musty odor of the building itself, the acrid smell of fear. "Your daughter doesn't live with you, then?"

"No. Chloe shares a flat with a friend, near Westbourne Grove. She's twenty-one, and you know how kids are. She's very independent."

"But you speak to her every day on the phone?"

"No," Yarwood said again. "It's just that I'd been trying to ring her since the fire. I didn't want her to read it in the papers or see it on the telly. I thought she might worry."

"Have you spoken to her flatmate?"

"No. No one's answered the phone or the door. Look, that tape . . . the time said ten o'clock, and the fire didn't start until after midnight, so there's no reason to think . . ." Yarwood gave Kincaid a look of appeal.

"Mr. Yarwood," Kincaid said gently, "unless we find some proof that your daughter left the building again, or we can get in touch with her, I'm afraid we do have to consider her as a possible victim. She fits the parameters given by the pathologist."

Michael Yarwood pressed both hands flat against his face, but not before Kincaid had seen his lips twist in a spasm of distress. "Let me see the body," he said, his voice muffled.

"There's nothing you could recognize. I'm sorry."

Yarwood was silent for a moment. Then he dropped his hands and stared hard at Kincaid. "DNA, then. Can't you do a DNA test?"

"I'm sure we can get a DNA sample from your daughter's flat. We could also take a sample of your blood, if necessary, and we can check your daughter's dental records if they're easily available. But it seems to me we're jumping the gun a bit here. First, have you any idea *why* your daughter was at the warehouse?"

"No. I can't imagine."

"Do you have any idea how your daughter got into the warehouse?" put in Bell. "Did she have a key?"

"No, of course not. Why would I have given her a key?"

"Did she have access to your key, then?" Kincaid asked.

"N—" Yarwood hesitated. "Well, I—I suppose it's possible. I left the key at the flat—I had no reason to carry it around with me."

"And Chloe has access to your flat?"

"Of course she does. It's her home."

"So she could have copied the key," stated Bell, making a note.

"Again, I suppose it's possible, but I can't imagine why she'd do such a thing. Why are you assuming she did?"

Kincaid leaned forward, so that only the width of the tabletop separated his face from Yarwood's. "The way I see it, there are three possibilities. One, your foreman lied about locking the door and he left the building open. But in that case, how would Chloe have known she could get into the building?

"Two, whoever entered the building picked the lock. It's obvious from the CCTV footage that your daughter and her companion entered almost immediately, which makes that option highly unlikely.

"Three, your daughter had a key, more than likely a copy she had made from yours. And that implies premeditation on her part. Do you get on well with your daughter, Mr. Yarwood?"

"What sort of question is that?" Yarwood rose out of his seat until he was halfway across the table. "What the hell are you getting at?"

Kincaid didn't back away. "I'm wondering if your daughter had any reason to set fire to your warehouse."

After a moment, Yarwood sank back into his chair. "No. Chloe wouldn't do something like that," he said slowly, but Kincaid thought he heard the slightest hesitation.

"What about the man with her?"

"I don't know. I've never seen him before. Look, I've told you all I know. You've got to find out if that's my daughter. I can't bear—"

"We'll do everything we can," Kincaid assured him. "But first we're going to need some information from you."

"And you'll keep this from the press?"

"Until we have a definite identification—"

"Sir," interrupted Bell, "could I have a word?" She gestured towards the door, and after a moment's hesitation, Kincaid excused himself and followed her into the corridor.

"What—"

"Sir, shouldn't we be asking him about the gambling connection?"

Kincaid made an effort to control his own impatience. It showed restraint on Bell's part that she'd bothered to consult him at all, rather than charging ahead with the questioning on her own. "Look, Maura, we're dealing with a man who thinks he may have lost his only daughter. We can't in good conscience accuse him of something based on completely unsubstantiated rumor. We'll talk to him about it if and when we have something to back it up—"

"I doubt you'd be so delicate if you didn't have instructions to treat the man with kid gloves," she retorted, her dark eyes snapping with disapproval.

Kincaid's forbearance vanished. "I'm not treating Michael Yarwood differently than I'd treat anyone else in such circumstances. And you, Inspector, are out of line."

The interview room door swung open and Cullen came out. "Keep your voices down, for God's sake. Do you want to broadcast to the entire station?" He glared at them both, then added, with his usual peacemaker's instinct, "Look, I've got Chloe Yarwood's address. I say we find out if the girl's really missing before we go any further with this. Maybe she just doesn't want to talk to Daddy."

Kincaid turned to Cullen. "Right. Okay, Doug, you and I will pay a visit to Chloe Yarwood. Inspector Bell, I'd like you to stay here and look into a couple of things." He told them about his encounter with Tony Novak. "Run a welfare check on the wife. Then see if you can get an address for him, and send somebody round to have a word."

"Sounds like a nutter, guv," put in Cullen. "His wife's probably done a runner with the kid to get away from him, just like he said."

"Probably. But we can't afford to leave any stone unturned at this point, and I don't like the connection with the shelter. It's just too close for comfortable coincidence."

Bell scribbled down the names and Laura Novak's address in grim silence, then said, "You'll tell Mr. Yarwood he can go, then? I'm sure he'll appreciate your diplomatic skills."

She directed a tight smile at them both and walked away.

"Bit hard on Inspector Bell, weren't you, guv?" Cullen said as they crossed the river yet again and snaked through the City, heading towards Notting Hill in Kincaid's car. "You always encourage *me* to say what I think."

"I don't encourage you to be insubordinate," Kincaid snapped. "Inspector Bell has yet to learn the difference between offering an opinion and questioning a senior officer's judgment."

"So you sent her to the salt mines because she disagreed with you? Anyone could have checked up on Tony Novak."

Kincaid took his eyes from the road long enough to give Cullen a quelling glance. "I'm beginning to think the inspector's a bad influence on you, Dougie. You'd better watch yourself."

Greeting this admonition with the silence it deserved, Cullen stared pointedly out the window.

Great, Kincaid thought. Now he had two sullen detectives on his hands, and he still had to account for authorizing Gemma to conduct interviews on someone else's patch. His day seemed to be rapidly deteriorating.

And yet, aggravated as he was, he began to wonder if

Cullen was biased simply because he fancied Maura Bell, or if Bell's criticism had been justified. Would he have been harder on Yarwood if he hadn't been worried about the fall-out from higher up? It was an unpleasant thought, and to top it off, he suddenly realized he'd completely forgotten about passing Rose Kearny's notes on to Bill Farrell.

Having navigated her way through the warren of buildings that made up Guy's Hospital, Gemma eventually found her way to the administrative section. A young woman sat at the front desk in medical records, her long nails clicking on her computer keyboard as she typed. She looked up as Gemma entered, a slight frown creasing her brow.

"Can I help you?" she asked. "Do you have clearance to be up here?"

Gemma produced her warrant card, which she'd needed to get through the main security checkpoint, although on Winnie's earlier visit her dog collar seemed to have worked just as well. "Hi, I'm Inspector James, Metropolitan Police. I just wanted to ask a few questions about a member of your staff, Elaine Holland."

The young woman dropped her hands from the keyboard and appraised Gemma with frank interest. "Someone came yesterday, too, a priest. Nice lady. I'm Tasha, by the way." Her smile revealed deep dimples in her cheeks. She was dark-skinned, with a round, friendly face emphasized by her elaborately plaited hair. Her long nails, Gemma noticed when Tasha reached across the desk to shake her hand, were lime green, each one decorated with its own unique design. "Everyone else is out at the moment—we've a skeleton staff on the weekends—but I work with Elaine. Isn't it unusual to call in the police just because someone misses a day of work?"

Pulling up a chair, Gemma explained, "She's been missing from home since yesterday morning. After twenty-four hours we begin to get concerned. I understand she didn't call in sick yesterday?"

"No. And that's unheard of for Miss Conscientious. You'd expect Elaine to give two weeks' notice if she were going to take a long lunch." There was enough satisfaction in Tasha's voice to make Gemma suspect that Elaine hadn't minded criticizing those who didn't meet her standards—and that Tasha had not cared much for her officemate. Nor could she imagine, from what she knew of Elaine, that Elaine would have found this bright, outspoken girl her cup of tea.

"Did she give you any indication before yesterday that she might be planning to go somewhere, or that there was anything unusual going on in her life?"

"No. But then Elaine's not one to sit down for a good girly gossip."

"Has she any particular friends in the department?"

Tasha thought for a moment, idly rubbing the tip of one of her long thumbnails. "No, not really. I suppose if she were going to talk to anyone, it would be me, just because I'm the most available body. But when she does get in the mood to talk, it's not because she's interested in what anyone else has to say. It's more like every so often she has an urge that needs satisfying—a sort of vocal masturbation," Tasha added, giving Gemma a cheeky grin.

Gemma smiled back, refusing to be shocked. "What sort of things does she talk about when one of these . . . um . . . *urges* strikes her?"

"Oh, it's usually some sort of rag about the disgraceful state of the government, or her glorious childhood in the Gloucestershire countryside with Mummy and Daddy. Sometimes you'd swear she's a relic from the Great War, instead of a woman in her thirties."

"I take it she's not a fan of the Labour government, then?" asked Gemma, making a mental note that Elaine wasn't likely to have volunteered for Michael Yarwood's election campaign.

"No. And I can tell you something else," Tasha added, "she didn't come from Gloucestershire."

"How do you know?" Gemma asked, interested.

"Because I was born and bred right here in Southwark, and I know a Southwark accent when I hear one. I belong to a local drama group," Tasha confided, "and accents are my forte. I'd guess Elaine Holland's never spent more than a month outside the Borough."

"Where am I from, then?" Gemma asked, fairly confident that her years in the job disguised any dead giveaways from her old neighborhood.

"Is this a test?" Tasha asked, grinning. "Okay, let me think." She closed her eyes, making a great show of concentrating. "London, obviously. Um, north of the river, but not within the sound of Bow Bells. Not posh, though . . . and I think North East rather than North West. I'd say Wanstead, or thereabout."

Gemma laughed aloud. "Got it within a mile. It's Leyton. I grew up in Leyton High Road."

"So you'll take my word about Elaine?"

"I will. And I'll come see you at the Old Vic one of these days. Your talents are definitely wasted here."

"It pays the bills. And it's all right, really." Tasha looked a little ashamed. "I suppose I shouldn't have been catty about Elaine. I mean, I hope nothing's happened to her. I just assumed she'd finally got a wild hair. Or gone off with that guy she's been hinting about."

Gemma nearly bolted out of her chair. "What guy?"

"I don't know," said Tasha, sounding less sure of herself. "She's never really said anything. It's just the last few months, there's been something different . . . a sort of smugness whenever anyone else is blathering on about their boyfriends. She listens with this little cat-who's-got-the-canary smile. And then . . . one of the other girls is getting married, and she made some comment about spinsters. I don't think she really meant it as a dig at Elaine, not directly, but Elaine just went off. I'd never seen her like that. 'I'll bloody well show you,' she shouted, and slammed out of the office."

"When was this?"

"A couple of weeks ago. A half hour later, Elaine came back in, as calm as you please, and never said another word about it."

Gemma struggled to fit this in with the secret wardrobe and her suspicions about Elaine's relationship with Fanny. "Tasha, did it ever occur to you that Elaine might be gay?"

"Gay?" Tasha frowned. "Well, you never know these days, do you? But even with the severe suits, no, I never really considered it."

"And did Elaine ever talk about her home life?"

"She said she had a nice flat, near the river. But as she never invited anybody round, she could have been taking the piss, I suppose."

"She never mentioned her flatmate?"

"No." Tasha looked surprised. "She has a flatmate?"

"She's shared a house with another woman for a couple of years. It was her flatmate who reported her missing."

"Oh. The lady priest said it was a friend."

Trust Winnie to be discreet, Gemma thought. Seeing the light of speculation in Tasha's eyes, and conscious of time passing and the boys waiting, she decided to wind up the interview. Gesturing at the laminated ID tag clipped to Tasha's blouse, she said, "We've not been able to find a picture of Elaine, but she must have an ID photo."

"Personnel will have it on file, I'm sure. I could show you—"

"I'm sure I can find it." Smiling, Gemma stood. "Thanks, Tasha. You've been a great help." She turned back as she reached the door. "One more question. Did Elaine often work late?"

"Elaine? She's as regimented about that as she is about everything else. She clocks in and out on the dot."

"Okay." Kincaid broke the silence a few minutes later as they passed Paddington Station and swung into Bishop's Bridge Road. "Maybe I was a bit hasty with Bell. And snarky with you. Sorry."

"Tact doesn't seem to be Bell's strong point," Cullen answered equably.

"While it is yours."

"Well, I try." Cullen smiled.

"Don't get too cocky. I'm not saying she was right. I don't like shooting in the dark, and we simply don't know enough yet. Nor am I going to badger a man who's afraid he's lost his child, regardless of his position."

"Do you think he was telling the truth about why he was trying to ring her?"

"No. But I haven't figured out why he would lie." Bishop's Bridge had morphed into Westbourne Grove, and Kincaid pulled up at a stoplight. "What was that address?"

Cullen consulted his notes. "It's Denbigh Road. Do you need me to check the map?"

"No. I know the street." Denbigh Road ran parallel to Portobello, but the mere block's separation made the difference between a quiet backwater and a teeming hive of activity.

Having passed the natural foods market on Westbourne Grove where Gemma liked to shop, Kincaid turned left into Denbigh Road. Although Notting Hill was becoming increasingly expensive and gentrified, there were still unreconstructed pockets, and Kincaid wondered which sort of flat Chloe Yarwood inhabited.

The address, which he found easily, turned out to be a prewar mansion block, in solid and unpretentious red brick. The first-floor flat was listed under Tia Foster's name. They rang the bell, and after Cullen explained briefly who they were, Tia Foster buzzed them in.

Chloe Yarwood's flatmate answered the door wearing tight jeans and a loose white cotton sweater, rubbing at her dripping hair with a towel. "Sorry," she told them. "I've just got back from a few days' holiday in Spain. Had to wash off the travel grunge." She was an elegant-looking woman in her midtwenties, her lightly tanned face free of makeup, her shower-damp hair a dark blond. More attractive than pretty, she had the good bone structure that promised her looks would last into middle age. "You said you were wanting Chloe?" she asked when they'd introduced themselves.

"Have you seen your flatmate recently, Miss Foster?" Kincaid asked.

"Not since I left for Spain on Wednesday. Look, can I get you some coffee or something? I was just making a pot."

"Yeah, that'd be great," Cullen answered before Kincaid could decline. "Can I give you a hand?" Cullen added, following her into the kitchen with the alacrity of an eager puppy. Kincaid wondered if his partner's enthusiasm had something to do with the fact that the girl didn't appear to be wearing a bra beneath her thin cotton sweater.

Taking the opportunity to examine the flat rather than its occupant, Kincaid looked round the room. The place had definitely been upgraded. Pale wood floors gleamed throughout, the creamy paint was new, the ceiling fitted with high-tech light fixtures. And because the mansion block had been purpose built, the rooms, unlike those in many flats in converted Victorian villas, were spacious and well laid out. How could two young women afford a place like this? Was Michael Yarwood contributing to his daughter's upkeep?

There were signs, however, that money was not unlimited. An expensive leather sofa anchored the room, but the rest of the furnishings were sparse and looked like they might have come from Ikea. The abstract prints on the walls were obviously inexpensive reproductions.

As Cullen came out of the kitchen carrying a tray with cups and a cafetière, Tia reappeared minus the towel, running a brush through her hair. She was still barefoot, however, and glancing at her slender, tanned feet, Kincaid was reminded of the Victorians' fascination with a briefly bared ankle. Sometimes a slice was more alluring than the whole cake.

"So what's my little roomie been up to that the police want a word with her?" asked Tia as she settled herself on the sofa, one foot tucked up beneath her. Abandoning the brush, she lifted the cafetière and filled the cups with an easy grace, but the glance she gave Kincaid was sharper than he'd expected.

"Her father's worried about her," Kincaid answered, accepting the cup she handed him. "He's been trying to get in touch with her for a couple of days with no luck."

"So he called the police? That seems a little excessive, even for Mr. Yarwood. And a senior officer." She gave Kincaid an assessing look.

"Did he call here asking for her?"

"There were a couple of messages on the answerphone, yeah."

"But you weren't concerned about Chloe?"

"I'm not Chloe's keeper. It wouldn't be the first time she's gone off for a day or two. She does her own thing."

"Would you mind looking to see if any of her things are missing?"

"But I'm sure—well, okay, I suppose I can do that." Tia Foster stood up with a look that said she thought he was wasting her time, and disappeared into the rear of the flat.

Leaning closer to Kincaid, Cullen said quietly, "Don't you think we should—"

Kincaid raised his hand, mouthed, "Just give it a minute."

Tia came back, shaking her head. "I can't tell that she's taken anything, but that doesn't mean—" She must have seen something in their faces because she paused, looking alarmed for the first time. "What?" she asked. "What aren't you telling me?"

"We have CCTV footage of Chloe Yarwood entering her dad's warehouse about ten o'clock on the night before last," Kincaid said, placing his coffee cup carefully on the table. "Two hours later a fire was reported in the building. The firefighters found the body of a woman who has yet to be identified."

"Oh, my God." Tia sank onto the sofa, graceless as a marionette whose strings had been cut. Beneath her even tan, Kincaid could see the color leach from her face. "And you—you think it's Chloe? But . . . that's just not . . . I know she's a bit of an idiot sometimes—you know, reckless—but she couldn't be *dead*."

Kincaid had never known recklessness to be proof against death; in fact, it was much more likely to be the opposite. "How do you mean, reckless?"

"She's just a kid. She likes to party, stay out late, that kind of thing. Look, I know Michael Yarwood doesn't like me, that he thinks I'm some sort of bad influence on his daughter, but I never meant . . . I didn't realize she'd be so eaten up with it . . ."

"Eaten up with what?" asked Cullen, apparently picking the last part of her statement to unravel first.

"I *know* people. I grew up in Chelsea. My family has money. I can't help that any more than Michael Yarwood can help having been born into a family of bricklayers, or whatever they were. But Chloe, Chloe was so impressed with it all . . . the right people, the right parties, the right clubs . . . it really went to her head.

"At first I thought it was kind of cute, you know—made me feel a bit like the fairy godmother. I thought she'd get over it, that she'd see it for the crap it is, but she didn't, and she was . . . out of control.

"I—I'd asked her to move out. If she was in that warehouse—if something happened to her because . . ."

"Why would Chloe have been there because you asked her to move out?" Kincaid asked, not sure he was seeing the connection. "You didn't put her out on the street, I take it?"

"No, no. I told her I needed someone in the flat who could pay half the mortgage, that I was worried about my job and about continuing to meet my commitment. My parents made me a gift of the deposit on this place so that I could get onto the property ladder, but that was it. Chloe was supposed to be paying me rent, but she was always behind, and lately she hadn't been paying me at all. At first, I didn't mind so much, but . . ."

"I'd say you were bloody generous to put up with it as long as you did," Cullen remarked stoutly. "But I still don't see what that had to do with the warehouse."

"It was the flats," Tia explained. "Chloe got the idea she could talk her dad into letting her have one of the flats when they were finished. I don't know why she thought that—he'd kicked her out of his own place because she wouldn't stay in school or keep a job—he certainly wasn't going to pay to set her up on her own. But she kept asking me to let her stay until the flats were ready. I thought she was just stalling for time. That's why, when I got back and heard those messages from her dad, and she wasn't here, I was a little . . . relieved." Tia dropped her head into her hands and rocked back and forth. Her hair, drying now, fell across her face like wisps of barley. "I'll never forgive myself if something's happened to her," she whispered.

"So Chloe wouldn't have gone there needing a place to sleep," Kincaid mused. "And why take the guy with her when she still had a room here, and plenty of privacy with you out of town?"

"What guy?" Tia's eyes grew wide with trepidation.

Kincaid drew out the CCTV photo and handed it to her. "Do you recognize him?"

"Oh, God." She shook her head, not as a negative but in apparent dismay. "It's Nigel. Nigel Trevelyan."

"You're sure?"

"Absolutely. I'd recognize that wanker anywhere."

"Would he have hurt Chloe?"

"No way. He's a poseur. Goes round in motorcycle leathers and chains, with his earring and his bandana, when the closest he's ever been to a Harley is a push-bike. And all the working-class thing is pure bollocks—his family lives in Ealing, overlooking the golf course. Nigel wouldn't say boo to a fly."

"Do you know how we can get in touch with him?"

"Not a clue. I mean, Chloe hangs out with him, but I wouldn't be caught de— Oh, God, sorry, I didn't mean that." Tia's eyes filled with tears and she gave a little hiccupping sob.

Cullen moved over to the sofa, as if his physical presence might comfort her. "Don't worry about it," he told her gently. "Everyone says things like that. It's just a figure of speech."

"We don't know for certain that it *is* Chloe in the warehouse," Kincaid reminded them. "We'll need some samples for the lab. Hair would be best. If you could tell me—"

"Chloe's things are on the right-hand side of the lav in the bathroom. I hadn't even unpacked my stuff yet, just used what I needed for my shower straight out of my travel kit. That's how I knew she hadn't taken her things—her hairbrush is still there."

Leaving Tia to Cullen's ministrations, Kincaid excused himself and found the bathroom. The sink had been set into an oak dresser, leaving a generous amount of space on either side. The left-hand side was clear, the right covered with opened bottles, spilled cosmetics, and a purple plastic hairbrush, its bristles matted with brown hair. There was also a tooth glass, its rim smudged with traces of lipstick and saliva.

Kincaid bagged both items, then stood, gazing at the snapshot that had been stuck into the edge of the gilt-framed mirror. It was a casual shot of the two girls, arms round each other's shoulders, laughing into the camera. Chloe was easily recognizable from the CCTV image, but the color and sharpness of the photo seemed to give her substance. And here her youth was obvious, as it had not been in the brief glimpse captured by the hidden camera.

Although Kincaid had empathized with Michael Yarwood's shock and worry, his sympathy had been abstract. Now, for the first time, he made an emotional connection between the laughing, pretty girl in the snapshot and the burned thing in the warehouse. Chloe Yarwood had become real.

He stood for a moment with his eyes closed, resting his hands on the basin's edge. Dear God, he hoped the body they'd found did not belong to this girl, not just for her father's sake, but for her own.

11

The debilitated old house in the city, wrapped in its mantle of soot, and leaning heavily on the crutches that had partaken of its decay and worn out with it, never knew a healthy or a cheerful interval, let what would betide.

CHARLES DICKENS
Little Dorrit

AS SHE WAS running late for tea, Gemma phoned the boys and asked them to meet her at Erika Rosenthal's house in Arundel Gardens, only a few minutes' walk from their own.

Before leaving the hospital, she'd visited Personnel and asked them to make her a copy of Elaine Holland's ID photo. Now, she tucked the small color likeness into her windscreen visor and glanced at it every so often as she drove towards Notting Hill. Whatever her imagination had conjured up from the various things she knew—or thought she knew—about Elaine, it had not been the haunting face that looked back at her.

There was an austerity in the magnolia-pale skin, the jaw-length auburn bob, the eyes that looked dark in the photo but that Gemma suspected held the same red-gold highlights as the hair, the prominent cheekbones, the rather thin mouth set in an uncompromising line—*that* she had expected. But when Gemma visualized the addition of a bit of makeup, the relaxing of the firmly held mouth, she knew the results would be stunning. She began to have a little clearer picture of the woman who had held everyone at arm's length but kept a secret wardrobe tucked away in her cupboard.

She was still mulling over the contradictions when she reached Arundel Gardens. Rather to her surprise, Erika, who had never been demonstrative, greeted her with a hug.

"Gemma, how lovely to see you. The boys are here already, and have made a start on the tea and sandwiches."

"I'm sorry about having to cancel on such short notice last night," said Gemma as Erika ushered her into the house.

"Not to worry. I'm afraid these days I find I'm just as happy to stay in by the fire with a book. And I will get to meet your young man eventually, I'm sure."

Gemma thought it would amuse Kincaid, who had recently inched past forty, to be referred to as her "young man"—it made him sound like a callow suitor paying court—but she was a little concerned about Erika. Her friend seemed more frail than when Gemma had seen her last, and when she had hugged Gemma, her bones felt as delicate as a sparrow's. But Erika's back was as straight as ever, her snowy hair swept as neatly into its twist, her bright black eyes sparkling with their usual humor.

Gemma had first met Erika Rosenthal the previous year, when the older woman had reported a burglary. Shortly afterwards, when Gemma was researching a case, she'd run across Erika's name on a scholarly monograph on the history of goddess worship and had consulted her professionally. They had become friends, and Gemma tried to visit her as often as her chaotic schedule allowed.

Now in her nineties, Erika was alert and independent, her mind sharp and engaged. Gemma often used her as a sounding board when she was stumped over a case and, more and more frequently with Hazel so far away, confided feelings she was unlikely to reveal to anyone else. Erika's wisdom and sense of perspective gave Gemma a comfort she'd never experienced, and it devastated her to think that her friend might be beginning to fail.

Entering the sitting room, she found the boys huddled over Erika's little piecrust table, attacking a huge plate of sandwiches.

"Don't scold them for not waiting," Erika entreated. "I told them to go ahead. Boys need feeding regularly."

"Like tigers," added Toby, looking pleased with himself. "Look, Mum, Erika's made scones, too." Another table held a plate of scones and the teapot.

"Oh, Erika, you shouldn't have gone to so much trouble," said Gemma, "especially when I meant to treat you."

"Nonsense. It's nice to have someone to bake for. I won't do it for myself."

Sitting down on the red-brocaded settee as Erika insisted on pouring her tea, Gemma looked round the room with her usual pleasure. Having grown up in a household ruled by the telly and by what her mother referred to as "practical" furnishings, she loved the rich and cluttered collection of books and paintings and the antique German furniture Erika had accumulated to replace the things lost by her family during the war. The room always held a large bouquet of flowers, and then, of course, there was the piano. Until Duncan's unexpected gift of a piano of her own the previous Christmas, Erika's baby grand had been the object of Gemma's envy.

Now, she looked at it with a pang of regret for her missed lesson as she accepted a still-steaming cup of tea from Erika. "Did you get your cabinet organized?" she asked Kit when she'd placed a few sandwiches on her plate.

"Um, not entirely," said Kit, with a glance at his brother. "Toby was helping," he added, putting it tactfully.

"I can imagine. Sorry to leave you in the lurch." She stopped herself from adding *Something came up.* It was a phrase used much too often in their household.

Kit's shrug spoke volumes. As she looked at the two boys sitting side by side, she thought how it never failed to amaze her that they were not, in fact, related by blood. Both had straight blond hair and blue eyes, but while Kit looked like both his late mother and Duncan, Toby was surely a changeling. He resembled neither her nor her deadbeat ex-husband, Rob.

Watching them, she realized that Toby, usually an unadventurous eater, was wolfing down smoked salmon and cucumber sandwiches as if he ate them every day, while Kit was merely picking. She'd hoped that the morning's expedition would have taken his mind off his worries over Monday's hearing, but it had obviously not done the trick.

Seeming to sense that Kit was troubled, Erika made an effort to draw him out as they finished their tea, asking him about his interests and collections. "And what field do you want to study eventually?" she added. "Botany? Zoology?"

"Um . . ." Kit looked a bit taken aback by being put on the spot but said gamely, "My friend Nathan's a botanist, and that's really cool . . . but I like animals, too. I'd like to study animal behavior like Konrad Lorenz or Gerald Durrell. And . . . then there's anthropology, and paleontology, and geology . . . I don't know how I'll choose."

"You will have to narrow it down a bit for practical purposes," Erika agreed, "but a diversity of interests is a good thing. It contributes to analytical thinking. And I believe that the problems the world faces today can only be solved by those who can synthesize ideas and think outside the traditions of their disciplines."

Setting down her cup, Erika stood and went to one of the bookcases lining the wall. She ran a finger down the spines, then pulled out a book and handed it to Kit. "You might enjoy this. Stephen Jay Gould was a Harvard professor of geology and zoology, with a lifelong interest in paleontology. He was a brilliant and original thinker whose interests were as varied as yours."

"Thanks." Kit examined the book, his face alight with interest. "I'll take good care of it."

Toby, meanwhile, bored with books and biology, had slipped from his chair and begun to sidle round the room, his hands clasped carefully behind his back in the "don't touch" position he'd been taught.

Suddenly, he paused, his body tensing like a retriever on point, and forgot himself so far as to reach out with a finger. "Mummy, look! There're little men, and horses!"

"It's a chess set, silly," Kit told him. He joined his brother, the book clasped under his arm.

Gemma had noticed the set before, but as she didn't play, she hadn't paid it much attention. The intricately carved pieces sat on a small table against the far wall, with a chair drawn up on either side.

"It was my husband's," said Erika. "One of the few things he managed to smuggle out of Germany."

"Don't touch it, either of you," warned Gemma, alarmed, visions of irreparable damage dancing in her head.

"No, it's quite all right," Erika assured her. "Do you play, Kit?"

"A little. My da—Ian—showed me a few moves."

"Why don't you teach your brother, then? Go on," she added as Gemma started to protest again. "I promise it's indestructible." As the boys began arguing over who would take the black and the white pieces, Erika sank back in her chair as if suddenly exhausted.

Gemma stood and began gathering the tea things. "We've

tired you out. Let me do the washing up; then we'll let you rest."

"I have more than enough time for that," Erika said with an unexpected touch of wistfulness. "And I like having the boys here. Back in my teaching days the house was always full of students." She roused herself. "But I will let you help with the washing up, if you promise to let me keep you company." Together, they cleared the dishes and carried them into the kitchen.

When Gemma had filled the basin with soapy water and persuaded Erika to sit at the kitchen table, Erika said, "I see you've been in the papers again. I've been following your case. Is there any more news about the missing child?"

Gemma shook her head. "No. And every day that passes makes it less likely she'll be found."

"Oh, I *am* sorry, my dear. It must be terribly hard for everyone concerned."

Gemma could only nod. To all appearances, the six-year-old had simply walked out of her front door while her mother had been busy in the kitchen, then vanished in broad daylight. The ordinariness of it terrified Gemma more than anything else.

"You cannot protect your children from everything," Erika said softly, as if she'd read Gemma's mind. "You can only do what seems sensible, and trust in fate."

Gemma spun round, her soapy hands dripping on the kitchen floor. "How can you, of all people, trust in fate?" Erika, a German Jew, had lost every single member of her family during the war.

"Because the only other option is to live in constant fear, which to me seems hardly worth doing. And I prefer to put my energies into nurturing minds like your son's. Has he heard from his father—or should I say 'stepfather'? I'm never sure what to call him."

"I can think of several things to call Ian," said Gemma,

with a grimace of irritation. "But Kit hasn't heard from him lately, no. Pressures of the new term at his university, and pressures of the new wife, apparently." She turned back to her task. "But he has sent an affidavit for the family court judge, saying that as Kit's legal guardian, he believes it best for Kit to live with us rather than be uprooted to Canada, and he feels that for Kit to have any contact with his grandmother would be damaging to his emotional well-being."

"And yet the grandmother still insists on pursuing custody?"

"Yes. Our first court hearing is Monday."

Erika considered this in silence for a few moments, then said, "Even my tolerance has limits. Someone needs to shake some sense into that woman."

Dusk was painting shadows in the corners of the garden as Rose got up from the computer, shoving her chair under the desk in a gesture of frustration. The conservatory off the kitchen, with its built-in computer nook, had been one of her father's last projects. Ordinarily, it was her favorite room in the house and she loved working or reading there, daydreaming as she gazed out into the garden.

That afternoon, however, she'd looked from the clock to the phone to the computer and back again, growing increasingly edgy and unsettled. She'd had a run and a shower, and tried to nap, but her sleep had been disturbed by half-remembered nightmares. Giving up on rest, she'd made coffee and pulled up the fire brigade database once again, hoping to see something she'd overlooked earlier, while she waited for Station Officer Farrell to call.

But the phone had not rung, and as the hours passed she felt more and more foolish for having attempted to contact him. Why had she thought she'd discovered something the investigating team wouldn't turn up on its own? And what good would it do even if she had? There was nothing anyone could prove, or that would help the investigators predict the location of another fire. Her guv'nor had been right; she should have kept her nose out of it.

The fading daylight told her she should be hungry. Padding barefoot into the kitchen, she peered into the fridge but found nothing appealing. Her mum had gone out for a meal with friends, and Rose couldn't be bothered cooking just for herself.

There was, however, half a bottle of her mum's Australian Chardonnay, and after a moment's deliberation, Rose poured herself a glass. She wasn't much of a drinker. Although she sometimes went to the pub with the lads after a day tour of duty, she usually nursed a half pint through the evening. Tonight, though, she thought the alcohol might help her relax.

Taking her glass to the open conservatory door, Rose gazed out into the garden. The day had stayed warm, and the faint breeze that had made the humidity bearable seemed to have faded with the sunset. She took a deep breath, trying to dispel the lingering sense of claustrophobia that had plagued her all day. It was absurd—she was used to wearing a mask, and she had never panicked in a fire, even as a raw recruit. Why should she feel now as if she had a weight on her chest?

She thought back to her meeting with the superintendent from Scotland Yard, the only time that day that the heaviness had lifted. Duncan, he'd said to call him. A nice name, and he was bloody good-looking, too. He hadn't made fun of her theory, but perhaps he'd just meant to be kind. She was wondering about his partner, and about his reluctance to discuss his domestic situation, when her mobile rang.

She scrambled back to the computer desk where she'd left her phone, flipping it open with one hand while she juggled her wine in the other.

"Hey." The voice was not Station Officer Farrell's, but one much more familiar.

"Bryan," she said, making an effort to disguise her disappointment.

"What's up, Petal?"

"Not a lot." Away from the station, she didn't bother complaining about the nickname. "You?"

"I thought you might fancy a drink."

It was the first time he'd ever rung her off duty and asked her to do something socially, and she heard his slight hesitation.

"Um, I don't think I'm up for it," she said awkwardly. "What with the early start tomorrow and all."

"I just thought you might want some company." Bryan paused, then added, "Are you all right, Rose?"

They hadn't really had a chance to talk since she'd been called on the carpet by Wilcox, and for a moment she was tempted to tell Simms what she'd been doing. She knew she could trust him to keep it to himself, but it was clear from the concern in his voice that he thought she needed looking after, and she didn't want to encourage that. Nor was she in the mood to have her ideas shot down, however kindly.

"I'm okay," she said. "I'm fine, really. We'll talk tomorrow, yeah? I'll see you at roll call in the morning."

"Right. Cheers, then."

When they'd rung off, she walked slowly back to the garden door. There she stood for a long time, cradling her still-untouched glass of wine against her chest, searching the darkening sky for a telltale smudge of smoke.

Having quickly familiarized herself with Fanny's kitchen, Winnie had prepared supper, pasta with a simple marinara sauce, some cheese she'd bought at Borough Market, and a salad. She'd hoped that something both light and comforting would encourage Fanny to eat, but she'd watched in growing frustration as Fanny pushed the food around on her plate, and she'd felt guilty for her own appetite.

"I'm sorry," Fanny said at last. "You've done so much already—I hate for you to think I don't appreciate it. It's not your cooking, I promise you. It's just—I can't—"

"Don't worry about it." Winnie stood and gave her a pat on the shoulder. "I'll do the washing up, then we can have a cup of tea and a biscuit. And"—she delved into the bag she'd brought with her—"I thought we might watch a video."

She kept a collection that she thought of as her "ailing parishioner kit." Through experience, she'd discovered that prayer had its place, but that there was nothing more healing to those who were ill or worried than a good belly laugh. Tonight she'd pulled out two of her personal favorites, *A Fish Called Wanda* and *Waking Ned Devine,* plus some old episodes of *Fawlty Towers.* They were all irreverent, but in her opinion reverence was highly overrated, and she even had a secret fondness for the ecclesiastical absurdities of *Father Ted.*

"Oh, Winnie." Fanny seemed to sag in her chair. "I don't think I could manage it. Could we just have the tea . . . and chat?"

"Of course. I'll just help you settle in for the night, shall I?"

Winnie made short work of the dishes, and when she'd put the kettle on she turned to see Fanny fingering the videos she'd left out on the table.

"Elaine would never have watched these," said Fanny, looking up at her. "Nor my parents. I remember how much my mother hated *Fawlty Towers* when I was growing up. There's nothing the Chinese find more offensive than rudeness, and to her Basil Fawlty was the devil incarnate. *'That awful man,'* she called him."

Winnie filled their mugs and sat down at the table. "I'll bet you watched it on the sly, then."

"I did, whenever I could manage." Fanny grinned, re-

membering, and Winnie realized it was the first time she'd
ever seen a real, unfettered smile on her friend's face. The
difference it made was astonishing. "And worried about getting caught," Fanny went on. "It was probably the worst
thing I ever did. They had such expectations, my parents,
and I never wanted to disappoint them."

"What about Elaine?" asked Winnie, beginning to see disturbing parallels between Fanny's home life and her relationship with Elaine Holland. "What did she like to watch?"

"Oh, serious things. Old movies, sometimes. I didn't like
to complain. She . . ."

"She what?" Winnie prompted when Fanny didn't continue.

"She—she could be . . . unkind." Fanny gazed down at
her mug, as if unwilling to meet Winnie's eyes.

Holding herself very still, Winnie measured her words.
"Unkind, how?"

"Oh . . ." The cat, Quinn, came in through his door and
jumped into Fanny's lap, kneading her with his front paws.
"She—she would say I was lucky to have her . . . that no one
else would want to be saddled with me, the way I am."
Fanny stroked the cat's back and he butted his head against
her shoulder, purring loudly. "She would say I was never
going to get better, that I was fooling myself. But that was
only when she'd had a particularly bad day, and I thought it
was all right, really, because she'd had such a hard time in
her own life."

Looking down, Winnie saw that the knuckles on the hand
she'd wrapped around her cup were white. "What sort of
hard time?"

"I at least had parents who cared for me. I mean, they
were strict, but I *mattered* to them, more than anything else.
Elaine . . . Elaine's mother committed suicide when she was
twelve, in their shower, so that Elaine would find her when
she came home from school. What kind of mother would do

that to her own child? And after that, her father cared nothing for her, but when he got sick she took care of him until he died."

"She told you this?"

"In bits and pieces, most of it when she'd been particularly . . . cross. She was—she could be—she *did* care for me, in spite of how it sounds."

"You're very forgiving," Winnie managed to say. "But you know that neither of the things she said about you were true."

Fanny looked down at her body in the chair. "It's getting harder and harder to imagine anything else."

"That will change, I promise," said Winnie, vowing that she would make sure of it.

At least Fanny had begun to speak of Elaine in the past tense, which Winnie could only see as a positive step. Whatever had happened to Elaine Holland, Winnie hoped that Fanny, having made such a confession, would not be willing to take her erring roommate back with open arms. And as much as it shamed her, Winnie found herself wishing, just for a moment, that Elaine Holland would never walk in Fanny's door again.

Kincaid leaned against the doorjamb, watching Gemma in the bath. The tub, an old-fashioned roll-top, was one of the things Gemma loved most about their house, and tonight she'd made the most of her retreat. Candles flickered, the water foamed with something flowery, and a piano nocturne drifted from the CD player. All were signs that she'd had a particularly stressful day.

"Is this the ritual bath?" he asked lightly.

"It's much easier on the goat this way," she said without turning, but he heard the smile in her voice. She'd pulled her hair up on top of her head, and sat with her arms wrapped round her knees, exposing the slender line of her neck and the curve of her back. In the candlelight, her skin looked pale as alabaster. "Are the kids in bed?" she asked.

"I've read to Toby, and Kit's curled up with a book he says Erika gave him." He'd helped Kit arrange the last of his birds' eggs and bits of stone and bone in his display case, and had promised to try to figure out some way to light it. "The cabinet's great, by the way. He seems pleased."

"He's had a good day, I think, between that and Erika. He's quite impressed now with her being a famous historian, with oodles of published papers."

"*Oodles?* Is that in the dictionary?" Grinning, he crossed to the dressing table stool and sat down so that he could see her face.

"Do I care?" She flashed a smile at him, then said, "Duncan, do you suppose we'll be an embarrassment to him one day?"

"What? You think he'll be apologizing for 'my parents the plods,' as he's accepting his Cambridge degree? Let's hope he has the opportunity," he added, sobering as he thought of Eugenia's custody suit.

"Duncan, this case . . . you won't let anything keep you from making the hearing on Monday . . ."

"Of course not. I've discussed it with Doug. He'll cover for me if necessary." He took off his watch and began rolling up his shirtsleeves. "Shall I do your back?"

"Please."

He took her nylon bath scrubby and lathered it with soap. "If I get the DNA results from Konnie tomorrow, we'll at least be able to narrow things down from there. Maybe then we'll be able to make some real progress."

Cullen had taken the samples they'd collected from Chloe Yarwood's flat back to the station, and had sent them off to the lab immediately, flagged for Konrad Mueller's immediate attention.

Kincaid had updated Gemma on Michael Yarwood's identification of the girl in the CCTV image as his daughter, and she'd shared the results of her interview at Guy's Hospital with him. While interested in what she'd learned, he'd decided there was no point in trying to trace Elaine's phantom boyfriend until they had the results of the DNA tests, and that copying her photo for the team could wait until the next morning. He had, however, set Cullen the immediate task of trying to find Nigel Trevelyan, the man who had been with Chloe Yarwood on the night of the fire.

Kneeling by the tub, he began soaping Gemma's neck, working his way down to her shoulders with a circular motion. When he had lather the consistency of shaving cream, he dropped the nylon ball in the tub and began massaging her shoulders and back with his hands.

"Um . . . can I hire you on a permanent basis?" Gemma asked, leaning into the pressure.

"Depends on the benefits. I'm open to offers." Her skin slipped like satin under his fingers. He began to think about the possibilities of the bath rug, and whether or not the boys were well and truly down for the night.

"Gemma—"

She turned suddenly, splashing him. "I've just remembered. You never told me what happened before you came to Fanny's house, when you were at the shelter."

Sighing, he sat back on his heels. He knew her well enough to realize she wouldn't be sidetracked until her curiosity had been satisfied. He told her about Tony Novak accusing the shelter of helping his wife and daughter disappear. Earlier in the evening he'd heard from Maura Bell, who'd said they'd had no luck finding either Novak or his wife. There was no one at the Park Street address Kath Warren had given him for Laura Novak, and although they'd found an address on Borough High Street for a Dr. Antony Novak, there was no answer there, either.

"There's a missing child?" said Gemma, a note of alarm in her voice.

"We don't know that for sure," he answered reasonably. "It's more than likely that the wife has taken off with the daughter, if they're really even missing at all."

"If that were the case, wouldn't she have asked for Kath Warren's help?" Gemma sloshed water on her shoulders, rinsing off the suds.

"Maybe Kath wasn't telling me the truth."

"Why would she lie, if there's nothing illegal about helping someone relocate?"

"All right, then," Kincaid said, a little aggravated over the mood obviously lost for the moment. "Maybe Laura Novak didn't trust Kath Warren not to tell Tony? Or Tony not to find out on his own? After all, Tony has had access to the shelter, and possibly to the shelter's records."

"How old is the little girl?"

Kincaid searched his memory for details. "I think Kath said she was ten."

"How long have they been missing?"

"I don't know. He buggered off before I had a chance to ask him."

Gemma leaned back into the curve of the tub, her expression thoughtful. "What were you talking about when Novak ran off?"

He frowned. "Kath was saying she hadn't seen the wife and daughter, and then she introduced me—"

"By rank?"

"Yes. And then you called, and when I turned round from answering the phone, he was gone. Maybe he thought I was going to nick him for assaulting Kath."

"Or maybe he'd done something he didn't want to tell the police."

"If he'd hurt his wife or his daughter, why would he have been accusing Kath of abducting them?" Kincaid argued.

"At this point, you don't know what sort of a nutter this guy is," Gemma countered. "You've got to talk to him again.

And make every effort to find his wife and daughter. What if—"

"Gemma—" He stopped himself telling her he knew perfectly well how to run an investigation, because he was beginning to have a niggling doubt as to whether he'd given Tony Novak's missing wife enough weight. "Look, I'll look into it myself in the morning, starting with Laura Novak's house. If she's not there, I'll canvas the neighbors—"

"I'm going with you." Gemma sat up and reached for a towel.

"Gemma, that's not necessary—"

"You need Cullen and Bell for other things. And I want to come."

He moved out of her way as she pulled the plug and got out of the tub. Her face was flushed pink from the heat, and set in the stubborn expression he knew well.

"Gemma," he said slowly, "it's not your fault you haven't found the little girl that's missing."

She put her foot up on the edge of the tub and gave great attention to drying her toes. "I know that," she said, but she didn't meet his eyes.

He watched her in silence, knowing there was nothing he could say that would convince her, any more than he would be able to convince himself if it had happened on his watch.

She had been all right until the light started to fade.

The woman who had brought her to the house had come twice during the day, locking the door when she left each time. The first time, that morning, she'd brought Harriet breakfast on a tray—a bowl of instant oatmeal and some dried fruit. She hadn't spoken at first, and it was only when Harriet saw she meant to put the tray down and leave that she'd got up the courage to speak.

"Why have you brought me here?" she asked, still huddled under her blanket. "Where's my dad?"

"Your father wants you to stay here for a few days," the woman said, turning back from the door.

"My dad wouldn't leave me in this place."

"No? Maybe your father has a little surprise planned for you."

"Let me talk to him," Harriet begged.

"He's not here right now. But you'd better do what he wants." The woman reached for the doorknob again.

"My mum." Harriet stood up, the blanket still wrapped round her shoulders. "My mum will be worried about me. She'll find me."

"I don't think so." The woman smiled, and Harriet felt cold in the pit of her stomach.

"Wait, please," said Harriet in desperation. "I have to use the toilet."

"Use the pail." The woman gestured towards the old tin pail Harriet had noticed against one wall.

"But I—" It was too late. The door swung shut behind the woman, and Harriet heard the locks click into place.

She'd cried then, big gulping snotty sobs that made her chest hurt and her throat ache. When the sobs began to subside, she realized there was nowhere to wipe her streaming eyes and nose except the tattered cover around her shoulders. Still hiccupping, she sniffed as hard as she could, then fastidiously blotted her nose with the edge of the blanket.

After a while, she gave in to hunger. The oatmeal had congealed into a cold and slimy mass, but she ate it anyway, then nibbled at what she thought were dried apricots.

Eventually, she used the pail, as well, because she had no choice, then pushed it into the very farthest corner of the room.

With her stomach filled, a terrible sleepiness came over her again. She fell upon the bed, curling herself once more beneath the blanket.

She woke sometime later, as suddenly as she had fallen

asleep, and this time with perfect clarity. She knew instantly where she was, and how she had got there, although she still had no idea why.

The light had changed. The sun had moved away from the window, and as she had no other way of telling time, Harriet thought it must now be afternoon. She was hungry again, and beginning to feel thirsty.

Time passed. She gazed out of the window at the gray rooftops, and when she tired of that, she thumbed through the books in the bookcase. There were a few of Enid Blyton's Famous Five adventures, an Arthur Ransome, a very tattered edition of *Black Beauty,* and a copy of *Peter Pan.* Had this been a child's room, wondered Harriet, some long time ago?

The room had grown warm and stuffy as the afternoon lengthened. She thought about breaking out one of the windowpanes, but realized she'd have no protection from the air if it turned cold in the night. Nor was she sure what sort of retribution such an action would bring.

She realized that she was beginning to smell, as was the pail in the corner of the room. It occurred to her that she had never in her life been dirty or failed to have clean clothes. Trying to ignore her growing thirst, she settled against the wall with one of the Enid Blytons. Her mother was always nagging her about reading when she should be doing other things, but here there was nothing else *to* do. The thought of her mother made her throat ache again. Blinking, she stared resolutely at the page until the feeling eased.

It was only when she found herself squinting to make out the print that she realized the light was fading. She had put down the book when she heard the creak that signaled footsteps on the stairs. She waited, heart thumping, hoping it was her dad come to take her away.

But the woman came in alone, with a tray, as she had that morning. This time it held some biscuits, more of the dried fruit, and what looked like some sort of tinned meat. There was also, Harriet saw to her relief, a glass of water.

"Where's my dad?" she said, straightening her stiff legs as she pushed herself up against the wall.

"He's been . . . delayed. Maybe he's forgotten about you."

This was a mistake on the woman's part, because if Harriet knew one thing, it was that her dad would not forget about her. Fear struck through her, worse than anything she'd felt before. Had something happened to her dad? Something that had kept him from coming for her?

She thought about trying to bolt through the door, but the woman seemed to read her mind. "I wouldn't try it," she said, with the smile Harriet had seen earlier. "The front door locks from the inside and I have the key. There is no phone. *And* I'd have to drag you back up." Her tone made it clear that Harriet would not want her to do that. She smiled again and went out, locking the door behind her.

As the footsteps faded, Harriet fell on the food, devouring the stale biscuits and the disgusting tinned meat. Even the water tasted stale and flat, as if it had been stored for some time. She drank a little of it, then realized she'd better save as much as she could—and that the more she drank, the sooner she'd have to use the pail again.

While she'd finished her brief meal, the room had grown dimmer. Harriet had already noticed that there were no lamps. Now she realized there was no ceiling fixture, either. Trying to quell her rising panic, she searched along the walls, moving furniture when she could. When she'd completed the circle, she did it once more, then went back to the bed and sat. There were no electrical outlets in the room, no paraffin lamps or candles, not even a match. There would be no light.

She lay down and closed her eyes, but the darkness seemed to press on her eyelids. When the panic threatened to choke her, she got up and fumbled her way to the door, kicking at it and shouting until she'd worn herself out, but the house was silent as a tomb.

Crawling back to the safety of the bed, she stared into the encroaching gloom. After a while, she began to realize that it had not got any darker. She could see her hand, when she held it in front of her face, and the window stood out as a silvery rectangle. It was the reflected light of the city, and it gave her a strange comfort to think that there were people outside this house, moving and laughing and talking, eating and drinking. She was not entirely alone.

12

"Look here. Upon my soul you mustn't come into the place saying you want to know, you know."

CHARLES DICKENS
Little Dorrit

THE RAIN THAT had threatened all day on Saturday passed through in the night, but it did not clear the air. Kincaid woke to an overcast sky, and when he walked out onto the small balcony off their bedroom, the pavements shone greasily with damp. The air felt pregnant with moisture.

Leaving Gemma sleeping, he'd slipped out of bed and quietly bathed and dressed, but when he came in from his perusal of the weather, she sat up and blinked at him sleepily.

"Is it nice?" she asked, yawning.

"No, not very. Rather damp and looming." He sat on the edge of the bed.

"Will it be all right for the boys?" They had arranged for Wesley to take the boys to the park that morning, and then to his mother's house for a meal. It would be a family gathering, filled with chatter and music and West Indian food, and Kincaid had convinced himself the outing would provide the most distraction for Kit.

"Should be, unless it pours buckets. You know boys are oblivious to the finer nuances. Should we try to slip out without waking them?" He knew that Toby had crept into Kit's room last night, and he'd heard them still up, talking and giggling, when he went to bed.

"Too late." Gemma sat up and pushed the hair from her face. "Can't you smell the bacon? When Kit was cataloging his choice of professions for Erika yesterday, I wonder that he forgot executive chef."

Like any teenager, Kit had to be dragged from bed on school mornings, but on weekends he was often up early, pottering about in the kitchen. He'd confided once to Kincaid that he used to make breakfast for his mother, but had made Kincaid promise to keep the information to himself.

Gemma would be touched if she knew, Kincaid thought. She walked a fine line between trying to be a mum to Kit and not making him feel as if she meant to replace his mother. He didn't envy her the job—in a way, his own was made easier by the fact that Ian had let Kit down so badly.

"Go on," said Gemma, giving him a gentle shove. "I'll be down as soon as I'm dressed. I want to get away as soon as possible."

A night's sleep had obviously not changed Gemma's mind about accompanying him to Laura Novak's, and in spite of the procedural difficulties, Kincaid realized that he was pleased at the prospect of having her with him.

The terraced row of houses looked Georgian in its four-square simplicity, its only ornamentation the scrollwork arches above the glossy black front doors and the white shutters framing the ground-floor windows. Although not obviously ostentatious, Laura Novak's Park Street address spoke of financial comfort. In London, location was everything, and this house had it all—no more than two or three minutes' walk from the river in one direction and Borough Market in the other, and another minute or two past Borough Market would bring you to London Bridge Station. It was also, Kincaid mused, a mere hop and a skip from Michael Yarwood's Southwark Street warehouse.

"It's very close, isn't it?" Gemma said uneasily, echoing his thoughts as they got out of the car.

Locating the number Kath had given him, he looked up at the house. Although the day was already warm and many of the other flats had windows cracked open, Laura Novak's were sealed and her curtains drawn. The flowers in the window boxes looked parched and wilted, in spite of the brief shower in the night.

Kincaid rang the bell and they waited, listening, but there was no answer.

"Could she be hiding from Tony?" whispered Gemma.

"Bloody suffocated if she is. Let's give the neighbors a try." He nodded to the right.

This time their ring was followed by the quick tapping of heels, and the door was flung open by a small Asian woman. "Jamie, how many times have I told you—" She stopped, staring at them in surprise. "Sorry, I thought you were my son. He's always forgetting his keys. Can I help you?"

Producing his warrant card, Kincaid introduced himself and Gemma. "We wondered if we might talk to you about your next-door neighbor, Laura Novak."

"Why?" she answered with a frown of concern. "Is Laura in some kind of trouble?"

"We're just making a welfare check at this point. She hasn't been seen for a couple of days."

"Would you like to come in? Oh, I'm Monica—Monica Karimgee, by the way." She led them down a hallway and into a bright kitchen at the back of the house. The room smelled of coffee and cinnamon buns, and the pages of the *Guardian* were spread across a small oak table.

"Sorry to disturb your peaceful Sunday morning," said Gemma, with the genuine warmth that made her so effective in interviews.

Monica Karimgee smiled and gestured at the table. "It's my vice, reading the Sunday paper from cover to cover, and I always make an effort to get my husband and son out of the house. I tell them I'm encouraging father-son bonding, but my motives are really more selfish." She was a pretty woman in her forties, a little plump, her glossy dark hair lightly threaded with gray. "Would you like some coffee? I've just made a pot."

"Yes, please. It smells wonderful," answered Gemma, and Kincaid concurred. Sitting where she indicated at the table, he examined their surroundings as Mrs. Karimgee fetched mugs from a cabinet. The coffee machine was German and looked as though it required programming by a computer; the rest of the kitchen was German and high-tech as well. Kincaid glanced at Gemma for signs of envy, but she looked merely comfortable and interested.

"Mrs. Karimgee," he began when she joined them, "when—"

"It's Ms., if you insist, not Mrs. My husband's name is Hodge. Why don't you just call me Monica?"

"Right, then." Kincaid smiled and sipped carefully at his coffee. It was as good as it smelled, and he regretted that she hadn't offered whatever smelled so enticingly of cinnamon, as well. "Monica, when did you last see Laura Novak?"

She thought for a moment before answering. "Sometime during the week. I'm not quite sure, but I think it must have been Tuesday or Wednesday."

"Did you speak to her?"

"No. I just saw her coming in with Harriet as I was getting the post. It *has* been awfully quiet next door over the weekend, come to think of it, but I just assumed it was one of Harriet's weekends with her dad and that Laura was working. No, wait"—she frowned as she thought—"that can't be right. I know Harriet was with Tony last weekend because he and Laura had a row when he brought Harriet back. Laura's very strict about visitations and she'd never agree to Tony having Harriet two weekends in a row."

"This argument," said Gemma, "did you hear what it was about?"

Monica fidgeted with her cup and looked away. "I don't want to sound like a snoop. It was unavoidable, really. My office is at the front of the house—I'm a commercial illustrator and I work from home—so if someone's shouting in the street it's a bit hard to ignore. All I can tell you is that Laura seemed to be angry with Tony, but then that's not unusual. I worry about Harriet—it can't possibly be good for her, all the dissension."

"No," Kincaid agreed, thinking of the damage their own difficulties with Eugenia had caused Kit. "Do you know why Laura's always angry with Tony?"

Again Monica looked uncomfortable. "Look, I really don't want to gossip. Surely that's their affair."

"Under ordinary circumstances, yes," Gemma told her earnestly, "but Tony Novak has reported both his ex-wife and his daughter missing. The more we know about what was going on between Tony and Laura, the more likely we are to get to the bottom of this quickly."

Monica blanched. "But you said Laura—Harriet's missing, too?"

"Her father thinks so, and there's no answer next door. You're sure you didn't see any signs that Laura and Harriet were going away for a weekend?"

"No. It is odd, though, now that I think about it," Monica said slowly. "On Friday—Friday morning, it would have been—I think I saw Tony's car. I just happened to look out the window, then I had a phone call, and when I looked out next it was gone. It's a dark green Volvo sedan, not all that common. When Tony and Laura split up, Laura kept the house and Tony got the car—not a great sacrifice for Laura, as she thinks it wrong to own a nonessential automobile."

"A nonessential car?" Kincaid echoed, puzzled.

"You know. She's very green-minded—one should use public transport at all times. I daresay the world would be a better place if we all went along with that, but most of us aren't willing to make Laura's sort of sacrifices."

"So if Laura had suddenly decided to take Harriet away somewhere for an extended period, she couldn't just have popped a few things in the boot and taken off," Kincaid said, thinking aloud. "She would have had to hire a car or a taxi."

"But why would Laura want to take Harriet away?" Monica asked.

"Perhaps she was afraid of Tony. It appears he has a bit of a temper."

"Tony?" Monica looked surprised. "It's Laura who's always flying off the handle, not Tony."

Kincaid thought of the man he'd met yesterday at the shelter. Had Tony Novak kept his aggressive tendencies well hidden outside the family, or had yesterday's behavior been an aberration? "You're sure you didn't actually see Tony, just his car?"

"I'm positive."

"Did you hear anything from next door during that time?"

Monica shook her head. "No. And the car can't have been there more than five or ten minutes, tops. I wasn't on the phone for that long."

Gemma leaned forward, creating a little zone of intimacy between the two women. "You said before that it was Laura who was always angry. Was it Laura who wanted to end the marriage?" she asked with an air of frank curiosity that invited confidence.

"Oh, yes, she made that clear to anyone who would listen. I don't know if it was one woman or many, but Tony obviously got caught out. Well," Monica added, "with Tony's looks I suppose it wasn't surprising he should be tempted to play away from home—I suppose even Heathcliff needed some light relief occasionally." As soon as the words were out of her mouth, she looked ashamed. "Oh, I'm sorry. That was really uncalled for. Look, I really do hope nothing's happened to Laura. It's just that she's not an *easy* person. And Harriet—Harriet's a great kid. Surely she's all right?" There was an appeal in her voice.

"Does Harriet get on with her dad?" Kincaid asked, side-stepping the implied question.

"Adores him. And vice versa. He must be frantic with worry."

That, Kincaid thought, certainly described Tony Novak's state the previous day. But in that case, why had he not informed the police of his concerns? And what had he been doing at the house on Friday morning?

"We will need descriptions of Laura and Harriet, if you wouldn't mind," he told her.

"But didn't Tony—"

"We just need a verification."

Gemma pulled out her notebook for the first time.

"Well, Laura's in her midthirties, about my height, but thin, with curly dark hair and dark eyes. And Harriet—Harriet's about average size for a ten-year-old. She's thin like her mother, and she inherited her mother's hair, but she looks more like her dad."

"Eye color?" asked Gemma, her pen poised.

"Gray. A dark gray." Monica looked increasingly distressed.

Kincaid finished his coffee with regret and pulled a business card from his pocket. "If you think of anything else, or you see Laura or Harriet, please call."

Monica studied the card, then looked up at him. "I didn't really take it in when you introduced yourself, the fact that you were a superintendent. Aren't you a little overqualified for a welfare call?"

"There's a possibility that Laura Novak's disappearance may be related to some other matters we're investigating, but I'm afraid that's all we can say at the moment." Before she could pursue it further, he stood, and Gemma followed his cue.

Monica saw them to the door, her pleasant face etched with worry. When they reached the threshold, she stopped suddenly. "What about Mrs. Blakely—Bleckley—something like that. Have you spoken to her?" Seeing their blank expressions, she went on. "The woman who keeps Harriet when Laura has to work nights. When Tony and Laura were together, they made sure to schedule night duties so that one of them could be home, but now Laura has to use a child minder. Not that I haven't offered to have Harriet here, but Laura didn't like to be beholden to anyone."

"Can you give me an address?"

"No, not exactly. I know she lives in those cottages on Redcross Way, across from the school. That made it convenient for Harriet to get to school on the mornings she had to stay." Her lips curved in a half smile. "Harriet's always telling my Jamie that the woman's a witch. I've had to reassure him that's there's no such thing."

"I hope you're right," Kincaid said with a passing thought for his former mother-in-law.

"Did you by any chance notice a little bias on behalf of Tony Novak?" said Gemma as they climbed back into her car. "How often do other women side with the straying husband rather than the wronged wife?"

"Monica Karimgee wasn't just forgiving his apparent lapses, she was almost justifying them," mused Kincaid.

"Which makes me think that either she's smitten with him herself or that Laura Novak does not endear herself to people."

Gemma gave him a sidelong glance. "You didn't tell me he was good-looking."

"Didn't occur to me. But I suppose he is, in a dark and brooding sort of way. Hence the Heathcliff reference. What I don't understand is why, if it wasn't his weekend to have Harriet, Novak was so sure she and Laura were missing." Rubbing his thumb over his chin, Kincaid stared at the house. "And what was he doing here? I doubt very much that he's welcome to come and go as he pleases. Did Laura let him in? Or did he go in on his own?"

"Maybe he saw something in the house that made him think Laura had taken Harriet, but he didn't want to admit he'd been inside. But that wouldn't explain why he was there in the first place. And you'd think, given the hostile state of their relationship, that Laura would have changed the locks." Gemma fished her *A to Z* from the driver's door pocket. "What about this child minder? She might be able to tell us something." Redcross Way, she saw from the map, was very close, just the other side of Union Street.

Glancing at his watch, Kincaid said, "Possibly, but I think the most urgent things on our agenda are finding Tony Novak, and barring that, getting a warrant to search Laura Novak's house. And right now I've got to meet Cullen and Bell at Borough station. I'm late as it is."

Gemma touched his arm. "I want to be there when you interview Tony Novak. I promise I won't interfere," she added, forestalling his protest. "I'll be quiet as a mouse."

"Right." He raised both eyebrows, an indication of extreme skepticism.

"And while you're at the station, I'll see if I can find Mrs. Whatever. Then I'll ring you."

"I don't suppose I could stop you, anyway," he said with resignation.

Gemma smiled and put the car into gear. "You should know better."

When Gemma had dropped Kincaid at the top of Borough High Street, outside the police station, she looped back around to Union Street and turned right into Redcross Way. She saw the primary school immediately and, across the street, a parched little park fronting on a row of almshouses, undoubtedly the cottages Monica had mentioned. There was nothing for it but to knock on doors.

She had success on her second try. A sweet-faced little white-haired woman answered the door and blinked up at her.

"Excuse me," said Gemma, "but do you know where I could find Mrs. Blakely?"

The woman stared at her so blankly that Gemma wondered if she might be deaf, or senile, but at last the woman said, "Oh, is it Agnes Bletchley you're wanting? That'll be next door, and good luck to you." She slammed the door before Gemma could reply.

After that reception, Gemma tried the cottage next door with some trepidation. She could hear the television blaring even through the closed door, so she knew someone was at home. She knocked, waited, then knocked again more loudly.

She'd raised her fist to try once more when a voice shouted from inside. "Just hold your damned horses, will you?" The door swung open and a woman leaning on a stick scowled out at her. "What do you want?"

"Mrs. Bletchley?"

"What's it to you?" She was tall and angular, with short hair dyed a lifeless brown, and a long face scored with hatchet lines of perpetual discontent.

Gemma showed her warrant card. "I'd like to talk to you about Harriet Novak."

"What's the little brat done? Robbed a bank?" Mrs. Bletchley snickered at her own humor, then added ungraciously, "I suppose you'd better come in, then." She turned away, leaving Gemma to follow her into a dark little sitting room dominated by the still-blaring television. The remainder of the room was stuffed with a three-piece suite covered in a flowered moquette fabric. The furniture clashed horribly with the threadbare carpet, and the acrid smell of cat urine made Gemma flinch. What on earth had Laura Novak been thinking to leave her child here? she wondered in horror.

"Mrs. Bletchley," she said, trying to pitch her voice above the noise of the telly, "can you tell me when you last saw Harriet?"

The woman lowered herself onto the settee but didn't invite Gemma to join her—not that Gemma was at all eager to sit on the furniture, but standing made it difficult for her to look Mrs. Bletchley in the eye.

A yellow cat as bony and angular as its mistress slunk in from the kitchen, stared balefully at Gemma, then began washing its paw.

"When did you last see Harriet?" Gemma repeated, shifting her position until she was blocking the woman's view of the television.

With a grimace of irritation, Mrs. Bletchley lifted the remote and muted the telly. "No need to shout. Bloody nuisance, that child. Always complaining about this and that. *Missy doesn't want fish fingers for her supper, she wants beef burgers. Missy doesn't want cornflakes for her breakfast, she wants frozen waffles.* Does she think I can afford those on my pension?"

Her patience rapidly deteriorating, Gemma said, "Mrs. Bletchley—"

"If you want to know when I saw her last, she was getting into that car."

Gemma's heart seemed to dive into her stomach. "What car? When was this?" She sat down in spite of herself and leaned closer to the old woman.

"Well, it was on the Friday morning, when else would it have been? I'd come out with the cats, after she left for school. I could see her across the yard, hanging about by the school gate. Then a car pulled up and she got in."

"Are you saying that Harriet stayed with you on Thursday night?" asked Gemma, trying to find a solid point of reference.

"What else would I mean? Her mother had to work, rang me at the last minute. Bloody inconvenient, wasn't it, as I had nothing to suit little Missy's taste. In my day—"

"Mrs. Bletchley, did you see Laura Novak on Thursday night?"

"She didn't stop except to pay me. Cash, I always ask for, so as not to have to bother with the bank."

"What time was this?"

"Nearly ten, it must have been. The news was coming on as she left. At least I didn't have to feed the child supper."

"Did Laura say anything to you about going away?"

Mrs. Bletchley looked at her as if she were daft. "I told you she didn't stop. In and out, always in a hurry, that woman."

Gemma was beginning to feel desperate. "Did Harriet say anything about going away?"

"What's all this about going away? Why should she talk to me about going away?"

"Mrs. Bletchley, Harriet and her mother appear to be missing. Can you tell me about the car you saw Harriet getting into?"

The woman shrugged. "It was dark. Newish. Blue, maybe, or green." She frowned and the hatchet lines deepened. "I think it was green."

"Dark green?" Gemma's heart plunged a little further as she took in the implications.

"Are you deaf?"

"I'm sorry. I just need to make sure. Could it have been a Volvo?"

Rolling her eyes, Mrs. Bletchley didn't deign to answer.

"Did you see the number plate?" tried Gemma.

"Do I look like I could see the number plate across that yard?"

"Okay." Gemma took a breath. "Could it have been Harriet's father who picked her up?"

Mrs. Bletchley glared at her with undisguised dislike. "How would I know? Never seen the man, have I? And the windows were dark. She got in from the school-yard side, so I never saw inside the car at all."

Gemma realized then that she'd insisted on pursuing this case partly out of concern for Harriet Novak, but partly in hopes that a positive resolution would ease her conscience over the child she'd failed to find. Now she felt as if she were caught in a repeating nightmare. "Mrs. Bletchley," she said, and it seemed to her that the words were weighted with lead, "I'm going to need a description of the clothes Harriet was wearing on Friday morning."

Kincaid found Doug Cullen leaning against the watercooler outside their temporary incident room in Borough High Street Station, grasping a paper cup as if his life depended on it. Cullen looked pale, and behind his spectacles, his eyes were puffy and red-rimmed.

"Whoa, mate," Kincaid said, grinning. "Night on the tiles?"

"I wish." Cullen straightened up, draining his cup and tossing it accurately into the waste bin. "Clubbing, yes. Fun, no. I got the names of some spots where Chloe Yarwood hangs out from Tia Foster. Thought I might find the boyfriend. This Trevelyan bloke's got no phone number listed, and no driver's license."

Kincaid would have been more impressed with his sergeant's sacrifice of his evening if he hadn't suspected Cullen of wanting an excuse to ring Tia Foster again. "No luck, I take it?"

"No. And I wish they'd make bloody smoking illegal," Cullen added, rubbing at one eye, just as Maura Bell came up to them.

"So who died and made you king?" she asked, giving him a defensive glare. She'd livened up her black suit that morning with a deep pink sweater, and her hair looked freshly washed. Kincaid wondered if the effort had been made for Cullen's benefit, and if Cullen had failed to notice.

"I did find out something, though," Cullen continued, ignoring the barb. "A bloke at one of the West End clubs recognized Nigel Trevelyan. Said the guy's a real sponger, always coming up with schemes to separate people from their money."

"Including Chloe Yarwood? Or Chloe Yarwood's father?" Kincaid suggested. "That could prove interesting, if it's true. Maybe he convinced her that her dad needed to collect the insurance on his warehouse."

"Then they torched the place together?" said Cullen, looking brighter.

"Aren't you overlooking a few things?" asked Bell acidly. "How does that account for the body, unless Trevelyan killed Chloe and left her there, and in that case how would he gain from Yarwood's insurance settlement?"

Cullen absently rubbed at his eye again, knocking his glasses askew. "What if Chloe came up with the idea herself? Maybe she needed money, and she thought that if Dad had a sudden cash infusion, he'd help her out. And it backfired on her."

The comment brought Kincaid a sudden clear vision of the charred body, and of Chloe Yarwood's young face in the photo he'd found in her bathroom.

"We'll talk to Yarwood again today, see if we can get some answers," he said. "But first, we need to find Tony Novak. I've just spoken to Laura Novak's neighbor. She says she hasn't seen mother or daughter since sometime last week, but that she glimpsed Tony's car outside the house on Friday morning."

"I checked with the hospital," said Bell. "Tony Novak didn't show up for his scheduled shift on Friday morning, and neither did his ex-wife. But I don't understand why you're wasting time on what sounds a simple domestic when we've proof Chloe Yarwood was at the scene."

Kincaid locked eyes with her. "I'm not discounting any-thing—or anyone—until we get the results of those DNA samples. That includes Laura Novak, Elaine Holland, and my aunt Martha if she happens to turn up missing between now and then. Is that clear?"

"Sorry, guv," Bell said after a moment, dropping her gaze. The capitulation was so unexpected that Kincaid wondered if Cullen had had a word with her. "Will we be needing a warrant for Laura Novak's house?"

"Get it in process. In the meantime, I'm going to try Novak's flat again."

"I've sent a constable round twice with no luck," Bell protested. "What makes you think you'll do any better? Didn't you say he ran away from you at the shelter?" Bell's efforts at concurrence obviously hadn't lasted long.

"Then we'll get a bloody warrant for his place as—"

"Guv," broke in Cullen quietly, "Station Officer Farrell's here, and I'd swear he's smiling."

Looking up, Kincaid saw Farrell coming down the corri-dor. While he wasn't sure he'd go so far as to call it a smile, the fire investigator's long face bore an expression of cau-tious enthusiasm.

"Got something for us, Bill?" he asked.

"Possible murder weapon," said Farrell as he joined them.

"Charred fragment of a two-by-four, buried under debris. Your classic blunt instrument. Luminol brought up a blood-stain on the underside, which was somewhat protected from the fire. The lab will check the blood against the victim's."

"The way this case is going, we may find one of the work-men cut his thumb," Kincaid murmured, but he was pleased to have something concrete to go on.

This time Farrell did actually smile. "If that's not good enough for you, we found several partial prints on the board as well, one in the blood. If you come up with a suspect, we may be able to place him at the scene. Or if you're really lucky, the guy has a record and the database will give you a name."

Kincaid thought suddenly of Rose Kearny's suspected se-rial arsonist. Arsonists often began with petty crimes. If the man existed, he might well have a record. Patting his jacket pocket, he found to his relief that he still had the papers. "Do you remember the firefighter who came to the scene?" he asked, handing Farrell Rose's list and map.

"The young woman?"

"I ran into her yesterday. She's convinced that some of the fires that have occurred in Southwark the past few months form a pattern. I said I'd ask you to ring her—her mobile number's on the sheet."

Cullen grinned. "Sounds like you've got yourself a nutter, boss, but at least she's good-looking." This earned him a dis-gusted glance from Bell and a scowl from Kincaid.

Farrell, on the other hand, after an initial look of skepti-cism, was scanning the papers with interest. "Why didn't she take this to her guv'nor?" he asked.

"She was off duty yesterday. Said she didn't want to wait until her tour began this morning. And I think her guv'nor warned her off pursuing it."

"So would I, in his place, and I'd recommend her for a stress debriefing," said Farrell, folding the papers. "But as

I'm not her boss, and it looks as though she might have come up with something interesting, I'll give her a ring."

Realizing there was still something in his pocket, Kincaid fished out the photo Gemma had given him the previous evening and handed it to Bell. "Elaine Holland. From her hospital file. Can you get it into the system?"

"How did you—" she began, but Kincaid was saved by the ringing of his phone.

Gemma had parked across from the primary school and, having escaped from Mrs. Bletchley, sat for a moment in the car, trying to make sense of what she'd learned. She stared at the school's bright blue iron fencing and low brick buildings, picturing a ten-year-old girl, her curly dark hair pulled back with an elastic, wearing jeans and trainers and carrying the inevitable backpack, getting into a dark green car.

Had Harriet been loitering deliberately by the gate, waiting by some prearranged plan? Or had she been surprised to see her dad when the car had pulled up beside her?

But if Tony Novak had picked up Harriet, why had he accused Laura of taking her? Could he have left Harriet at Park Street when Monica Karimgee had seen his car there, and then Harriet had later been taken somewhere by her mother?

Or could the green car have been mere coincidence? What if Harriet had not been picked up by her father at all? For all Gemma knew, Laura Novak had hired a green car and fetched Harriet herself, or it might have been a stranger who had enticed Harriet away. The thought made her blood run cold.

Realizing she wasn't going to get any further without more information, Gemma pulled out her mobile phone and rang Kincaid.

When he answered, she gave him a condensed report of her conversation with Mrs. Bletchley, adding, "Laura Novak must be daft, to leave her child with that woman. It wouldn't surprise me if she'd buried Harriet in the garden, except she hasn't got one."

"Gemma, did you say Laura Novak told the child minder that she had to work on Thursday night?"

"Yes. Why?"

"Because we've been in touch with the hospital. Laura was scheduled to work Friday during the day, but she didn't show up or call. Nor did Tony Novak."

"Laura lied to Mrs. Bletchley?"

"So it would seem."

Gemma felt more confused than ever. Lying seemed out of character for a woman so devoted to her principles that she refused to drive a car. Why would Laura Novak have done such a thing? And where was she now?

"Tony Novak didn't show up, either?" she repeated. "We have to talk to him."

"Hang on a sec," said Kincaid. Gemma heard the murmur of background conversation, then he came back on the line. "Here's the address. I'll meet you there. But, Gemma, don't go in without me. He could be dangerous."

Gemma parked the car in front of Guy's Hospital, as she had the previous day, and walked round the corner into Borough High Street. As she looked for the address Kincaid had given her, she passed the George, the last of the ancient galleried inns of Southwark. The Tabard and the Queen's Head had long since disappeared, but the George, with only one of its galleries intact, had not only survived but did a booming business.

Tony Novak had certainly gone for convenience, she thought as she found the address a bit farther along. It was a block of flats over a shop front, not particularly inviting, but merely a stone's throw from Guy's Hospital.

She was about to push the entrance buzzer when a parting of the pedestrian traffic revealed a man sitting on the curb, a few yards farther along. He was hunched over, his head cradled in his hands, his feet in the gutter. People were giving him a wide berth, as they usually did the drunk or the homeless, although you seldom saw either sitting half in the street, and the man looked ill as well as unkempt.

Although the distraction was unwelcome, Gemma couldn't pass by without attempting to help.

She smelled the sour stench of alcohol before she reached him and felt a bit more sympathy for those who hadn't bothered to stop. From a few feet away, she said, "Excuse me, sir. Are you all right?"

When he didn't respond, she crouched down and looked at him more closely. He was dark-haired and tall—that much was apparent even in his present position—and slender. His clothes, although rumpled, seemed clean and of good quality, and on his wrist, bared where his shirt cuff had fallen back, was an expensive-looking watch. The man was no vagrant, and Gemma had a sudden flash of intuition. If she was wrong, she had nothing to lose.

She touched his shoulder. "Tony."

This time he raised his head, slowly, and stared at her with bloodshot eyes. His face was long and thin, and covered with several days' worth of stubble, and his eyes were hollow, but Gemma could see that under better circumstances he would be handsome. He didn't speak.

"Tony," she said again. "My name's Gemma." Here she hesitated but decided that if she wanted to gain his trust she'd better be honest from the beginning. He didn't look in any state to run off. "I'm a police officer, and I think you need some help."

He stared at her a moment longer, then grasped her arm with surprising strength. "You've found her. Harriet. Tell me—is she—"

"We haven't found your daughter. We're hoping you can help us do that. But first, let's get you up to your flat, okay? Can you stand?"

"Don't know," he mumbled, but let her pull him to his feet. He swayed a little but seemed steady enough to walk without help. Gemma began to think he was not so much drunk as hungover and exhausted.

He had not lost his keys, at least, and Gemma let him lead the way up the stairs to his flat. She had to help him unlock the flat door, and once in the sitting room, he sank down on the nearest available chair as if his legs had given notice.

The flat was no more inviting from the inside than it had looked from the street. Obviously hastily converted to take advantage of the property boom, it had cheap fittings, and the walls and ceiling were already beginning to show patches of damp. The sitting room held a few pieces of non-descript furniture, and an open suitcase spilled its contents onto the floor.

"How long has it been since you've had anything to eat, or any sleep?" Gemma asked, as Tony looked in danger of nodding off again.

"Don't know. Don't remember." He frowned and rubbed at his stubble. "Couple of days, I think."

"Right." Gemma went into the tiny kitchen and took stock. There was part of a loaf of bread on the counter and some cheese and butter in an otherwise pathetically empty fridge. "You're going to have something to eat, and then we'll talk." She buttered bread and sliced cheese for a sand-wich as the kettle boiled, then made a big mug of strong, sweet tea.

When she returned to the sitting room he had closed his eyes, but he sat up and took the food from her without protest. After the first bite, he wolfed down the sandwich as if suddenly starving, then gulped at the tea, even though it must still have been scalding.

When he looked up at her again, his eyes were more clear and focused. Picking at his shirt, he said, "God, I stink. Must have spilled the bottle."

"Yeah." Gemma smiled. "You do. But that can wait. First we need to talk about Harriet."

His dark eyes filling with tears, Tony said on a sob, "Oh, God. It's my fault."

Gemma controlled her start of alarm. "What's your fault, Tony?"

"I should never have left her."

"Left Harriet?"

Just then the buzzer sounded from the street door. Tony jerked as if he'd been shot, then stood up, looking round wildly. "Laura—she'll kill me—"

"It's not Laura," Gemma said, gambling that she was right. She pressed the release for the street door latch. "It's my friend Duncan. You met him the other day." She gave Kincaid a minute to climb the stairs, then opened the flat door before he could knock. At his startled expression, she gave a quick shake of her head and held up a hand in warning before turning back to Tony.

"Tony and I are just having a chat," she said. "About Harriet. He's very worried about her."

Tony sat down again slowly, his expression wary.

She saw Kincaid take in the open suitcase, but he followed her lead and pulled up a chair without speaking.

"Tony," she said quietly, as if they hadn't been interrupted, "where did you leave Harriet?"

He looked from Gemma to Kincaid, then back at Gemma. "With a friend," he whispered. "It was just for a few minutes. I—I had something to do."

"Was this after you picked Harriet up from school?"

His eyes widened, but after a moment he nodded. "It was a treat. I was taking her out for the day, for a treat."

"Did Laura agree that you should take Harriet out of school for the day?"

"God, no." His face twisted in a grimace. "It was going to be our secret, Harriet's and mine. But then I had to—she wanted some things from the flat, and I said I'd get them, but I couldn't take her with me."

Gemma felt Kincaid's stir of impatience, but she nodded as if it all made perfect sense. "So you left her with your friend, while you went to the flat. Was Laura there?"

He looked at her blankly. "Laura? Of course not. She was at work, or I'd never have gone."

"Okay," she said. "So you picked up Harriet's things. Then what happened?"

He rubbed a trembling hand across his stubble again. "I was supposed to meet them—Harriet and my friend. But they didn't come. And I realized I'd no idea how to get in touch with her."

"Your friend?"

"Beth. Her name's Beth. I—" He shook his head. "We'd been going out for a while, but she always came here. She said there was someone else, and I never—"

"But you must have had some way to reach her?"

"Only her mobile, and now it just goes straight to voice mail. She said she worked at an estate agent's here in the Borough, so yesterday I went round to every office, but no one knew anyone called Beth."

Kincaid could contain himself no longer. "Are you saying you don't know this woman's last name?"

"It was only casual sex, for God's sake. I never thought— I never meant—"

"You left your daughter, on the spur of the moment, with a woman whose name you didn't even know?"

"It wasn't like that," protested Tony. "I needed help, and I couldn't think of anyone else to ask, anyone who didn't—"

"Know your wife," Gemma finished for him, the light dawning. "Is that why you didn't want to leave Harriet on her own, because you were afraid she'd call her mum?" She looked at the suitcase, crammed with clothing, a little girl's T-shirt spilling over the side. "You weren't packing for a day away, Tony, that much is obvious. You'd never have thought you could just take Harriet off for a day without Laura suing to revoke your custody. And you'd have been in trouble with the hospital for failing to let them know you were going to be absent." She tilted her head to one side, thinking, then said slowly, "Unless it didn't matter, because you weren't coming back. Where were you taking her, Tony?"

He stared at her defiantly, and for a moment she thought he would deny it. Then he closed his eyes, and the tension seemed to seep from his body.

"Prague," he whispered. "I was taking her to Prague."

13

❧

There is a passion for hunting something deeply
implanted in the human breast.

CHARLES DICKENS
Oliver Twist

"**IT'S A BEAUTIFUL** place, Prague, the city of the spires,"
Tony went on dreamily, as if repeating a story he'd told himself many times. "My family's Czech. I thought they could
help us. There's always a need for qualified doctors in Eastern Europe—I was sure I could find a job, start over."

"Wait a minute," Kincaid said, his voice rising in disbelief. "I don't care what you meant to do. Why the hell did
you come bursting into the shelter accusing Kath Warren of
helping your wife abduct your child, when all the time you
knew you'd left Harriet with someone else?"

Tony Novak raised his head and blinked at him. His hungover state was still evident in his glazed and red-rimmed
eyes, but he spoke clearly enough. "At first, I thought Harriet might have asked Beth to take her home, or to the hospital, and that Harriet might have told her mother I'd taken

her out of school. Laura would've gone spare, I can tell you—packed everything up and walked out, just to spite me.

"But then, the longer I tried to find Beth, the odder it seemed that she'd just vanished without a trace. If Beth had taken Harriet to Laura, why wouldn't she have rung me, or met me where we'd arranged, to tell me what happened?"

"Did Beth know what you meant to do?" asked Gemma.

Tony nodded, draining the last of the tea Gemma had made him. "I'd rung her the night before. I told her I thought Laura was planning to abduct Harriet—that Laura had been threatening me with it for months, and then on Sunday when I brought Harriet back late, she was furious. She said it would be the last time I'd have that chance, and I could tell she meant to do something drastic. I was afraid if I didn't take Harriet, I'd never see my daughter again."

"But why did you need to go to the house, after you'd picked Harriet up? Surely you could have bought Harriet anything she needed?"

"I had to get her passport. Laura kept all the legal documents, and I couldn't get Harriet into the EU without her passport."

"Then why not pick Harriet up after you'd got the passport," Kincaid said, "rather than involving Beth at all?"

"I needed Harriet's key. When I dropped off Harriet and Beth, I kept Harriet's backpack. And I had to pick Harriet up before school started, because once she'd gone inside, the school wouldn't release her to me. Laura's instructions, thanks to the shelter's advice," Tony added, his face tightening with anger and resentment.

Kincaid stood and paced a few steps. The smell of sweat and stale alcohol in the small, stuffy room was making him edgy. "Where did you let them out of the car?" he asked, trying to keep Tony on track.

"We talked for a bit. I told Harriet I had a surprise for her, a treat, but that first Beth was going to take her shopping.

Then I dropped them at London Bridge Station and said I'd pick Harriet up there in three hours. I wanted to be across the Channel before Laura realized Harriet hadn't come home from school."

"You didn't think Harriet would object to leaving her home and her mother?" Gemma asked sharply, her disapproval obvious for the first time.

Tony rubbed at his face again, avoiding her gaze. "Harriet loves me," he said. "She never wants to leave me after our weekends together, and I know she was worried that Laura meant to separate us. I thought—I thought I'd explain things to her once we'd left England, ask her to give it a try. If she didn't like it after a few weeks, she could go home. And I meant to let Laura know Harriet was safe, as soon as we were well away."

"It's still inexcusable, taking a child away from her mother—"

"What gives mothers special dispensation?" Tony retorted, anger flaring again. "What would you do if someone was going to take your child away from you? How would you feel?"

Kincaid saw Gemma glance at him, eyes wide, and he knew they were both thinking of Kit.

"Tony," she said, "why would Laura be so determined to separate you and Harriet? Is there something you're not telling us?"

"What?" He glared at her. "You think I mistreat my child? Is that what you're suggesting?"

"No. I—"

"Then you can just bloody well fuck yourself." He half rose from the sofa, his fists clenching. "I told you, I love my daughter. I've never done anything worse than have her back a few minutes late from one of our weekends." He sank down again, his face contorting, and pressed his knuckles hard against his mouth to stop it trembling. "Oh, Jesus. I couldn't bear it if something's happened to Harriet."

"Then why—"

"Laura's jealous. That's the truth of it. She's always been jealous of the fact that Harriet preferred me to her. When she found out about the women I'd been seeing, that was just an excuse to end the marriage, because she could never admit the truth, even to herself."

Kincaid's first response was to put Tony's statement down to self-justification, the bitter fallout of a failed relationship. Then he thought of Kath Warren's tactfully expressed dislike of Laura Novak and of the equally unflattering portrait painted by Laura's next-door neighbor. But if Tony's assessment was accurate, did that tell them anything about what had happened to Harriet?

He said, "Tony, if Laura had been planning to disappear with Harriet, don't you think Harriet would have told you?"

"Laura can be . . . harsh, if she feels Harriet's disobeyed her. Harriet might have been afraid to speak."

"She didn't say anything when you picked her up on Friday morning?"

"No. But I didn't give her a chance. Beth was there and I—I put Harriet off when she tried to talk to me. I thought she was just worried that her mum would be angry I was taking her out of school. I didn't think it would matter, once we were gone."

Leaning forward, Gemma said intently, "I don't see how Laura could have gone away with Harriet without alerting the neighbors. She'd have to have taken a few things—"

"You don't know Laura. She could have had an emergency getaway kit stashed at the hospital—"

Gemma was shaking her head. "Tony, none of this makes sense. Laura wasn't at the hospital. She didn't show up for work on Friday. And she left Harriet with the child minder on Thursday night, saying she had to work night duty, but she didn't. We've checked."

He stared at her. "What?"

"You're *sure* she wasn't at home when you went in to get Harriet's passport?"

"Of course I'm bloody sure! Do you think she'd have let me walk merrily out of the house with Harriet's passport in my pocket?"

"If she wasn't at work and she wasn't at home, how could Beth have left Harriet with her?"

"But if Laura didn't take Harriet, it must have been Beth, and that makes even less sense," protested Tony. "Why would she do such a thing?"

"You tell us," Kincaid said, still prowling the room. He could tell his movements made Novak nervous, and he wanted the man unsettled. "You're the one who knew this woman well enough to take her into your confidence."

"But I—" Tony picked up his empty mug, tilted it, set it down again. "I told you, she never said much. Odd, really, as most women tell you their life stories in the first five minutes."

Gemma raised an eyebrow at this, but didn't comment. Taking Tony's mug, she stepped into the adjoining kitchen and snapped the kettle on. She plopped a tea bag and a few spoonfuls of sugar into the cup in the few seconds it took the water to boil, then carried the tea back to Tony. "How did you meet her?" she asked, perching again on the edge of her chair.

"In the George. One night a couple of months ago. I'd never seen her in there before. She was . . . different. Most women who come into a bar alone, they're either obviously looking for company, or they're obviously just there for a drink. But Beth . . . she had this aloofness, yet at the same time she never stopped watching everyone. It was as if she was working out what made them tick, and she didn't much like what she saw. But when I saw her studying me, I offered to buy her a drink, and she accepted." He looked as if it still puzzled him. "Then later . . . she went home with me. After that, she'd come over a couple of times a week, but we never talked much." Tony stopped to sip at his still-steaming tea.

"Can you describe her?" Kincaid asked.

"Um, midthirties, medium height, brown hair . . . not beautiful, really, but attractive in an unusual sort of way."

Another missing brunette? Kincaid's eyes met Gemma's and she gave her head a barely perceptible shake, as if warning him not to pursue it further. He let her continue.

"Tony," she said quietly, leaning forward until she could almost touch him, "we're going to need you to come down to the station to make a formal statement."

Panic flared in his eyes again. "I—I can't—I've got to find Harriet—"

"We're going to help you find Harriet. I promise you." She touched his knee lightly. "But you have to cooperate with us. There's nothing you can do on your own that you haven't already tried."

"I—"

"You get yourself cleaned up. We'll wait for you."

"But I—" Tony picked at his shirt again, holding it away from his body as if suddenly aware of his revolting state. "All right." He stood, still a little unsteadily, but when he looked at the open suitcase his eyes filled with tears.

"Here. Let me help you." Gemma quickly knelt beside the case, fishing out shirt and trousers, clean socks and briefs with the practiced efficiency of a mother of boys. She bundled the articles into Tony's arms and nudged him in the direction of the bathroom.

When he'd disappeared behind the closed door, Gemma turned back to Kincaid. Her face was strained.

"You realize we now have four missing women that potentially fit the description of one body?" he said.

Gemma knelt and dug through the suitcase again. "And a missing child who very well may not be with her mother." With a grunt of satisfaction, she pulled out a framed photograph and sat back on her heels, studying it for a moment before handing it to Kincaid.

The girl stared into the camera with the defiant seriousness of a child refusing to smile for the photographer. She had wiry dark hair pulled back tightly from her thin face, and her gray eyes held an adult intelligence. She might, Kincaid thought, be heartbreakingly beautiful in ten years' time.

Dusting off her knees, Gemma came to stand beside him. "I'm not so sure there are four missing women," she said, touching Harriet Novak's face with a fingertip. "Do you still have Elaine Holland's photograph?"

Kincaid frowned at her. "No. I gave it to Bell. What are you—"

"Think about it. Elaine Holland left work every day on the dot, but several evenings a week she told Fanny she had to work late. She'd been hinting recently to a coworker that she had a boyfriend. She had clothes tucked away that Fanny never saw. She lied to Fanny about having a mobile phone, yet Tony had no number for Beth other than a mobile phone. And the physical description . . . Elaine has a striking face. Not beautiful, but you can see how a man could be fascinated—"

Kincaid's phone rang. He snapped it open with a grimace of irritation, but his impatience vanished when he heard Konnie Mueller's voice. He listened, nodding, then said, "And nothing yet on the other one? Okay. As soon as you have a result. Right."

As he rang off, Gemma said, "Konnie?"

He nodded. "He's narrowed our options by one. Whoever—and wherever—Elaine Holland may be, she didn't die in Thursday night's fire."

*　　*　　*

It was another ordinary Sunday lunch in the Warren semi-detached house in Peckham—Kath's sixteen-year-old son shoveling his food, eager to finish and get out of the house; her thirteen-year-old daughter picking at hers, eager to resume an interrupted phone call in her room; Kath's husband, a commercial traveler home for the weekend, eager to make the most of his well-deserved Sunday-afternoon nap.

Kath, who had long tried to practice a daily litany of counting her blessings, felt a tide of irritation threaten to swamp her. She slammed plates coated with congealing gravy into the sink and, for once, walked off and left them.

"I've got to go in to work for a bit," she called out as she grabbed her handbag and keys.

"I'll drive you," her son volunteered. "What about that crazy guy?"

"I'll be fine." Tony Novak had not made another appearance, and Kath had more pressing things to worry about.

As she climbed into the car she realized she'd added another lie to the tally that had grown past counting. It wasn't that she had to go in to work, but that she couldn't bring herself to stay away.

When she reached Southwark Street, she found that the crime scene tape still fluttered round Yarwood's warehouse like the ribbon on a giant Christmas package, and that the smell of burning lingered in the air like a fog. She ducked her head as she walked by, wondering if she would ever be able to pass the building without seeing the ambulance men maneuvering their burden carefully out the door.

The shelter's residents were unsettled as well. She'd spent yesterday—without Jason's help—comforting and consoling, and trying to quiet the rumors flying round the shelter like contagious ghosts.

She found Jason where she'd expected, in the office, head bent over a filing cabinet. She stood in the doorway for a moment, watching him, knowing he was aware of her presence, but that he wouldn't look up until she spoke.

He wore jeans, as he usually did when he took Sunday duty, rather than the designer shirts and ties he favored during the week, and the contrast between the rough clothes and the elegant planes of his face made the breath catch in her throat. God, one would think that knowing oneself for a fool would be enough to effect a cure, but the self-knowledge only made her despise her desire.

"How was your visit with your aunt?" she asked, when the silence had gone on as long as she could bear.

Jason looked up. "Great-aunt. She fell. She needed Mum to stay with her, and you know my mother doesn't drive. It couldn't be helped, Kath." His voice was cool, dispassionate, the message clear. She was nagging, and he wasn't going to apologize for leaving her in the lurch on a chaotic Saturday—or for anything else.

She came into the room and perched on the edge of her desk, making a pretext of straightening papers. "You missed all the excitement. Tony Novak showed up, accusing us of helping his wife run off with their child."

Frowning, Jason paused with a paper half into a folder. "Dr. Novak? Why would he do that?"

"He says Laura threatened him, and now she and the little girl have both disappeared."

The paper slid neatly into its ordained spot and Jason closed the file drawer. "Not very smart to give advance warning, if she meant to do a runner. It's odd that she didn't come to us for help, though."

Kath rubbed her thumb across the rough edge of a fingernail. "I thought maybe there was something you weren't telling me."

"Me?" His wide, mobile mouth twitched in irritation. "Don't be daft, Kath. You know Laura's not that fond of me. If she'd come to anyone, it would have been you." He studied her. "Look, if this is about the other night, something came up."

"I waited," she said, the words spilling out like acid. "And you played me for a fool."

"It's not always about you, Kath. Did that ever occur to you? You've no idea what it's like for me, living with— My mum's difficult. It was a bad night."

"Your mum?" she spat back. "I lied to my kids—"

"And it's not my sodding fault if you feel guilty. Give it a rest, Kath."

They stared at each other, poised on the edge of a full-fledged row. Then, to her surprise, Jason looked away. "I did come, you know," he said. "But you were gone. And it's just as well we weren't both here when all hell broke loose." He flashed her one of his smiles, and she felt her anger start to melt.

Standing, he came over to her and ran his fingertip very lightly from her cheek to the corner of her mouth. She turned her face into his hand with as little volition as a moth flying into a flame.

"Am I forgiven?" he said softly.

"I—" She glimpsed a shadow at the office door, a whisper of movement that was somehow familiar. "Mouse?" she called out. "Beverly?"

But there was no answer, and when she went out into the corridor, no one was there.

"It's not protocol," hissed Maura Bell. She'd drawn Kincaid down to the far end of the corridor outside the interview room at the station. A shocked Tony Novak, having identified the photo of Elaine Holland as the woman he knew as Beth, waited inside the room, while at the other end of the corridor, Gemma spoke animatedly to Doug Cullen.

"I don't care if it's bloody protocol." He glanced over at Gemma, then jabbed a finger at Bell. "She's the one who got

Tony Novak to cooperate. She's the one who made the connection between Elaine Holland and Beth. She's the one who insisted we had a child at risk. She's going to sit in on the interview if she bloody well wants."

"We don't know that the child isn't somewhere with her mother," protested Inspector Bell.

"We don't know that Tony Novak didn't bash his wife over the head in the ten minutes he was inside her house. We won't know until we get the search warrant. If you want to be useful instead of obstructive, why don't you see if you can hurry the damned thing up?"

"Excuse me, ma'am." Bell's sergeant had appeared at her elbow. "A Mrs. Teasdale is here to see you. She says she's Chloe Yarwood's mother."

When Bell hesitated, Kincaid said, "You've got another interview room?" At her nod, he went on. "I'll take her up personally. We'll have to put Novak on hold until we see what the former Mrs. Yarwood has to say—in fact, cut Novak loose when he's signed his statement, but have a constable keep an eye on him. I'd just as soon wait to talk to him again until we've searched his wife's house, but I don't want him disappearing on us."

"Is there—is there any news on Chloe Yarwood, sir?" asked the sergeant, with a quick glance at her boss.

"Not yet. The lab hasn't finished running the match, and I hate to think what Konnie Mueller is going to say when I ask him to run a sample from Laura Novak's flat."

Gemma and Cullen had joined them and were listening intently.

"Sir—ma'am—" said the sergeant, obviously having difficulties with the issue of temporary authority, "that warrant's just come through. I was coming to tell you when the duty sergeant rang up about Mrs. Teasdale."

Kincaid considered, trying to work out the most expedient division of labor with the least amount of territorial piss-ing on Bell's part. "Doug, why don't you and Gemma go along to Laura Novak's house with the uniforms? Maura, you and I will talk to Mrs. Teasdale. Then when we've finished we'll meet the others at Park Street." Bell might think she'd drawn the plum job, but the truth was that he trusted Gemma's assessment of whatever they might find at the Novak house as well as his own.

Maura Bell drew breath as if to protest, then seemed to think better of it. Turning to the sergeant, she said, "Right. You'll need a locksmith—"

"No, we won't." Gemma's lips curved in a very small smile. "We've got Tony Novak's keys."

Sundays were supposed to be civilized, Rose thought grumpily as she hung her turnout coat on the drying rack for the second time that day. A day of rest, a day of roast beef and Yorkshire pud, of dozing in front of the telly or taking the kiddies to the park.

God knows she'd hoped for a quiet day after a night of dream-haunted, interrupted sleep, but instead they'd had half a dozen road traffic accidents, as many medical calls, and two fires. Both had been nuisance fires, one in a rubbish skip, the other brush set alight on waste ground at the edge of a park, but both times when she'd seen the smoke her mouth had gone dry and her hands had been unsteady as she pulled on her gear.

Surely she was just tired, and not losing her nerve, she thought as she pushed a stray hair from her face with a grubby hand. What she felt seemed more a bone-deep foreboding than fear.

There was certainly no one she could talk to about it. Even if she had been tempted to confess to Simms, he'd been distant and abrupt with her all day. Last night's phone call hung unmentioned between them.

Nor had she heard from Station Officer Farrell, and she'd

begun to think she'd made a complete ass of herself. She'd meant to talk to her own guv'nor about her theory, but as the day went by the prospect seemed less and less appealing. If she had any sense, she'd take Wilcox's advice and forget the whole thing.

When she'd washed up, she wandered into the kitchen. Their lunch had been interrupted by the bells an hour ago, and bowls of congealing chili con carne still stood on the table. Steven Winston came in, whistling tunelessly, and popped his into the microwave, but after a moment's hesitation Rose scraped hers into the bin. The smell made her feel nauseous, and the last thing she needed was to sick up her lunch on the next shout.

She made up her mind to speak to Bryan Simms, see if she could clear the air between them. At least she could tell him she appreciated his concern. She left the control room and went down to the turnout bay, where she found Bryan washing the mud off the appliance from the last shout.

"Hey," she said, grabbing a towel and following along behind him.

"Hey, yourself." His voice was casual, but he didn't meet her eyes.

"Busy day, yeah?" she offered, but this brilliant sally met with no more than a nod.

She stopped in midswipe. "Look, Bryan. About last night. It's not that I— It just wasn't a good—"

"You two are gluttons for punishment," said a voice behind her, and she spun round, startled. It was Simon Forney, the other half of Castor and Pollux, and the look he gave her was speculative. He was assigned to the pump ladder, and had not been needed on the last shout. "Someone rang you while you were out. Station Officer Farrell, the arson bloke. Said you didn't answer your mobile. He left a number where you could reach him." Simon handed her a Post-it with an unidentified number scribbled on it.

Rose felt a flush of excitement, quickly dampened by the wary looks on both men's faces. She'd left her bloody mobile in her locker. She'd have to retrieve it, then hope she could snatch some privacy to ring Farrell back. "Bloody nuisance," she said, thinking quickly. She made a face. "I've already told him everything I—"

The bells went with a deafening clamor, and the men turned away, running for their gear. After an instant's hesitation, Rose followed, feeling more alone than she had since her first day at Southwark station.

14

So near the fire as we could for smoke;
and all over the Thames, with one's face in the wind,
you were almost burned with a shower of firedrops.

SAMUEL PEPYS'S
description of the Great Fire of London in 1666

HARRIET WOKE AS the room began almost imperceptibly to lighten. She lay in the narrow bed, watching as the shadows gradually took on familiar shapes, and as the square of window grew from a slightly lighter black, to pearly rose, to a dull gray. It was funny, she'd never realized how long it took for night to become day, and vice versa, because she was always doing other things.

When she could see well enough, she climbed out of bed and used the pail. Then she stood at the window, her face pressed to the murky glass. She heard church bells, faintly, and then the whoop of a fire engine's siren. Were they coming for her? But the sound grew fainter until at last she heard only the echo in her mind.

After a bit, as the light grew stronger, she began to prowl

the room, reexamining every nook and cranny, as if something different might have materialized in the night.

She was now more certain than ever that the room had once belonged to a child. There was the small bed, with its odor of old and secret accidents. There was the wooden stool, which she found, on closer inspection, bore the faint remnants of a painted design. In one of the drawers of the chest beneath the window, she discovered a chipped wooden horse and a yellowed deck of playing cards.

And of course there were the books, all worn and fragile, as if the pages had been turned again and again, as she had turned them the past two days. It was in *Peter Pan,* on the blank page before the back cover, that she found the writing. Tiny and cramped, done with a dull pencil, each line the exact repetition of the next.

I promise I will be good.

The words made Harriet feel sad and frightened, but nothing frightened her as much as the scratches around the keyhole of the door. What had happened to the child who tried to get out of this place?

She curled up under the worn blanket, even though the room was warm and stuffy, clutching the copy of *Peter Pan* to her chest. Her stomach was beginning to ache with hunger, as if something were gnawing it from the inside. It was getting late, she could tell that by the light, and the lady hadn't brought her any breakfast.

Where was her dad? Why would he have left her here in this house, with this strange woman? Why had he picked her up from school, especially when it wasn't his weekend? She screwed her face up in concentration, trying to sort out the fuzziness in her mind.

She remembered that her dad had said it was a treat, and that he'd looked a little odd, nervous and excited, his long fingers tapping on the steering wheel. She remembered that the woman had turned and smiled at her, and that her dad had told her the woman's name, but she couldn't remember what he'd said. It was as if there were a blank space in her brain where the memory should be, all mixed up with the Starbucks and hot cocoa.

Had the woman put something in her drink that made it hard for her to remember? Things only came back to her in a nauseating jumble of images that reminded her of the kaleidoscope her father had given her one Christmas.

Suddenly, Mrs. Bletchley's face came into focus, creased in a suspicious scowl. Mrs. Bletchley had been watching, from the cottage yard, and Harriet had wondered if the old cow would tell her mother that her dad had picked her up from school. Her mum would be bloody furious.

The thought made her stomach churn. Would her mother keep her from seeing her dad ever again? A little whimper of distress escaped her and she pressed her hand to her mouth. She loved her dad, but she hated it when her mother was upset. Her mum was always feeling sorry for people, except for her dad, and everything he did made her angry. He tried, he really did, but somehow everything always seemed to go wrong.

She felt a longing for her dad then, so fierce that her throat tightened on a sob. She wanted them all to be home, in their own house, together. When she was very small, it had been different. Her parents had laughed, and her mother had sung to her when she'd tucked her into bed at night.

Was it something she'd done that had made things change?

Harriet pulled the blanket tighter, and after a while she dozed again, but it was a fitful and feverish sleep. She woke suddenly, sweating, and then she realized she'd heard the creak of footsteps on the stairs.

She sat up, her heart thumping in panic. She had to get out. There must be a way, if she could just think how, if she were just clever enough. Maybe if she could distract the woman, she could make a dash for the door. Maybe the lady had been lying when she'd said only she could open the front door. Maybe there really was a phone, or maybe there was someone else in the house who would help her.

Harriet knew she had to make an attempt—she couldn't bear to be shut alone in this room another minute.

When the door opened, she stood and tried to smile.

As she waited in the second interview room, Maura Bell wasn't sure if she was flattered or insulted that Kincaid had chosen her to join him in talking to Yarwood's ex-wife. Not that she liked to admit that his decision mattered to her—yet as infuriating as she found his easy authority, there was a small part of her that wanted his approval.

Nor did she want to admit that she'd been hoping for a few minutes alone with Doug Cullen. She was beginning to think she'd imagined the chemistry between them on Friday night, and she felt a fool. Seeing the obvious camaraderie between Doug and Gemma James hadn't improved her mood one bit, and she frowned as she thought of them searching Laura Novak's house together. It was bad enough that Kincaid had brought James into the investigation without so much as a by-your-leave—

The opening of the interview room door interrupted her uncharitable thoughts. Kincaid ushered in a small woman in a lilac trouser suit, saying, "Mrs. Teasdale, this is Detective Inspector Bell."

Mrs. Teasdale offered her small, cool hand, leaving no doubt that she'd been a well-trained politician's wife, and Maura saw that her perfectly manicured nails matched her suit. Maura guessed her to be in her very well-preserved midforties, but not even the flawless makeup and carefully styled strawberry-blond hair could hide the lines of stress round her eyes and mouth.

"I've come about me daughter," she said as she took

the chair Kincaid held out for her, and the high voice and unaltered working-class accent caught Maura by surprise. "My Chloe. I want to know if you've found her—if you've found . . . anything? Mick says—" She stopped, clutching at the handbag she held in her lap. "He says you're certain it was her, going into the warehouse." Her eyes, pale beneath her mascaraed lashes, darted from Kincaid to Maura.

"Both your husband—ex-husband—and Chloe's flatmate have identified her from the CCTV photo as going into the warehouse, yes," Kincaid answered. "But we're not sure of anything more at this point. There are tests—"

She shook her head, cutting him off as if refusing to contemplate it. "He's keeping something from me. He's in some kind of trouble, and if he's hurt Chloe—" As she clenched her hands, her nails scored the soft leather of her handbag.

Kincaid hesitated, as if trying to decide which point to address first, but before Maura could speak he said, "Why do you think he's in trouble, Mrs. Teasdale?"

"He told me he wants to sell the house. He says he's found a buyer."

Maura frowned. "I'm not sure I under—"

"It's a listed building. Just round the corner from the Tate. I've been trying to get him to sell it for years, even before the divorce, but he wouldn't have it. Oh, no, he said, it was only fitting that the member of Parliament for the Borough should show respect for the old places." Venom had crept into her voice. "Never mind that it was built for pygmies and the plumbing only works when it's in the mood. Never mind that it's worth a small fortune these days, and Trev—that's my husband, Trevor—Trev and me could use the cash for our business." She leaned forward and tapped a nail on the table with a brittle sound that made Maura's teeth hurt. "I'm telling you," Michael Yarwood's former wife went on, "he's into something, and he's got our Chloe mixed up in it somehow. He's gone out, and he wouldn't tell me where he was going."

Was the woman more interested in snitching on her husband than in finding her daughter? wondered Maura. Had she not understood that Chloe might be dead? She'd taken a breath to speak when Kincaid fixed Mrs. Teasdale with a sympathetic smile.

"Mrs. Teasdale—it's Shirley, isn't it?" he asked. When Mrs. Teasdale nodded, he went on. "Did you ever know your husband to have a problem with gambling?"

She stared at him as if he were daft. "Michael? Gambling? He was brought up Chapel—he can hardly bring himself to have a drink."

"Then what sort of trouble do you think he might be in?" asked Maura, trying to emulate Kincaid's tone.

Shirley Teasdale seemed to sag in her chair, her momentary umbrage forgotten. "I don't know. He won't talk to me, but I know him—I know he's keeping something back. He's never forgiven me for Trev, but this is our daughter. He keeps saying she must be all right, but . . . she'd have rung me, wouldn't she?" The look she gave them was pleading. "I can't imagine why she wouldn't have rung me."

"I'm sure Chloe must confide in you, about her life, boyfriends, things like that," Kincaid said. "Do you know anything about the man she was with in the video, Nigel Trevelyan?"

Shirley hesitated, and it seemed to Maura that even the crisp lilac suit lost a little starch. "You have to understand. Chloe likes to tease her dad with things. I think . . . I think she likes knowing she can make him angry. It's like waving a red flag under the nose of a bull. She said . . ." Her voice dropped to a whisper. "She said if her dad knew about Nigel, he'd kill him. But it's not Nigel that's dead, is it?"

As she drove the now familiar route between Borough High Street Station and Park Street, Gemma glanced at the dashboard clock and gave a little groan of dismay. It was already

midafternoon. She should be home; the boys would be back
from their outing with Wesley, and she'd let the weekend
slip by without doing any of the things necessary to prepare
for the coming week. Tomorrow would be especially difficult, as she planned to take the afternoon off for the court
hearing.

"Are you okay?" asked Doug Cullen, beside her.

"The boys will be home on their own by now. I never
meant to abandon them for the entire day."

"If you need to go, go," he said, with his usual earnest-
ness. "I'll do the search, then wait for Duncan. No one could
expect you to do more on this case—"

"And I should mind my own business, at least according
to Detective Inspector Bell." She softened the words with a
smile. "Can't say I blame her." She wasn't used to encoun-
tering such obvious hostility from other female officers, and
she was surprised by how uncomfortable it made her feel.

"She's all right, really," Doug said quietly. "When you get
to know her a bit."

When she glanced at him, he was studying the spots on
her windscreen with great deliberation. Gemma seemed to
remember hearing him say the same thing once about Stella
Fairchild-Priestly, but with less conviction.

"I suppose you've not had much time for Stella this weekend," she ventured, her curiosity roused.

"She's away. Another country house party." Doug didn't
meet her eyes. "And I suppose I'm in the doghouse for not
joining her."

Gemma had always wondered what the very polished
Stella saw in a lowly detective sergeant who didn't share her
social aspirations, but if he was developing an interest in
prickly Maura Bell, he might be jumping out of the frying
pan into the fire. "Doug," she began, meaning to deliver the
standard warning about the pitfalls of relationships on the
job, then realizing how absurd that would sound coming

from her. And besides, Doug and Maura didn't normally work on the same patch, and who better to understand the demands of the job than another copper?

Having reached Park Street, she pulled up the car in front of Laura Novak's house and said instead, "I want to come in with you, Doug, just for a bit. But thanks for the offer." She'd come too far not to see for herself if the house held any clues that would tell them what had happened to Laura and Harriet.

Nor could she go home until she'd done one other thing. Fanny Liu would have to be told that her flatmate was alive, and that she might have abducted a child.

Gemma knocked and rang the bell, then stood listening for a response. The air was hazy and still, the neighborhood quiet, as if its inhabitants had all decamped for fresher climes. She heard the rustle of Doug's jacket as he shifted beside her, and the quick rhythm of her own breath, but there was no sound from within the flat. Next door, the curtains were drawn.

Slipping on a pair of latex gloves, Gemma put the key in the lock and called out, "Police! We're coming in." Her voice echoed back at her, an intrusion into the close silence, and she felt a bit silly.

The door swung open easily and they stepped into the hall. The house smelled stale and a little musty, as if no one had been home in several days, but there was no dreaded hint of decay.

Gemma let out a breath she didn't realize she'd held.

"No body, then," said Doug, and she knew he'd been thinking the same thing. "There'd be no question, in this warm weather."

"I thought, when Laura left Harriet with the sitter on Thursday night and lied about having to work, that she might have meant—"

"To kill herself?" Doug's eyes widened behind his round glasses. "That hadn't occurred to me. I was thinking more along the lines of Novak having conveniently forgotten to tell us he'd offed his wife when he stopped by on Friday morning."

Gemma stooped to gather the mail scattered on the tile floor. There was nothing more personal than a few advertising circulars and credit card solicitations—one still addressed to Dr. Antony Novak—and a couple of bills. The postmarks bore Thursday's and Friday's dates, so Gemma assumed the mail represented both Friday's and Saturday's deliveries.

On a narrow table against the wall, more mail was neatly stacked, but when Gemma examined it she found only envelopes marked "Resident" and a few pizza delivery menus.

An umbrella stand in the corner contained a large black umbrella and a cricket bat, while a few pegs mounted on the wall held a woman's fleecy jacket and a smaller Gap anorak in dark green. Harriet's, Gemma thought, her heart contracting. Kit had one that was identical.

Doug moved forward, opening doors, peering into empty rooms, and Gemma followed. The house was long and narrow, with the same beautiful proportions and detailing as the neighbors' next door, but here no effort had been made to highlight the period features. A sitting room faced the front of the house, then came a dining room, then the kitchen—all neat enough, but none showing any evidence of visual or sensual flair. The furniture was of good quality, and a few pleasant prints were hung haphazardly on the magnolia walls, but Gemma saw little that reflected a personal life. The house obviously belonged to a woman whose interest lay in other things. For the first time, Gemma wondered about Laura Novak's background. There were no family photos, not even of Harriet.

"No sign of a struggle or of a hurried exit," she said as

they reached the kitchen. Nor was there any obvious sign that a child inhabited the house. The refrigerator, unlike her own, held no school reports or drawings, and there was no sign of a calendar marked with family schedules. "Look, Doug," Gemma added, frowning, as she drew closer to the sink. "This is odd, don't you think? For a woman this tidy, she's not done the washing up."

Two plates, two glasses, and a saucepan had been stacked and hastily rinsed. The pot still bore traces of what looked like marinara sauce, and there was a very faint smell of spoiled food.

"Maybe she meant to come back and finish up?" suggested Doug. "That's what you do, when you're in a hurry. Or at least that's what I do."

Was this Thursday evening's supper? wondered Gemma. Mrs. Bletchley said Harriet had already eaten when she arrived. Had Laura meant to come straight back after she'd dropped Harriet at the sitter's? And if so, what had prevented her?

"Let's have a look upstairs," she suggested, and let Doug lead the way back to the stairs in the entrance hall. The first floor contained two bedrooms and a bath, the front-facing room obviously Laura's. It was more feminine than Gemma had expected, papered in pale blue and cream, with cream curtains at the window and a cream quilt on the double bed. The bed was made, but a blouse and trousers had been left tossed across a chair. Beneath the chair lay a pair of shoes, one turned over on its side. There was no sign of packing, or indication that anything had been removed from the room or the wardrobe.

A white-painted dressing table held a few cosmetics and a hairbrush, and in a silver frame, a black-and-white photo of a toddler with curly dark hair. Harriet, wondered Gemma, or Laura herself?

Lifting the brush with a gloved hand, Gemma saw hair nestled in the bristles. "Doug—"

"I've got it," he said, opening the evidence collection bag he'd brought with him and taking the brush from her.

Gemma thought of all the times she and her sister had sat at their mother's dressing table, using her hairbrush and trying out her lipsticks. "We can't be sure that some of the hair doesn't belong to Harriet," she said.

Using a pair of tweezers, Doug carefully transferred the dark, curling strands into the bag. "It should be a close enough match, regardless."

Leaving him to it, Gemma glanced briefly into the bathroom. Towels hung on the warmer, bottles of shampoo and bubble bath crowded the tub's edge, and on the basin, a ceramic cup held two toothbrushes.

She carried on into the back bedroom, undoubtedly Harriet's. The hastily made bed sported a navy coverlet with gold stars. Under the window, brightly colored plastic crates held a jumble of books and school projects, and above the desk, a corkboard was jammed with drawings and photos of pop singers and movie stars, cut from glossy magazines.

Next to the desk stood a wardrobe, one of its doors half open, spilling out a jumper and a pair of frayed-bottomed jeans. Opening the doors all the way, Gemma checked the built-in drawers and found them stuffed to bursting with T-shirts and panties and mismatched socks—all expected, and all heartbreakingly ordinary.

Hearing a step behind her, Gemma turned as Doug came into the room. "I've had a look upstairs," he told her. "There's a box room and an office. The boffins will have to have a go at the computer, but I found this under the desk blotter." He handed her a piece of scratch paper. In blue ink, in a neat, firm hand, was a list of women's names.

Mary Talbot. Amy Lloyd. Tanika Makuba. Clover Howes. Ciara Donnelly. Debbie Rufey.

The first three and the last had been checked off; the fourth and fifth bore tiny penciled question marks.

"It could be anything," said Gemma. "An invitation list for a birthday party, or a school outing. A professional group . . ." She took out her notebook and copied down the names, then glanced up at Doug. "But it was under the blotter?"

"Just a corner showing. There was nothing else obviously interesting on the desk itself, just the usual bills and household paperwork, and stacks of literature from different causes, mostly neighborhood things—meals for the homeless at St. John's Waterloo, the food bank, family violence outreach. Oh, and the file drawer containing personal documents was standing half open. Seems to support Novak's story about the passport."

Gemma's phone rang. Even from her pocket the sound was unexpectedly loud in the quiet house. Her first guilty thought was of the boys, needing her at home, but a look at the ID told her it was Kincaid.

When she answered, he said without preamble, "I've just had a call from Konnie Mueller."

Gemma felt her doubts dissolve, leaving a hard and implacable certainty, and a spasm of grief for a woman she would never meet. "It's not Chloe Yarwood, is it?"

"How did you know?"

She thought of the dirty dishes in the sink, the kicked-off shoes, the unopened mail, all the small telling details of a life interrupted. "Because Laura Novak didn't run off with her daughter," she said. "Because when Laura Novak walked out of this house on Thursday night, she had every intention of coming back."

"We need to talk," said the message from Kincaid as Gemma checked her voice mail an hour later. "Ring me and we'll meet somewhere . . . How about the Anchor, Bankside."

Gemma stood by her car in Ufford Street, having just come away from an exhausting visit with Winnie and Fanny

Liu. When she'd told Fanny that Elaine Holland's DNA did
not match that of the victim of the warehouse fire, Fanny
had pressed a hand to her mouth, stifling a sob of relief.

But Fanny's relief soon turned to dismay when Gemma
explained, as gently as she could, that they thought Elaine
might have abducted ten-year-old Harriet Novak. She told of
Elaine's masquerading as the mysterious "Beth," of her affair
with Tony, of her agreeing to help him kidnap his daughter,
then of her disappearance with Harriet on Friday morning.

As Gemma spoke, Fanny seemed to retreat further and
further into herself, mutely shaking her head and clutching
at the shawl in her lap. "No," she whispered when Gemma
stopped. "No. I don't believe it. I don't believe any of it. She
was . . . we were . . . I thought we were . . . happy."

"I don't think there's any doubt. Tony Novak identified
Elaine's photo. It explains so many things, including why
she left without telling you on Thursday night." Gemma
reached out and took Fanny's cold hand in her own. Beneath
her fingers, the bones felt as delicate as a bird's. "Do you
have any idea why she would have taken a child? Or where
she might have gone?"

"No. I—no. No, I can't imagine."

"Did she ever say—" began Gemma, then stopped as she
saw Winnie give a barely perceptible shake of her head.
"I'm sorry," she said instead, and pressed Fanny's hand before letting it go. "I know this is a shock. We can talk more
tomorrow." Even as she spoke, impatience gnawed at her.
She knew Winnie was right, that she couldn't push Fanny
past the limits of her physical and emotional endurance. But
she also knew that Harriet's safety might be at stake, and
that no one knew Elaine better than Fanny. "Ring me
tonight, please, if you think of anything at all," she added,
standing to go.

Fanny's tears had stopped. The face she turned to Gemma
was bleak and empty as a paper husk, and she drew herself

up with obvious effort. "She's not coming back, ever," she'd said then, coldly, clearly. "She might as well be dead."

Gemma felt the skin tighten between her shoulder blades as she remembered Fanny's expression. There was nothing more cruel than betrayal, and here they had a web of betrayals. There was Laura, who had perhaps meant to betray Tony; Tony, who meant to betray Laura; and Elaine, who had betrayed both Tony and Fanny. But while Tony's and Laura's motivations seemed at least understandable, Elaine's did not.

And if it was Laura Novak who had died in the warehouse, who had killed her? Where were Elaine and Harriet, and how did Chloe Yarwood fit into it all? For if they had proof of anything, it was that Chloe Yarwood had been in the warehouse that night.

Kincaid was right; they had to talk.

Setting a fire in daylight took nerve and cunning, but he had both, and he was more than ready for the challenge. Since the burning of the warehouse on Thursday night, he had slept only feverishly, his brain teeming with images of flames and shouting firefighters.

The pleasure had been more intense than any he'd experienced, and yet it had left him with a niggling shard of discontent. He'd held the open flame of the pocket lighter to the furniture—oh, yes—but he'd missed the careful planning and plotting that had preceded his other fires; it had been like orgasm without foreplay. Now he knew he had to own the fire from beginning to end, and the desire to get it right drove him like an itch under his skin.

But this one, this one he'd worked out well in advance. He knew the building from a job he'd had some years ago, and he'd marked it then on the map he carried always in the back of his mind. The place was perfect, a neglected Victo-

rian warehouse, set back from any main thoroughfare. This meant not only that he'd be less likely to be seen, but that the blaze would have more time to take hold before it was reported. And best yet, he knew the building had an illegal propane tank. Once he'd set alight the cardboard boxes accumulated on the ground floor, the warehouse would burn like fury.

They would come, the firemen—firefighters, he corrected himself, his lip curling at the politically correct term—like little gods in their coats and helmets and boots, and he would show them.

He thought of the photograph he kept by his bed, a faded sepia image of a Victorian fire company, all Southwark men, in full regalia. They might look like Gilbert and Sullivan caricatures to the modern eye, with their luxuriant whiskers and pointed helmets, their mongrel dogs in their laps, but these men had been real firefighters who had fought real fires. Heroes. They had been heroes the likes of which the fire service would not see again.

They had breathed smoke like dragons, and they had conquered fire with the poor means at their disposal. And if sometimes the fire had conquered them, there had been no shame in it.

Stepping out of the shadows, he crossed the empty road and eased open the ground-floor door of the warehouse. He'd cut the padlocks the previous night, on his way home from work, gambling that the damage wouldn't be noticed on a Sunday. He looked round the cavernous space, adjusted a cardboard box filled with the crisp packets he'd collected for the purpose, and pulled his lighter from his pocket.

Oh, they would come, these great new firefighters, little gods in their arrogance—and then they would run like rats.

Kincaid was waiting for her on the terrace of the Anchor, leaning on the railing overlooking the Thames. The day had stayed damp and dull, and now water, sky, and the City across the river seemed to meld one into the other, like a Turner painting with all the color leached out.

"Samuel Pepys watched the City burn from here, did you know that?" He gestured at the prospect as Gemma joined him.

"From the Anchor?"

"I don't think the Anchor was built until a century or so after the Great Fire. But somewhere near here, on the Southwark bank. It must have been terrifying, but thrilling in a way, as well," he added, his gaze fixed on the distance.

Gemma had no patience at the moment for daydreaming about fires. They had more concrete matters to deal with. "I've rung the boys," she said, accepting the half pint of cider he'd bought for her. "They've been home to let the dogs out and have gone back to Wesley's. They're having a jam session, apparently, with Wes's cousins, and eating until they're sick."

"That's good for Kit." Kincaid looked relieved. "He's hardly touched anything for days."

"I've got to get home soon," said Gemma, her guilt over her absence only slightly tempered by the knowledge that the boys were in good hands. "I want to be there when they get back."

"I know. But I'll be a while yet." Running a hand through his hair, as was his habit when he was tired, or exasperated, he sighed, then drank off some of his pint. "God, what a day. I've rushed Laura Novak's hair sample to Konnie. He's not happy, I can tell you, but he said he'd start on it straight-away." He turned from the river to study Gemma's face. "You've not much doubt, have you, that it was Laura's body in the warehouse?"

"No. I don't think Laura took Harriet. And if she's not with her daughter, there's only one thing that would keep her from moving heaven and earth to try to find her. But if Laura's dead, who killed her, and why?"

"Novak's the obvious suspect," Kincaid said. "Maybe he decided he couldn't keep Laura from taking Harriet back, even in Czechoslovakia, so he arranged to meet her Thursday night. He killed her, intending to take Harriet out of the country the next day, before Laura's death was discovered. And he'd have wanted to delay identification of the body, hence the stripping and the fire."

Gemma was shaking her head even before he'd finished. "Why would Laura have arranged to leave Harriet with Mrs. Bletchley if she were just meeting Tony for a talk? Why would she have lied about having to work that night? Why would she have agreed to meet Tony in an empty warehouse? That wouldn't make sense even if they'd been on good terms. And"— she waved a hand to stop him from interrupting— "you didn't see Tony's face when you rang the bell at his flat and he thought it was Laura. He was genuinely terrified."

"He'd also been on a bender and was barely coherent. Maybe he was having guilt-induced hallucinations. Like Lady Macbeth."

"Now you're really stretching it." She wrinkled her nose at him.

Kincaid grinned. "Admitted. But tell me if you've a better idea."

Resting her elbows on the railing, Gemma gazed out at the river, as he had done. A train rumbled by over the railway bridge, but the pedestrian walkway along Bankside was fairly quiet. The weekend was winding down, the time she could give to this case was running out, and it seemed they'd made little progress. "Why would Laura have gone to Michael Yarwood's warehouse? Is there some connection between them we haven't seen?"

"I've got Doug out looking for Yarwood as well as Chloe. Yarwood's ex-wife says he's not been home since earlier today, and that he's desperately trying to raise money, even trying to find a quick buyer for his house, which he's always refused to sell."

Gemma frowned. "That might make it more likely that he torched the warehouse for the insurance money, if it weren't for the small matter of the body—"

"Not if he needed immediate cash. Insurance payouts are never quick."

"Forget the fire for a bit," Gemma said slowly. "What would you think if you had a missing child and a prominent father trying to raise immediate cash on the quiet?"

Kincaid stared at her. "Ransom. Bloody hell."

"It could be an attempt to collect Yarwood's gambling debts. They—whoever he's in hock to—lured Chloe to the warehouse, snatched her, then set the place alight to prove they meant business."

After a moment's thought, Kincaid said, "It might be plausible but for two things. Yarwood's ex-wife, who has nothing kind to say about him, swears he'd never gamble. And—"

"The body." Gemma grimaced and rubbed at her face. Her head was starting to ache. "It doesn't explain the body, whether it's Laura's or not. And none of this is getting us any closer to finding Elaine and Harriet Novak."

"Did you have any luck talking to Fanny?"

"No. She was too shocked. I'm not sure she took it in, about Harriet. Winnie's promised to stay on with her."

"I'll talk to Fanny again tomorrow," he said. "And to Tony Novak, and to Yarwood, if we can find him."

"You won't have much time." The thought of the court hearing hovered in the back of her mind like a shadow, and she felt her stomach knot.

"I know." He touched her shoulder, turning her to face him. The reflection of the river had turned his eyes gray as slate. "It'll be all right," he said, and she wasn't sure if he meant to reassure her or himself. In the distance, a siren began to wail, then another. After a few moments, the sound faded away.

Fanny sat, chill and silent, as the light in the green room faded to gray. She seemed not to hear Winnie's soft queries, or to feel Winnie's chafing of her hands, or to notice the butting, purring overtures of Quinn, the cat.

Winnie lit the lamps and the candles, hoping to restore some sense of normality. Then she made a cup of tea, to warm her hands if she could not warm Fanny's. She sat close beside Fanny's chair and saw her own face reflected in the darkening window, lit by the flickering candle flame.

The petition came to her without thought. She had said it every night since her ordination, so that it was now as automatic as breathing. As the words ran through her mind, she realized she was speaking them aloud, her voice a rising and falling murmur of sound.

"Keep watch, dear Lord, with those who work, or watch, or weep this night, and give your angels charge over those who sleep. Tend the sick, Lord Christ; give rest to the weary, bless the dying, soothe the suffering, pity the afflicted, shield the joyous; and all for your love's sake. *Amen.*"

When she'd finished, the silence seemed deeper. Fanny sat with eyes closed, her face so pale and pinched that Winnie began to think she had better call a doctor. But before she could rise, the cat jumped up in her lap. She stroked him for a moment, then put him down, and when she glanced at Fanny once more, she saw that her face was wet, her eyes open.

At first, the tears slipped silently down Fanny's cheeks, as if she were unaware of them. And then her mouth began to twist, her shoulders to shake, and she was crying with the grief of the bereaved.

Winnie pulled her chair as close as she could and wrapped

her arms around Fanny's thin shoulders. "It's all right," she whispered. "You'll be all right."

"How could she do it?" choked out Fanny. "How could she let me think she loved me?"

To this Winnie had no immediate answer. She could only keep patting Fanny's back, and when the sobs subsided to an occasional gulp, she provided a clean handkerchief from the pocket of her cardigan and sat back to let Fanny blow her nose.

"I think," Winnie said slowly, when Fanny looked up at her with red and swollen eyes, "I think perhaps she was in terrible pain. I know there are people who are simply wicked, who hurt others for the pleasure of it . . . but because Elaine was good to you in so many ways, I can't find it in my heart to believe that of her. She said, didn't she, that her mother committed suicide and her father died from an illness when she was young? That might have—"

"She said a lot of things that turned out not to be true," countered Fanny. "Why should we believe that?"

"Why would she have lied? Unless . . . unless there was something worse . . . something she couldn't bear to talk about or perhaps even to remember." Winnie shook her head. "We're grasping at straws, love, and we may never know the truth."

"I can understand, a little, about the doctor. I mean, people have affairs all the time . . . And it's not as though there was anything physical, really, between us." Fanny looked away, as if ashamed to have mentioned it. "There were only things that I might have . . . misinterpreted . . . But why . . . why would she take a *child?*"

"Did Elaine want children?" Winnie had seen it in her pastoral work, women—single or married—who reached a certain age and found themselves suddenly obsessed with the desire for a child so strong that it drove them beyond reason. It was a thought she'd kept in the back of her mind, a slender thread of hope on which to hang the safety of Harriet Novak.

"No," whispered Fanny, the brief animation fading from her face. "No. She didn't care for children at all."

Rose sat in the rear cab of the pump, with Bryan and Steve Winston. Seamus MacCauley was driving and Station Officer Wilcox rode beside him. Beneath her heavy tunic, she could feel her T-shirt plastered wetly to her back. The day had gone from bad to worse—two more nuisance fires, one in a rubbish tip and the other in an abandoned car, two medical calls, then a road traffic accident that had injured an unrestrained child. She'd never had a chance to dry out properly from the morning's fires, much less the afternoon's, nor had she had any opportunity to return Station Officer Farrell's call. And now they were on their way to another fire.

"Better gear up," said Bryan. "We're almost there." In this warm and humid weather, they resisted pulling up their Nomex hoods as long as they could. The fire-resistant fabric stopped any air circulation inside their tunics, turning their already sweltering coats into sweatboxes.

They were headed west, along Webber Street, the pump ladder careening along right behind them. A fire had been reported in a warehouse tucked back between Webber Street and Waterloo Road. As they slipped on their hoods and re-settled their helmets, the pump swung round a curve and Rose saw the smoke.

"Christ," said Steven, his voice filled with awe. The building was old—Victorian, Rose thought, although with none of the architectural grace of the Southwark Street warehouse—and in poor repair. Its concrete surround was cracked and patched with weeds, a wire fence sagged listlessly to the ground in places, and broken windows gaped like sightless eyes. From the third- and fourth-floor windows, smoke dark as coal pumped furiously out. It looked as though a bomb had gone off in the place.

Pedestrians milled about in the street, shouting and pointing. MacCauley had to sound the air horn to scatter them so that he could maneuver the pump into a position near the hydrant. As soon as they rolled to a stop, Rose could hear the fire, crackling and hissing and groaning like a live thing. As they spilled out of the appliance she felt her chest tighten.

"Seamus," Wilcox shouted, "get on to Control. Tell them to make pumps four. Then get us police backup, and get these people out of the way until the police get here to take over crowd control." He turned to the others. "You three, rig in BA. We'll need to get a hose in through the main doors and make an assessment."

Wilcox turned to the ladder crew. "Get us entry, then get a ladder up to the roof. And someone have a look round the back side, see what the status is there."

Both crews sprang into action. It was chaos, but it was the controlled chaos of those who knew their jobs and were prepared to give whatever was required of them. As Rose settled the BA pack on her back and handed in her tally, marked with her set number and the amount of air in her cylinder, she felt the tightness in her chest ease. A rush of adrenaline surged through her, making her feel light-headed and razor-sharp. She was going to be okay.

She had comms, the breathing apparatus radio, and would be responsible for letting Wilcox know what they found inside. As they unreeled the hose, the ladder crew broke down the remainder of the fence and charged at the main doors, axes swinging. The doors splintered under the blows and Rose had a brief glimpse of the padlock flying, then she and Bryan and Steve were pushing through, Bryan at the tip.

A blast of heat jetted out, knocking them back. They crouched, moving forward again, Bryan sending controlled pulses from the hose into the dense black smoke. The jets turned instantly to roiling steam, and Rose felt her face sear through the faceplate of her mask.

Bryan pulsed the hose another half a dozen times, but there was no change in the temperature. They could see nothing but black clouds of smoke mixed with steam, and then, out of the corner of her eye, Rose caught a flicker of flame within the fumes: flashover.

"Guv!" she shouted over the radio. "It's all going to shit in here. We can't control it!"

"Back out!" Wilcox yelled in her ear. "Get out now."

She grabbed Bryan and Steve and pulled at them, feeling the heat of their tunics even through her gloves. "Out," she repeated. "We're moving out."

They backed out the way they'd come, Bryan continuing the short bursts from the hose, Rose keeping a grip on them both. She only knew they'd reached the door when Bryan's helmet materialized in front of her.

As they staggered away from the building they heard a rumble and a pop, and a jet of flame shot out, licking at them. "Jesus," she heard Steve say again as they scrambled away.

When they reached Wilcox and MacCauley, they pulled their masks off, and Rose took a deep, gulping breath. In the distance, she heard the faint double tone of sirens.

"We're going to have to tackle this bastard from the outside," said Wilcox. "And we're going to need help. I've made it pumps six. Get the hose back on the door—"

"Hey!" The shout had come from the crowd. A man's finger pointed upwards, and Rose caught a glimpse of a pale face, and the blue arm of a uniform sleeve. "There's somebody in there! I saw somebody in there!"

"Where?" said Wilcox, scanning the building.

"Third floor," the man called out. "In the window. Third from the left. A face."

Rose looked, saw nothing but billowing smoke.

"Persons reported," Wilcox called over the radio. "I'm sending crew up." He turned to Rose and Bryan. "The ladder crew's venting the roof. You two will have to take a look."

Bryan gave her a quick bright grin, then they moved in unison, raising the ladder and hauling up the hose, Rose leading the way. She felt a moment's relief that the constraint between them had vanished; then she thought of nothing but the job at hand.

When she reached the window, she grabbed the frame and straddled the sill, feeling her way with her foot. She could feel the wood's heat through her gloves, but there was no flame showing inside, only the dense, oily smoke.

"Okay," she said as her foot found solid floor. Swinging her other leg over, she inched forward, testing the surface with the toe of her boot. She kept hold of the window frame with one hand and groped outwards with the other, exploring the darkness like a blind person in an unfamiliar room.

She'd expected, if there had been someone at the window, to find them crumpled beneath it, but she felt only the solid floor. Bryan climbed in behind her, bumping against her as he crouched and steadied the hose on his knee. He gave two bursts of the jet, and this time she felt the temperature drop.

"Anybody here?" Bryan shouted, his voiced muffled by his mask.

Rose listened, her senses straining, hearing nothing but the hiss and crackle of the fire.

Rising, Bryan pulsed the hose again, then stepped forward. Rose felt a sudden vacuum beside her, heard an exclamation cut short. She swung her arm out wildly, towards the spot where Bryan had stood a moment before, and almost lost her balance as she encountered only air.

"Bryan!" She fell to her knees and inched forward, her hands sweeping in an arc through the smoke. When her knee touched something solid she gasped in relief, but her exploring fingers felt not a leg, but the round shape of the charged hose.

"Bryan!" she shouted again, panic rising in her throat. She felt along the hose until she touched the nozzle, then swept her hands across the floor in front of it. He must have caught his foot on something, fallen, but she could find him, she could get him out.

She tried to think calmly, to regulate her breathing. She couldn't afford to use up all her air. Keeping one hand on the stationary hose as a guide, she crept forward, her free hand patting the floor. Vaguely, she heard a voice shouting into her headset, but she shut it out. Her world had narrowed to the tips of her gloved fingers.

Then, the floor disappeared beneath her hand. She jerked back instinctively, then felt again. Nothing. She ran her hand sideways, touched the hard edge of the floor, then she reached forward again. Nothing. The other side was the same. The floor dropped away in front of her, as far as she could reach.

"Bryan!" she screamed, but only her own voice echoed back inside her mask.

She kept calling, gripping the edge of the pit, until strong arms came round her from behind and pulled her away.

15

Oh, Captain Shaw!
Type of true love kept under!
Could thy Brigade
With cold cascade
Quench my great love, I wonder!

GILBERT AND SULLIVAN
Iolanthe, 1882

WHENEVER HARRIET CLOSED her eyes, the darkness seemed to press against her eyelids with a smothering weight, so she stared at the paler patch of dark she knew was the window. She had no idea how long it had been since nightfall; she'd lost all perception of the passage of time.

She shifted slightly on the narrow bed but kept her left arm tight against her chest. She thought her arm was broken, but not badly. Her mum had told her about fractures—with a compound fracture the bones might stick right through the skin, but a simple fracture was just what it sounded, a clean break.

Her forearm was swelling, and it hurt to move it, but the skin wasn't broken and nothing felt jagged when she probed gently with her fingers. Still, she felt feverish and nauseated, and miserably thirsty.

At last, in spite of her discomfort, her eyelids fluttered, and she drifted towards the edge of sleep.

Oh, God, she was falling, falling, she couldn't stop herself . . . the dark wooden banisters flashed by in a sickening whirl and she felt the impact as the hard steps came up to meet her . . . then hands gripped onto her ankles, the weight of a body crushed the breath from her lungs, and a searing pain tore through her arm.

Harriet jerked awake, gasping, her arm throbbing from the involuntary movement. Slowly, she eased herself up until she was half sitting against the wall. After a bit the falling sensation faded away, but she couldn't stop the images replaying in her mind.

She had stood up, and smiled.

The lady had paused, a slight look of surprise on her face, then she'd carried on into the room and set the tray she carried on the low chest.

"It's warm in here," Harriet managed to say, even though her heart was thumping. "Could I—could we—could we have the window open a bit, for some air?"

The woman had turned and gazed at her with a very strange look, as if she'd forgotten Harriet could speak. Then she had stepped to the window and touched one of the fogged panes, her fingers lingering on the glass in what seemed almost a caress.

"It doesn't open," she said, her voice rusty. "It hasn't opened for years. You'll have to live with the heat."

Harriet stared at her, then at the books, and at the narrow bed, and a dreadful knowledge filled her. "This was your room," she whispered. "These were your books. You wrote in them. You wrote—"

"Only when I was bad," said the woman. She smiled. "But then, I was bad quite often."

"But why did you— How could you bring me here, when you knew . . ."

"I didn't intend to, not at first." The woman frowned as she spoke, as if it puzzled her. "But your father . . ." Her eyes fixed on Harriet, sharper now. "Your father was going to leave, and he never thought of taking me with him . . . I don't think he'd have even bothered to tell me he was going if he hadn't needed my help . . ."

"But—"

"I couldn't have that, you see."

Her dad didn't know, then. He didn't know where she was. Harriet felt a rush of relief that he hadn't put her in this place, then a cold fear as she realized what that meant. Desperate to keep the woman talking, she said, "No. No, you couldn't. It was selfish of him. My mum's always saying he's selfish." She flushed with shame at her disloyalty, but she had to go on. "I'm sure he's sorry. He should have known better."

"Yes, he should." The woman looked pleased at Harriet's understanding.

"If he's learned his lesson," Harriet said carefully, trying to keep her voice level, "maybe you could let me go."

"Oh, I don't think so," the woman said, as if she'd given it long consideration. "Because then I'd be in trouble, and I don't want to be in trouble."

"I wouldn't tell."

"Yes, you would." Her face hardened, and Harriet knew her deception wasn't going to work. From the corner of her eye, she glimpsed the door, not quite pulled shut. She had to take her chance, but she needed a distraction.

"Are those your cards?" she asked, nodding towards the chest. "I saw them, the playing cards, in the drawer. I could play with you, if you like."

There was a softening, a flicker of pleasure, perhaps of memory, in the woman's eyes, and then she glanced towards the chest. In that instant, Harriet dived at the door, yanked it fully open, and plunged down the stairs.

The steps were steep and hard, the carpeted runner worn thin as tissue. Harriet skidded on the first step and tumbled, crashing down, and the woman came behind her like a fury. She'd fallen on Harriet, pinning Harriet's slighter body beneath her, ignoring her cries of pain. Then she pulled her to her feet and marched her back up the stairs.

"You tricked me," she hissed, her breath panting hot in Harriet's ear. "You tricked me, and you're going to be sorry." She shoved Harriet into the room, slamming the door so hard the walls shook and the china basin on the chest made a chinking sound.

For a long time, Harriet lay where she fell, too afraid to move. The room brightened, then grew dimmer as the sun passed its zenith. At last, driven by the pain in her arm, she shuffled across the floor and climbed up on the bed. Shivering in spite of the heat, she pulled the blanket round her.

The hours passed, the room grew gray as the afternoon faded to evening, and nothing stirred in the house. Harriet's head swam with hunger as well as pain. She'd had nothing to eat or drink since last night's meager supper. The tray still sat on the chest where *she* had left it, hours before. Trying not to make a sound, Harriet got up and crossed the room.

Congealed oatmeal, dried fruit, a cup of warm, flat water. Harriet drank all the water, no longer caring if she had to use the pail, then made herself eat a few bites of the oatmeal and nibble a piece of fruit. But she had felt ill, too dizzy to stand for long, and she soon crawled back into bed.

Now, as she lay staring into the dark, her stomach cramped with emptiness.

She recalled again what she'd seen, in the brief minutes of her flight. A landing. An open door. A room as dusty and disused as the one that held her. The bottom of the stairs had yawned dark as a cavern—there had been no light, no sound, anywhere in the house.

Harriet thought of the meals she'd been given; the dried food, the stale water. Then she thought of the utter silence that surrounded her, and of the way she heard the sound of the boiler and the grumble of the plumbing when she lay in her own bed at night.

This house was dead, she realized, abandoned. There was no power, no water, and no one had lived here for a long time, until the woman had brought her here.

It made it worse, somehow, to think of the house so desolate, so empty, and she felt very cold and very afraid. Suddenly, she wanted her mother more than she had ever wanted anything in the world. She cried out in the darkness, but her mother didn't come.

Kincaid groped for the alarm, trying to shut off the insistent ringing. His fingers found the Snooze button, but the sound didn't stop. "Bloody hell," he muttered. It was the phone, not the alarm.

Squinting at the digital readout of the clock as he fumbled for the handset, he saw that it was only a few minutes after six, and that a dusky light had just begun to show at the gap in the bedroom curtains. Gemma groaned and pulled the pillow over her head as he got the phone to his ear.

"Kincaid," he croaked.

"Duncan, it's Bill Farrell here. Sorry to ring so early, but I thought you'd want to know."

He pulled himself up against the headboard, coming fully awake. "Know what?"

"There was another warehouse fire in Southwark yesterday evening, just before the day watch ended. I was off duty yesterday, so another team took the initial investigation. I didn't hear about it until I got up this morning."

"What hap—"

"I only know it was a bad fire, fully involved, and that a firefighter was killed."

"Jesus." Kincaid remembered Rose telling him she was working a day tour yesterday. "Do you know who it was?"

"Not yet. I'm meeting Martinelli at the scene. I thought you might want to come. It's just off Waterloo Road—at Webber Street."

"Give me half an hour."

When Kincaid hung up, he found Gemma awake and watching him, her eyes wide with alarm.

"Another fire in Southwark," he said, before she could ask. "I've got to go."

He drove east, into a glorious rising sun, and tried to think of anything other than Rose Kearny. The city was just coming to life, its pulse quickening in anticipation of the coming day, and when he crossed the Thames at Waterloo, the water reflected the sky in a molten sheet of pink. Such beauty seemed incongruous with death, and it made the dread weigh more heavily on his heart.

As he turned off the Waterloo Road, following Farrell's directions, he realized how close the fire had been to Ufford Street and Fanny Liu's house. Then he saw the blackened hulk of the building, stark against a sky turning quickly to gold. The roof of the warehouse had fallen in, and the remaining walls stuck up like jagged, rotting teeth. The surrounding yard was filled with piles of burned debris and broken fencing, and the rank smell of the fire penetrated the car. The perimeter of the blue-and-white crime scene tape fluttered lightly in a rising breeze.

He recognized Bill Farrell's van parked in the road, and saw Farrell himself, gazing up at the remains of the warehouse. With him was Jake Martinelli, and Scully.

The men turned to greet him as he climbed from the car, and the dog wagged her tail in recognition. Kincaid bent to stroke her, burying his hands in the thick ruff of fur on her neck. Still clasping the dog, he looked up at Farrell. "Did you—"

"I stopped by the station. It was a young firefighter named Bryan Simms. He was Rose Kearny's partner."

Kincaid felt a flood of relief, then shame. Why should this death be any less tragic because he had not known the victim? Why did it matter so much to him, that Rose was safe?

Seeking a moment's distraction to get his emotions under control, he rubbed the dog's head and said to her, "Have you got a job today, girl?" Scully licked his ear, obligingly. Then he stood, turning to Farrell. "How did it happen?"

"They'd had to abandon an interior attack when a person was reported on the third floor. Simms and Kearny went up on the aerial ladder. There was no flame showing, so they went in through the window." Farrell looked away, gazing at the building. "The smoke was heavy; they were blind. It was an unsecured lift shaft. He fell to the bottom. It was three hours before the crews could get the fire damped down enough to get to him." He rubbed at his jaw. "Wouldn't have mattered, though, if that's a blessing. Some falling debris partially protected the body. There was enough left that they could tell he'd broken his neck."

"Oh, Christ." Kincaid swallowed. "And Rose?"

Farrell shrugged. "They've given her leave, of course. It wasn't her fault, though I doubt she'd believe it. The floor within four or five feet of the window was solid, so they had no warning of the drop. Simms stepped in front of her."

"What about the person on the third floor? Did they get him out?"

"They didn't find anyone—at least not yet. We'll see what my lads turn up when it's full light."

"Was she right?" Kincaid asked, thinking of the papers Rose had given him, and that he had carried around so carelessly for a day. Had he been in some way responsible for this? "Was there a pattern?"

"There was a propane tank in the building," said Martinelli. "We won't know if an additional accelerant was used until we get the lab results. But like the other fires, there seems to be only one obvious point of origin. And the overhaul crew turned up a few bits of cardboard that could have been used as the initial fuel."

"And we found this, this morning." Farrell pointed at the ground a few yards from the twisted doors. Kincaid moved closer and peered down. It was a heavy-duty padlock, rusty from exposure, but a bright gleam of metal showed where the linkage had been sheared clean through.

"The entry crew—"

"They didn't cut it. This was done before the fire."

Kincaid looked up and met Farrell's eyes.

"We may not find any more hard evidence," said Farrell, "but I'd stake my career that this was arson. He's clever, but he's not clever enough. And I'm going to nail the bastard to the wall."

Rose had held on to a flicker of hope until they carried Bryan's body out of the ruins of the fire.

She'd made a sound then, and Seamus MacCauley had tried to hold her, to turn her away, but she'd pushed herself free of his encircling arm. The others had stepped back in silence, had let her walk beside Bryan to the waiting ambulance. She owed him that, and so much more.

Their relief had arrived, an hour into the fire, but the entire watch had stayed on, watching and waiting. You didn't leave a mate, not like that. The paramedics had stood by as well, even though any hope that they would be needed faded as the fire blazed unabated, and the minutes lengthened into hours.

The pumpers poured out hundreds of thousands of gallons, and it seemed, for a long while, that the water only fed the flames. Then the roof had begun to cave, the inrush of oxygen sending up sparks and new tongues of fire, but it had been the beginning of the end. The glow had dimmed, the fierce heat fading, until she had felt the night air cool against her face. At last, the ladder crew had gone in, to search out the last stubborn, smoldering pockets, but victory had come at too great a price.

Rose reached out as the stretcher slid into the ambulance, but Station Officer Wilcox stilled her hand with his own, and the doors clanged shut.

As the ambulance pulled away, he said, "He didn't suffer, Rose. And there was nothing you could have done."

She looked at those gathered round her, their eyes red-rimmed, their faces stained with snot and soot, and she knew she couldn't belittle their grief by giving way to hers. Nodding, she stepped back.

Steven Winston and Simon Forney came up to her. "We're taking you home, Rose," said Steven. "I'll drive you, and Simon will bring your car."

"But I can—"

"Just do as you're told and don't argue for once, Kearny," interrupted Simon, and the familiar hectoring tone had eased the tightness in her chest.

She rode with Steven in silence, after they'd dropped their gear at the station and Simon had picked up her Mini. There was nothing to say, and when they reached the house in Forest Hills and Simon had handed over her car keys, they'd stood in awkward silence for a moment.

"Get some rest, Rose," Steven had said, and she noticed that when he'd washed up at the station, he'd missed a streak of soot along his left cheek. "A day or two, then we'll see you back on duty."

"Right. A day or two," she'd agreed, and gone in.

She found her mother sitting up in the reading chair in the conservatory, a book facedown in her lap.

"Rose?" she called, putting the book aside and standing

up. In her dressing gown, with her face scrubbed free of makeup and the gray showing visibly in her blond hair, she suddenly looked all of her fifty-two years. "Rose, Officer MacCauley called me. I'm so sorry." She reached out, but Rose stepped away from her.

"No, Mum, please. I can't. I just can't." She couldn't bear sympathy now—it would dissolve the fragile glue that was holding her together. Steven and Simon had known that.

After a moment, her mother nodded and sank back into the chair. "Can I get you something to eat? Or something hot to drink?"

"No, Mum. I just want to sleep." Rose leaned down and quickly brushed her lips across her mother's forehead. "But thanks. I—we'll talk in the morning."

Once upstairs, she showered, scrubbing her skin until it stung, then fell into her clean white bed. But the forgetfulness of sleep, so longed for, evaded her. She dozed eventually, in fits and starts, always waking with the same urgent feeling of having forgotten something crucial, of needing to be somewhere, needing to do something, if only she could remember what.

She woke fully when the first light of dawn began to pale the windows, her mind suddenly preternaturally clear and alert. Throwing on a sweatshirt and jeans, she left a scribbled note in the kitchen and snuck quietly out of the house. The early-morning air smelled clean and fresh, making her think suddenly of the year her father had helped her throw a paper route. There had been a secret pleasure in getting up together while the world still slept.

She chased away the thought before it could progress to longing—she had no time for that now—and climbed into the Mini. Laying a copy of the map she had made carefully on the passenger seat, she drove north to Southwark.

Traffic was still light, and nothing impeded her as she drove slowly past the scene of every fire she'd marked on the map. The Southwark Street warehouse was last on her list, and last on her route. There, she parked the car and got out. After a moment's hesitation, she turned towards the river. She needed to walk, needed the physical movement in order to sort out all the ideas tumbling wildly through her mind.

She cut through Borough Market, which bustled with the early-morning wholesale trade, as it had for centuries. Then she crossed the cathedral yard and climbed the stairs to London Bridge.

When she reached the bridge's center, she stopped, gazing first at St. Paul's to the northwest, its dome glowing golden in the light of the rising sun. Then she turned back to the south, until she could see the square tower of Southwark Cathedral. She remembered reading somewhere that this was the only spot in England from which one could see two cathedrals, and she thought that on another day, she might find that a wondrous thing.

Then her gaze swept on, to all that lay beyond. She recalled what she had thought she'd known about the fires, and what she had seen that morning, and the pattern began subtly to shift. The shadowy form flitting from fire to fire took on clarity, and substance, and moved easily into the nightmare of last night's blaze.

She saw him in her mind, she understood what made him act, and then—then she saw something so terrible that she sagged against the railing, her hand pressed to her mouth to stop the rising bile.

The squeal of car tires tore Kincaid's attention from the remains of the padlock. A jaunty red Mini swerved, too fast, round the corner into Webber Street, then jerked to a halt behind his car. As the dog began to bark at the unexpected commotion, Rose Kearny got out and ran towards them.

She halted before Farrell, her breath coming hard, her eyes wide and dilated.

"Rose!" said Kincaid. "What is it? What are you doing here?"

She glanced at him, then turned her attention back to Bill Farrell. "I rang the station. They told me you were here. I've just realized—I was wrong—or at least only partly right—about why he sets the fires. He *has* picked sites that haven't required added accelerant because he wants to prove he's smarter than we are, but that's only been an added convenience, icing on the cake."

Martinelli, who had quieted the dog, looked baffled. "What are you—"

"I've looked at the map, and I've looked at the sites themselves, one after the other. I think he's re-creating historic fires."

"I don't understand," said Farrell.

"Well, maybe not the first one, the Waterloo lockup. That might have been a practice run, testing his skills. But the others have been either Victorian warehouses, or he's re-created an aspect of a Victorian warehouse fire." Impatiently, Rose shoved a stray hair behind her ear, and Kincaid saw that her hand was trembling. "Look at the contents. Groceries. Paint. Fabric."

Understanding began to bloom in Farrell's craggy face, but Kincaid was completely at a loss.

"Tooley Street?" said Farrell, and she nodded.

"Scovell's warehouses and Cotton's Wharf. Tea, rice, sugar. Paint. Rum. Hemp, cotton, and jute." Rose turned to Kincaid. "The Tooley Street fire burned for two days, in 1861. It did over two million pounds' worth of damage. It was the worst fire to strike London since the Great Fire, and it wouldn't be equaled until the Blitz."

Martinelli was nodding now too. "It's wild, but yeah, I can see it. But why?"

"I don't know why," said Rose. "But I think he's escalating—building up to something much bigger than anything we've seen. And—" She stopped, her hands clenching and unclenching at her sides.

"What?" said Farrell gently. "Tell us, Rose."

She took a ragged breath. "I think—I think I saw him. Last night. The man who shouted that there was someone in the window on the third floor. It was a bogus call. There was never anyone in this building. But he wanted us to go in. He wanted to kill a firefighter. And I saw him. I saw his face."

"Can you describe him?" asked Farrell, his voice tight now.

"Tall. Youngish. Dark hair, pale skin." Rose closed her eyes, frowning with the effort of recollection. "And his sleeve . . . it was dark blue, a uniform sleeve."

"Bloody fucking hell," said Martinelli, and at the anger in his tone Scully growled and raised her hackles. "Are you saying it was a fireman? A fucking fireman?"

Rose shook her head. "No—I don't know. It wasn't a brigade uniform. I'd have seen that instantly. This was something else, almost like a mock-up of a real uniform. But wait— Say he has a grudge, this guy, against firefighters. Or maybe not just firefighters, but the whole brigade. Look at the dates of the fires, from the first one. When was the last hiring take-up?"

"Jesus." Farrell rubbed at his beard furiously, as if it had caught a cinder. "You think this guy might have been a rejected applicant? And you think you'd recognize him, if you saw him again?"

Rose nodded once.

"Right," muttered Farrell, half to himself. Then he grasped Rose by the shoulder. "We'll go to the station, pull the entire brigade files if we have to. Jake, can you oversee the forensics team when they get here?" He turned to Kincaid. "And, Duncan, I still don't see where the Southwark Street body fits into this, but if Rose is right, Bryan Simms's death is a homicide. Can you—"

But Kincaid's phone was ringing, and he excused himself, turning away as he unclipped it from his belt.

When he answered, Konnie Mueller said, "Bingo."

"Sorry, Konnie—what was that?"

"I said 'Bingo,' mate." Konnie sounded tired but jubilant. "One out of three is not bad. You've got a match on all points. Your Jane Doe is—or was—Laura Novak."

16

. . . a being, erect upon two legs, and bearing all the
outward semblance of a man, and not of a monster . . .

CHARLES DICKENS
The Pickwick Papers

KINCAID FELT A growing unease as he returned to Borough
High Street Station. They'd made progress, with the discovery that Bryan Simms's death was a possible homicide, and
the positive identification of Laura Novak as the victim in
the Southwark Street fire, but he couldn't shake the sense
that he was missing something crucial, and that his time was
running out.

He'd taken what action he could, leaving the search for
the arsonist in the capable hands of Bill Farrell and Rose,
and mobilizing every resource in the search for Harriet
Novak and Elaine Holland, but now he had to face giving
Tony Novak the news about his ex-wife.

He'd had Novak brought into the interview room where
they had spoken the previous day. The man looked a bit
more tidy this morning, clean-shaven and dressed in a

pressed shirt and chinos, but more hollow-eyed and gaunt than ever.

Cullen had rung while Kincaid was at the fire scene, saying he was still trying to trace Chloe Yarwood and Nigel Trevelyan, so Maura Bell would be assisting with the interview.

"Is there some news about Harriet?" demanded Tony as soon as Kincaid and Maura had taken their seats.

"No, we've heard nothing about your daughter," Kincaid said, unwilling to keep him in suspense any longer than necessary. "But I have to tell you that Laura is dead. I'm sorry."

"Laura?" Tony sounded shocked, but it seemed to Kincaid that there was the slightest easing of tension in the man's body, as if the news had been expected. "But why— How did you—"

"We informed you yesterday that we were going to search your ex-wife's house, Mr. Novak," said Bell. "Her DNA sample matched that of the victim of the warehouse fire."

"Dear God," Tony whispered, blanching. "That fire . . . Laura . . . I can't—"

"We think she was already dead when the fire started, if that's any comfort," Kincaid told him. "She didn't suffer from the burns."

"But who would— You don't think Beth—"

"What time did Beth—Elaine Holland—leave you on Thursday evening?"

"It wasn't late. Before ten, I think."

Was it possible, Kincaid wondered, that Elaine had left Tony's flat, somehow lured Laura to the warehouse, killed her, then returned to Fanny's in time to watch the ten o'clock news without a speck of blood on her? And what would she have done with Laura's clothes? She had no car, and she couldn't possibly have walked out of the search area in that time. Nor did that explain the fire.

"Why would she do such a thing?" Tony asked.

"I don't think she did." Maura leaned towards Tony as if inviting a confidence. "I think Laura found out what you meant to do. I think she left Harriet with the sitter and came to confront you. You argued. Things got out of control. Maybe you didn't mean to kill her, but she was dead, and you had to dispose of the body. You took her to the warehouse, stripped her of any identification, then set the place alight. Then you drove out of London and dumped her clothes."

Tony stared at her as if she'd gone utterly daft. "I live in Borough High Street, for God's sake. How am I supposed to have carried Laura's body out to my car without anyone noticing?"

"Wrapped in something, of course," retorted Maura. "People carry rubbish out all the time, and no one thinks anything of it."

"That's bollocks, and you know it." Tony had begun to let his temper show, and Kincaid had to give Maura credit for knowing how to wind up a suspect. Wearing a black leather coat and a bright blue sweater this morning, she looked tough and surprisingly sexy. He sat back, content to let her play bad cop for the moment.

"Okay," she said, and smiled, but before Tony could relax, she dived at him again like a pecking gull. "Maybe Laura didn't find you out, but you were afraid she would. Maybe you tried earlier on Thursday to get the passport, and a neighbor saw you. You knew it was only a matter of time before Laura heard you'd been in the house, and then she'd never let you get your hands on Harriet. So you lured her to the warehouse—"

"You think Laura would have agreed to meet me in a deserted building?" Tony shook his head in disgust. "You really are daft."

"I didn't say she agreed to meet you. I think you needed Elaine Holland's help for more than one thing. You got

Elaine to call Laura that night, pretending to be an abused woman who needed her help. You knew that was the one appeal she couldn't resist."

"No," said Tony, but he was beginning to look frightened.

"That would explain why Laura left Harriet with the sitter—perhaps she thought she'd have to bring this distressed woman back to her own house.

"Of course you didn't tell Elaine you meant to kill Laura," continued Maura, her eyes alight with conviction. "She came to help you with Harriet on Friday morning, just as you'd agreed. Then, when she learned about the fire and the body, she realized what had happened. That's why she took Harriet, to keep her safe from you."

It was good, Kincaid admitted, inspired, even. But there was one problem with Bell's scenario. He didn't believe it.

There were too many gaps. It didn't explain what Chloe Yarwood had been doing at the warehouse that night, or what had happened to her. It didn't explain Elaine Holland's strange and secretive behavior with Fanny, or how she could have managed to disappear with a ten-year-old child without leaving a trace. Why, if she had believed Tony guilty of murder, had she not come to the police?

Nor did it leave a place for Rose Kearny's arsonist, unless that fire had not been part of the pattern—and yet it fit too well. After last night's blaze, he was convinced that Rose was right and they were dealing with a serial arsonist.

And then there was Gemma. Kincaid had learned to trust Gemma's instincts, and Gemma didn't believe Tony Novak was a murderer.

Tony turned to Kincaid with a look of desperate appeal. "Tell her. Tell her it's not true. I'd never have hurt Laura."

"I'm sorry, Tony," Kincaid said with genuine sympathy. "We have to follow up every possibility. Our forensics teams are searching your flat and your car."

Tony stared at him as if he'd just become Judas Iscariot;

then he leaned forward, gripping the table edge until his knuckles turned white. "Search all you want. Think what you want. I don't care what you do. Just find my daughter."

When they had first interviewed Tia Foster, Doug Cullen had made note of her saying that Nigel Trevelyan's family lived near the golf course in Ealing. He'd found two telephone listings that seemed likely prospects, and had tried both numbers on a regular basis over the weekend, without result. This morning one of them had answered. The woman had sounded Punjabi, and had disavowed any knowledge of a Nigel Trevelyan.

Having exhausted all his other leads for Chloe, and having found Michael Yarwood in his office at last, but ensconced in a committee meeting, Cullen had decided to check out the second address in person.

He'd also had another agenda, a personal one, and had been glad of an excuse that allowed him to drive west from his flat in Euston, rather than south to the Borough. It took him half an hour in morning traffic to reach Kensington High Street, and the closer he got, the more reluctant he became to carry out his intentions.

But he knew if he backed out now, he might never get his courage up again, so he steeled himself and went on. He found a parking spot on a back street behind St. Mary's Church, and walked quickly to the High Street.

It was too early for the shops to open for business, but when he peered in the window of the home furnishings boutique, the sales assistant recognized him and unlocked the door with a smile.

"Doug! What are you doing here?"

"I've come to see Stella," he said, feeling his mouth go dry. "Is she in yet?"

"In the stockroom. Go on back."

He made his way through aisles filled with ribbon-tied

linens and bundles of dried flowers, silk-tasseled lampshades, vases, mirrors, gardening implements—the inclusion of which he found very odd—and things he couldn't even put a name to. He felt, as he always did in this place, like the proverbial bull in the china shop.

The scent of potpourri wafted out from the stockroom, and he stopped for a moment in the doorway, stifling a sneeze. Stella stood with her back to him, carefully refolding a flower-sprigged quilt. She wore a twinset in a pale yellow that set off her icy blond looks, with the cardigan tossed casually over her shoulders, and pearls. She was flawless, and faultless, and he'd come to the terrible realization that he didn't love her.

"Maddie," she said, sensing a presence behind her, "if you could hand me another bolt of the raffia—"

"Stella."

She whirled around, dropping the cord she'd lifted to tie round the quilt. "Dougie! What are you doing here? Are you— Is everything all right? I've been ringing you since Friday. You said you'd come down if you could get away—"

"I know."

She'd left half a dozen messages on his voice mail, the first few cross, the last, uncharacteristically for Stella, sounding uncertain, and even a little frightened. "I'm sorry," he said. "It's this case. We've had a woman murdered, and now her little girl is missing." He saw her mouth began to thin in an expression of disapproval and irritation, as it did whenever he talked about a case, and he held up his hand to stop her.

"Stella, don't. This is not going to change. I'm not going to change. You're not going to change. I think it's time we gave it a rest."

She stared at him. "I— You don't mean—"

"I'm good at my job, Stella. I can't go on apologizing for it."

"But things will be different, when you're promoted—"

"No, they won't. I'll only have more responsibility, and you wouldn't like it any better." He smiled at her, trying to ease the sting. "Besides, there must be dozens of blokes with trust funds dying to take you away for a country weekend."

Her pale blue eyes grew hard. "Meaning you don't care?"

"No, of course I care. I only meant—"

"You've found some bloody policewoman to shag, haven't you, Dougie?" she spat at him, crossing her arms tightly beneath her small breasts.

"No, I—I only want what's best for both of us," he protested, cursing the flush he felt staining his cheeks. "Stella, listen—"

"You always were a lousy liar, Doug, and too innocent to walk God's earth. What do you think I've been doing all those weekends you couldn't be bothered to join me?" She saw his shock and smiled. "What did you expect, Sleeping Beauty?" Turning away from him, she began retying the folded quilt. "Now, just bugger off, will you, and don't keep your prison wardress waiting." The raffia snapped in her fingers.

The address in Ealing wasn't on the golf course, but near enough that Cullen thought Nigel Trevelyan might have felt justified in fudging his geography a bit. The house was detached, built of rose-colored brick with white trim, set back on a tree-lined road.

As he pulled up across the street, Cullen saw yellowed newspapers piled in the shadow of the porch, and a collection of advertising circulars decorating the doorknob. He swore aloud. No wonder the people hadn't answered their bloody telephone.

Now he really *was* buggered. He'd used up his last lead, and a good part of a morning that could have been spent pursuing something more productive. The day, which had begun with such promise, had darkened, and a splatter of raindrops rattled across the windscreen on a gust of wind.

Well, he could at least talk to the neighbors, find out if he had the right Trevelyans. He sighed and reached for the door handle, then sat back, resting his hands on the steering wheel, as he replayed Stella's parting words once again. Stung pride and guilt and relief jumbled all together in his mind, and he couldn't begin to sort them out. There would be time for that, he knew, and time for regret, as well, but now he had a job to get on with.

Checking for oncoming traffic before reaching again for the door handle, he glanced in the side mirror and froze. A girl was walking up the street towards the house and his car. Young, brunette, she trudged head down, hands laden with two plastic carrier bags. He caught only a glimpse of her face as she shrugged her hair back with an irritated twitch of her shoulder, but he would have known it anywhere. He had seen it, over and over, on a loop of security cam videotape.

Chloe Yarwood looked younger than she had in the film, and thinner. Her skirt was too short, and made her white legs look oddly vulnerable, rather than sexy. As she passed the car, he reached for the cold coffee in his console and glanced away from her as he sipped. That was the one good thing about his old Astra—the car that had so humiliated Stella— it attracted no notice at all.

Once Chloe had passed him, he watched her again, openly. She turned into the drive of the house and walked, not towards the front door, but towards the back of the property, and he saw what he hadn't noticed before—there was an outbuilding at the end of the drive, set back behind the house. When she reached it, she transferred both bags to one hand, unlocked the door, and slipped inside.

Cullen jumped out of the car and followed. He didn't want to give her time to get comfortable. There were no cars in the drive and he hoped he'd caught her alone. It was only

as he knocked on the door that he remembered Nigel
Trevelyan didn't have a driving license, but then it was too
late for caution.

There was no answer, and not a peep of sound from
within. The quiet seemed suddenly to hold a palpable sense
of fear, and he knew she was listening just the other side of
the door.

"Chloe Yarwood? I'm Detective Sergeant Cullen, from
Scotland Yard. I'd like a word with you." He waited, then
knocked again. "Come on, Chloe. I know you're in there. If
you don't open up I'll have to call for a patrol car. I'm not
going away."

Another long minute passed. "Chloe!" He'd raised his
hand again when the door swung open. Chloe Yarwood
stared out at him. She looked ill, and terrified, and relieved.

"I'm sorry," she whispered. "I thought you were *them*."

The story came out in bits and starts, between small hiccupping sobs. Cullen sat beside her on an old sofa covered with
a woolen horse rug. The place had obviously been converted
from a garage at some point in its history. The floor was still
concrete, covered only with a couple of dirty rugs, and the
interior walls were unfinished. There was a small cooker and
fridge to one side, and a curtain that he assumed hid the
bathroom facilities. The room's only ambience came from
the half-dozen Harley-Davidson posters tacked to the bare
board walls. It was cold, even now, on a fairly mild day, and
Cullen thought the place must be unbearable in winter.

"Where's your friend Nigel?" he asked, wanting to settle
that little matter straightaway.

Chloe seemed to take it for granted that he knew who
Nigel was. "Gone to France. His family's there for the
month. They have a farm in Normandy."

"And he didn't take you with him?"

"He didn't want any trouble. I can't blame him. It wasn't

Nigel's fault—none of it was. He said I could stay here, as long as I wanted."

"That was good of him," said Cullen, and Chloe nodded, seemingly unaware of the sarcasm.

Now that he knew he didn't have to worry about Nigel Trevelyan popping in unannounced with a shotgun or a blunt instrument, he relaxed a little and studied her more closely. It was hard to see a trace of the smiling girl in the photo Kincaid had found at Tia's flat. "Why don't you start from the beginning, Chloe, and tell me why you went to your father's warehouse on Thursday night."

"You know about that, too? How did you—"

"Security cam in the building across the street. It caught you and Nigel going in."

"Oh." She didn't ask who had identified her from the photo, and he didn't volunteer the information.

"Come on," he encouraged. "What were you doing in the place?"

"There were these blokes, see." She pulled at the hem of her skirt, which had ridden up even farther when she sat down. "I'd been to this club, in the West End. My mum gave me a little money, when I moved out from Dad's, but then Tia didn't charge me rent . . ."

"And?"

She hesitated, picking at a spot on her cheek, then locked her fingers in her lap and said with a sigh, "There were cards. I won a bit at first. But then I lost. They let me keep playing, these blokes, saying I'd be sure to make it back. And it was fun. It was like, every time, anything was possible. But I kept losing."

So it was not Michael Yarwood who had been gambling, but Chloe. It all began to make sense. Doug didn't bother to tell her that the mark always lost, and that the only reason they'd let her ride so long was that they'd seen the potential for making a bigger profit.

"And then"—she gave another little hiccup—"then one night they turned me away from the table. They—they told me how much I'd lost." She paled even at the memory of it. "They said I had to give them the money. When I said I didn't have it, they said I'd have to get it or—or they'd hurt me."

"They wanted you to ask your dad?"

Nodding, she tugged harder at the skirt. "But I couldn't. He'd kill me. I mean, it was one thing to make him mad over things like moving out or not finishing my school course, but this—something like this could ruin his career." She shook her head. "I couldn't. They gave me a few days, and I thought if I just didn't go back to the club . . ."

Cullen groaned inwardly. And to think Stella had called *him* innocent. "But they came to you."

"First at Tia's. Then they came to Nigel's friend's flat, where he'd been staying. I don't know how they knew . . ."

If the police had an information network half as good as the London gangsters', thought Cullen, they'd solve every case on the books. Chloe Yarwood had been a perfect pigeon, had possibly even been marked before she ever set foot in the club. Had the gallant Nigel been in on it? he wondered.

"So I thought . . . maybe I could stay at the warehouse at night, and just hang out somewhere in the daytime, you know, where no one knew me, until . . ." Her expression was bleak. She'd have realized by that time that they weren't going to forget about her, but she'd been cornered.

"You had a key to the warehouse?" Doug prompted her, gently.

"I'd made it for a lark. I'd told Nigel that Daddy was going to give me the top-floor flat, when it was finished, and I'd wanted to show it to him. I got him to go with me that night. He was going to leave for France, after the blokes came round his flat, and I didn't want . . ."

"You didn't want to be alone."

"No." She glanced up at Cullen, then back at her hands. "We went in, and I showed him round a bit. I had a torch. We went upstairs . . . and after a while, we heard voices. I thought—I thought it was those guys, looking for me, but then we heard a woman. It was a woman and a man, and they were arguing. There was something—I don't know." Her shoulders jerked. "I got really scared. We got our—Nige and I got put together again, you know? And then we ran down the stairs, as quietly as we could, and out the back door.

"Nige left. He went—I don't know, to another friend's, I think. He—he didn't want to take me with him. But I was afraid to go back to Tia's, and I kept thinking about the woman I'd heard. She'd sounded frightened. I walked for an hour or two, and then I went back.

"But the warehouse was on fire. It was . . . terrible. The heat and the smoke, and the shouting. I thought maybe *they'd* done it, to show me they meant business. And then, the next morning, when I heard about the body, I thought maybe they'd thought it was me . . . or, I don't know what I thought. I just wanted to disappear, and I couldn't bear my dad finding out it was all my fault . . . His building . . . He loved that building . . ."

"Chloe . . ." Doug tried to sort out the relevant bits of her story. "Could you or Nigel have started the fire? Did either of you smoke, or light a match, while you were there?"

"No." She looked horrified. "We don't smoke, and I told you, I had a torch. Why would I light a match?"

He thought about the CCTV film and what it had not shown. "Chloe, did you unlock the back door before you and Nigel went upstairs?"

"Well, yeah. I was showing him my private entrance, like, and we looked up at the balconies. Then we went up. I never thought of anyone coming in—"

"When you and Nigel ran out, did you see anything? Did you see the man and the woman?"

She shook her head.

"Did you recognize the voices?"

"No." She frowned and chewed on a fingernail. "No, but I heard her say something like 'How could you, of all people, when you knew what would happen?' It didn't make any sense."

"And him? Did you hear what he said?"

"No. It was just that one bit, as we went out the door."

"Do you know what time it was, when you left the warehouse that first time?"

"We can't have been there more than half an hour," she said slowly. "Half-past ten, maybe."

"Good girl." He patted her shoulder. "One more thing, and then we'll get you out of here. Did you ever know a woman named Laura Novak?"

"No. Who is she?"

"Right." Doug stood up, avoiding the question. It would be some time before they released Laura Novak's name. "Get your things together, luv. You'll need to come into the station with me, to make a statement, but first we're going to your dad's office."

"My dad?" Her voice rose in a squeak. "But I don't want him to—"

"Chloe, your dad's been desperate with worry," he said, adding with certainty, "The blokes from the club went to him, probably when they didn't get anything out of you on the first try. Your dad thought the fire was a warning to him that they'd kill you if he didn't find the money. And then, for a while, after he saw the videotape, he thought the body was yours."

At daybreak, Harriet got up and crossed the room to the chest by the window. Trying to ignore the growing pain in her arm, she ate the last of the apricots and picked at the dried crust of oatmeal in the bowl. Then she tilted the water glass above her mouth, licking at the last drops. That made her dizzy, and she crawled unsteadily back to bed.

She waited, then, for the sound of footsteps and the creaking of the door, at first with dread and then, as her hunger and thirst grew worse, with dread and longing, but no one came.

After a while, even that ceased to matter so much. Her arm was swollen and hot to the touch, and she shivered and sweated in turn.

She thought she heard the patter of rain against the window, but the sound faded away as she drifted in and out of a restless sleep. In her dreams, she wandered in a long corridor filled with endless rows of doors, hearing voices she could never quite reach.

As noon approached, Kincaid called Maura Bell and Cullen into their temporary office. "Maura, will you take charge of coordinating the searches of Tony Novak's flat and car? Doug, you can take the statements from the Yarwoods. I've got to go, but I'll be back as soon as I can." He meant to get a bite of lunch, then to meet Gemma, Kit, and their solicitor at the family court. "You'll let me know if there's any news about Harriet?"

"Right, guv," said Cullen, then he hesitated a moment before adding, "Good luck with the hearing."

Kincaid nodded his thanks and left the station, his mind occupied with sifting and sorting what they'd learned to date.

When Gemma had called a few minutes earlier to say she'd pick Kit up from school, he'd told her about Rose Kearny's theory, and the news about Laura.

She'd listened in silence as he confirmed what she'd already guessed. After a moment, she said quietly, "You know

Harriet's running out of time, don't you? Every hour she's missing lessens our chances of finding her alive."

"I know," he told her, "but I've run out of ideas." They'd put out an all-points bulletin, now that they were sure the child was not with her mother. He and Bell had sent uniformed officers to interview the children and personnel at Harriet's school, to reinterview hospital staff who had worked with Laura and with Elaine Holland, and to search for any useful background information on Elaine.

At least they had reunited one child with a parent. Michael Yarwood, Cullen said, had crushed his daughter to him in a spasm of relief, then shaken her and called her an idiot, then hugged her again. Yarwood admitted that the men from the club had threatened him, and that he'd feared Chloe dead when he couldn't reach her after the fire. He'd gone on in desperate hope, trying to raise the money, trying to find Chloe, and cursing the involvement of Scotland Yard.

"I couldn't very well protest when the AC asked you to look into things," he'd said to Kincaid when he arrived at the station. "Not without buggering my own pitch."

"You should have been honest with us from the beginning," Kincaid had told him, but without great conviction. In Yarwood's place, he might have withheld the truth, too.

"Do you think those bastards were responsible for this?" Yarwood asked, beginning to sound like a crusading politician again. "Do you think they killed that poor woman as an example? Or because they thought she was Chloe?"

Kincaid thought back over what Cullen had told him. "No. First of all, I don't think they wanted Chloe dead. That would have meant killing the goose before it laid the golden egg. And from what Chloe's told us, it seems pretty obvious that the victim knew her killer."

"Then why kill her in my warehouse? And why burn it?" Yarwood shook his head. "I'm sorry. That sounds callous. I only meant—"

"We don't know. We don't know if the fire was set as the last attempt to hide the victim's identity, or if there was an unrelated motive. We may never, in fact, prove that the fire was set at all." Kincaid couldn't broadcast the fact that they suspected they might be dealing with a serial arsonist turned murderer, not to someone with Yarwood's media connections, and not when Yarwood stood to gain by making such news public.

But the conversation had started him thinking about Rose's theory again, and as he paid for his sandwich at a takeaway near the station, he had an idea. Glancing at his watch to make sure he could squeeze in a few more minutes, he went back into the station and found Sarah, the sergeant who had helped with the CCTV video.

"Can you print me another still from the tape?" he asked. When he'd shown her what he wanted, he ate his sandwich while waiting for the photo, then drove to Southwark Fire Station.

He found Rose and Bill Farrell sequestered in an unused office, surrounded by a mountain of files. They both looked tired and discouraged. The London Fire Brigade only hired new staff irregularly, and then they were inundated with thousands of applications for a few hundred positions.

"No possibles?" he asked, and they both shook their heads.

Rose sat on the floor against the back wall, her knees drawn up, a box of files beside her.

Kincaid handed her the print he'd made. "Maybe this will help."

She took it and stared at it. "What—where did you get this?"

Hearing the excitement in her voice, Farrell joined her and bent to look.

"It's the man who walked by the Southwark Street warehouse a few minutes after Chloe Yarwood and her friend went inside. He only hesitated a moment as he passed, so we didn't think anything of it. Do you recognize him?"

"Yes. I—I think so." She looked at the time stamp on the print. "But this was only a little after ten. The fire wasn't reported until after midnight."

"Maybe he came back," Kincaid suggested.

"At midnight?" asked Farrell.

"Or earlier, if he killed Laura Novak." Kincaid told them what they'd learned from Chloe Yarwood. "We've no way of knowing exactly when she died, and even if it was nearer ten than twelve, we don't know how long he spent . . . preparing the body."

Rose flinched. "But why this particular woman? I mean, I can understand, in a bizarre sort of way, his wanting to kill a firefighter if he has some sort of grudge against the brigade. But why Laura Novak?"

Kincaid thought again of the words Chloe had overheard. Could Laura have learned about the fires and confronted the arsonist? But how could she have discovered something like that? What connection could she have had with this man?

His phone rang and he snapped it open, irritated at the interruption when he knew he was in danger of running late for Kit's hearing. It was Maura Bell.

"Guv, we've found another body."

"What? Where?" He felt a sick dread. "It's not Harriet—"

"No. But you'd better come. It's Crossbones Graveyard, just behind the Southwark Street warehouse. And we've met her. It's Beverly Brown, the young woman who reported the fire."

"The woman from the shelter? Mouse?" He saw instantly the pinched little face, the hair with its badgerlike white streak.

"Yes. And it looks like she's been strangled."

17

Let us be moral. Let us contemplate existence.

CHARLES DICKENS
Martin Chuzzlewit

THEY MET IN the judge's chambers. It was a comfortable room, anchored by a long, polished, mahogany table. The Honorable Sophie O'Donnell, an attractive woman in her fifties with smartly styled, blond-streaked hair, sat at the head.

On one side were Kit's maternal grandparents, Eugenia and Bob Potts, and their solicitor, a rabbity-faced man named Cavanaugh; on the other, Gemma, Kit, and Miles Kelly, their solicitor. It was shaping up to be the battle of the Irish, thought Gemma, but she couldn't summon a smile. The large clock on the wall behind the judge read straight up two o'clock, and Kincaid hadn't arrived.

Neither party had spoken to the other. Eugenia was in full war paint, her fair hair freshly lacquered, but it seemed to Gemma that her clothes hung too loosely and there was a feverish look to her eyes. Bob merely looked diffident and distressed, the classic henpecked husband, and Gemma wondered if he might someday snap and bite the hand that had led him such a merry dance.

Miles Kelly glanced at Gemma, raising very black eyebrows over very blue eyes, and she gave a tiny, worried shrug. Beside her, Kit sat silent and strained. She'd bought him new gray flannels and a navy blazer for the occasion, and he looked painfully grown up.

The judge glanced at her watch and cleared her throat. "I think, Mr. Kelly, that we should begin, but we seem to be missing your client."

"I know Superintendent Kincaid is on his way, Your Honor," replied Kelly with his most charming smile. "Perhaps he's been detained in traffic. If you could give us just a few more moments—"

Gemma jumped as the mobile phone clipped to her waist began to vibrate. A quick glance at the caller ID told her it was Kincaid. After looking at the judge, who nodded permission, she excused herself and moved a few steps away from the table, turning her back to the room before she answered.

She listened briefly, spoke in monosyllables, and rang off. Then she stood for a moment, trying to get her dismay under control before she faced the others.

When she turned round, Kit said, his voice tight, "He's not coming, is he?"

"Something's happened, Kit," she answered quietly, then spoke to the judge. "Your Honor, Superintendent Kincaid has been unavoidably detained on urgent police business. He apologizes to the court and asks if we can reschedule this meeting at a later time."

"Do sit down, Ms. James," said the judge, sounding very displeased.

As she slipped into her chair, her face blazing with embarrassment, Gemma caught the flash of triumph in Eugenia Potts's eyes.

"This is very irregular," Judge O'Donnell went on, frowning. "Under ordinary circumstances I would not be inclined to grant such a request, but considering the nature of Mr. Kincaid's job, I will think about it." Before Gemma could breathe a sigh of relief, she continued: "However, I must say this gives me serious doubts about Mr. Kincaid's suitability as a guardian for Christopher."

Seeing the protest forming on Kit's face, she raised a hand to silence him. "I've had a brief discussion with Christopher before we began this meeting, and I'm aware of his feelings on the matter. I've also looked over Christopher's father's rather unusual petition requesting that you, Ms. James, and Mr. Kincaid be allowed to provide care for Christopher until he comes of age.

"I'm always most reluctant to disrupt what seems to be a stable home situation, particularly when a child has suffered a loss." She fixed Gemma with a sharp eye. "But the demands of a police officer's job are both heavy and unpredictable, as Mr. Kincaid has demonstrated today, and as both of you are officers of senior rank, I'm not sure you can provide the sort of environment Christopher needs. And as neither of you has any blood tie to the boy, and we don't know what Christopher's mother would have wished for him, I'm inclined to give consideration to his grandparents' petition for custody."

Gemma felt Kit's physical recoil. She touched his arm in reassurance and leaned forward. "Ma'am, may I speak?" When Judge O'Donnell nodded, she said, "You're right. The job is demanding and unpredictable. But there are two of us, and one of us has always managed to be there—"

"That's all very well for the time being. But you'll forgive me, Ms. James, if I say I've seen no evidence of a long-term commitment on the part of you and Mr. Kincaid."

A black pit seemed to open before Gemma. How could she answer that? "I—"

"There's also the matter of Christopher's education. His grandparents have assured the court that they have the means to send him to public school—"

"I don't want to go to public school," broke in Kit, tears of fury starting up in his eyes. "I like it where I am—"

"Your Honor." Eugenia spoke for the first time. "It's just this sort of disrespectful behavior that concerns us. Christopher is obviously living in a household where this is considered acceptable. Nor is he being encouraged to show the interest in his future fitting for a boy his age—"

"You don't know anything," Kit shouted at his grandmother. "I'm going to Cambridge. Lots of kids from comprehensives get into Cambridge—"

Judge O'Donnell rapped her knuckles sharply on the table once. "That's enough, son. I'll not tolerate displays of temper in my chambers, nor reward them." When Kit subsided, his hands clenched in his lap, she turned to Eugenia. "Mrs. Potts, it does worry me that Christopher seems to feel a great deal of hostility towards you."

Eugenia seemed to pale beneath her makeup, but she smiled. "He has some childish grievance over a dog. I'm sure, in time, that it can be overcome."

Clapping a hand on Kit's shoulder, as if fearing the boy might not be able to restrain himself, Miles Kelly said hurriedly, "Ma'am, may I remind you that Kit's father, Ian McClellan, feels that Mr. and Mrs. Potts have never given Kit the proper emotional support in his grief over his mother's death."

"You may remind me all you like, Mr. Kelly, but I don't have to give it credence. It doesn't seem to me that Mr. McClellan has demonstrated much in the way of emotional support himself, by taking a job in Canada and leaving his son behind in England."

Eugenia whispered urgently in Cavanaugh's ear, and when she'd pulled away, he addressed the judge. "Is Your

Honor aware that at the time of the late Mrs. McClellan's death, she and Mr. McClellan were separated? That Mr. McClellan was, in fact, living in the south of France with a young woman? We feel this demonstrates a long-standing lack of responsible behavior concerning his son—"

"That's enough, Mr. Cavanaugh," said the judge with a glance at Kit. "We will adjourn this hearing until further notice." She sighed and stood. "I may very well find that neither party is a fit guardian, without evidence to the contrary."

She had seemed pathetic in life; death had not given her dignity.

Kincaid looked down at Beverly Brown's twisted body. It lay at the far end of a vacant expanse of cracked and weed-infested concrete. Her head was pillowed on a drift of wind-blown rubbish, her small, sneaker-clad feet pushed against the bottom of a rusted metal barrel.

When Maura Bell had said Crossbones Graveyard, he'd thought of a churchyard, with a bit of grass and headstones; not this wasteland, its fence adorned with fluttering ribbons and a few faded wreaths.

"What is this place?" he asked Maura, who stood beside him. She'd been called out immediately when the body had been reported and had identified the victim herself.

The police surgeon had certified death, and they were now waiting for the arrival of the pathologist, the photographer, and the forensics team. The wheels of justice ground slowly, as always, and he tried to control his impatience. The time made no difference now—he'd known by two o'clock that there was no possible way he could get to Kit's hearing. But he couldn't think about that now—his personal concerns would have to wait until he had put this case behind him.

"It was a medieval cemetery, an unconsecrated burial ground for prostitutes and others who couldn't afford proper burial," Maura answered. "When London Transport began work here on the Jubilee Line extension a few years ago, they started digging up bodies. Work was stopped, and the place has been in limbo since. London Transport want to use the property for part of their travel hub; the local residents want a park, with some sort of fitting commemoration for those buried here. Meanwhile, the heroin addicts have a field day."

"I suspected she might be a junkie, when we met her," he said, remembering the girl's edgy pallor.

"She could have met someone here, looking for a buy."

"Maybe. But dealers don't usually strangle their clients." The bruising was clearly visible on the girl's exposed throat.

"A rape gone wrong?" suggested Maura.

"Not unless he dressed her again." He shook his head. "I don't believe this was a random killing, and neither do you. We're a few hundred yards from the warehouse where Laura Novak was killed, not to mention the fact that it was Beverly Brown who reported the fire."

"Could she have seen something else that night?" Maura mused. "But if so, why didn't she report it?"

"Maybe she didn't realize what she'd seen. Maybe she was protecting someone."

"Or maybe she was frightened," Maura said slowly.

"With good reason." He thought of the two little girls, now motherless, like Harriet Novak. Whoever this bastard was, he had to be stopped.

And what of Harriet? Gemma was right, time was running out. He tried to put aside the fear that Harriet was already dead, that they would find her body tossed away like a bit of rubbish, as Beverly Brown had been.

"If this was the same killer," said Maura, "why no attempt to hide the victim's identity this time? Or to hide the body? She wasn't even covered."

Kincaid glanced round the barren lot. "Lack of means? Lack of opportunity?" He grimaced as a gust of wind blew grit in his eyes and a fat raindrop splashed against his cheek. The rain had been teasing since midmorning, advancing and retreating like a shy schoolgirl, but now the sky to the west looked thunderous. "Let's get that tarp up," he called out to the uniformed officers. "The Home Office pathologist won't be happy if her trace evidence gets washed away."

When a car pulled through the cordon of patrol cars and Kate Ling got out, he found he wasn't surprised.

"Duncan," she said as she reached them. "If you really want to see me every few days, you could just buy me a drink."

"Hullo, Kate. You remember Inspector Bell, from the other day?"

Already pulling on her gloves, Kate nodded at Maura. "I hear you got an ID on the warehouse corpse."

"News travels fast in exalted circles," Kincaid told her. "That's about all we've got, so far, and now . . ." He gestured at the body before them. "This young woman was a resident at the women's shelter across the street from the warehouse."

Kate squatted, graceful even in such an awkward position, and gently tilted the girl's head back with her gloved fingers. "There are obvious signs of manual strangulation, as I'm sure you're aware." She pulled back the eyelids, then stretched her hand across the throat, matching her own hand to the bruises. Her finger and thumb fell short on either side by half an inch. "Not a particularly large hand, either, but he—or she—seems to have been strong enough to subdue her single-handedly."

"Right-handed?"

"Looks that way."

"Could she have been sedated?" asked Maura.

"Did she shoot up, you mean?" Kate pushed up the right sleeve of the girl's sweater, then repeated the process with the left. "There are some tracks, but nothing that looks terribly recent. Unless she injected somewhere else."

"Can you tell if she fought her attacker?"

The pathologist lifted the hands in turn, examining the fingertips.

Beverly's nails were bitten to the quick, and one cuticle bore a smear of dried blood. "Hers?" Kincaid asked, bending down to look more closely.

"I think so, but . . ." Kate isolated the middle finger on the right hand. "Even as short as her nails are, we may have some trace evidence here." She looked up. "You know I can't tell you much more until I get her on the table. I can't even be absolutely certain that strangulation was the cause of death."

He raised an eyebrow. "Time of death? Come on, live dangerously, Doc."

"You never give up, do you?" asked Kate, flashing him a grin. Then she turned back to the body, checking the exposed skin of the arms for lividity, testing the limbs and neck for rigor. "I'll have to get a temp, but off the cuff I'd say at least twelve hours. But if you quote me, I'll deny it." She stood up and reached for her instruments. "Oh, and livor mortis seems to be very well defined. I don't think she was moved from this spot."

"Well," said Kincaid. "At least this time we have an idea where to start."

Gemma had driven Kit back to school, insisting that he finish his afternoon classes. He hadn't objected. He hadn't spoken at all during the drive from the court to Notting Hill, and his silence worried Gemma more than any angry tirade.

When she stopped the car, she said, "It'll be all right, Kit. We'll work things out."

He'd given her a look that told her he knew it was an empty promise, and when she tried to hug him, he pulled away. As she watched him walk into the school gates, she felt a rush of helplessness, followed by a fury that left her trembling.

Not trusting herself to talk to Kincaid over the phone, Gemma had rung Doug Cullen for directions to the crime scene. She'd left her schedule free for the afternoon, as she hadn't known how long the court proceeding would take, and she decided that anything pending could wait a bit longer. She was going to Southwark.

Now she ducked under the tape strung round the edge of the rubble-strewn vacant ground, then stood for a moment, picking out Kincaid's figure among the group huddled round a tarp at the far side of the lot. Their faces were briefly illuminated by the photographer's flash and she recognized Kate Ling and Maura Bell.

Kincaid looked up then, and when he saw her, he came quickly to meet her.

His smile of greeting faded as he saw her face. "Gemma. Is everything okay? How did it go?"

"It was a disaster. It was bloody well dreadful, if you want to know." All her pent-up anger and worry spilled out in a flood of bitter words. "It couldn't have been worse if we were axe murderers. Eugenia seemed plausible, while we looked like irresponsible parents—not that the judge could see that we had any qualifications to *be* Kit's parents. Without proof that you're Kit's natural father—"

"I'll talk to her—I can explain—"

"And the worst thing about it was that at least part of what she said was true. Ian *is* irresponsible. And we're *not* always there for Kit. You weren't there for him today."

Kincaid looked devastated, and Gemma knew that if she'd meant to wound him, she'd succeeded.

"I know I let him down," he said in appeal. "I'll make it up to him somehow. Surely the judge will see reason." He gestured towards the group gathered round the body. "I couldn't leave today. I had no choice."

"You did have a choice. You chose the job," she spat back at him. But even as she said it, she saw the mortuary attendants lift Beverly Brown's small form onto a body bag, and she wondered whether she would have done the same.

When Kincaid and Maura Bell rang the bell at the shelter, the door buzzed open immediately. The stairs seemed steeper than the last time he'd climbed them, the stairwell more dank and airless. His legs felt leaden and his shirt, still damp from the sudden soaking they'd received at the graveyard, clung to his skin as tenaciously as Gemma's words haunted his conscience. As he followed Maura upwards, he was grateful to her for pretending she hadn't witnessed their very public row.

They found Kath Warren waiting for them in the first-floor corridor, an anxious expression on her face.

"We've just now rung the police," she said. "I didn't expect to see you so soon."

"Why? What's happened?" Kincaid asked as they followed her back into the office. Kath moved a stack of files from a chair so that they could sit, but neither accepted the offer.

Jason Nesbitt was on the phone, but he quickly rang off and stood up to shake their hands. "It's Mouse," he said. "Beverly Brown. She seems to have gone walkabout on us. The girls woke up this morning and came looking for their mummy, so she must have gone out sometime in the night."

"I thought you had a sign-out system?" Kincaid said with a quick glance at Maura. He wanted to hear what Kath and Jason had to say before he revealed anything.

Kath looked uncomfortable. "We do, but Bev didn't sign out, and Shawna, the girl on the desk last night, didn't see her leave." She sighed. "Shawna's not always as dependable as she might be. We may have to do away with the telly in the staff room."

"Why have you waited until now to report her missing? Weren't you worried about her?" Maura sounded more puz-

zled than accusing, and Kincaid thought it a giant leap in fi-
nesse.

"It's not the first time this has happened," Kath said reluctantly. "The last time she managed to sneak back in before she was missed, and we only learned what had
happened when the children talked about waking up in the
night and missing her. The residents aren't given the security code, you see—they have to be buzzed in—but sometimes they piggyback on one another. We thought she'd turn
up this morning, trying to bluff her way out of it, but . . ."
She looked at the clock.

"What happens if the residents go absent without leave
like that?" Kincaid asked.

"We try to give the women every chance, if we can see
they're making an effort, but Bev's pushed it too far this
time. It sets a bad example for the others. I'm afraid she'll
have to go."

Kincaid caught Maura's quick glance, and this time he
nodded.

"That's one decision you'll be spared," Maura said,
watching their faces intently. "Beverly won't be coming
back. She's dead. Her body was found near here a few hours
ago."

There was an instant's silence that seemed to stretch, vi-
brating like a high-tension wire. Kath stared at them, one
hand pressed to her mouth. Jason sank to the edge of the
desk, his eyes wide.

"You're sure?" whispered Kath. "You're sure it's her?"

"There's no question," Kincaid said. "I'm sorry."

"Oh, shit. The daft little cow." Jason had tears in eyes
now. "Look, it's all my fault."

The others all stared at him in surprise.

"She's a repeater. Mouse." When Kincaid and Maura
looked at him blankly, Jason made an effort to explain. "She
can't stay away from her husband. He's not a bad bloke,

really—has a steady job as an electrician. They only row when she goes back on the drugs, and then he tries to shake some sense into her. After that, she comes in here for a few weeks, then they make it up, and she goes back to him. Until the next time."

Kath was shaking her head. "But, Jason—"

"I suspected it. I suspected she was seeing him again. But I didn't say anything because I didn't want to get her in trouble. And now—he must have—" His mouth twisted with distress.

"Jason." Kath went to him, touched his arm. "It's not your fault. You couldn't have prevented this."

"We will be interviewing Beverly's husband," Kincaid put in, "but I think you might be jumping to conclusions a bit here." He had their attention now, and there was something interesting in the tableau they presented, Kath's hand hovering protectively over Jason's shoulder. "Earlier this morning we identified the body in the warehouse fire as Laura Novak. That makes two women with a connection to this shelter that have died in the last four days. That's too much of a coincidence for my taste."

Kath gasped as if she'd taken a body blow. "Oh, my God. Laura. But Laura . . . Laura hardly knew Bev. Why would—Oh, God," she said again. "I can't believe Laura's dead. I thought she must have gone away somewhere, with her little girl."

Kincaid noticed that the offering of comfort was one-sided. Jason made no move towards Kath but sat absently loosening the collar of his designer shirt, his face blank with shock.

"We'll need to get Beverly's husband's name and address, as well as any other contact information," Kincaid began, but Kath interrupted him.

"But then, if Laura's dead . . . Where's Harriet?"

"We don't know," Kincaid answered, but he was suddenly

distracted. The tab on one of the files Kath had transferred from the chair to the corner of the desk had caught his eye. *Clover Howes,* it read. It was an odd name. Where had he heard it before?

The skies opened up just as Gemma reached her car, dumping a brief deluge as if providing fitting punctuation to her conversation with Kincaid. She sat, thinking, while the rain pounded roof and windscreen.

She'd been unfair. She knew she'd been unfair; she knew that with this new death, and Harriet still missing, he needed all his focus on the case, but she hadn't been able to stop herself.

Bloody hell, she was useless. She'd failed the missing six-year-old. She'd failed Harriet Novak. She'd failed Kit today in the hearing. Had she even, a mean little voice whispered in her mind, failed her own unborn child? Everyone said nothing could have prevented her miscarriage, but deep in her heart she'd never quite believed it.

No! She pounded her palms on the steering wheel until they smarted. She'd been down that road before—she certainly wasn't going that way again. There was too much at stake.

Then she realized the rain was letting up, the shower moving away as quickly as it had come. A few straggling drops splattered against the windscreen as a watery sunlight emerged. When Gemma rolled down the car window, the air smelled so clean and full of promise that she felt ashamed of herself for even such a brief descent into self-pity. She'd always prided herself on her determination; it was time she demonstrated some evidence of it. She wasn't going to give up, not on Kit, not on Harriet, and it was Harriet who needed her help most urgently.

Frowning, she tried to recall everything that she had learned about Elaine Holland since her first phone call from

Winnie. Then she put the car into gear and drove to Ufford Street.

To her astonishment, as she pulled up to the curb in front of Fanny's house, she saw Winnie wheeling Fanny's chair down the ramp. They both waved to her as she got out of the car.

"What's happened?" she asked, hurrying to them. "Is everything all right?"

"We decided it was high time Fanny got out for a bit," explained Winnie. "We're going for a drink at the Hope and Anchor."

"Will you join us?" Fanny smiled, and Gemma realized she did look better. Her eyes were clear, and her face seemed less pinched, as if a constant pain had eased.

"Nothing would suit me better." Realizing that she'd been dreading entering the close confines of the house, Gemma thought it no wonder Fanny seemed relieved.

They walked companionably down the street, Winnie pushing Fanny's chair, and when they reached the pub the staff made much fuss over settling them at a table. It was a slow time of the afternoon and the place was empty except for a few solitary patrons with newspapers and a man tinkling idly, softly, at the keys of the upright piano. He segued from bits of Gershwin to Cole Porter to random snatches that Gemma didn't recognize, and the sound made her feel unaccountably sad.

When they'd got their drinks—Pimm's for Winnie and Fanny, a half pint of cider for Gemma, who wanted to keep a clear head—she told them everything that had happened since she'd seen them the previous day.

"Fanny, I don't want to distress you," she went on, "but I want to talk about Elaine. I've just realized how many different stories she told about her background, and I thought if we could put them all together, we might find something in common."

"I don't mind, really." Absently, Fanny rotated her glass in the center of the beer mat. She wore a pearl-buttoned cardigan fastened to the throat, and her cheeks looked faintly pink from the warmth or the excitement of the outing. "I feel—I don't know. Once I knew she wasn't coming back . . . It's as if I was carrying a weight, but I never realized it until it was lifted." Her face fell. "But Elaine—wherever she is—I don't like to think of Elaine with a child."

Nor did Gemma. "Elaine told Tony Novak that she was married to a commercial traveler, and that she worked at an estate agent's here in the Borough.

"She told her coworkers at Guy's that she grew up in Gloucestershire and only came to London when her parents died, but the girl I spoke with swore that Elaine's accent was native to the Borough."

"And she told me that her parents had emigrated from Canada," said Fanny, "that her mother committed suicide when she was a child, and that she took care of her ill father until he died."

Gemma realized suddenly that the music had stopped and the piano player was gone. She had never seen his face. For a moment she wondered if she had imagined him, as Elaine had imagined entire lives. Aloud, she mused, "We know the first story was a complete fabrication. Could one of the others have been the truth?"

"What I wonder," said Winnie slowly, "is whether she told Tony Novak her parents were dead?"

"You think that's the common thread, her parents' deaths?"

"There's something else." Winnie fingered the silver cross she wore beneath her collar. "Fanny, before Roberta left, did Elaine ever stay when Roberta brought you communion on Sundays? Because I remember that when I first came, I never saw her, but after a few weeks she began to hover in the doorway, and then after another week or two she would come into the room, a bit like a stray animal gaining confidence. I assumed it was the church she disliked, but what if it was the priest? What if she was afraid of the priest?"

Gemma frowned. "I'm not following you."

"Maybe Elaine was afraid of Roberta."

"Elaine was never home when Roberta came during the week," said Fanny. "And now that I think of it, the few times Roberta dropped by unannounced on a weekend, Elaine went straight up to her room without meeting her. And then on Sundays, of course, she was always out of the house."

"That settles it, then." Winnie's pleasant face glowed with missionary zeal. "We'll ring Roberta straightaway."

Winnie had drawn her mobile from her belt and flipped it open when Gemma felt hers vibrate. Gemma pulled her phone from its clip, murmuring, "Sorry, sorry," and feeling absurdly like a dueling gunslinger in an old western.

It was Kincaid. She found her throat suddenly tight and had to swallow before she answered. "Hey," she said lightly. "I'm sorry about—"

"Gemma, hang on a second." She caught the muffled slur of his voice as he spoke to someone else, then he came back on the line. He hadn't heard her, she realized. He hadn't heard her at all.

"Gemma, listen," he said without preamble. "I need your help. Do you still have the list of names you and Doug found in Laura Novak's house?"

18

❧

"But we never knows wot's hidden in each other's
hearts; and if we had glass winders there, we'd need
keep the shetters up, some on us, I do assure you!"

CHARLES DICKENS
Martin Chuzzlewit

SHE HADN'T THOUGHT of what she would do with the
child. She hadn't thought past wanting to hurt *him,* to pun-
ish him for discarding her without even a thought of apology, as if she had never been more than a convenience.

Nor had she meant to come back to this house ever again.
She'd locked it up after her mother's funeral, set up an account out of her parents' estate to pay the taxes, so that
there'd be no connection with the new name she'd taken,
and walked away. Why she hadn't sold the place, she'd
never quite been able to fathom. When she tried to think
about it, her mind slithered sideways and the memories
crowded, clamoring, at the gates she'd refused to breach.

But then Tony had betrayed her; she had taken his daughter—oh, so easily—and there had been nowhere else to go.

And the house had settled back around her, the smells and sounds fastening into her flesh like little claws, making it more and more difficult to separate the past from the present.

The room drew her—but no, there was another child in the room now, a different little girl who had been bad. Or had she? The confusion made her feel ill. She hadn't slept, despite the pills she'd taken from Fanny, nor had she eaten much. The bits of food she'd found in the pantry stuck in her throat, dry as the dust of the years gone by.

When she tried to close her eyes, she saw the stairwell spinning, the bottom rushing towards her like a vortex. What had she done? No, she hadn't meant the girl to fall, hadn't pushed her, no, not this time.

Or had she?

All she knew for certain was that she had to get out, out of this house, before it devoured her. But where could she go? Not back to Fanny's, not back to her job at the hospital—all that was finished, a life that seemed as distant as another universe. But . . . she had created a new life before; she could do it again. A new name, a new place, a new story—any story but this.

But what of the child? She climbed the stairs and stood outside the door. There was no sound from within. What would she find if she looked inside?

She should open the door, she knew, but the fear swept through her, leaving her trembling and sick. What child would she let out, if she opened the door? Would she ever be free of the little girl who had lived in that room?

At last she turned and retraced her way down the stairs, and as she went out of the house, she locked the door behind her.

Rose wiped her hands against the legs of her jeans for perhaps the hundredth time. Her fingertips had begun to crack from the hours of contact with the dry and dusty paper, and her throat felt parched as sandpaper. She had shifted position from table to floor and back to the table, but her back ached as if she'd been carrying hose all day.

"Want some coffee?" Bill Farrell asked as he set another stack of folders beside her. The initial reserve she'd felt with him had evaporated over the long day, and by now she'd almost forgotten to think of him as a senior officer.

"No, thanks," she said, looking at the cups littering the room. "If I get any more buzzed I'll have to run laps round the room while I read these bloody things." She stared in dismay at the number of boxes yet to examine and tried not to rub the dirt on her fingers into her eyes.

At least the photo brought by Superintendent Kincaid had allowed them to organize their search more efficiently. Farrell had begun by winnowing out only applicants who were male and Caucasian for Rose's perusal—with the help of the photo he was able to narrow his selection to those applicants whose photos bore at least some resemblance to the man caught by the security cam.

But in the end, it was Rose, rummaging through a fresh box on her own while Farrell had gone for more coffee, who found the file.

"Holy shit," she whispered, looking from the application photo to the print, then staring back at the file in stunned astonishment.

When Farrell came back into the room, she was standing, waving the folder at him. "You're not going to believe this. His name is Jimmy Braidwood."

"What?" Farrell set the coffee down among the files on the table, careless of the sloshing, and coming to stand beside her, looked at the file. "You're not serious? As in James Braidwood?"

James Braidwood had been the celebrated superintendent of the London Fire Engine Establishment, and he had been killed in the great Tooley Street fire of 1861, crushed under a falling wall. "Yeah. Although it's just 'Jimmy' on the application, not 'James.' No wonder this guy has such a thing about Victorian fires."

"And you're sure it's him?"

She looked again at the photos, comparing them both with her memory of the man glimpsed so briefly at the scene of the fire, and a rush of nausea made her swallow hard. "Yes. And look," she added, flipping through the file. "He aced both the written and physical exams. It says he was rejected due to psychological assessment. There's a note attached by the interviewer."

She read it aloud. *"Mr. Braidwood demonstrates a profound lack of the cooperative skills needed in today's firefighting environment. He also displays a marked bias against females and persons of color, and in my opinion, suffers from delusions concerning an imagined connection with the legendary James Braidwood, and is a likely candidate for antisocial behavior."*

Farrell whistled. "Good God. The bastard's a psychopath."

Rose's queasiness gave way to an icy calm. "We knew that," she said with cold conviction, thinking of Bryan Simms's burned and broken body.

Bill Farrell took the file from her and flipped back to the opening page. "At the time of application, he was employed by a private security firm—"

"The uniform." Rose saw again the flash of dark blue sleeve.

"And it gives his home address as Blackfriars Road. If we're right, he's certainly set his fires close to home."

"And he's escalating in leaps and bounds. What I don't understand is why he killed Laura Novak. Could she have somehow learned what he was doing?"

"There's no obvious connection between them." Farrell looked again at the CCTV photo, his brow creased in concentration. "From the video, it looks as if he happened to see the door that Chloe Yarwood had left open. But he works for a security firm, so he might have known, or guessed, that the premises across the street had a surveillance camera—"

"So he checks out the side entrance, just in case, and finds it unlocked, too," said Rose. "What if— We know that Laura Novak had a connection with the women's shelter, which overlooks that door. Maybe she was at the shelter for some reason, saw Braidwood go in, and confronted him."

"If she saw him, why didn't she just call the police?" argued Farrell. "And that doesn't account for the conversation Chloe Yarwood overheard, unless Laura knew him. His uniform alone wouldn't have been enough to prompt her comment." He shook his head. "I don't think we can go any further without more evidence. We'll have to—"

"I think we're running out of time, sir." Rose faced him, tense with the sense of foreboding that had plagued her since the first fire. "He took a huge risk yesterday. I think he's been working up to something, something big, and now he's out of control."

"What could—" Farrell stared at her, enlightenment and dismay dawning in his face. "You think he means to re-create Tooley Street, where Braidwood died a hero. Not just with similar fires, but the real thing. Hay's Galleria?"

"What would be more fitting?" Hay's Wharf, known as "the Larder of London," had, like Cotton's Wharf, been one of the great Victorian riverside warehouses. It lay between Tooley Street and the Thames, and been beautifully restored as Hay's Galleria, a Bankside complex filled with restaurants, shops, and crafts stalls. A fire there would be disastrous, and if started in daylight, as the last fire had been, could cost civilian lives.

"Dear God. If you're right, Rose, we can't wait. We'll have to bring him in now, and hope we can find substantiation. But we can't talk to him without police present." Farrell pulled out his mobile phone. "I'm calling Kincaid."

Kincaid had accompanied Maura Bell back to Borough station, leaving the uniformed officers to search Beverly Brown's meager belongings and contact social services regarding care of the children. But while Bell and Cullen tried to find an address for one Gary Brown, husband of the late Beverly, thought by Kath Warren to live somewhere in Walworth, he stood at the window overlooking Borough High Street and thought.

He knew he'd come across the name on the shelter's file somewhere else in the course of the case; it was simply a matter of dredging through all the accumulated information until he found the right bit.

When it came to him, he turned and said to Cullen, "Hey, Doug. Gemma copied out a list of names you found at Laura Novak's. Did you keep the original?"

"Sorry, guv. I left it for forensics, in case it had prints. Was it important?"

"I don't know yet." He remembered Gemma showing him the copy she'd made in her notebook. Would she have it with her now? He'd rung her to ask when Maura called out that she'd found an address for Gary Brown and that Brown had a previous conviction for assault. Covering the phone's mouthpiece, Kincaid said, "Gemma, hang on a second. Somebody find me a pen and some paper." When Cullen complied, he copied the list Gemma read to him. Clover Howes was one of the six names.

Ringing off, he said to Cullen and Maura, "I'm going back to the shelter. There's something we've missed here. I'd be willing to wager that these other women on the list were shelter clients, but what was Laura Novak's interest in them?"

"You think Kath Warren can tell us?" asked Cullen.

"It's worth a try. Maura, if you want to follow up on Brown—"

"I'll be damned if you'll send me haring after a domestic if you've got a real lead." She gave him a ferocious glare. "That's bollocks. I'm going with you."

Kincaid grinned. "Right, then. Brown can wait. Doug?"

"Count me in."

They found Kath Warren alone in the office, tidying up in preparation for the end of the day. Lines of exhaustion aged her usually pert face, and she looked up at them anxiously. "If this is about the children," she said, "we're still waiting for social services. I'll stay until they come. We haven't been able to locate any other family to contact—"

"No, Kath, sit down a minute, please," Kincaid said, motioning her back to her desk. "We just have a few more questions we need to ask you." She sat slowly, and Kincaid took the chair that had previously been occupied by the stack of files while Cullen and Maura stood unobtrusively at the back of the room.

He unfolded the list from his pocket and handed it to Kath. "Are these women all clients of the shelter?"

"What—" Kath glanced at the sheet, and he thought she paled beneath her makeup. "Where did you get this?"

"From Laura Novak's desk. Why would Laura have made a list of these names?"

Kath looked dismayed. "I'd no idea Laura knew. This wasn't something we were eager to advertise to the board of directors."

"What did Laura know, Kath? What's special about these women?"

The paper trembled in Kath's hand. "I told you the other day. Sometimes, when we place women in new situations, in spite of all our precautions, their abusers find them. These women—all of these women were tracked down by their husbands or boyfriends. One of them, Clover Howes, is dead. Her husband assaulted her with a poker."

"That's why you were moving her file," Kincaid said slowly. "Six women? In what time period, Kath?"

"A year." She put the sheet of paper down on her desk and smoothed it flat. "Six in the last year."

"That's pushing the law of averages, I'd say. And you didn't tell your board about this?"

"We . . . we wanted to try to resolve it. We suspected that one of the regular clients, like Beverly, might have been selling information to the other women's partners. Or even one of our own staff—I told you we'd had suspicions about Shawna, who works the night desk. We know she's taken bribes from the residents to overlook minor infractions."

"Like sneaking out at night?"

"Or alcohol in the rooms, that sort of thing. But we had no proof of anything more—"

"Wait a minute." The pieces had begun to fall into place, all too clearly. Motive, means, opportunity—and the fact that when Kath Warren said *we* she wasn't using the royal first person. He stood, leaning over the desk. "Kath, where's Jason?"

"Oh." Kath looked round, as if expecting Jason to pop up. "He left early. A family emergency, a sick auntie in Kent. He had to drive down on Saturday as well."

"Really? That's very interesting."

"Why? What are you talking about?" Kath sounded baffled, but she'd shrunk back from him.

Kincaid thought of the subtle relationship cues he had seen between the two of them, and changed tack. "Tell me what happened on Thursday night, Kath. What was Jason doing here?"

"He wasn't here," she protested, more firmly than he'd expected.

"How can you be so sure?"

She looked at him, then at Cullen and Bell, who had moved up quietly to flank him on either side, and seemed to come to a decision. "Because I was. And he never came."

"Was he supposed to?" asked Maura, with surprising sympathy.

Kath swallowed and looked down at her hands, as if avoiding their eyes made her shame easier to bear. "He was supposed to meet me here at half-past ten. I'd told Shawna she could take a couple of hours off to see her boyfriend. But I waited and waited, and Jason never came. So if you're thinking he had something to do with Laura's death, you're wrong."

Kincaid thought of Laura, making a list of women and checking off names as she discovered what had happened to them; of Laura, dropping Harriet at the sitter's before ten o'clock, making up a story for Harriet and the sitter, because she meant to investigate something that was not appropriate to discuss with a child, and she didn't know how long it would take. She had meant to go home that night, after she'd had a look round the shelter office on her own—that's why she'd left the washing up in the kitchen sink—and she'd meant to go to work the next morning. But she never got to do either.

"Kath," Kincaid said, "what time did you actually get here on Thursday night?"

"A few minutes after half-past ten. I got held up at home, with the kids."

Kincaid thought of Jason coming in early, quietly, seeing Laura Novak digging through the files. Perhaps she'd been asking questions already that had made him suspect she knew something, so he moved back into the shadows, watching, and when she left, he had followed her. Or had he gone ahead and waited, knowing she would pass by him on her way home?

What had happened then? Had he ducked into the shelter of the warehouse door, and discovering it unlocked, pulled Laura in when she walked past? Or had he confronted her in the street? Perhaps as they began to argue, he had pushed her against the door, and it had swung open, and a terrible opportunity had presented itself.

You, of all people, should have known, Laura had shouted in the darkness of the warehouse. Jason had known all too well what would happen to women trying to make new lives, if their abusers found them.

Kincaid thought of Jason's designer clothes, no doubt bought with money earned from others' misery, and he remembered the way Beverly Brown had flinched away from him when he passed. Kincaid had assumed it was dislike, but perhaps it had been fear. Poor little Mouse, up that night with a fretfully ill child—what else had she seen from her window? And how had Jason lured her to a rendezvous in a deserted graveyard?

He thought of Jason's easy tears when they'd told him of Beverly's death, of his casting suspicion on Beverly's husband by his willing assumption of guilt, and fury coursed through him.

Jason had choked Beverly Brown, as he'd choked Laura, but in Laura's case he must have hoped he could prevent any connection being made between the shelter and the victim. Why he had set the fire after taking so much trouble to disguise Laura's identity, Kincaid still hadn't worked out, but he knew enough.

"We're going to need Jason's address, Kath, then we'll take you straight to the station so that you can make your statement. After all"—his smile held no humor—"we wouldn't want you making any urgent phone calls."

Gemma and Fanny listened intently as Winnie spoke to Roberta from her mobile phone. Winnie had given a brief synopsis of what had happened and then had described Elaine. "Yes," she said now. "Elaine Holland, that's right."

Winnie's body slumped as she listened to the reply, her face growing glummer by the minute. "Right, Roberta, thanks. I'll ring you la—" she'd begun when Gemma grabbed her arm.

"Winnie, wait. Tell her to hold on. Look, there's no point in giving her Elaine's name. I doubt that's any more real than anything else she's said about herself. Does Roberta have a fax?"

"There's one in the vicarage office."

"I've a copy of Elaine's photo. Tell Roberta to expect a fax. We can go to the police station—"

"No. I've a fax in the church office. We can send it from there," offered Winnie, her eyes beginning to sparkle again. She passed this on to Roberta, adding that they would soon call her back.

As they walked from the pub back to the church, their progress slowed by Fanny's chair, Gemma's impatience was tempered by dread. She feared they were wrong, and she feared that if they were right, they were too late.

When they reached the church office, Fanny suddenly put a hand on the chair's wheel and brought it to a jerking halt. She twisted around so that she could look at Winnie.

"Winnie." Her face had lost its animation, and she looked small and frightened. "I'm not sure I want to know. Maybe it would be better if I could just go on thinking of her as she was. As Elaine."

Winnie seemed to consider this. "Do you think so?" she asked. "I can take you home, if you want." She held Fanny's gaze, her face gentle with understanding, and after a moment, Fanny sighed.

"I can't, can I? I know too much to go back, and it was never real. None of it was real." She wheeled the chair forward of her own accord, and Winnie and Gemma followed.

The tiny office was cramped with Fanny's chair and warm from the heat that had built up during the afternoon. As Winnie fed the photo into the fax machine, Fanny looked away until Gemma had tucked it back into her bag.

"There's a speakerphone," said Winnie. "Shall I—"

Gemma nodded. Winnie dialed, and after a moment Roberta's voice filled the room, rich and warm, with the huskiness of the chronic asthmatic.

"It's just coming through now, Winnie. Let me—" Roberta fell silent.

"Roberta," said Winnie, "are you still on the line?"

"Dear God," whispered Roberta.

"What—"

"I'm sorry, love." Her voice came through more strongly. "It's just— I'd never have thought."

"Do you know her?"

Gemma could hardly breathe.

"It's Elizabeth Castleman," said Roberta. "Her parents were parishioners of mine. They were elderly—Elizabeth was a child of their dotage, I suppose. They died, both of them, several years ago, after extended illnesses. Elizabeth looked after them."

"Roberta, what is it?" prompted Winnie, hearing the hesitation in her friend's voice.

"They were churchgoing people. You know it's not our place to judge, Winnie, but their ideas were . . . harsh. And their house, it was a terrible place. Old, dirty, and neglected. I paid pastoral visits the last year or two, and I always dreaded them. I remember Mrs. Castleman telling me they cared nothing for material things, that it was the spirit that mattered, but there was no love in that house."

"And Elizabeth?" Winnie asked quietly.

"She must have been past her midtwenties by the time they died. Like a moth trapped under glass, I always thought her. Pale and futile. Then Mr. Castleman died in his sleep, and a few weeks later Mrs. Castleman fell down the stairs. It often happens that way with elderly couples, even those bound more by habit than fondness. But . . . I don't know. I don't feel comfortable speculating even now."

Gemma leaned nearer the speaker. "Roberta, this is Winnie's friend, Gemma. I know Winnie's explained that this is a police inquiry and a little girl's life may be at stake. Please tell us if there's anything you remember that might help."

After a moment, Roberta's gusty sigh came over the line. "It's just that I'd visited the day before Mr. Castleman died, and he seemed very strong. I know that doesn't mean anything, heart failure can happen at any time. But . . . I remember Elizabeth, standing in the corner, watching with such intensity, as if she were waiting for him to die. Then Mrs. Castleman, only a few weeks later, such a dreadful accident. And then, at her mother's funeral, just for an instant, I'd swear I saw a look of triumph on Elizabeth's face."

Fanny clasped a hand to her mouth, and Winnie sank onto the corner of her desk, her eyes wide with horror.

"You think she killed them," said Gemma.

"I—I suspected it. But I told myself it was purely fancy, and the coroner ruled death from natural causes, in both cases. I wanted to be charitable. I let it go."

"Roberta, what happened to the house?"

"I don't know. I never heard it had sold. And Elizabeth just disappeared not long after her mother's funeral. I always assumed she'd moved away from the area, found somewhere free of old memories."

"Where is it?"

"Why, it's just off Copperfield Street, near All Hallows Churchyard. Not far from you at all."

Jason Nesbitt lived on a council estate, near the junction of The Cut and Waterloo Road, not far from Ufford Street. The estate was early-sixties purpose-built, with all the concrete-block charm that implied. Some of the small balconies had been cleaned and decked out with late-season flowers; most held a jumble of rusted household items, the overflowing detritus of crowded low-income living. All the walls were liberally decorated with graffiti.

They had dropped a shaken but still protesting Kath Warren at the station to give her statement, and Kincaid had called for uniformed backup to meet them at the council estate. If Kincaid was right and Jason Nesbitt had killed at least two people, he wasn't going to take his team in unprotected.

They found the flat on the back side of the estate. The paint on the door was bubbled and flaking, and half the number hung askew. There was no bell.

"Definitely no urban regeneration going on here," muttered Cullen, a sure sign that he was nervous.

Kincaid pounded on the door. He'd expected reluctance or refusal to answer at all, since Nesbitt had vanished from the shelter like a man with flight on his mind. He'd sent one of the uniformed officers round the back to cover the balcony and windows, and fully intended to wait at the front until they could get a warrant, if there was no response to his knocking, but the door swung open almost immediately.

Jason stared out at them, then gave a panicked glance towards the rear of the flat. His hair stood on end, his tie was loose, and the tail of his lilac shirt hung half out of his trousers. "Keep it down, will you? Me mum's asleep in the back." His carefully cultivated accent seemed to have slipped, as well as his tie. "Look, I've already told you everything I—"

"And you've been very helpful, so I'm sure you won't mind if we come in and ask a few more questions," Kincaid said.

"I've got to go. My auntie's not well—" The blood ran

from Jason's face as he glimpsed the two uniformed officers behind Cullen and Bell. "What—"

"I don't think you lads need come in quite yet," Kincaid told the uniforms, then stepped neatly by Jason. When Cullen and Bell followed, Jason retreated to the center of the room.

The place was a tip, and stunk of alcohol, old cigarettes, and unwashed flesh. Not Jason, Kincaid thought, as the young man had always appeared scrupulously clean at work. At the back of the room an open suitcase lay on the floor, half filled, not with clothes, but with expensive electronics.

"Taking the telly, too, are you, Jason?" Kincaid asked conversationally.

Maura looked round the room appraisingly. "I'm surprised someone hasn't relieved you of this stuff, in this neighborhood. Or of your car." They'd spotted his new-model Renault, reluctantly described by Kath Warren, on the side street nearest the flat.

"Is this what you normally pack for a visit to your sick auntie?" Kincaid poked about in the suitcase. "Kent, I think Kath said? And you drove to Kent on Saturday as well. You're a very conscientious nephew."

Jason swiveled another panicked glance at the front door, then the rear of the flat. "Look, tell me what you want, then bugger off, okay? I've got to go."

"Were you in such a hurry on Saturday, too?" Kincaid asked mildly. "Friday must have been hard for you, waiting, with the police all over everything like flies. Where did you keep Laura's clothes, in the boot of your car? And yours, too—you must have got blood all over one of your expensive shirts. A shame, that." Kincaid felt his phone vibrate, an unwelcome distraction. He ignored it and let the call go to voice mail.

"Is there really an aunt in Kent?" asked Maura, taking the ball. "Or did you just drive outside London somewhere and chuck the things in a roadside bin? Only thing is, you'd be surprised at what people manage to find and turn in to the police. Nosy buggers, humans."

A sheen of sweat had appeared on Jason's brow, and his eyes rolled wildly. "Don't know what you're talking about," he said, but his voice cracked.

"And then there's the forensics," Maura went on with a smile. "In spite of all the shows on the telly, people still underestimate the forensics. You will have left traces in your car, Jason, and we will find them. A smudge of Laura's blood, a single hair. Oh, and we found a fingerprint in the blood on the board you used to bludgeon Laura—a good print, very clear."

"And that's not to mention Beverly Brown," Kincaid added. "The pathologist found skin cells under her fingernails. That's the problem with choking people, they do tend to struggle a bit. Did she see you arguing with Laura that night, from her window?"

"I don't know what you're talking about," Jason shouted at them, his voice rising into a sob.

"There's one thing I don't understand, though. Why did you set the fire in the warehouse, when you'd already bashed Laura's face in?"

"I didn't set any fire," said Jason, shaking his head, spittle forming on his lips. "You don't understand. You have to let me—I have to go—"

The smell of urine reached Kincaid's nose, and he looked away from the spreading stain on Jason's trousers, feeling sick. "You don't seem to understand, Jason. I doubt you're going anywhere for a long time. We're processing a warrant for your arrest for the murders of Laura Novak and Beverly Brown. We may be able to charge you as an accessory in the death of Clover Howes as well.

"What did Laura find out, Jason? Did one of the women's husbands have an attack of conscience and talk to her? Or did she threaten to track them all down until one of them admitted the truth?"

Emotions flitted across Jason's mobile face—fear, caution, then venom won out. "Laura was an interfering bitch who could never keep her nose out of things that didn't concern her," Jason spat at them, his face contorting with hatred. "She should have—"

"Jason!" The woman's voice came from behind Kincaid. "Jason, I told you to keep yer bloody noise down, din't I?"

Kincaid turned and stared, appalled. Past middle age, blowsy, the woman had a rat's nest of peroxided hair and a mask of makeup that had slipped down her face as if she were melting. She was clad only in a stained wrapper that revealed far too much of her sagging breasts, and she reeked of gin, but not even the weight and the paint could completely disguise the resemblance to her son.

"Jason, did you get me ciggies, like I asked yer?" She looked round at the detectives blearily. "Who're these wankers? Get 'em out of me frigging sitting room before I knock yer silly."

"Shut up, Mum." Jason looked at the others, and his mouth twisted in a bitter smile. "You self-righteous bastards," he said, levelly now. He made a gesture encompassing the flat and his mother. "You fucking, self-righteous bastards. Why don't you ask yourselves what you would do to get out of this?"

The window of the flat above the Indian takeaway was flung wide. A curtain at its edge moved lightly with the breeze, then hung still again. The sound of a radio could be heard, faintly, above the noise of the busy road.

Rose and Bill Farrell stood on the pavement, studying the place as unobtrusively as they could manage. They were both wearing civvies, and had left the FIT van a block away.

They didn't want to put the wind up Braidwood until they'd had a chance to talk to him.

"Someone's living there," said Farrell. "Let's have a word in the takeaway." They went in, assaulted by the smell of hot oil and spices, and Rose felt herself salivate from hunger while her stomach cramped with anxiety over what they might discover. She let Farrell go up to the counter.

"We wondered if you knew the guy who lives upstairs?" Farrell asked the dark-skinned Indian working the cash register. "We were looking for a Jimmy Braidwood."

"Don't know his name. Funny bloke. Never speaks. No *hi, how are you, how's the weather*—you know what I mean?"

"No chitchat," offered Rose, smiling, and the man smiled back.

"I have to remember that. Chitchat." He looked at them more closely. "You official something? No badges, but you have that look."

Farrell produced his identification. "Fire investigator. Do us a favor, though, don't tell your neighbor we were asking about him before we've had a chance to talk to him."

"Hey. The guy's done something wrong, I don't want to talk to him." His teeth flashed white as he grinned. "You take him away, maybe I get a pretty neighbor. But if you want to talk to him, you better talk soon." He glanced at the clock on the shop wall. "Guy usually leaves for work about now. Some security job."

Farrell and Rose both thanked him, but the lingering smile he reserved for Rose.

"I should take you round with me more often," Farrell teased as they stepped out onto the pavement again.

"Now what do we do?" asked Rose. They had left messages for Kincaid and for Jake Martinelli, explaining their situation, but neither had yet responded.

Farrell rubbed his beard. "I say we go ahead. We're just

going to have a friendly chat, see what he has to say for himself—assuming it is Jimmy Braidwood in this flat. I've told Kincaid and Martinelli to meet us here, and Martinelli to bring the dog, just in case this guy's left any trace of accelerants about."

"Won't we need a warrant?"

"Not if he lets us in, and for that we'll depend on your charm. Like I said, it's just a friendly visit."

Rose couldn't quite see how you could accuse someone of arson in a friendly way, and as much as she liked Bill Farrell, she had a brief wish for Kincaid's comforting presence.

There was no bell at the flat's street entrance, and the door opened easily. From the bottom of the stairs, they could see that the door at the top stood open, and as they began to climb, Rose realized she no longer heard the radio.

Farrell stopped at the top landing and rapped on the doorframe. "Mr. Braidwood?"

As Rose slipped up behind him, she saw a small room, drab and dingy, but neat as an army barracks. A man stood at an ironing board in trousers and cotton vest, carefully ironing a blue uniform shirt. He was thin, thinner than she'd realized, but his bare arms were well muscled. His acne-pitted cheeks were hollow, and his eyes, when he glanced at Rose, seemed curiously flat and passed over her without a sign of recognition.

She shuddered and made an effort to keep her expression pleasantly neutral.

"What can I do for you, folks?" said Braidwood. Turning off the iron, he set it on the end of the table, then slipped into his shirt, buttoning each button with careful deliberation. "I'm afraid I don't have much to offer in the way of hospitality."

He didn't invite them to sit but didn't seem to object when Farrell led the way farther into the room. Rose could see now that the walls held a collection of framed Victorian prints, many from the *Illustrated London News,* showing

Southwark warehouses and docks, and the horse-drawn engines of the original London Fire Establishment.

"We're from the fire brigade," said Farrell. "We'd like to ask you a few questions about the fire on Southwark Street last Thursday night." When Braidwood merely looked at him, Farrell went on. "A security camera recorded you looking in the open warehouse door a short time before the building burned."

"I may have," Braidwood answered slowly. "But is that a crime, Mr.—what did you say your name was? Farrell?"

"Most citizens would have reported an unsecured door," countered Farrell, "especially someone in your profession."

"My profession?" Braidwood gazed at them and Rose couldn't tell if the flat eyes were interested or mocking. "How is it that you know my name and my job from a CCTV film?"

"We know quite a bit more than that, Mr. Braidwood," said Rose. "You see, I saw you at last night's fire, directing firefighters to save someone who didn't exist—deliberately putting firefighters at risk. It seemed to me that only a person with a grudge against the fire brigade would do such a thing, so we started looking through the files for applicants who had been fairly recently rejected. We found you, and your file photo matched the CCTV film, as well as my description.

"We also found that you have an obsession with James Braidwood and with Victorian fires. You like to re-create them, and you are especially fascinated by Tooley Street, where James Braidwood died."

Braidwood's eyes held open dislike now, and a spark of respect. "That's very clever of you, but it doesn't prove anything about anything."

"Oh, but we will," said Farrell. "Now that we know who you are and where you are, we'll be rechecking every bit of forensic evidence from those fires—not just the last two, but the half-dozen before that. And then we'll be checking your work schedule and your movements against the times of the fires, we'll be checking into your background—and we'll be searching your premises for trace evidence connecting you to the fires. So, you see, we're all going to be very busy together for a good while."

"Don't mock me," snapped Braidwood, and for just an instant, Rose glimpsed the blazing anger that hid behind the flat, expressionless eyes. "You think you're so clever," he went on. "But you're not clever enough. I've always been one step ahead of you.

"Do you think I'll let you paw through my life, my things, as if I were some sort of exhibit?

"Yes, I set those fires—although Southwark Street was an unexpected gift, divine intervention, I like to think—"

"And the woman who died in the fire?"

Braidwood shrugged. "Not down to me. I didn't know she was there until they pulled her out the next day. But it was a nice touch, I thought. I would have tried it again." He turned to Rose. "Now, as to your firefighter, he really should have been more careful. The fire brigade is not what it used to be," he added with a sigh.

Farrell dug his fingers into Rose's shoulder, paralyzing her before she could react.

"I told them that," Braidwood went on, "but they wouldn't listen."

Rose could feel the tension in Farrell's fingers. He said with great sincerity, "I'm sure they'll listen now, Mr. Braidwood."

Braidwood showed his yellowed teeth, and the menace in the smile made Rose really afraid for the first time. "Oh, I'm sure they will. The question is, will *you* live to tell them what fools they were?"

Reaching down behind his ironing board, he lifted a gallon can and in one fluid motion twisted off the top and sloshed the liquid all over himself. Then he swept his arm out in an arc, flinging the liquid towards them, and threw the can into the door. As the fumes hit Rose—it was acetone, dear God, acetone—she saw what Braidwood was lifting from the corner of the sofa, where it had been concealed behind a cushion. It took her brain an instant to process such a familiar thing in an unexpected circumstance, then it all clicked and she shouted with terror. It was a road flare, and she saw his hand grip the cap to twist it.

"Rose, out!" Farrell was shouting in her ear. "Out the window. It'll blevy! Jump, God damn it! Jump!" He was pushing her and she was climbing, sliding, and then with a gasp dropping to the pavement, wrenching her ankle as she fell.

She looked up at Farrell, half out the window, hands grasping the sill, when there was a great whomp of sound and a ball of flame blew out the window and Farrell was falling, crumpling to the ground. She hobbled to him, pushing bystanders out of the way, shouting, "I'm a firefighter, let me through." One of his legs was twisted at an odd angle, and the tops of his hands and his forehead were burned, but he was conscious and shouting, "That crazy bastard!! He's going to burn down the whole goddamn road. Get the pumper—make it pumps two—"

"I'm calling, Bill, I'm calling," said Rose, who had managed to fumble her phone from her pocket and make her fingers push the right buttons. "Just lie still, please, they're on their way, and there's an ambulance coming, too."

"That crazy bastard," he said again, but with less force, and she knew the shock and pain were setting in.

Looking up, Rose saw Kincaid and Martinelli running towards her, and they were lifting her, hugging her, and shouting questions over each other.

But before she answered, Rose knelt and put her arms around Martinelli's dog, burying her face in Scully's soft coat until she could choke back a sob.

Then she looked up once more at the fire blazing above her, and just for an instant, she thought she saw Jimmy Braidwood, dancing in the window like a human torch.

Gemma slowed the car as she passed the small rectangle of All Hallows Churchyard. Some part of her mind noted the gate's graceful iron flowers, echoed by the stone arch beyond it, even as she searched for the street name Roberta had given them.

"Here," said Winnie beside her, pointing, and Gemma made a sharp, screeching left turn.

Scanning the faded numbers, she quickly found the one she sought and stopped the car with an unexpected stomp on the brake. "This is it. This must be it."

She and Winnie slid out of the car and stood staring at the house before them in dismay. Its flat front was as inhospitable as a prison, its windows opaque with years of grime. To one side, a wall the height of the ground floor sported coils of spiked wire and a frosting of broken glass.

"It looks like no one's been here for years," said Gemma. But as she looked more closely she saw that the sill of the door was free of accumulated rubbish and that the windowpane nearest the door had a spot about the size of a fifty-pence piece rubbed clear of grime. "No, I take that back," she whispered. "She has been here, and recently."

"What should we—" began Winnie, but Gemma was already striding towards the door.

She pounded the tarnished knocker against the wood, calling out, "Elaine Holland! Police! Open up!"

The house seemed to stare back at them in malevolent silence. Gemma tried the door, but the latch held fast. She pounded once more, then stepped back, her hand smarting from the effort. There was no sign of a watching eye at any of the windows.

"Can you get a warrant?" asked Winnie worriedly.

"Warrants take hours." Gemma moved back several more paces, until she stood in the street and could survey the entire house and its heavily fortified yard. "And there's certainly no other way to get in." The wall was impossible to scale, the windows French-paned, and she suspected that even if she could gain access to a latch, the windows wouldn't open. Still, it was worth a try, and if Elaine was inside it might get a reaction.

There was nothing in the street of accommodating size and weight, so she popped open the boot of her car and pulled out a spanner. She cracked the pane above the center sash smartly, then tapped the glass out. No one in the neighboring houses stirred—the entire street seemed eerily abandoned.

Gemma could see the latch now. She reached in and flipped it open, then pushed upwards on the sash, straining until her arms ached. The window didn't budge. "Okay, that's out. These windows haven't been opened for a very long time."

"Then we'll have to wait," Winnie said. "Although I hate to think—"

"No. We're not going to wait." Gemma rubbed her sweaty palms against the jacket of her best suit, flipped open her mobile phone, and hit the speed dial for 999.

When Control answered, she gave her name, rank, and location. "There's smoke coming out of the house," she said, "and we think a child is trapped inside. I can't rouse the resident." She suspected the panic in her voice sounded genuine enough.

Winnie gaped at her as she hung up, then looked frantically back at the house. "But, Gemma, I don't—"

"When they get here, tell them you saw smoke coming from the back of the house, over the roof." Gemma could already hear the two-tone of the siren and she sprinted to her car, pulling it up well out of the way.

Rejoining Winnie, she said, "I'll be in enough trouble without blocking access," but she was grinning with the euphoric rush of having taken action.

The fire brigade's pump ladder careened around the corner, air horn sounding, and screeched to a stop. As the crew jumped out, Gemma showed the officer her badge and gave her explanation once more. One of the firefighters banged on the door and tried the latch, but the door didn't move.

"A fire, ma'am? Are you sure?" asked the officer. He'd had time to examine the prospect himself and had seen no sign of smoke.

"Yes." Gemma pointed over the roof. "I definitely saw smoke coming from the back."

"All right, ma'am. On your head be it." The officer studied the map brought to him by his driver, then added, "No way to get in from the back. Place is a regular fortress." He gestured at his men. "Okay, lads. Let's have some fun."

One of the firefighters took an axe to the door, reducing the heavy barrier to kindling within a few minutes. The leading firefighters rushed in, Gemma and Winnie right on their heels. Ignoring the furious shouts of the officer, Gemma ran from room to room. There was no sign of Elaine or Harriet, or any evidence that the house had recently been occupied at all.

"Thought you said there was a fire, ma'am," said one of the firefighters, coming out of the kitchen. "Have to admit the bloody old place is a firetrap, though."

"Upstairs. It was upstairs, in the back. The smoke was curling over the top of the house."

"Right, then." He motioned to his partner. "Let's have a look-see." They climbed, Gemma trying to make herself invisible as she trod in their wake, with Winnie behind her.

The first-floor rooms were empty, and to Gemma the air seemed impregnated with age and illness, barely masked by the odor of dust. She felt an unwanted stab of pity for the child who had grown up in this place, but the pity only fueled her rage towards the woman that little girl had become.

"She's gone," murmured Winnie. "Elaine's gone, isn't she?"

Gemma sensed she was right—there was no watchfulness here—and her heart gave a lurch of despair. Had she taken Harriet with her?

But another, narrower flight of stairs continued upwards. Following the firefighters, Gemma looked back only once, to give Winnie a reassuring glance, then had to drag her mind away from the vision of old Mrs. Castleman tumbling down the dark chute.

When they reached the top landing they found only one door, locked. The leading firefighter pounded, then looked at Gemma and shrugged. She nodded. "Step back, then, ladies," he said, and swung his axe.

The old locks were no match for the force of the blade. The door swung wide and the smell hit them like a blow, a sickening miasma of human waste, illness, and fear. Peering past the bulk of the firefighters' shoulders, Gemma took in the chest with its ewer and basin, the bookcase, the pail in the corner. She pushed forward, and the firefighter let her by.

Then she saw the bed, and the frightened, feverish eyes of the little girl who lay huddled beneath the tattered blanket.

"Jesus Christ," said the firefighter, shaking his head, his weather-beaten face creased with horror. "I'll swear to any amount of smoke you like, ma'am."

But all Gemma's focus was on the child, still alive, still aware. Safe. Moving to the bed, she dropped to her knees. "It's all right, sweetheart. It's all right now," she whispered, and then she lifted Harriet in her arms.

19

Grief never mended no broken bones,
and as good people's wery scarce, what I says is,
make the most on 'em.

CHARLES DICKENS
The Pickwick Papers

THE WEATHER HAD changed at last, bringing a light frost in
the night, followed by a bright, crisp day. As Gemma drove
through northeast London, she saw that the city had suddenly taken on an autumn tint, and above the faint flush of
color in the trees the sky looked impossibly blue.

She followed the familiar road that led to Leyton, but on
this day her destination was not her parents' bakery but
Abney Park Cemetery in nearby Stoke Newington. She'd
promised Kincaid she'd meet him at Bryan Simms's funeral,
but she'd been delayed at work by a meeting with her
guv'nor. Knowing she'd missed the church service, she'd
headed directly to the cemetery instead.

Abney Park, like Kensal Green in Notting Hill, was one
of the great Victorian cemeteries, built when churchyards

could no longer hold the multitude of dead. As she drove through the gates into the rambling grounds, she stopped and glanced at the map she'd downloaded from the Internet, comparing it with the directions to Bryan Simms's grave site.

But as she scanned the page, James Braidwood's name jumped out at her. The great Victorian fireman was buried here, she saw, in a monument on the main drive. Putting the car into gear, she drove on, gazing at the marble tomb as she bumped past it.

What, she wondered, would happen to the poor remains of Jimmy Braidwood, who had had no family to claim him?

She soon saw that her map was superfluous, as parked cars filled the roads like arterial blood pumping out from a heart. She followed the main track until she saw the crowds, then found a spot for her little Ford and walked back, leaving the road for a rough, grassy track. Her long russet coat provided a welcome protection against the chill breeze.

As she crested a rise, she looked down upon a sea of mourners, almost all in navy-blue uniforms. The fire service had turned out to honor its own.

She stood at the back of the crowd for a few minutes, listening as an occasional snatch of the burial service drifted to her on the wind. Then she moved to one side and edged her way through the packed bodies until she could see the mourning party.

The pallbearers, all firefighters, sat to one side, ramrod straight in their dress uniforms. On the other side of the grave sat Bryan Simms's family, recognizable by their dark skin. Her throat tightened and she blinked until the feeling eased. The tears made her feel a hypocrite—she had never met the young man. And yet she knew that he had been brave, that he had been loved by friends and family, and that he had died needlessly. Surely that was reason enough to grieve for anyone.

A glimpse of the minister in his vestments made her think of Winnie, and of their conversation the previous day as they'd parted outside Guy's Hospital.

"Gemma, I wanted to tell you straightaway," Winnie had said. "I'm going back to Glastonbury. It's sooner than expected, but Roberta's doctor says she's well enough to come back to London, especially with the cooler weather coming . . . and I think everything that's happened has made her feel her parish needs her."

"But you've done so much—"

"No, no." Winnie shook her head, cutting off Gemma's protest. "I've done no more than Roberta would have done, had she been here." She touched Gemma's arm gently. "I'll miss you especially. We've become so close these last days. But I miss my parish, and I miss Jack. It's time for me to go home." She smiled and hugged Gemma hard. "We won't lose touch, though. We're family, after all."

Gemma had returned the hug, then let Winnie go, but the sharp pinch of separation was still with her. It seemed to her that the past year had been made up of losses. First her baby. Then Hazel, gone so far away, and now Winnie. Was that what you learned as you grew older, that life was made up of a series of losses?

And now Kit . . . She couldn't bear the thought of losing Kit, and the disastrous court hearing on Monday had made the possibility seem very real.

It wasn't Kincaid's fault—she knew that. It was the bloody job, and she'd have been forced to do the same in his position. And yet . . . unreasonable as it was, she still felt he had let them down, and she knew he sensed her disappointment.

This added to the constraint that had begun to build between them over the question of trying for another baby. She knew the tiny separation could grow into a chasm if they weren't careful, but she somehow couldn't bring herself to bridge the gap. It wasn't that she didn't want to talk to him, but that she didn't understand her own hesitation well enough to explain it to anyone else.

The minister's voice rose, bringing her back to the scene before her, and he lifted his hand in final benediction. The pipes keened, and as the uniformed pallbearers stood to make their last salute, Gemma saw that one was female. This must be Rose Kearny, whom Gemma had not met, but she knew that Kincaid had been particularly drawn to her. Tall, fair, and coltish, even with her blond hair restrained in a knot—something about the young woman struck a chord in Gemma's memory.

The mourners shifted and began to drift away. Gemma caught sight of Kincaid at last, standing a few yards back from the pallbearers. As she began to make her way down the slope, she saw Rose Kearny come up to him and, after a brief conversation, slip her arms around him. Kincaid returned the hug, a little awkwardly, then they stepped apart.

Another firefighter approached, the dark-haired fire investigator with the sniffer dog, whom Gemma had seen briefly the day of the first fire. After a moment, he and Rose walked away side by side.

Kincaid turned and saw her. "Gemma! I thought you hadn't made it."

"That was Rose, wasn't it?" she said as she reached him.

"Oh." He flushed as he realized she'd seen the embrace. "That wasn't what—"

"No, no, I know that. It's just—" She studied him. "You don't see it, do you?"

"See what?" He frowned, puzzled, and she thought of the strange ways that grief could disguise itself in the labyrinth of the human heart. Kit's mother had had that same fair grace, that same look of innocence burnished by intelligence.

"It's Vic," she said, touching his cheek. "She reminds you of Vic."

* * *

Kincaid left the cemetery with every intention of driving straight back to the Yard. Instead, he found himself winding west through the early-afternoon traffic and then on the M4, heading towards Reading.

He rang Cullen. "Listen," he said when Cullen picked up. "I—I've got some personal business. Cover for me for a couple of hours, will you?"

Cullen hesitated, as if about to ask a question, then said, a touch too heartily, "Right. Let me know when you're on your way in."

It occurred to Kincaid to be thankful he'd signed out a motor pool Rover rather than driving the Midget to the funeral—his mother-in-law had always hated that car.

How could he not have seen that Rose reminded him of his ex-wife? It was more than a fleeting physical resemblance. He thought of Vic as she had been at twenty-two or twenty-three—she'd had that same air of quiet gravity, of taking life just a little too seriously.

The realization jabbed him like a pike, opening a wound he thought he'd plastered over, and then, to his astonishment, he'd found himself thinking of Eugenia.

What must it be like to lose a child, to have every reminder of that child bring fresh pain, and yet to know that the loss of that pain was a death in itself?

When he reached Reading, he exited the motorway and drove to the quiet suburb where Vic had spent her childhood, and where Bob and Eugenia Potts still lived. He pulled up in front of the house and stopped the car.

The brick semidetached was one of identical dozens built in the sixties, when they had represented the ideal of middle-class affluence. Now, they seemed merely dreary, and stultifyingly dull. The house hadn't changed, although the garden seemed more neglected than when he'd been there last. It was here Eugenia had brought Kit when his mother died; it was from here that Kit had run away.

Kincaid had always wondered how such an environment could have produced Vic—it had seemed as unlikely as a stone hatching a butterfly. And yet there must have been something in this household, in this family, that had nourished her uniqueness.

The net curtain at the front window twitched—identical curtains were probably twitching all down the street. It was his cue to charge the citadel or die trying. He brushed a bit of imaginary lint from his lapel—his best dark suit, along with the sober Rover, might buy him an entry point—and got out of the car.

Bob Potts opened the door before Kincaid could ring. His father-in-law's hair had thinned to reveal shiny pink scalp, his gray cardigan bagged at the elbows. He had become an old man. "Duncan," he said. "You shouldn't have—this isn't a good—"

"Bob, please. Just give me a few minutes. Let me talk to you both."

"You don't understand. I don't want her upset." Bob Potts had spent forty years trying to prevent his wife from being upset, and the effort had sucked him dry. "She—"

"Hear me out. What can it—"

"Let him in." The voice came from the darkened room beyond the door.

As Bob stepped back, his shoulders drooping in resignation, Kincaid followed. It took his eyes a moment to adjust to the dimness, then he made out his mother-in-law, seated in the worn armchair near the fire. One of the electric bars was lit, an unheard-of concession for a crisp and sunny afternoon, and the room was stuffily warm.

She, too, had aged visibly. He had not seen her since the spring, since the first letter had come from her solicitor, and his own solicitor had banned any direct contact between them. Her frame seemed to have shrunk, and the flesh sagged at her cheeks and jaws.

"Duncan. You had better sit down," she said. Eugenia had never been one to forget the proprieties, even under duress. "I'm surprised you could find the time to drive to Reading, when you couldn't manage to appear at Christopher's hearing."

Kincaid bit back a retort. He'd long ago learned the folly of trying to justify himself to Eugenia, especially where his job was concerned. "I want to talk to you both about Kit. I want to see if we can reach an understanding, without lawyers, for his sake."

"You've given up your advantage, so now you want us to give up ours?" she asked, a gleam of malice in her eyes. "Why should we make any concession to you?"

"This isn't a chess game," he snapped, his anger flaring. "This is a child we're talking about, and a child's life. We need to consider what's best for him."

"And that has *nothing* to do with you. Christopher is our grandson, and only we have the right to make decisions concerning him."

"Yes," Kincaid said, as levelly as he could manage. "He is your grandson. But he's my son, and I will not let you continue to make his life a misery."

The spark of anger faded from Eugenia's eyes, and her face settled into a frozen mask. "I will not discuss this with you. Now, get out of our house."

"Why can't you face the truth? Is it because you still blame me for Vic's death?" He realized he was shouting and made an effort to lower his voice. "Eugenia, please. Listen to me. I understand how you feel. I understand that every time you look at Kit you see Vic, and that it hurts you terribly, but that you can't bear the pain to stop because that's all you have left of her.

"But you have to let him go. Kit is not his mother, and he deserves to live his own life. You have to let him go . . . and you have to let her go. It's the only way you'll heal."

She stared at him in silence, her eyes hollow, and for an instant he thought he'd reached her. Then she said, "How dare you tell me what I feel? You always were an arrogant bastard. You know nothing, *nothing*, do you hear me?"

Bob cleared his throat, a nervous stutter of sound. "You'd better go now, Duncan. You'd better do as she says."

Kincaid stood. "All right. But let me tell you this. I will do whatever it takes to keep my son with me—whatever it takes. And if you keep on with this, you will rue the consequences. Do you understand me?"

When neither of them replied, he turned away and let himself out of the house. As he got into the car and pulled away from the curb, he realized his hands were shaking from the flood of fury and adrenaline.

He felt oddly and surprisingly liberated, as if he'd crossed some unexpected Rubicon. He had meant it. He would do whatever it took to keep Kit with him, even if it meant sacrificing his job, or his life as he knew it.

He would never know, now, if Tony Novak had been justified in taking his daughter, but he knew that were he faced with giving Kit up to his grandparents, he would do the same.

It was evening by the time he reached Notting Hill again. Dusk was stealing round the brown house with the cherry-red door, and a welcoming light shone out from the windows.

The dogs barked as he came in, then leapt at his knees, tails wagging. He greeted them and went through to the kitchen. Gemma stood by the table, still in her workclothes, going through the post.

"Where are the boys?" he asked, kissing her cheek.

"Upstairs." She looked up at him, frowning in concern. "Where have you been? You didn't answer your phone, and Doug said you were out."

"I went to see Bob and Eugenia. They're not going to budge, Gemma. They mean to take him away from us, and I won't let them do it. I don't care what it takes, even if it means giving up the job. If we have to go away somewhere, make a fresh start, would you—"

"You would do that for me?" It was Kit, standing in the kitchen doorway.

Kincaid turned and saw his son's face lit with surprise, and a wondrous dawning hope. "Yes. You're my son, Kit. I won't let you go."

"What . . ." Kit hesitated, then seemed to come to a decision. "What if I had the test? Would that help?"

"It might. But I thought you didn't want—"

"And if it's not true, if I'm not really your son, will you still—"

"Kit, do you think I love Toby any less because we don't share genes?" He glanced at Gemma and saw that her eyes were bright with tears. "What matters is that we're family. We stick together, okay?"

Kit took a breath and grinned. "Right. Okay. Then I'll do it."

They celebrated with the boys' favorite takeaway pizza and a riotous game of Scrabble in the sitting room, the boys' shouts punctuated by the dogs' barking. Kit radiated an infectious joy new to Kincaid, and he wondered if he was seeing his son for the first time as he'd been before grief entered his life.

Toby, charged up by an excitement he didn't understand, bounced round the room like a table-tennis ball, until Gemma laughingly shepherded him upstairs for his bath.

Later, when both boys were in bed and Gemma lay curled in Kincaid's arms, she said, "Will the test be enough, do you think?"

"I hope so. We'll see."

She turned a little, until he could just make out her profile in the dark. "And did you mean what you said, about being willing to give up everything?"

Kincaid felt he'd stood at the edge of a chasm and found himself willing to leap. If he'd been given a reprieve by Kit's decision, at least he knew he possessed enough courage for the plunge. "I think so, yeah."

"Even the job?"

He traced a finger along her bare shoulder. "I'd like to think I'm more than the job."

"Oh, I think you're much more than that," she said softly, and kissed him.

It was only much later, as he lay drowsily beside her, listening to her breathing steady into the slow rhythm of sleep, that the realization struck him. When he'd asked her if she would be willing to give up the life they'd built, for Kit's sake, she had not given him an answer.

Harriet had had to stay two days in hospital, for observation. Her arm had been set, and the doctors had said she needed fluids and rest. She didn't remember much of the first day, only her father, sitting beside her bed, gaunt and unshaven. He'd cried when he'd told her about her mum, gripping her good hand as if it might keep him from drowning, but Harriet couldn't find anything to say.

It seemed to her that she'd known, somehow, that her mother was gone, when she'd cried for her as she lay on the bed in the dark house. Now she just felt numb, as if it had all happened to someone else, or to her a long time ago. Her mind wouldn't go any further than that; she couldn't visualize what her life was going to be without her mother in it.

She slept again, and when she woke she had visitors. Her father spoke to them, then went out, leaving her alone with the newcomers. She recognized the policewoman with the pretty red hair who had found her, and the priest who'd been with her, with her kind face and funny collar.

With them was a small Asian woman in a wheelchair. When the others had greeted Harriet, the woman rolled her chair up to the bed and took Harriet's hand. Her thin face bore lines of pain, as if she'd been ill, but there was also something calm in it that Harriet found comforting.

"I'm so sorry about your mother, Harriet," the woman said, her soft voice strained with the effort. "And I'm so sorry about what happened to you."

Harriet didn't understand who she was or why it should matter to her so much, but she nodded as if she did.

The woman looked relieved and smiled. She pulled something wrapped in tissue paper from her bag. "This is for you—not for here, of course, because you can't light it—but for when you get home."

Harriet couldn't manage the tissue paper with one hand, so the woman helped her pull it away, lifting out a candle in a square of pale green glass. It smelled sweet and made Harriet think of something nice, but she couldn't quite remember what it was. "Thank you," she said, and the woman seemed pleased.

"We'd better let you get some rest," said the priest, and as they moved towards the door her father came back into the room.

"Have you— Is there any news of her?" he asked the policewoman in a low voice.

"No, nothing yet," she answered.

"And—" Her father shifted uneasily and rubbed at his chin. "Will I— Will there be . . . charges?"

"No," the policewoman said again. "No, I don't think so. You only took your daughter out of school, after all."

When they'd gone, Harriet thought about asking her dad what he'd meant, but instead she drifted off to sleep again.

She had one more visitor, on the second day. Her dad had gone down to the canteen for coffee when Mrs. Bletchley sidled in the door, looking warily round the room. She wore what Harriet knew to be her best dress, and a smear of orange lipstick like a gash across her mouth.

She gave Harriet a brusque nod, then stood awkwardly at the foot of the bed. "Just came to say sorry about your mum," she blurted at last. "A good woman, your mother. You shouldn't forget it. She remembered them as was less fortunate than her." Mrs. Bletchley nodded again, as if satisfied with her pronouncement, then frowned at Harriet. "Don't suppose you'll be coming to stay, now."

"No," Harriet answered cautiously. "I shouldn't think so."

"Well. There's that, then." Mrs. Bletchley turned away but stopped at the door. "You could maybe stop in sometime after school," she said, not looking at Harriet, but there was an odd expression on her face.

Harriet struggled to cover her surprise. "I—yeah, okay, I suppose I could do that," she said. Mrs. Bletchley made a funny sort of screwed-up face, then nodded once more as she went out, leaving Harriet to try to make sense of it all. When her dad came back, she didn't mention the odd visit. It seemed, somehow, to be something that should be kept between her and Mrs. Bletchley . . . and her mum.

Her dad came to the hospital for her in his car, on the evening of the second day, and she saw that the back was filled with all the bits and pieces from his flat. They drove to Park Street, and when he pulled up in front of the house, Harriet saw Ms. Karimgee still working at her desk next door. She lifted her hand in a wave, and Ms. Karimgee waved back.

They went into the house in silence. Harriet walked from room to room, wondering what to do. None of the ordinary things seemed right. Where did she begin this new life, without her mother?

Hearing sounds from the kitchen, she went in and saw her father at the sink, doing the washing up. She stood, stricken with the realization that she'd never see her mum in that spot again, and the world felt as if it were caving in beneath her feet.

Her dad turned and saw her. He dropped the pan and dish-cloth and came to her, scooping her into his arms. Cradling her carefully, so as not to jar her arm, he sat down in the kitchen chair and held her in his lap. Her head just fit beneath his chin, and she could feel his heart beating in his chest.

"We'll be all right, won't we, Harriet?" he whispered, smoothing her hair. "We'll take care of each other."

"Yes," she said. "We will."

Turn the page for an exciting sneak
preview of the next
Duncan Kincaid and
Gemma James mystery
from award-winning author

Deborah Crombie

Water Like a Stone

1

❧

November

Mist rose in swirls from the still surface of the canal. It seemed to take on a life of its own, an amorphous creature bred from the dusk. The day, which had been unseasonably warm and bright for late November, had quickly chilled with the setting of the sun, and Annie Lebow shivered, pulling the old cardigan she wore a bit closer to her thin body.

She stood in the stern of her narrowboat, the Lost Horizon, *gazing at the bare trees lining the curve of the cut, breathing in the dank, fresh scent that was peculiar to water with the coming of evening. The smell brought, as it always did, an aching for something she couldn't articulate, and an ever-deepening melancholia. Behind her, the lamps in the boat's cabin glowed welcomingly, but for her they signaled only the attendant terrors of the coming night. The fact that her isolation was self-imposed made it no easier to bear.*

Five years ago, Annie had left behind her husband of twenty years as well as her job with South Cheshire social services, and had bought the Horizon *with money accumulated from her interest in her family's shipping business. She'd imagined that the simplicity of life on a boat seventy feet long by a mere seven feet wide, and the physical de-*

mands of working the boat on her own, would keep her demons at bay. It had worked for a while. She'd developed a deep love of the cut, as the traditional boating people called the canal, and an unexpected strength and pride in her own skills. Her explorations of the inland waterways had taken her from Cheshire to London, then back up the northern industrial route to Birmingham and Manchester and Leeds, until she sometimes imagined herself adrift in time, following the route of all those hardy people who had gone before her.

But lately that ghostly comfort had begun to fade, and she found herself returning more and more often to her old haunts, Cheshire and the stretch of the Shropshire Union Canal near Nantwich. Her memories came thronging back, and against the horrors she'd seen in child protective services, the measure of her own life seemed woefully inadequate. She'd been too afraid of loss to make her own mark against the darkness, to stay in her marriage, to have a child, and now it was too late for either.

She turned back towards the lamp-lit cabin, drawn by the thought of the white wine chilling in the fridge. One glass, she told herself, just to ease the evening in, but she knew her discipline would fail as the long hours of the night ticked away. Just when, Annie wondered, had she become afraid of the dark?

Ahead, the cut curved away between the overarching trees, offering the elusive promise of vistas unseen, unexplored, and a chill little wind snaked across the water. Scudding clouds blotted the rising moon and Annie shivered again. With a sudden resolve, she leapt to the towpath. She'd take the boat up the cut to Barbridge before the light faded completely. There, the bustle and sounds from the old canalside inn would provide a welcome distraction. Perhaps she'd even go in for a drink, leave the bottle of wine safely corked, panacea for another night. Then first thing in the morning *she'd move on, away from this place where the past seemed so much more present.*

Kneeling in the soft turf with her hand on the mooring strap, she felt the vibration on the path before she heard the rapid footfalls, the quick pant of breath. Before she could move, the hurtling shape was upon her. She saw the boy's wild, white face, felt the lash of his sodden clothing as he stumbled past her. He muttered something she didn't quite catch, but knew it for a curse, not an apology.

Then he was moving away from her, and she imagined she heard the sound of his footsteps long after his slender shape was swallowed by the darkness.

December

Gemma James would never have thought that two adults, two children, and two dogs, all crammed into a small car along with a week's worth of luggage and assorted Christmas presents, could produce such a palpable silence.

It was Christmas Eve, and they'd left London as soon after lunch as she and her partner, Duncan Kincaid, could get away from their respective offices, his at New Scotland Yard, hers at the Notting Hill Division of the Metropolitan Police. They had both managed a long overdue week's break from their jobs and were on their way to spend the holiday with Duncan's family in Cheshire, a prospect that Gemma viewed with more than a little trepidation.

In the backseat, her five-year-old son, Toby, had at last fallen asleep, his blond head tilted to one side, his small body sagging against the seat belt with the abandon only managed by the very young. Geordie, Gemma's cocker spaniel, was sprawled half in the boy's lap, snoring slightly.

Next to Toby sat Kit, Duncan's thirteen-year-old, with his little terrier, Tess, curled up beside him. Unlike Toby, Kit was awake and ominously quiet. Their anticipated holiday had begun with a row, and Kit had shown no inclination to put his sense of injury aside for the sake of family harmony.

Gemma sighed involuntarily, and Duncan glanced at her from the passenger seat.

"Ready for a break?" he asked. "I'd be glad to take over."

As a single fat raindrop splashed against the windscreen and crawled up the glass, Gemma saw that the heavy clouds to the north had sunk down to the horizon and were fast obliterating the last of the daylight. They'd crawled up the M6 past Birmingham in a stop-and-start queue of holiday traffic, and only now were they getting up to a decent speed. "I think there's one more rest stop before we leave the motorway. We can switch there." Reluctant as she was to stop, Gemma had no desire to navigate her way through the wilds of Cheshire in the dark.

"Nantwich is less than ten miles from the motorway," Kincaid said with a grin, answering her unspoken thought.

"It's still country in between." Gemma made a face. "Cows. Mud. Manure. Bugs."

"No bugs this time of year," he corrected.

"Besides," Gemma continued, undeterred, "your parents don't live in the town. They live on a farm." The word was weighted with horror.

"It's not a working farm," Kincaid said, as if that made all the difference. "Although there is a dairy next door, and sometimes the smell does tend to drift a bit."

His parents owned a bookshop in the market town of Nantwich, but lived in an old farmhouse a few miles to the north. Kincaid had grown up there, along with his younger sister, Juliet, and as long as Gemma had known him he'd talked about the place as if it was heaven on earth.

By contrast, having grown up in North London, Gemma never felt really comfortable out of range of lights and people, and she wasn't buying his glowing advertisements for country life. Nor was she thrilled about leaving their home.

She had so looked forward to a Christmas unmarred by the calamities that had shadowed last year's holidays, their first in the Notting Hill house. And she felt the children needed the security of a Christmas at home, especially Kit.

Especially Kit. She glanced in the rearview mirror. He hadn't joined in their banter, and his face was still and implacable as he gazed out the window at the rolling Cheshire hills.

That morning, as Gemma had attempted a last minute sort through a week's worth of neglected post, she'd come across a letter addressed to Kincaid and bearing Kit's school insignia. She'd ripped it open absently, expecting nothing more than a fund-raising request or an announcement of some school activity. Then, she'd stood in the kitchen, frozen with shock as she scanned the contents. It was from Kit's head teacher, informing Kincaid of her concern over the recent drop in Kit's academic performance, and requesting that he schedule a conference after the holiday. Previous notes sent home with Kit by his teachers, the head had added, had come back with signatures the staff suspected had been forged.

Gemma had waited with tight-lipped restraint until Kincaid got home, then they'd confronted Kit together.

Things had not gone well. Kincaid, his anger fueled as much by Kit's duplicity as by concern over the boy's school performance, had shouted at his son while Toby and the dogs had cowered in the background. Kit had gone white and balled into himself as defensively as a threatened hedgehog, and Gemma found herself the peacemaker.

"It's too late to ring the head now," she'd said. "We'll have to wait until term takes up again after the holidays. Why don't we all calm down and not let this spoil our trip." Glancing at her watch, she added, "And if we don't get off soon, we'll never make it to your parents in time for tonight's dinner."

Kincaid had turned away with a shrug of disgust to load the last of the luggage into the car, and Kit had retreated into the stony silence he'd maintained since. It was ironic, Gemma thought, that although it was Kit who'd been called on the carpet, she felt that she and Duncan were the ones who had failed. They should have discussed how to handle things before they talked to Kit; perhaps they should even have spoken to the head teacher before tackling the boy.

Having recently come to at least a temporary resolution in the custody battle with Kit's maternal grandparents that had consumed much of their last year, they'd allowed themselves to be lulled into a false sense of security. Kit had at last agreed to have his DNA tested, and when a match proved Duncan to be his biological father, the court had awarded him custody dependent on the continuing evaluation of the boy's well being and the stability of his home life.

They should have known better than to take that achievement for granted, Gemma thought. It was too easy, and with Kit, things were never going to be easy. A simple paternity test was not going to magically erase the damage he'd suffered from his mother's death and his stepfather's abandonment.

As she glanced at Kincaid sitting beside her, she realized what had prompted his uncharacteristic display of anger that afternoon; fear that they might lose everything they had gained.

A rustle and a yawn came from the backseat. "Are we there yet?" piped up Toby. "I'm hungry."

"You're always hungry, sport," Kincaid answered. "And we're close. Just a bit longer."

"Will Grandma Rosemary have mince pies for us?" Toby, as always, had jumped from a sound sleep to a high-energy state of alertness without any apparent transition.

Gemma found it both amusing and touching that Toby, who had never met Duncan's parents, had adopted them as comfortably as if they were his own family, while she, who had at least met Duncan's mother once, felt as if she was facing a difficult job interview or a root canal. What if they didn't like her? What if she didn't live up to their expectations for their son? Kit's mother, after all, had been an academic, a well-respected Cambridge don, while Gemma had gone straight from secondary school into the police academy, and no one in her family had ever graduated from university. Her parents were bakers, not intellectuals, and her mother's most literary endeavor was an addiction to Coronation Street.

"Yes, lots and lots of mince pies," answered Kincaid. "And turkey tomorrow for Christmas dinner."

"What about tonight? I'm hungry tonight." Toby leaned as far forward as his seat belt allowed, his eyes wide with interest.

"Your Auntie Jules is cooking tonight's dinner, I think, so you'll just have to be patient. And polite," Kincaid added, sounding a little uneasy. He didn't often talk about his sister, and Gemma knew he hadn't seen Juliet or his niece and nephew since Christmas before last.

Toby drummed his shoes into the back of Gemma's seat. "Why? Can't she cook?"

"Um, she was always better at making things with her hands when she was a little girl," Kincaid said diplomatically. "But hey, if Gemma can learn to cook, anything is possible."

Without taking her eyes off the road, Gemma smacked him on the arm. "Watch it, buster, or you'll get worms in your food from now on." Toby cackled, and to Gemma's relief, she thought she heard a faint snicker from Kit.

"How is Father Christmas going to find me if I'm not at home?" asked Toby. "Will I have a stocking?"

"Don't be such a baby," said Kit. "You know there's—"

"Kit, that's enough," Kincaid said sharply, and the slight rapport of a moment ago vanished instantly.

Gemma swore under her breath and gripped the steering wheel a bit tighter, but before she could think how to mend the breach, Toby shouted, "Look, Mummy, it's snowing. It's going to be a white Christmas!"

The large flakes drifted into the windscreen one by one, light as feathers, then came more thickly, until the swirling mist of white filled Gemma's vision.

"A white Christmas," Kit repeated from the backseat, his voice flat with sarcasm. "Oh, joy."

"Bloody Caspar." Juliet Newcombe swung the pick hard into the three-foot swath of plaster in the wall of the old dairy barn. "Bloody Piers." She swung again, with equal force, enlarging the hole left by her first blow.

The light was fading fast, and the bitterly cold wind blowing off the canal held the metallic scent that presaged snow. She'd sent her crew home hours earlier, to spend Christmas Eve with their families, and it was only her stubbornness and her fury that had kept her on at the building site long past knocking off time.

Not that she didn't have a good reason for working late. The conversion of the old dairy barn on the Shropshire Union, between Nantwich and Barbridge, was the largest commission she'd landed since striking out on her own in the building business, and a spate of unseasonably bad weather earlier in the month had thrown the project weeks behind schedule. She leaned on her pick for a moment, surveying the progress they *had* made.

Set where the gentle sweep of pasture met the canal, the place would be a small gem when it was finished. The building was a single story, constructed of traditional Cheshire red brick and slate roofed. At some point in its history, outbuildings had been added to the original single-roomed barn, so that the structure now formed a U with the wings facing the pasture. The main building hugged the edge of the cut, and the windows they'd set into the frontage gave a wide view of the water and of the arch of the old stone bridge that crossed it.

Of the half-dozen narrowboats moored below the bridge, one sported a welcoming light and a wisp of smoke from its chimney. Perhaps its owners lived year-round on the boat and were making preparations for a cozy Christmas Eve.

"A cozy Christmas Eve," she repeated aloud, and gave a bitter laugh. Her eyes prickled as she thought of her children—Sam, with his ten-year-old's innocence still intact, and Lally, fighting to maintain her wary, adolescent cool against the excitement of the holiday. They were at her parents', waiting to meet their cousin, her brother Duncan's newfound child.

Cousins, she supposed she should say, recalling that the woman her brother lived with had a small son of her own. Why hadn't they married? she wondered. Had they discovered that the secret of a happy relationship was not taking each other for granted? Or were they just cautious, not wanting to make a mistake that could bind them to years of misery? She could give them a bit of advice, if they asked her.

Then, guiltily, she remembered that she had no corner on misery. They had lost a child, this time last year, a baby born just a few weeks too early to be viable. Her face flushed with shame as she thought of her failure to call, or even to write. She had meant to, but somehow she could never manage to find the words that would bridge the gap that stretched between her and the older brother she had once adored.

And now they would be here, tonight. They were all coming to her house for a festive Christmas Eve dinner before midnight mass at St. Mary's, and she would have to play "happy families."

Caspar would be civil, she was sure, the perfect host, and no one would guess that her husband had just that afternoon accused her of sleeping with his partner, Piers Dutton.

The rage swept through her again and she swung the pick hard into the crumbling plaster. She had to go home, she had to face them all, but first she would finish this one task, an accomplishment that was hers alone and untainted by lies. She would breathe with the rhythm of the blows and think of simple things, making a doorway from the front of the barn into what had once been a feed store. The old barn's history stretched away from her like a ribbon; the generations of farmers who had found shelter here on frosty mornings, had huddled inside on evenings like this, finding an escape from the searching wind.

One of them had plastered over what she guessed had been a manger, leaving a smooth, graying swath that broke the uniformity of the red brick walls. It had been a good job, neat and careful, and in a way she hated to destroy it. But the barn's new owners wanted a doorway from what would be their kitchen/living area into the back of the house, and a doorway they would have.

As the hole in the plaster widened enough to give her purchase, she hooked the tip of the pick into the plaster and pulled. A piece came loose, but hung, still attached by what looked to be a bit of cloth. Odd, thought Juliet, peering at it more closely. The barn had grown dim with the approaching dusk. She extricated the tip of the pick, then switched on her work lamp and trained it on the wall. She touched the stuff with her fingers. Fabric, yes—something pink, perhaps?

She inserted the pick again and pulled, gently, until she dislodged another piece of the plaster. Now she could see more of the material, recognizing the small pattern as leaping sheep, a dirty white against stained pink. It looked like a blanket her children had had as babies. How very odd. The fabric seemed to be nestled in a cavity that had been only lightly covered with the plaster. Shifting her position so that her body wasn't blocking the light, she tugged at the material, freeing a little more. It seemed to be wrapped round something, another layer of cloth . . . pinkish cloth with a row of rusted snaps.

It's a doll, she thought, still puzzled—a black baby-doll in a pink snap-suit. Why would someone put a doll inside the wall of a barn?

Then, she realized that those were tufts of hair on the tiny head, that the face was not brown plastic but leathery skin, that sockets gaped where there should have been eyes, and that the tiny hands curled under the chin were curves of bone.

Juliet jumped back as if scalded, and heard the high, thin sound of her own scream echo from the barn's cold walls.